IT WASN'T EXACTLY THE USUAL WAY TO MEET THE WOMAN OF HIS DREAMS . . .

Malcolm rose up on his elbow and glared at the woman in front of him.

"You bloody shot me!"

Crimson flooded her pale cheeks, but she didn't reply.

"I don't know what kind of game you're playing, but you'd better untie me before I—" he said.

"I'm glad to see you're feeling better." She placed a breakfast tray on the table beside his bed. "I was beginning to be concerned. I thought you might like some breakfast."

"And how am I supposed to eat, trussed up like a Christmas goose?"

She frowned. "I could feed you myself, I suppose—no, you'd choke in that position. Perhaps I could untie one of your hands if you gave me your word as a gentleman that you would refrain from attempting escape."

Malcolm suppressed a laugh—had his father bothered to marry his mother, he would have *been* a gentleman. As it was . . . .

"Say that I do give my word—What's to stop me from calling for help from whoever is outside that door? If I tell them I don't know you, that I've been kidnapped—"

"No one will believe you. I've told them that you're my cousin, and have suffered an injury that has caused a certain amount of mental disturbance."

He surveyed her with grudging respect. She was thorough, he'd give her that. Still, he'd talked his way out of more than one tight spot over the years. "I fear I have a rather pressing need to attend to. One that will require, to put it delicately, the use of both hands," he gestured at the chamberpot in the corner of the room, ". . . unless, of course, you'd care to help?"

The question hung between them for a moment before she took his meaning and blushed a fiery red. "Oh," was all the answer she made, but her actions spoke volumes. Freed and alone in the room, Malcolm chaffed his numb wrists and plotted his escape.

What he needed was a good plan.

And a hostage . . . .

IT WAS THE BEGINNING OF A BEAUTIFUL RELATIONSHIP!

ALEXA SMART

A TOUCH OF PARADISE

PINNACLE BOOKS
KENSINGTON PUBLISHING CORP.

PINNACLE BOOKS are published by

Kensington Publishing Corp.
850 Third Avenue
New York, NY 10022

Pinnacle and the P logo Reg. U.S. Pat. & TM Off.

First Printing: June, 1996
10 9 8 7 6 5 4 3 2 1

Printed in the United States of America

"[The gods] distributed the whole earth into portions . . . And Poseidon, receiving for his lot the island of Atlantis, begat children by a mortal woman . . . All these and their descendants were the inhabitants and rulers. [They] had such an amount of wealth as was never before possessed by kings and potentates, and is not likely ever to be again . . . such was the vast power which the god settled in the lost island of Atlantis.

"For many generations, as long as the divine nature lasted in them, they were obediant to the laws . . . employ[ing] themselves in constructing their temples, and palaces, and docks. [But] when this divine portion began to fade away in them . . . they were filled with unrighteous avarice and power. Zeus, the god of gods, who rules with law and is able to see such things . . . want[ed] to inflict punishment on them, that they might be chastened and improved . . .

"[And so] in a single day and night of rain all your warlike men in a body sunk into the earth, and the island of Atlantis in like manner disappeared, and was sunk beneath the sea."

—Plato, from his *Dialogues,* 350 B.C.

"The fact that the story of Atlantis was for thousands of years regarded as a fable proves nothing."

—Ignatius Donnelly, from his
Atlantis: The Antediluvian World, A.D. 1882

Prologue

Boston, Massachusetts
Midsummer, 1883

"Sounds like a right good crowd," Wilkie Foote allowed, stepping forth from the darkened wings to twitch the backstage curtain. He peered past the resulting gap in the dusty black drapery to the audience beyond the sputtering footlights, then gave a satisfied nod.

Indeed, the staid auditorium fairly boiled with activity. Beneath the prim glow of gaslit chandeliers, black-suited, mustachioed gentlemen juggled walking sticks and doffed black silk hats, while their satin-and-lace draped ladies preened. Lavish fabrics and bright feathers swirled in a kaleidoscope of color and texture, and the accompanying tide of genteel conversation rose and fell in waves of enthusiasm.

What caught Wilkie's attention, however, was the abundance of precious stones in evidence.

From emerald stickpins to diamond tiaras, the enticing flash of jewels was everywhere. This audience was composed, not of scholars in search of new theories to mull over, but of high-society types eager to embrace the latest fad. Just the sort of people who gladly would part with a bit of blunt to support a fashionable cause.

Just the sort of people he and his partner routinely preyed upon.

Wilkie dropped the curtain and rubbed his chapped hands in anticipation. "Ev'ry toff in the city is 'ere," he eagerly informed the well-dressed man beside him. "An' they got money to burn, by the looks o' 'em. This is the best scam yet, Malcolm—"

"Sir John," his companion corrected, as he stroked his dashing brown mustache and then checked the time on his gold pocket watch. "Sir John Abbot, late of Berkshire in West Sussex, England. Do try to remember that, Wilkie . . . and do try to avoid using the word *scam*. It sounds so uncouth."

Uncouth.

Aggrieved, Wilkie fidgeted with the cuff of his gaudy servant's livery, then glanced at the younger man's garb. The contrast was unmistakable . . . sleek black trousers and a crisp white shirt topped by a black silk tie and a well-tailored black evening coat. The man himself was equally impeccable, with his pomaded hair and neatly trimmed mustache and sidewhiskers. His fingernails were so highly buffed that Wilkie fancied he could see reflected there his own pockmarked face and unruly shock of blond hair.

" 'Tain't 'alf fair," he grumbled. " 'Ere, I put together all those fancy letters fer ye, but I always 'ave to play the valet. As for yer bleedin' name, 'tain't 'alf easy keepin' up wit' it, seein' 'ow ye change it ev'ry week."

"We have had this discussion countless times before," the younger man said. He snapped shut his timepiece, so that the engraved coat-of-arms with its snarling wolf momentarily glinted in the dim light. "Your contribution to our work is immeasurable, given your talent at forgery. Still, I fear you fall short in the areas of proper dress and deportment, not to mention in your manner of speech. That is why I take the role of Sir John. As for changing my name, I believe it's time to do so again."

"You don't mean we're quittin' this 'ere game?"

"I think it best, after our stop in New York City."

Momentarily forgetting his own grievance, Wilkie shrewdly narrowed his pale blue eyes. "Yer thinkin' 'ow as that bleedin' pirate, O'Neill, 'as followed us all the way from Savannah, right?"

"I have my suspicions. At any rate, I believe Sir John will conveniently disappear once we have collected this week's contributions to our . . . scholarly fund."

"Lor', I almost forgot." Wilkie fumbled in his breast pocket and withdrew an envelope. "This came after you left the 'otel," he explained, handing over the post addressed in a woman's firm, graceful hand to the fictitious Sir John. "I'd wager 'ow it's from one o' them society females wot wants a titled gent for 'erself."

Wilkie noted the faint curl of distaste that twisted his partner's patrician lips at that observation, and he smothered his own answering grin. Throughout their travels on this side of the ocean, they had encountered numerous examples of that uniquely American phenomenon . . . fresh-faced young heiresses anxious to marry into the English aristocracy, possessed of doting fathers willing to pay a princely sum for the privilege.

"I fear you are correct, Wilkie," the man conceded, scanning the enclosed sheet of ivory bond before reading it aloud.

"My dear sir, I have followed with great interest the newspaper accounts of your exploits and am intrigued by your theories—so much so that I would like to discuss a substantial monetary contribution to further such commendable scientific study. I understand that you are to be here in New York City two days hence . . . Thursday. A prior engagement prevents me from attending your scheduled lecture that evening, but perhaps you will do me the kindness of stopping by my town house

beforehand—three o'clock would be most suitable—so we might talk. Respectfully, Miss Halia Davenport."

"Sounds right promisin'," Wilkie exclaimed over the growing buzz from the unseen audience. "Just pop over an' whisper a few sweet words in 'er ear, then take 'er blunt. You want I should send 'er a reply 'ow as you'll be there?"

"It would seem the thing to do." Malcolm frowned as he refolded the missive. "The name Davenport sounds familiar, somehow. I do believe I will consult my notes before I make that visit—"

"Sir John!" An unctuous voice drifted from the darkened hall behind them. A moment later, Horace Melbourne, founder of the Society to Promote Free Scientific Thought, appeared at the corridor's entrance.

Melbourne paused long enough to mop his balding pate with an oversized handkerchief; then, spotting the pair, he tucked away the square and trotted over to join them.

"My dear fellow, the response to your appearance this evening is gratifying, nay, unprecedented," he burbled, grasping Malcolm's hand and pumping it with what Wilkie privately considered to be typical American overenthusiasm. "Every seat in the house is taken, so perhaps you would care to begin?"

Not waiting for a reply, Melbourne released his hold and with the same vigor swept through the curtain toward the lectern waiting at center stage. As the accompanying polite applause died away, Wilkie caught snatches of the man's pompous introduction.

"Sir John Abbot . . . eminent classical scholar . . . all the way from England . . . startling revelations . . ."

A second, equally restrained ovation followed this uninspired bit of pedantry. Wilkie glanced over at his partner, who nonchalantly smoothed a nonexistent wrinkle from his waistcoat, only to frown.

"Damn it all, Wilkie, I forgot my lucky watch fob," he

muttered as he transferred his anxious glance from the stage curtain to his flat midriff. "I can't go out there, not without it."

" 'Ere now, it's just a cheap bit o' stamped metal," Wilkie reassured him in an indulgent tone. " 'Tain't nothin' lucky about it—just ask the poor bloke what you stole it from."

"I suppose you are right." His expression, however, remained unconvinced as he strode past the yards of drapery and out onto the stage.

Lad sets too bloody much stock by 'is so-called good luck pieces, Wilkie thought with an undignified snort as he took up his position at the curtains. He waited until the applause died away, then adjusted the velvet hangings so that he remained hidden from the audience and yet had a clear view of the proceedings on stage.

Settling himself against a discarded section of wooden scenery, he folded his arms and waited for the show to commence. He had heard the same speech nigh on a dozen times and understood but a portion of it; still, he never tired of seeing his partner at work.

"Ladies, gentlemen, distinguished guests," began the younger man's silken voice . . . the same voice that had parted many a woman from her virtue and many a gentleman from his blunt. "I am honored by your presence here today—"

The tongue o' an angel an' the conscience o' old Nick, 'isself.

Wilkie shook his head in admiration as the younger man began to weave the well-rehearsed threads of his tale across the loom that was his audience. Through the years, Malcolm had used that same talent to talk the pair of them into the finest homes and pocketbooks that London and the Continent had to offer . . . and talk them out of a tight spot or two, as well. In the process, they had amassed and spent more than one respectable fortune, yet something kept his friend ever in search of some newer, more elaborate swindle.

"—what most scholars refuse to believe, even in the face of hard evidence."

Malcolm's voice rose on a quiver of passion, then broke off as he slowly surveyed his audience. Wilkie, who had been silently mouthing the familiar words along with him, paused. Even tucked away as he was behind the curtain, he could tell that the audience's earlier air of polite interest had sharpened to palpable curiosity.

"I, too, was skeptical at the start," Malcolm finally went on, "but a decade of study has convinced me that these documents which have fallen into my hands are indeed genuine. And so, ladies and gentlemen, I am privileged tonight to speak the words that have been denied to countless other scholars for more than two millennia."

"I, Sir John Abbot, have rediscovered the long-lost continent of Atlantis."

Chapter 1

New York City

Halia Davenport paced the cramped study of her modest brownstone and mulled over her choice of weapons. It was a limited selection, at best. Still, she methodically reviewed each one, spreading them out in her mind like a surgeon arranging his scalpels and speculums upon a tray.

The fireplace poker? No, it was unwieldy and too apt to be wrenched from her grasp. She hesitated over the wicked-looking carving knife she knew was sheathed in a wooden block in the kitchen downstairs, then rejected it on much the same grounds.

She gave a moment's more consideration to the crossed pair of foils hanging over the mantelpiece. At her father's urging, she had long ago acquired a rudimentary knowledge of swordsmanship; still, she could hardly picture herself marching a man through the city streets at the point of a blade. She was left with one choice.

With an air of determination, she settled in the worn leather chair behind the battered expanse of her father's desk. Until just a few days ago, its contents had remained undisturbed since his disappearance in the Caribbean almost three months earlier.

She had clung for several weeks to the hope that he would

be found—adrift on a makeshift raft, perhaps, or else aboard some foreign vessel. That had not happened. However, other disturbing events had compelled her to keep a careful watch over her father's papers.

First, had come the anonymous letters. Then, several weeks after Arvin Davenport had been declared missing, some unknown person had broken into the library and made off with a portion of his notes.

She reached for the drawer pull. Her previous look had not turned up the document she sought, a missing page from her father's final journal. How long that page had been gone, she was not sure. She might have guessed that her father had himself removed that sheet, perhaps having blotted it beyond use, save that the page in question appeared to have formed part of a longer entry. Even then, she might not have thought twice about it, had not the entire book vanished from the study shelf a fortnight ago, only to mysteriously reappear in the same spot a week later.

But why take just that single page, when the tiny library was filled with scholarly dissertations?

Halia shook her head. Only she knew of Arvin Davenports's secret obsession, a fixation that would have earned him the scorn of his fellow scholars, had they known. And only a fellow antiquarian would have more than a passing interest in the subject.

Still troubled over those questions, she reached for the flat, rectangular black morocco box that she had discovered in her first search of the desk. She had not bothered to open it then, instinctively sensing what lay within its ominous-looking confines. Now, she gingerly placed it on the desktop, then unfastened the stiff latches and raised the lid.

The revolver nestled jewel-like upon a layer of red velvet, far larger than she had imagined. The harsh gleam of its polished steel barrel contrasted with the soft glow of its pearl-inlaid handle . . . male and female elements combined to form a work both deadly and beautiful.

Halia eased the weapon from its case. Then, with a shiver of loathing, she hefted it in both hands in imitation of the gunfighters she had seen portrayed upon the lurid covers of countless penny dreadfuls. The pistol fitted her grasp as if it had been molded to her hands.

She laid the pistol back on the desk, then rubbed her fingers along her skirt in a reflexive attempt to banish the taint of it. She had never known her father to own any sort of weapon, save for the antiques that were part of his research. No doubt he had purchased the gun a few weeks before his death . . . but why?

She blinked back a sudden onrush of tears and let her gaze linger upon the tiny silver-framed photograph propped atop the desk. It was a formal portrait, taken last year after their final trip together to the Caribbean. Father and daughter met the camera's impassive lens with keen gazes rendered an identical shade of tan by the film, though in reality his eyes were the bright blue of a sunlit sea and hers, the pale green of a storm-tossed ocean.

Critically, she studied her sepia image. Though she often had overheard herself described as a beauty, to her mind she merely possessed that particular collection of classical features traditionally prized by artists. Her gown in the photograph reflected that same timeless tradition, white and simply draped. Even her riot of blond curls, bleached almost white by the tropical sun, had been tied up in a classical style more suited to a figure on a Greek fresco than to a modern young woman of almost five-and-twenty.

The man posed alongside her had cared even less for current fashion. Halia allowed herself a fond smile at the memory. Her father had refused the photographer's suggestion that he tame his unruly, golden mane with pomade. Moreover, he had disdained the requisite stiff collar and neat cravat, preferring his usual outfit of trousers, loose shirt and oversized waistcoat. The resulting image called to mind, not so much a scholar as a buccaneer—a comparison that no doubt would have pleased him.

She bit her lip and tore her gaze from the photograph; then, almost as an afterthought, she scooped up the palm-sized picture and stowed it in her reticule. With more deliberation, she reached for the thin gold chain which had lain beside it. Those delicate links were threaded, in turn, through the center of a worn gold disk that was the last gift her father had bestowed upon her.

Centuries' worth of pummeling by waves and sand had long since rendered the coin almost square. A scattering of raised Greek letters were visible on its reverse, but she could only hazard a guess as to what the inscription might have been. The image on its obverse, however, was still discernible . . . a crowned and bearded man of regal mien who brandished a trident.

Poseidon, Greek god of the oceans.

Arvin's discovery of this particular coin had given him final proof that his years of calculations had led him, at last, to the site he sought. Most scholars, she knew, would have dismissed the tiny relic as a poorly preserved numismatic specimen. What set the coin apart from other similar finds was the fact that this one had been dredged, not from deep within the Mediterranean, but from the crystal blue waters of the Caribbean.

She slipped the chain over her head and carefully concealed the makeshift necklace beneath the high collar of her tucked and ruched white blouse. Barely had she done so than the mantel clock began its musical chiming of the quarter hour.

He is late, she thought with a frown, while a curl of nervousness wound through her chest. Not for the first time over these past few days, she questioned the wisdom of what she was about to do. Strictly speaking, she was about to embark upon a course that barely stopped short of criminal. But what alternative did she have?

The faint metallic staccato of the front doorknocker halted her musings. Halia scrambled to her feet and swiftly concealed the revolver in the skirt pocket of her black and tan walking suit, just as the echo of men's voices drifted to her from the hallway.

Christophe, showing in our distinguished guest.

Despite her apprehension, she managed a fleeting smile at the thought of her visitor's likely reaction to her manservant. Even at his most benign, Christophe projected an intimidating facade . . . and today, his mood was anything but genial.

Barely had she assumed a serene air than a measured rapping sounded at the study door. "Enter," she called, relieved to find that her voice betrayed no hint of her anxiety.

The heavy door swung open, revealing on its threshold a tall, dark-skinned man whose massive build called to mind some ancient Nubian warrior. He was dressed in white cotton trousers and a loose shirt dyed in a kaleidoscope of yellows, reds, and blues, the bright colors accentuating the ebony hue of his skin. As usual, he was barefooted—a state of affairs that always seemed to engender distress in her callers.

"Sir John Abbot be here to see you," Christophe intoned. His deep voice reflected both the musical cadence of his Caribbean birthplace and a stony distrust of their guest. At Halia's nod, however, he stepped aside and allowed the gentleman in question to pass.

"Do come in, Sir John . . ." she coolly began, only to find her words stumbling to a halt when the newcomer took a few bold strides beyond the threshold and then paused to make her an elegant bow.

"My dear Miss Davenport," the Englishman smoothly took up where she had left off, "my apologies for my tardiness. I fear I was called upon to render aid to a gentleman who had been set upon by . . . but I do ramble on, and that is another story. Now, let me just say that I am indeed honored to make your acquaintance. It is a rare pleasure to find a woman of your youth and beauty who also is dedicated to the scientific pursuits."

"Yes, well—" Halia began when he finally paused for breath, "th-that is, I . . ."

She broke off and bit her lower lip in annoyance, aware that she was blushing, yet helpless to stem that wash of blood that tinted her lightly tanned cheeks. She had expected oily lies and false compliments from this charlatan. What she had not foreseen, however, was that the man who spoke them would prove so—

—so presentable . . . even handsome?

"Please make yourself comfortable—Sir John," she went on, stumbling only a little over his name. "I trust that your journey from Boston was agreeable?"

While he made the proper pleasantries, she gestured him toward an overstuffed, wingback chair and then settled again behind the desk. A tight smile twisted her full lips as she listened to his replies and struggled to reconcile the earlier mental image she had formed of her unknown foe with the reality now before her.

His precise accent was that of an English gentleman, as was his refined manner. His hair was dark, and he sported a rather dashing brown mustache that, combined with old-fashioned sidewhiskers, gave him the look of a polished scholar. The sober cut of his elegant garb befitted a man of his title and downplayed his comparative youth while flattering his lean height.

At second glance, however, he proved to be not quite as attractive as she first had thought. What little she could see of his facial features beneath his whiskers tended toward the pleasant if undistinguished . . . mild brown eyes, well-formed if unexceptional nose, forehead, and chin. Taken together, those characteristics lent him an air of bland geniality that his victims had no doubt misinterpreted as trustworthiness.

She, too, might have fallen into that same trap, had she not possessed several damning bits of evidence that clearly showed this so-called Sir John Abbot was neither the scholar nor the nobleman he claimed to be.

The thought spurred her to her duty. "I am honored that you could spare a few moments from your busy schedule to accept my invitation," she began again once the man had finished his account of the trip. "Of course, I had hoped to hear your lecture tonight, but previous obligations prevented my attending."

"I quite understand, Miss Davenport . . . or might I perhaps call you Halia? Such an unusual name, but quite lovely. Greek, is it not?"

"Yes." *Indeed, was the man never at a loss for idle chitchat?* "My late father was a classical scholar of some note— perhaps you have heard of Arvin Davenport?" When he nodded, she went on, "He named me after a daughter of one of the Greek gods, Poseidon. Thankfully, my mother was able to dissuade him from his first choice."

"I would not dare hazard a guess," came his polite reply. "And your mother, she is also—"

"She died when I was ten," she shortly told him. "But you did not come here to speak of me. I believe we have another topic to discuss."

"A woman who comes to the point. I quite admire that trait. So, I must presume from your letter that you have some small interest in Atlantology?"

"To the contrary, Sir John, I have a very keen interest in Atlantis. I have studied the subject at great length, from Plato's accounts to the most recent works. You *are* familiar with Ignatius Donnelly and his theories, are you not?"

As surely he must be. The eccentric politician's recently published text concerning that lost continent had caused an international stir, both in scientific and lay circles. Indeed, Atlantis had become a *cause célèbre* with the fashionable set, so that the bogus Sir John likely had found it easy to ply his nefarious trade among their number.

Now, he gave a polite nod. "His is an interesting if wrong-headed approach toward solving the mystery," he flatly stated, punctuating that opinion with a dismissive flick of his fingers. "I fear that the good senator is so intent upon tying all the world's enigmas into one neat, convenient package labeled Atlantis that he has forsaken common sense."

"Then you do not believe his assertion that the ancient Atlanteans were the forebears of numerous other races?"

"Let us just say that I refuse to accept coincidental similarities in various languages and cultures as proof that a single group of people seeded half the world's populations."

"I see." Halia gave a thoughtful frown, aware that time was passing, but needing to plumb for herself the depths of the man's perfidy. "And what of his conjecture that a land mass once existed in the middle of the Atlantic Ocean?"

"Again, wishful thinking. No documentable evidence exists to warrant such an assumption." Then he tempered that blunt reply with an engaging smile. "I do trust that my answers have not inadvertently run roughshod over some pet theory of yours?"

"Not at all," she answered, struggling to suppress her surprise. Rather than falling in with the popular view, he had taken an opposite stance. Indeed, his opinions of Donnelly's findings corresponded with her father's and hers—perhaps too closely for comfort.

"But what of *your* theories, Sir John?" she persisted. "Surely you have formulated your own ideas as to the true location of Atlantis and the cause of its disappearance."

"Indeed, I have. Within the year, I hope to reveal my findings to all the world . . . which is why I have undertaken this lecture tour. As you know, scientific study depends as much upon generous funding as it does upon raw data and physical labor."

He paused and steepled his manicured fingers—so much for physical labor, Halia sourly thought—his expression now that of the earnest scholar. "Much as I am loath to play the role of supplicant," he went on, "it is a necessary evil to ensure my expedition's success. And if my theory as to where the ruins of Atlantis may be found is proved correct, which I am confident that it shall be, both my patrons and I shall reap reward beyond measure."

"Reward?" Halia echoed. "Are you perhaps referring to spiritual remuneration?"

"I am referring, my dear Miss Davenport, to gold."

He must have caught her suppressed sound of disapproval, for he once again flashed his engaging smile . . . a smile that might have disarmed a woman made of less stern stuff.

"I fear I have offended your scholarly sensibilities," he apologized. "Of course, my own motivation lies in the possibility of uncovering data that will point to unknown technologies, to alternate approaches to medicine, and the like. I myself have no need for money beyond the expenditures of my research, for my title brings with it a modest yearly portion that more than satisfies my needs."

When she merely arched one pale brow in response, he assumed a more serious mien. "You must believe me, Miss Davenport, when I tell you that in my view, the thought of wealth pales in comparison to the vast opportunities for expanding the world's knowledge. But surely you realize it is the lure of riches, rather than enlightenment, that prompts those outside the scientific community to support a cause such as mine."

"And support is what you seek of me, Sir John, is it not?"

"You did indicate such willingness in your letter . . . but perhaps such matters are best discussed in private?"

He ended with a questioning look at Christophe who, having allowed the Englishman past, had resumed his silent post in the doorway. Halia glanced from the dark-skinned man back to her guest, then coolly replied, "But what of the proprieties, Sir John? Surely you do not expect an unmarried woman such as myself to entertain a gentleman alone?"

She sensed rather than saw the flicker of irritation that passed through him, much like the momentary stirring of a tranquil pond caused by some unseen creature moving below its surface. This man, she realized, would not accede to her demands without a fight. As unobtrusively as possible, she slipped a hand into her skirt pocket and gripped the pistol butt.

In the next heartbeat, however, the Englishman had resumed his genial facade. "You are quite right. Indeed, I berate myself for making so thoughtless a suggestion. It is just that I am impatient to continue my work—"

"—which entails soliciting donations to fund a nonexistent research expedition . . . a practice better known as thievery."

"My dear Miss Davenport!"

"And I believe this is not the first such swindle you have perpetrated on an unwitting public. Previously, you have posed as missionary, and before that, you sold shares in a nonexistent diamond mine, and before that—"

"Really, this is all too distressing," he broke in again, the precise English accent taking on a razor sharp note of surprise. He shook his head, his dark gaze filled with pitying tolerance. "The fact that you happen to disagree with my Atlantis theory—though you have yet to hear it—hardly entitles you to accuse me of defrauding those who have heard and accepted my ideas. Your accusations border upon slander."

"My accusations are the unvarnished truth, a concept with which you obviously are unacquainted, Sir John—or should I call you Malcolm Northrup?"

His indulgent facade slipped away, replaced now by a chill politeness that somehow was more frightening than any display of anger. The lines of his face grew sharper, while his mild brown eyes narrowed and took on an almost predatory cast. The transformation, while subtle, was nonetheless disturbing—as if a house cat had unexpectedly turned tiger.

How had she ever thought that face bland? she wondered as she suppressed a sudden shiver.

"My name, Miss Davenport, is Sir John Abbot . . . late of West Sussex county in England," he coolly replied, rising from his chair. "I am unacquainted with any Malcolm Northrup, and I must confess I am at a loss as to why you bear me such ill will. Had you previously voiced doubts, I could have supplied you with numerous letters and documents attesting both to my identity and to the scope of my work. But now, I fear our visit has come to an end. If you will excuse me—"

"Not so fast, Mr. Northrup."

Halia slid back her chair and rose. "I have acquired evidence that you have made false claims of a scientific expedition to discover Atlantis," she countered, "while all the time you were pocketing every cent donated to the cause. Not only have you played falsely with the dreams of countless people, but you have made a mockery of the glory that was the lost continent. I fear I cannot allow such activities to continue unchecked."

"Indeed? And just how do you intend to stop me?"

He took a few steps toward her, halting when a wordless sound of threat issued from Christophe's direction. He gave the thickly built Negro an assessing look—though he and the servant were of a height, Christophe was almost double his size—then spread his hands in a deprecating gesture.

"Do forgive me, Miss Davenport," he went on, a humorless smile playing about his lips. "I was under the misapprehension that, here in America, a man is deemed innocent until proven otherwise. But seeing as you both already have made up your minds as to my guilt, I presume you now wish to turn me over to the proper authorities?"

Had she not been so nervous, Halia might have admired the cool aplomb with which he was handling the situation. As it was, she could only give thanks for her foresight in providing herself with a weapon so she could hold him at bay.

"I see that you have mistaken my intentions," she replied, drawing the pistol from her skirt pocket and leveling its barrel at his chest. "You see, you are not being arrested, Mr. Northrup. You are being kidnapped."

Chapter 2

"Kidnapped?"

The Englishman shook his dark head in disbelief; then, turning in Christophe's direction, he gestured peremptorily. "You, there, can you not see that your mistress is delusional? I suggest you disarm her, before she hurts someone."

"Miss Halia, she be knowin' what she be about," the Haitian grimly countered, folding his burly arms across his chest. "Now, you be doin' what she say."

"This is lunacy. I refuse to—"

"Oh, do cooperate, Mr. Northrup," Halia cut him short, a renewed sense of urgency gripping her as she heard the mantel clock chime again. Pausing to loop her reticule over her wrist, she clutched her pistol more tightly and stepped out from behind the desk.

"Lally and the luggage are safely at the wharf by now, are they not?" she asked Christophe, her question referring to the Haitian's older sister, who was also one of the Davenport household.

At Christophe's nod, she turned back to the Englishman. "I fear I do not have time to explain my actions just now, since our ship disembarks within the next hour. If you will just slowly move toward the door."

"What do you mean, *our* ship?" he demanded, a dull red flush distorting his features even while he ignored her command. "Surely you are not expecting me to accompany you on some sea voyage of sorts?"

"*I* am traveling to the island of Bimini in the Caribbean. *You* shall journey with us only as far south as Savannah, where you shall visit the banking establishment where you keep the ill-gotten fruits of your nefarious schemes. You will then withdraw those funds and turn them over to me."

"Funds . . . turn over . . . to you—"

"You heard me, Mr. Northrup," she cut short his choked protest. "I have information that a substantial sum—half a million dollars, to be exact—is deposited there. If you cooperate fully, I may even be persuaded to let you go free . . . if, of course, you give me your word you will cease defrauding our citizens in such a manner. The arrangement *is* more than generous," she finished, noting the sudden narrowing of his dark eyes.

He gave a harsh sound of amusement that was hardly recognizable as a laugh. "Generous? You will forgive me if I prefer to decline your offer and take my chances with your American court system, instead. I rather think they will view me as the innocent victim, considering that I am the one being held against my will by a self-confessed kidnapper and thief."

His words were laced with languid disdain now, and Halia realized in some alarm that he was calling her bluff. Unless she promptly regained control of the situation, he would simply walk away, taking with him any chance left her to finish the work her father had begun.

"The decision is yours, Mr. Northrup," she replied in a cool tone the equal of his. "You may accompany us without protest to the ship, or you may remain here bound and under Christophe's care while I turn over the evidence of your perfidy to our local authorities—"

"—the third alternative being that you will shoot me where I stand?"

"That is correct," she answered and in a fluid move

cocked her pistol. "Now, shall I instruct Christophe to bring the ropes, or will you start for the door?"

"Given the charming manner in which you have phrased your invitation, how can I possibly refuse? Besides which, I must admit to a horror of firearms—particularly those in the hands of women."

The bow he made her was a mocking one, as was the smile with which he favored her before he turned and began walking. Warily, Halia followed behind him.

At the doorway, Christophe moved aside to let them both pass, then fell in step behind her. They started down the narrow hall, their footfalls muffled by the threadbare red runner that led through the corridor to the front entry.

As they made their way Halia kept a good arm's length distance between herself and her captive. She let out her breath in a small sigh. Indeed, the entire affair was progressing more smoothly than she had dared hope. Though the man had yet to admit his culpability—either in the matter of his spurious identity or with respect to the greater crime of defrauding innocent people—she could almost believe that her desperate scheme might succeed.

By the time they neared the door, however, her arms had begun to ache from keeping the heavy weapon trained upon the man before her. And she was finding herself oddly distracted by the unavoidable sight of his broad shoulders emphasized by the expensive tailoring of his black jacket. Neither could she help noticing how his dark hair, longer than currently was fashionable, curled just above his collar. It gave him an almost rakish air that, for a painful instant, called to mind memories of her father.

The sound of the Englishman's cool voice promptly returned her to the matter at hand. "I must admit, this has been an illuminating experience," he began in a light, conversational tone, as if there were no pistol leveled at his back. "I can hardly wait for the next scientific gathering, to entertain my colleagues with my adventures. I am sure they will find the tale quite amusing—"

He broke off abruptly and swung about to face her, the fluid move momentarily catching her off guard. In the next instant, he had knocked the pistol from her grasp and sent her sprawling across the faded carpet with the force of that same blow.

Her outraged cry of protest ended on an undignified whoosh of expelled air. Struggling to regain her breath, she scrambled to her knees and frantically groped for her dropped weapon. An instant later, her fingers closed on its smooth grip . . . just as the Englishman reached the door.

Instinctively, she raised the pistol. Every thought fled her mind, save for the realization that he was about to escape and take with him all her hopes and dreams.

Dear God, his hand was already on the knob! She had to distract him somehow, had to divert his attention.

A blow from behind jostled her arm. The pistol erupted in a deafening explosion of smoke and fire that knocked her backwards again and set her ears ringing.

Barely had she registered the fact that she had fired the gun than a pair of beefy arms—Christophe's, she vaguely realized—hauled her upright. She clutched at the servant a moment to steady herself, glancing about the hall to see that the pistol's accidental discharge had not resulted in any apparent damage.

"I assure you, that was quite unintentional," she faintly apologized to the Englishman, who had halted in his tracks. "Perhaps this will serve to convince you that I am quite serious—"

She broke off as he turned and took an unsteady step toward her, his expression one of dazed disbelief. Then, slowly and almost deliberately, he slumped to the floor.

Halia stared for an uncomprehending moment at his prone form on the carpet before her. Then her heart lurched into her throat as stunned realization swept her, and she let the pistol drop from her suddenly nerveless fingers.

"Dear Lord . . . I-I killed him."

The words tore from her lips in an anguished whisper. Guilt and denial battled within her as she struggled with the enormity of what had just happened. Despise Northrup though she might as a liar and a cheat, she never had meant to harm him!

"We should notify someone, I expect," she finally said in a voice devoid now of emotion. "Do not worry, Christophe, I will explain to the authorities that you had no part in any of this."

"No, Miss Halia. The fault, it be mine." The servant gave her a sympathetic shake of his head, though his dark features remained impassive as he studied the still form at his feet. "I be tryin' to stop him, and I be bumpin' you."

"But I was the one pointing the pistol at him," she protested, desperately wishing she could block out the chilling sight before her yet unable to wrench her gaze from the Englishman's body. "Besides, I—"

She broke off with a gasp and dropped to her knees, reaching a tentative hand toward Northrup. "I-I thought I saw him breathe," she whispered, placing her palm on his chest while she made a silent, frantic prayer that her eyes had not deceived her. "He seems to be . . . oh, Christophe, I do believe he is still alive."

The Haitian made no answer but squatted next to her on the faded carpet. Halia watched as he ran his beefy hands over the unmoving man, then paused in his examination. A moment later, he drew back one hand from Northrup's temple so she could see the crimson blood that stained the paler inner skin of his ebony-hued fingers. He ignored her gasp and in quick succession rolled back the Englishman's closed eyelids, frowning at what he saw.

"What is it?" she softly demanded. "Is he—"

The Haitian glanced up at her, a white-toothed grin unexpectedly stretching his broad lips. "A lucky man, that. He still be alive. Now, be bringin' me some cloths and water, and I be fixin' him up for you."

Swept by a profound sense of relief, Halia silently complied. She returned a moment later with several clean lengths of cotton cloth and a pan of warm water. Struggling against the faintness that always afflicted her at the sight of blood, she knelt down beside the injured man once more and prepared to assist Christophe.

Almost immediately, the pan of clear water took on a bright pink tinge, while several cloths were stained crimson. Halia swallowed against the nausea that threatened. But she remained where she was, wringing out the bloodied cloths as Christophe used them and handing him fresh. The bleeding finally slowed, and she could see that the wound was not as serious as she had feared. It was merely a crease along one side of the Englishman's scalp.

With the last of the blood mopped away, she carried off the makeshift medical supplies, returning as Christophe whipped the snowy handkerchief from Northrup's breast pocket and fashioned it into a bandage around the man's forehead. Then, with a satisfied nod, he sat back on his heels and glanced up at her.

"We best be gettin' him to the ship now," he urged. "Lally, she be takin' care of him there. By tomorrow, he be better."

"I hope you are right."

She leaned back against the wainscoting and briefly shut her eyes against the wave of giddiness that swept her. She had struggled for days over her decision to abduct the Englishman, weighing that bit of duplicity against the chance that her actions could conceivably benefit multitudes. As it was, her conscience was already uneasy.

Never would she have been able to live with the knowledge that she was responsible for someone's death.

And he will *be better,* she firmly told herself, that belief bolstered by the fact she had seen countless other examples of Lally's healing skills. Unorthodox as the older woman's treatments were—a flamboyant combination of potions, powders and obeah spells—she had yet to lose a patient.

With that in mind, Halia gathered up her reticule and gingerly caught up the pistol, once more tucking it in her skirt pocket. Not that she had any intention of ever using the cursed thing again, she vehemently reminded herself, but she could hardly leave a loaded gun lying about the hallway.

Christophe, meanwhile, had propped the unconscious man over his shoulder and now stood waiting with his ungainly burden at the front door. Halia joined him there, sparing another anxious look at the Englishman.

His eyelids flickered for an instant, their lashes like sooty smudges against a face now as pale as the white linen handkerchief wrapped around his head. Then, just as she thought he might regain consciousness, he subsided with a soft groan.

She drew a deep breath against the sudden constriction in her chest. The Englishman bore little resemblance now to either of his earlier personae—the genial charmer or the cold-eyed criminal. Instead, he looked vulnerable and quite tragically handsome despite his awkward pose . . . rather like some Greek hero of antiquity fallen upon the field of honor.

"Do we be goin', Miss Halia?"

The Haitian's urgent question cut short her romantic musings. "Take him out to the carriage," she replied, more brusquely than she had intended, in her embarrassment. "I shall be along directly."

She opened the door and walked out onto the stoop, waiting as Christophe and his burden descended the few steps from her brownstone to the modest coach standing alongside the curb. To her relief, the street was relatively empty of both vehicles and passersby this afternoon, and no one showed any undue interest in this little drama.

While the servant stowed the unconscious man inside the carriage, Halia pulled the front door shut and locked it, mentally rebuking herself as she did so for her lapse into misplaced sentimentality. After all, she *had* been forewarned—

. . . a cold, craven man . . . cares only for his own comforts . . . not to be trusted for even an instant . . .

All three unsigned letters had contained those same dire exhortations, along with information regarding Northrup's true identity and urgings for her to help put an end to his nefarious schemes. Who her anonymous informant was, she could only guess—one of her father's friends, perhaps, or else an enemy of the Englishman's who somehow had learned of her connection to Atlantis.

Either way, she would be a fool to ignore that person's warnings.

With those disturbing thoughts in mind, she made her way down to the carriage. She accepted the Haitian's help in clambering inside it, then settled on the worn leather seat across from her unconscious traveling companion. Her own small valise, the only piece of luggage that had not accompanied Lally to the dock, took up much of the remaining legroom between them. After swift consideration, she pulled the pistol from the pocket of her gown and stowed it away in that bag.

"Don't be worryin' none, Miss Halia, you won't be needin' dat gun," Christophe assured her through the open window as he refastened the door. "This Englishman, he be sleepin' for a good while."

Halia nodded, rallying with some of her earlier spirit. "I am sure you are right," she replied. "To the wharf then, Christophe, and hurry. I fear this mishap has cost us much valuable time."

A moment later, the coach began its rumbling journey down the cobbled city streets toward the waterfront. She paid little heed to the familiar passing sights—rows of neat, anonymous brownstones all crowded together; humble wagons and carts jockeying with sleek carriages for position along the avenues; pedestrians, intent on their destinations, milling in steady streams down the sidewalks. Though she had lived most of her life here, she'd never felt quite at home in this city of stone and noise.

She turned her attention to the unconscious Englishman. Christophe had propped him in a position somewhere between reclining and sitting. The pose looked anything but restful, the less so because he was jolted against the backrest with every bump the coach encountered. Hardly the sort of treatment to inflict upon an injured man, criminal or not.

Impulsively, she reached for her valise and withdrew the new black shawl she had packed in anticipation of any inclement weather the sea journey might bring. She folded the loosely woven length of wool into a wide square. Then, assuming an awkward, half-standing position within the low-ceilinged coach, she leaned forward to tuck the blanket behind his shoulders for support.

The task proved difficult, for the Englishman was heavier than his lean build had led her to expect. She could feel the corded muscles beneath his jacket as she awkwardly maneuvered him about, could feel the warmth of his body through that fine woven fabric. Indeed, close to him as she stood, she could breathe in the unmistakable male scent of him . . . a scent that was shaving soap and warm flesh mingled with some spicy fragrance that reminded her of hot tropical nights and cool ocean breezes.

That last untoward thought brought the blood rising to her cheeks. How was it that this man—this criminal!—could make her behave like some giddy girl fresh from the schoolroom, rather than the woman of sense and purpose that she truly was?

Determinedly, she leaned over once more and had just managed to straighten the blanket, when another bump of

the coach unceremoniously tumbled her into the unconscious man's lap.

Halia choked back a cry of surprise and scrambled to regain her balance. She managed, in the process, to twist her
skirts quite wantonly about the Englishman's long legs and
to catch one hand beneath his waistcoat. She bit back another cry and resumed her struggles, fervently praying as
she did that the man would not choose this moment to come
to his senses.

Luckily, he did not.

By the time she recovered her footing and resumed her
own seat, she had convinced herself that her breathless state
was nothing more than the result of her exertions. After all,
she had no feelings for this man save contempt—that, and
the sort of neutral pity one reserved for any wounded beast.

Still, it was with a profound sense of relief that she felt the
carriage rumble to a stop a moment later. She had been
aware for some minutes of the dank, salty air sweeping off
the water. Here on the pier, that odor was joined by the
stench of rotting timber and dead fish—yet to her, drawn as
she had always been to the ocean, the familiar smell was as
sweet as any rare perfume.

"We be here, Miss Halia," Christophe unnecessarily
called as he swung off his perch to open her door. He helped
her onto the sodden wharf and removed her valise from the
coach, then spared the Englishman a suspicious look. "Dat
one, he not be giving you any trouble?"

"No trouble as yet," she lightly replied, though she felt
her pulse quicken and knew her answer for a lie. The man
did mean trouble . . . and not just to the success of her expedition. The sooner she was shed of him, the better.

"This is our freighter, then?" she asked in a swift change
of subject and indicated the aged vessel docked before them.

At the Haitian's nod, she studied it more closely. The *Esmeralda* had once been a proud vessel, and time had not yet
blunted her jaunty lines. Though wind and salt had taken

their toll on her, she was still sturdy—rather like a shabby dowager, Halia decided, who had fallen upon hard days but continued to hold her chin high.

With that whimsical thought, she caught up her valise and waited for Christophe, who now was exchanging words with the slight, dark-skinned man from whom he had borrowed the conveyance earlier in the day. Once a few coins changed hands, the Haitian turned back to the coach and lifted out their unconscious captive. With the Englishman safely hefted over his shoulder again, they started toward the ship.

"We shall proceed much as originally planned," she explained once they were out of earshot of the other driver. "I will still claim kinship with Mr. Northrup, but now we shall say we are taking him to our relatives in Savannah so under their care he may recuperate from his injuries."

"And do let us think positively," she added as they mounted the rickety gangplank. "The most difficult part of our plan is behind us, and Savannah is but two days' journey ahead. What other disaster could possibly befall us before then?"

Christophe grunted and rolled his eyes. "Me, I can be thinkin' of many. A gale, maybe . . . or else this ship, she could be sinkin' . . . or maybe—"

Halia paid scant attention, however, as the Haitian recited several other unlikely if unwelcome possibilities. By now, she was aware of a painful truth—that the sole threat to her grand plans did not lie in the sea or sky.

Rather, it rested with her.

Chapter 3

Malcolm Northrup lay flat on his back in a narrow and unfamiliar bed, eyes half-closed as he waited for the dire rumblings in his stomach to subside. It had to be early morning, he determined, for faint gray light seeped past his slitted eyelids. Where he had spent last night, he could not guess, but one thing was certain—wherever he had been, he'd had too bloody much to drink.

Odd, that he had no memory of overindulgence, though how else could he account for his aching head and the unsettling way the bed seemed to sway beneath him? What he could not explain away, however, was the leaden sensation in his arms and legs, rather as if those limbs were tied down to the bed. Suspicious all at once, he opened sleep-heavy eyelids to gaze about him.

"Bloody hell!"

His hoarse exclamation gave way to a steady stream of pungent curses as he discovered he was indeed bound spread-eagle to the narrow bunk. Thoroughly awake now, he tugged at his bonds only to find that his unknown captor had been most efficient.

He was dressed in the clothes he must have been wearing the previous day, save for his shoes and his jacket, which was hung on a peg on the wall across from him. Each of his ankles and wrists was tied to a different corner of the bed frame. The cords held just enough slack for him to raise his limbs several inches, but not enough for him to sit up.

When, after a few moments more struggle, the knots showed no sign of loosening, Malcolm lay back in disgust and swiftly considered his situation. Another look around showed that he was not being held captive in a room, as he first thought, but in a ship's cabin. By the same token, the steady rise and fall of his bunk was not an aftereffect of too much brandy, but was rather a response to the rhythmic swell of waves beneath the vessel. As for the pounding in his skull—

He managed with an effort to raise one hand to his temple, only to discover that his forehead was bandaged, with one side of his skull excruciatingly tender as if he somehow had been injured. He could identify a faint, unpleasant aroma—oddly reminiscent of burnt feathers and rutting beasts—that seemed to be emanating from the vicinity of that wound.

Malcolm grimaced. If only he could remember how he had come to this pass, if he knew who was responsible . . .

Seamus O'Neill.

The familiar name flashed through his mind the same instant a second realization hit. He hadn't been drinking, after all. Despite his precautions, O'Neill must have finally caught up with him. He had been bashed over the head and shanghaied by the bloody pirate! But where was Wilkie . . . and, more importantly, what had happened to the jewel that was the reason behind O'Neill's single-minded pursuit?

Where in the hell was the bloody emerald?

Emerald. Even as he recalled that the gem was safely vaulted away, the word conjured a sudden recollection—not of the stolen gemstone and its seafaring former owner, but of a young green-eyed, blond siren. He shut his own eyes, ignoring his throbbing temple as he willed memory to return. There had been something about a very large, dark-skinned man and a beautiful blond woman. Malcolm and the woman had been talking—no, arguing—and she had pulled a pistol on him . . .

Memory crashed back on him with painful clarity just as the cabin's louvered door opened, and *she* walked in, dressed in a braid-trimmed walking suit the same sea green color as her eyes. Malcolm rose up on his elbows and glared at her.

"You bloody shot me!"

His outraged accusation, bearing unmistakable echoes of his East End upbringing, stopped the woman. Crimson flooded her pale cheeks, while silverware and dishes clattered against the tin tray she carried. Pressing his advantage and not caring that he was supposed to be the genteel Sir John Abbot, he raged on, "I don't know what kind o' bloody game you're playin', but you'd better untie me before I—"

"I am glad to see you are feeling better. I—that is, we were beginning to be concerned. Yes, you have been unconscious since yesterday afternoon," she answered his unspoken question, "though I presume it was to be expected, given the fact you have a head wound."

Her composure apparently recovered, the woman—one Halia Davenport, if his memory continued to serve—let the door close behind her and started toward him. In that same unruffled tone that set his teeth on edge, she added, "I thought you might like some breakfast, Mr. Northrup."

Northrup! Damn it all, she really does know who I am.

While she settled the tray on a nearby table, he swiftly sorted through a mental list of his most recent victims, searching for some tie between this hitherto unknown woman and whoever was responsible for tracking him down. O'Neill, he promptly eliminated from that number—the pirate was too much the purist to let someone else do his dirty work. That left four score or more people who might want revenge for some past indiscretion of his. The realization did nothing for his aching head.

Aloud, he merely said, "And just how in the hell am I supposed to eat, trussed up like a bloody Christmas goose?"

She frowned. "I could feed you myself, I suppose—no, you would only choke in that position. Perhaps I could untie one of your hands so you could prop yourself up . . . that is, if you gave me your word as a gentleman that you would refrain from attempting escape."

His word as a gentleman.

Malcolm suppressed a bitter laugh. Little did the chit know that, had his father bothered to marry his mother, he *would* have been a gentleman. Hell, he would have been bloody Lord Sherebrooke, heir to the Northrup fortune, instead of the bastard son of that family's former underparlor maid. As it was, the closest he'd come was to take his father's name in a mocking sort of tribute to the man.

"Say that I do give you my word," he conceded in caustic tone, "what's to stop me from calling for help from whoever is passing by? If I tell them that I don't know you, that I've been kidnapped—"

"—I am afraid no one would believe you."

She moved a few steps closer. Her wide green eyes levelly met his gaze, while her full lips settled into charmingly stubborn lines that, had he been in a mood to appreciate such things, he would have found quite appealing. "You see, Mr. Northrup, the ship's staff has been informed that you are my cousin, and that you have suffered an injury which has caused a certain . . . mental disturbance. The crew would attribute any such claim you made to your illness. Now, if you will just give me your word you will not try anything, we can proceed with your breakfast."

He did not answer right away, but surveyed her a moment with grudging respect even as he pondered his own next move. She was thorough, he would give her that. Still, he had talked his way out of more than one tight spot over the years, and he'd be damned if he would let some simpering chit—and an American one, at that!—get the best of him.

"Your concern is most touching, Miss Davenport," he finally replied, resuming his best Sir John Abbot tones. "Unfortunately, I fear I have a rather more pressing need to attend to, one that will require, how shall I delicately put this, the use of both hands . . . unless, of course, you would care to help?"

The question hung between them for a moment before Halia took his meaning and blushed a fiery red. "Oh," was all the answer she made, but her confusion spoke volumes.

Malcolm suppressed a triumphant smile as he gently urged, "Do hurry your decision, Miss Davenport, before I have a mishap that embarrasses us both."

"Oh, my," she elaborated in a faint voice and then delicately cleared her throat. "I-I do suppose there is no way around this. If only Christophe had not gone on top deck already—"

"Knowing what little faith you have in me, I would have no objection if you wished to watch while I use the chamberpot," he interrupted in the same mild tone and was rewarded by her outraged gasp.

"Certainly not!"

With more haste than dignity, she loosened the loops that bound his wrists; then, snatching the ceramic pot from its shelf beneath the bedside stand, she all but thrust it into his arms.

"I shall be just outside," she flung over her shoulder as she fled toward the louvered entry. "Call me when you . . . that is, once you have—"

The rest of her words were lost in the slam of the door behind her. Grinning broadly, Malcolm chaffed his numb wrists and then eased himself into a kneeling position. The throbbing in his temple intensified, and he wasted a few precious seconds regaining his equilibrium.

Once the dizziness subsided, he made welcome use of the chamberpot—strategy notwithstanding, his earlier threats to her had not been without foundation. While he relieved his aching bladder, he took quick stock of his options.

It would be easy enough for him to cast off his other bonds and make an immediate escape. But not through the porthole, he decided, for he could see that it was far too small to accommodate him. He could instead make a bold exit via the door—and risk encountering Halia's oversized manservant who might even now be waiting outside for him to make such a move. In his current weakened state, he had no desire to go up against a man twice his size.

Malcolm refastened his trousers and made quick use of the washbasin and pitcher atop the bedstand, where those items were fitted into hollows to withstand the ship's rise and fall. His ablutions dissipated much of the odor that so offended his senses—no doubt he had fallen into the hands of some quacksalver while he was unconscious—and served to sharpen his thoughts.

Even should he make good his escape, he had but two immediate courses of action open to him. He could leap overboard and risk drowning. Alternately, he could spend the remainder of the voyage eluding the ship's crew, and probably every other able-bodied man aboard, who would be enjoined to hunt him down like the raving lunatic they had been told he was. Neither idea held any appeal for him.

What he needed was another plan.

What he needed was a hostage.

Halia leaned against the doorjamb outside the cabin and waited for the heat in her cheeks to burn away. If she wished to watch, indeed! She should have left the nursing to Lally, who would not have hesitated to keep an eye on the Englishman, even under such circumstances.

But Lally was tucked away in her own cabin, enjoying some much-deserved sleep. After yesterday's ritual that included various foul-smelling salves and appropriately hued candles, the older woman had remained with their captive until dawn, when Halia insisted upon relieving her. A vague sense of guilt had made her own vigil an uncomfortable one . . . after all, she *had* come within a hairbreadth of killing the man.

More unsettling, however, was the sight of him lying atop the narrow bunk, with dark hair tumbled over his newly bandaged head and long limbs stretched and tied. Had she not known better, she would have said that *he* was the one who had been cruelly used.

That feeling, combined with hunger, finally had driven her in search of the galley and breakfast. She had been more than a little nonplussed upon her return to find the Englishman awake. Still, she had managed to maintain an unruffled facade . . . that was, until he had indicated his need to relieve himself.

Halia blushed again, even as she frowned. Familiar with Northrup's background as she was, the idea of leaving him alone for even a minute made her uneasy. But, criminal or not, the man could hardly be denied the opportunity to attend to his physical needs.

She glanced at the timepiece pinned to her shirtwaist. He had been alone for almost five minutes, time enough for him to accomplish that particular activity.

"A-Are you quite finished, Mr. Northrup?" she hesitantly called through the louvered door.

She could hear the splash of water in the washbasin but was unable to see past the painted slats and into the cabin. Now, it occurred to her that he never had quite given her his word that he would not try to escape. Could she have made a mistake by trusting him even this far?

At his muffled reply, she reached for the handle and pushed the door open a few inches. *Please, let him at least have his trousers on,* came her silent plea as she peered inside.

The sight that greeted her, however, proved infinitely

more disturbing. The Englishman lay much as she had left him, flat on his back and with ropes still looped over his ankles, but now his eyes were shut and his head was lolling against the meager pillow. At her involuntary sound of dismay, he opened one eye.

"Never . . . should 'ave . . . tried," he gasped, his voice little more than a whisper. "S'dizzy . . . bloody 'ead feels like it's . . . fallin' off."

"Oh, my!"

Forgetting her suspicions, Halia let the door swing wide open and hurried toward the bed. "Do try not to move," she urged, guilt welling in her breast when he made a weak attempt to sit up. "I will make you more comfortable, and then I shall bring Lally back to attend you."

He made a faint sound of assent but otherwise remained still. Mindful of his wound, she propped the pillow more securely beneath his head and smoothed his now-damp hair from his brow. Then, belatedly recalling her responsibilities, she reached for one of the ropes that had bound his wrists. "It will take me just a moment to find her, but I fear I must retie your arms while I am gone."

"Whatever you say."

Barely had she registered the fact that his voice had lost its previous note of weakness than Northrup had caught both her wrists in a steel grasp. Before she could make any protest, he scissored his long legs around hers and neatly flipped her, so that she now lay pinned beneath him on the narrow bunk.

"A piece of advice, luv, from one criminal to another . . . never trust the other bloke."

"You—you untied yourself," she inanely replied, even as his chill words sent a shiver through her.

He gave her a humorless smile. "Bloody right I did. Now, let's discuss this kidnapping business, shall we?"

His face hovered scant inches above hers, and she could see that it was cool calculation and not a feverish glitter that lit his dark eyes. He had dragged her wrists above her head in a painful hold, while his legs securely pinned her lower body to the mattress in a pose fraught with a frightening intimacy.

"P-Please, let me go," she managed in a voice little better than a whisper.

He shook his head. "Not a chance, luv . . . not until we get a few things straight."

She bit back a wordless cry of distress. Never had she allowed any male of her acquaintance to take physical liberties with her beyond a brotherly kiss . . . yet here she lay, entwined with a strange male atop his bed and offering only token protest. The rational portion of her mind demanded that she scream for help, rather than calmly conduct any sort of conversation.

So why was she not screaming?

"I have found, Mr. Northrup, that I am much more articulate when sitting upright," she finally countered with as much dignity as possible, given the circumstances. "So if you will allow me—"

"Here now, what's goin' on?" roared a voice from the doorway. An instant later, Halia heard the thud of booted footsteps just before Northrup was lifted bodily from her.

With a gasp of relief, she sat up in time to see three burly sailors subduing the Englishman as he struggled in their grip. The tallest of the trio, knit-capped and bearded like his fellows, turned his attention from the skirmish long enough to glance her way.

"Are you all right, miss?" he demanded, his gray brows beetling in paternal concern. "The boys and me, we was walking by and saw what was happening."

"I am quite fine," she assured him a bit breathlessly as she got to her feet and smoothed her gown. "My, uhm, cousin is still suffering from his delirium, and I fear the poor man believes that I—"

"She . . . is not . . . my cousin," Northrup broke in.

Though he had ceased his struggles, his expression was anything but conciliatory as his gaze swept the trio who surrounded him. "I tell you, this . . . person is no relation to me," he went on in the strained tone of a man trying to contain his temper. "She's some bloody madwoman I'd never even met before yesterday. Now, she and her bloodthirsty band of servants have shot and kidnapped me, and I—"

"Come along, mate, and quietly now," a second crewman, blond and stocky, interrupted in a soothing tone. *Sotto voce,* he addressed Halia. "You want we should tie him up again, miss?"

"I do think that would be best, given the circumstances. But do mind his head . . . he *is* injured, you know."

It took all three sailors to restrain him. By the time they had refastened the ropes, the tall crewman was nursing a bloody nose, while his companions sported various bruises of their own."

"He won't be giving you no more trouble, miss," the former assured Halia as he tried to stanch that crimson trickle. "Should I send someone down to wait with you?"

She tactfully refused his offer and showed the stalwart trio out, then turned to meet the baleful gaze of her captive. Her earlier uncertainty gave way to a sense of pique, so that she gladly assigned him all fault for what had just transpired. By what right did he blame her for his predicament, when she had done her utmost to treat him as fairly as circumstances allowed? Indeed, the man was proving most provoking!

"That was most ungallant of you, Mr. Northrup," she hotly began. "I trusted your word, and you took advantage of my leniency . . . besides which, with an injury such as yours, you should not risk such exertion—"

"Stow it, luv," he rudely cut her short.

Halia bristled at this final breach of manners. Before she could explain to him the error of his ways, however, he continued in the same tone of chill fury, "Over the past twenty-four hours, you have shot me, kidnapped me, and made plans to rob me. Now, since I have accepted my fate with comparatively good grace thus far, perhaps you might enlighten me as to the point of all this?"

"The point?" she echoed and levelly met his gaze. "I thought I had made myself most clear on that matter from the very start. You see, we are using your ill-gotten funds for the very purpose that you promised your victims they were intended."

When he only stared at her, uncomprehending, she gave her head an exasperated shake. "Really, Mr. Northrup, you can be most dense. Why, we are setting off in search of Atlantis."

Chapter 4

"Dat man, he be trouble."

With that terse pronouncement, Lally seated herself at Halia's table in the center of the ship's elegant dining salon. Halia stared at her in dismay, not needing to know to which "man" the woman referred . . . and hardly daring to guess what he might have done now.

Her attention was temporarily diverted, however, by the stares that she could feel turned in their direction. A moment later, a muttered tide of conversation began to build.

A few of the more hostile comments—"don't know her place . . . damned darkie thinks she's good as the rest of us"—were audible above the general murmur. Others merely professed whispered amazement at her unconventional appearance. Here among this staid cross-section of American gentry, the Haitian woman stood out like a brilliantly plumed parrot set amongst a flock of sparrows.

Her yellow and crimson shift was wrapped sarong-like over her lush curves, the gleaming fabric an exotic contrast to her coffee-colored skin. She wore her black hair twisted into medusan braids that were, in turn, adorned with glass beads of every hue. Gold bangles the size of small saucers swung from her earlobes in tinkling counterpoint to the loops of gold that adorned both her wrists and throat.

She was handsome, rather than beautiful. Her thickly

chiseled features bespoke an undiluted African heritage, though she had been born in that melting pot that was the Caribbean. Though she must have been well into her middle years, Halia had never been quite certain of the other woman's age, for hers was the smooth, unwrinkled skin that many black women possessed and which any female might envy.

As always, Lally gave no indication that she heard or saw anything untoward. Whether her reaction was prompted by sheer pride or simple disinterest, Halia never was entirely certain. Lally's demeanor was that of a princess set among peasants and, indeed, she often claimed descent from tribal royalty. Halia had little doubt that the woman spoke the truth, especially at such moments.

Halia was unable to disregard the boorish behavior of other passengers. Indignation flared in her breast on behalf of the woman who was not so much employee as friend. Why, Lally had been like a second mother to her—had all but raised her after her own mother had died.

What difference did it make that her skin was of a darker hue and her clothing of decidedly flamboyant cut? She had as much right as any other passenger to be seated in the dining room, given that she held a first class passage.

With an effort, Halia returned her attention to Lally's words of a moment before. "Trouble," she echoed with a small sigh. "I presume you are talking about Mr. Northrup. Has he tried another escape, then?"

"Dat man, he better not be tryin' to get by me."

Lally's generous lips curved into a chill smile that boded ill for the man—or woman—who crossed her. Idly, she toyed with her glass of Chablis before her cool expression of amusement gave way to a heated frown.

"Dat trouble, it be for *you*. My spirits, they be tellin' me this."

"Really, Lally, you know I don't believe in spirits."

But the other woman did, Halia knew. Lally had never

bothered to conceal the fact she was a voodooienne . . . a practitioner of that spirit worship practiced in the Caribbean islands. For her part, Halia took pains to be respectful of the other woman's religion; still, she suspected that Lally's success as a voodoo priestess had less to do with supernatural intervention and more to do with the force of her personality.

Halia considered the matter a moment longer while her friend busied herself with the bowl of clear broth before her. She had witnessed several of Lally's public rituals—melodramatic blends of primitive superstition and solemn Roman Catholic liturgy. She could see how persons less attuned to the forces of logic than she might succumb to the power of such diversions. For herself, she admired the other woman's theatrical flare but gave no credence to the results.

It was only in the name of scientific zeal, she assured herself, that she would delve more deeply into this particular message from the beyond.

"Very well, what sort of trouble do the spirits claim that Mr. Northrup will cause us?"

"*You,*" the other woman corrected again. "It's you dat be gettin' the trouble. The spirits, they say you not to be givin' your heart to him."

"*Giving my heart to him?*" Halia echoed, feeling a blush steal over her cheeks. "Why, you make it sound as if I were considering Mr. Northrup as a suitor. Be assured that the only thing about him that interests me is his ill-gotten gains."

"You be tellin' yourself dat now, but my spirits, they know better. They know he be havin' designs on you, and you on him. Trouble, dat's what he be bringin' you."

And the rest of us.

Halia read those unspoken words in Lally's expression. The woman elaborated no further, however. She merely turned her attention back to her wineglass, as if the straw-colored liquid held the answer to this troubled vision. Halia felt her blush deepen, even as she chided herself for letting Lally's words have any effect on her.

She did not believe in voodoo prophecies, she sternly reminded herself. The fact that she experienced an odd flutter in the pit of her stomach whenever she was in the Englishman's presence was hardly a sign of tender feelings. More likely, it was the result of nervousness over what was to come . . . that, or an indication she did not yet have her sea legs.

With a decisive shake of her head, she dismissed Lally's doleful predictions. "So long as we keep him securely in his cabin, I fail to see how Mr. Northrup can be a problem. After all, we will be rid of him by tomorrow afternoon, when the ship makes port in Savannah. I assure you I am well able to guard my heart for that small space of time."

"The spirits, they be knowin' better."

With that final, sour warning, Lally reached for her utensils. She attacked her portion of beef with such vigor that Halia suspected the woman was picturing a certain Englishman being served up before her, instead. The mental image drew a reluctant smile from her.

Malcolm Northrup might be an accomplished swindler, but his suave manner would be no match for Lally and her voodoo spells.

"Here, lad, come a bit closer," Malcolm coaxed in his best Sir John tones. Doing his damnedest to ignore his throbbing head and the unsettling pitch of the ship, he arranged his features into an expression of benign supplication. "I do promise I won't bite you."

The lad in question, an overweight boy of perhaps ten years, remained where he stood and eyed him doubtfully. Clad in a miniature version of the white sailor suit and jaunty beribboned cap worn by members of the ship's crew, the lad had spent the past half hour since breakfast racing about the upper deck and generally annoying his fellow passengers. Having apparently tired of that particular sport, he had gallumped his way down to the main deck in search of new diversion . . . and unwittingly become the possible means of salvation for Malcolm.

"My momma says you're a crazy man and I'm not s'posed to talk to you," the boy finally declared, planting pudgy fists upon his hips. "She says she doesn't know why the captain even let you on board. She says it's a wonder you haven't murdered us in our cabins yet. She says—"

"Ah, but your dear mother has been sadly misled," Malcolm hastily cut short any further words of maternal wisdom. "I am hardly a lunatic and certainly no threat to anyone, least of all you."

"So why are you tied up?"

At the blunt question, Malcolm felt a muscle in his right cheek begin to twitch. *Bloody little begger could use a good caning,* he sourly determined and swept his gaze about the deck to see if perhaps more sympathetic assistance lay within hailing distance. As it was, however, the other passengers were giving him wide berth, presumably warned off by his ersatz cousin, Miss Halia Davenport.

Halia.

At the thought of the little green-eyed baggage, he bit back an oath. No matter how this unpleasant episode finally ended up, he would make her pay for the ignominy he had thus far suffered, particularly this latest bit of degradation. He spared a glance at his bound wrists, lashed by a yard's length of cord to the ship's wooden railing. Then, again schooling his features into a pleasant expression, he returned his attention to the boy before him.

"In answer to your very perceptive question, my dear lad, that is precisely why I am appealing to you. You see, I am no villain but am the victim of a terrible crime. It is the young woman with whom I am traveling who is not quite well. Indeed, she and her servants have taken me captive for nefarious purposes."

"N-Nefar—what?"

"Nefarious. It means vicious . . . immoral."

The boy gaped, bemusement and suspicion warring across his flabby features as he struggled with the unwieldy words. Finally, with a child's unerring reduction of matters to their basics, he blurted, "You mean, *they're* the bad ones?"

"I fear that is so," Malcolm confirmed with a sober nod. "Moreover, you are the only person on this entire ship to whom I have yet dared confide my plight . . . and you are the only one who can help me prove the truth."

"M-Me?"

With that squeak of a word, the boy moved a half dozen steps closer. Malcolm nodded again, suppressing his own triumphant response as he sensed that victory was, quite literally, almost within his grasp.

"The first thing we must do is cut me loose," he went on. "Perhaps your mother has a pair of sewing scissors in her valise that you might fetch, or else you might slip into the galley and borrow a knife—"

"Henry Robert Peterson, get away from that madman, at once!"

The frantic female screech from the deck above caused him and the aforementioned Henry to give a guilty start. As one, they jerked their gazes upward to see a plump, middle-aged matron in gray striped bombazine waving a parasol.

"But Momma, I—"

"Come here now, young man! And as for you"—she pointed her furled weapon threateningly in Malcolm's direction—"you are a monster, daring to accost my innocent son like that . . ."

She trailed off into a wordless sputter and clasped one plump, gloved hand to her equally ample bosom, which was heaving like a twin bellows. Young Henry, meanwhile, thrust out his lower lip in protest but moved to comply.

"Got to go now, mister," he muttered and clomped off in the direction of the stairs.

With resignation, Malcolm watched the redoubtable Mrs. Peterson reclaim her offspring and then scurry off, presumably in search of the captain. No doubt she would render a hysterical account of her child's presumed near abduction, after which Malcolm would find himself subjected either to constant scrutiny or total ostracism.

With a sound of disgust, he turned and propped his elbows atop the railing to gaze out over the gray water. He'd always been a poor sailor, prone to seasickness on even the calmest water, and his injury made him more vulnerable than usual to the ship's pitching. Still, even incipient queasiness could not dampen his enthusiasm for the sight before him.

Land . . . and more importantly, freedom.

"And not a bloody way to reach it," he muttered, swallowing back the salty taste that had risen in his mouth. Longingly, he gazed at the Eastern shore, a rolling rise of green-ridged white sand separated from the steamer by a smooth expanse of glittering blue water.

The shoreline lay a quarter of a mile away, he judged, perhaps a bit more. A strong swimmer could make the crossing handily. Unfortunately, he could not paddle a stroke.

"Enjoying the view, Mr. Northrup?"

At the sound of Halia Davenport's cool voice behind him, Malcolm spun about, only to be jerked back against the rail again as he stretched to the limit of the rope securing him. The rasp of hemp against bare flesh was another indignity that further soured his foul mood.

"I am sorry if I startled you," she apologized, though her chin was raised in a challenging gesture that robbed the words of much of their sincerity, "but I fear we have a few matters to discuss before we dock."

"Do we, now?"

Malcolm shot her a defiant scowl, reflecting as he did so, that it was bloody lucky for the chit that she was out of reach. Otherwise, his fingers would be wrapped around her slim throat by now, choking some sense into her. Indeed, he had pictured that very scene in vivid detail a dozen times over the past four-and-twenty hours that he had spent tied to his berth following his abortive attempt at escape yesterday morning.

Halia must have read something of his thoughts in his expression, for she took a prudent step back and chose a different tack.

"I am relieved to see you up and around," she began again in a composed tone, as if she habitually conversed with fettered gentlemen. "Lally said that your health was much improved this morning, so that she saw no harm in allowing you up from your bed to take the air. She is quite the healer, is she not?"

"A bloody miracle worker," he replied through clenched teeth as Halia was momentarily distracted by the approach of a grim-faced crew member. A look of distress marred her cameo profile as she swiftly made her way toward the seaman. Certain their discussion would entail his recent encounter with young Master Peterson, Malcolm shrugged and let his thoughts drift back to earlier that morning.

Though Lally's foul ointments did seem to have hastened his healing, he was in no mood to sing the woman's praises. Not when his pride—and certain other portions of his anatomy—still smarted from his other treatment while in her care. Hell, the bloody female had not so much allowed him from his bed as dragged him from it by the ear! Deterred from protest by the glowering presence of Christophe beside her, he'd had no choice but to let her tie his wrists before him and march him up on deck like a naughty schoolboy.

Malcolm's frown deepened at the memory. Once on deck, he *had* managed to twist free of Lally's crablike pinch long enough to take a step toward freedom . . . only to be felled by her well-placed kick to his hindquarters.

Dat be teachin' you, had been the Haitian woman's only comment, but her triumphant expression spoke volumes.

Head spinning, he had not even struggled when Christophe hauled him to his feet again and dragged him to the railing. Then, while the scattering of passengers gaped in interest, Lally had used a second length of thick cord to secure his bound wrists to the railing. Save for his brief encounter with young Henry, he had spent the next hour alone and in fair imitation of a cart horse awaiting its master's return.

Adding both servants to his growing list of malefactors, he turned his attention back to Halia. Her murmured exchange of words with the sailor ended, and Halia gave him a nod and rejoined Malcolm.

"I fear, Mr. Northrup, that you have caused no little distress among some of the passengers," she rebuked him, her full lips drawn into tight lines of disapproval. "A certain Mrs. Peterson claims you seized her child and threatened to cut his throat."

"I did no such thing!" Malcolm shot back and drew himself up with injured dignity. "I merely asked the bloody little . . . lad to bring me a knife so I could cut myself free."

"Oh."

He noted in grim amusement the flicker of relief that passed over her features before she resumed her disapproving air. "Be that as it may, Mr. Northrup, you have proved that I cannot trust you to remain unattended under any circumstances. The captain has requested—and I really must concur—that you should remain tied to your bunk for the duration of our journey."

The muscle in his cheek began to twitch again as he favored Halia with a smile that verged upon a sneer.

"You must forgive me, Miss Davenport, if I do not greet your announcement with any great enthusiasm. The fact that I have already spent a day and a night lashed to a narrow berth atop a mattress no thicker than *The London Gazette* has quite soured my spirits. Besides which," he finished with a gesture at his bandaged forehead, "I am surprised that you would give no better consideration to someone who has suffered an injury such as mine . . . and at your hand, I may add."

"I-I am quite sorry for that."

With those contrite words, her green gaze flickered away to leave him with a view of her delicately chiseled profile. He noted in satisfaction the swift flush that stained her golden cheek, along with the slightest trembling of her full lips that bespoke consternation.

And you bloody well should *feel guilty,* he thought with a trace of self-pity, for the gash along his temple continued to pain him. His wince as he settled back against the rail again was not entirely feigned. Neither was his impatience as he demanded, "So when the bloody hell are we due in Savannah?"

"By noon, or so the captain has assured me."

She turned back to him, her features composed once more. Not for the first time, Malcolm allowed that had the circumstances been different, he would have been tempted to seduce the chit. He had always had a weakness for green-eyed, blond sirens, no doubt due to the fact that his first lover—a woman of five-and-thirty to his fifteen years—had possessed hair the color of spun gold and eyes the color of emeralds.

Malcolm suppressed a wry twist of his lips that could not quite be called a smile. The woman in question had been as cold and hard as a cut gem, too . . . just as had all of the women with whom he had carried on prolonged affairs over the years. Most had been married, and none had wanted any sort of commitment from him, save for his undivided attention during the hours they had spent together in bed.

Swiftly, he revised his assessment of Halia, deciding that she would not have suited, after all. She was an unsettling

combination of cool logic and heated emotion, as change-
able as sea foam on the waves. He required of his women the
same characteristics as he sought in his whiskey—smoothly
aged, obscenely expensive, and sharp-edged enough that he
was never tempted to drink more than his fill.

She, on the other hand, would demand far more of a man
than a quick tumble. That did not mean, however, that he
could not extract some measure of enjoyment toying with
the chit until such time he escaped her clutches.

"So tell me, Miss Davenport," he blandly asked, "can
you suggest a way I might enjoyably pass the next few
hours, given the fact I am to be confined to my bed?"

He raised a sardonic brow and waited for her gasp of
mortified outrage at this not-so-subtle innuendo. Instead,
she coolly surveyed him from head to foot for a long moment. Then she favored him with a slow smile of promise
that sent instinctive anticipation humming through his
veins.

"Indeed, Mr. Northrup," she softly replied, "I know just
the thing to occupy you for a time . . . but I must warn you
that it will require the removal of your clothing."

Chapter 5

" 'In the interior of the temple the roof was of ivory, adorned everywhere with gold and silver and orichaleum; all the other parts of the walls and pillars and floors they lined with orichaleum.' "

Halia interrupted her reading to glance over the edge of her text at Malcolm. He contrived to look bored despite the fact he was again tied spread-eagle upon a berth . . . this time, sans shirt and trousers.

She averted her gaze. The missing garments had been consigned to Lally and her flatiron for some much-needed attention. In the interim, modesty was served by the ship's blanket that was draped across Malcolm's nether regions. Unfortunately, that woolen covering was of such a miserly length that much of Malcolm's torso was exposed to her gaze.

She bit her lip and willed herself not to blush. Her acquaintance with the naked male form was extensive, given her classical education. Had she not studied and cataloged any number of Greek and Roman marbles and frescoes, many of which depicted athletes in their traditional state of undress? The fact that those depictions were stone and plaster, rather than living flesh, should make little difference.

Still, she found herself more unnerved by Malcolm's state of undress than she cared to admit. In an attempt to keep her composure, she demurely addressed the wall above his head.

"It might interest you to know, Mr. Northrup, that most scholars believe orichaleum to have been some manner of copper or alloy. Likely, the metal was valued for its utilitarian properties rather than as a precious ore."

An inelegant snort was Malcolm's only reply to this bit of intelligence. Hastily, she resumed her reading.

" 'In the temple, they placed statues of gold: there was the god himself standing in a chariot . . . around him, there were a hundred Nereids'—those are sea nymphs, Mr. Northrup—riding on dolphins . . . there were palaces in like manner which answered to the greatness of the kingdom and the glory of the temple.' "

She skimmed the next few lines in silence, then gave a satisfied nod. "You should find this following bit quite enlightening. 'In the next place, they used fountains both of cold and hot springs . . . they constructed buildings about them . . . also cisterns, some open to the heaven, others which they roofed over, to be used in winter as warm baths.' "

"All the bloody comforts of home," came the muttered observation from her prisoner.

Halia frowned. "Really, Mr. Northrup, you are being most disagreeable. It was imperative we restore your clothes to some semblance of order, and that could hardly be accomplished any other way save by removing them. In the meantime, I am attempting to entertain you the best way that I know how—"

"Certainly not the *best* way, luv."

"—and I would appreciate a modicum of cooperation on your part," she finished in a rush, feeling her cheeks flame at his attempt to unnerve her.

To cover her confusion, she shut her book with an acerbic little snap. "Very well, I presume you must already be familiar with this text, anyway, since it was part of your charade.

If you do not wish me to read, perhaps you would rather discuss our plans for when we reach Savannah."

"Suit yourself."

His features were still arranged into an expression of carefully contrived ennui. Only the glint in his dark eyes spoke of angered impatience barely held in check. Doubtless, any cooperation on his part would have to be gained by way of bribe or threat.

Taking a deep breath, Halia began her explanation. "Just as soon as the *Esmeralda* docks, we will make our way to your bank—a branch of the Second Bank of the United States, I do believe. Once there, you will withdraw the entire half million dollars you have swindled from my fellow countrymen and then turn over that sum to me."

"And just what will you do, luv, if I decide I'd rather take a solitary little stroll, instead?"

"I would not entertain thoughts of escape if I were you," she countered with as much composure as she could muster. "You see, Christophe will have my pistol trained upon you from the moment you set foot ashore. And it would be equally foolhardy of you should you attempt to alert the bank officials as to my plans. If you do so, I will simply turn over to them a certain packet of letters I have with me . . . letters detailing in length your nefarious deeds."

At that last, Malcolm favored her with a humorless smile. "My congratulations, Miss Davenport. It would seem I have no choice but to cooperate. But even if I do go along with your mad scheme, what makes you think my banker will hand over that sort of blunt without question?"

"But I *expect* him to ask questions. Indeed, I would be most disappointed had you entrusted your ill-gotten gains to someone lacking common sense. For that reason, I have come up with a story I believe will serve quite well. You will simply tell your banker that I am your betrothed, and that you require funds to set up our new household."

"Betrothed . . . household?" he repeated, raising up on one elbow to regard her with a look of horror.

His action sent the blanket slipping to his waist, but that lapse of modesty was lost on Halia when he added, "Whatever my supposed crimes, Miss Davenport, surely none is so dastardly as to deserve that particular fate."

With an effort, she swallowed back the heated words that rose to her lips at this aspersion. How dare the rogue imply that marriage to her would be nothing short of punishment! Why, she'd received quite a respectable number of proposals over the years, with more than one swain claiming his heart to be irreparably broken by her refusal. Indeed, had she wished to give up her work, she could have long since been married to any number of fine gentlemen.

And as for this blackguard tied upon the bunk before her, he certainly was no prize, himself!

Not caring at this point if the man lay stark naked before her, she shot him a quelling look. To her dismay, the same humorless smile was again playing over his lips, and she realized that he had followed her chain of thought.

Her irritation redoubled. Might it not be worth the sacrifice of her goal for the pleasure of watching Christophe toss this would-be nobleman, ropes and all, into the gray waters of the Atlantic?

Reluctantly, she shoved aside the pleasant image of the man floundering in the waves. "I believe that my plan is quite workable, so long as you contrive to properly act the part," she said, instead. "By now, Lally will have pressed the worst of the wrinkles from your clothing, and Christophe has already procured a suitable shirt from one of the senior crew to replace yours. At least, you will appear the gentleman . . . even if you are not one."

That last comment earned her the faintest of sneers from her prisoner. "So let me get this straight," he said in a stiff tone. "We go to my bank, I let you have all my money, and you release me from your charming custody."

"Exactly."

She waited for Malcolm to launch into a volley of objections at her reply. Instead, he managed the suggestion of a bored shrug and said, "One last question, Miss Davenport. As you surmised, during my tenure as Sir John, I was forced to do a bit of study on the subject of Atlantis. It would seem that scholars and adventurers have been searching for the place for centuries now."

"Indeed."

Malcolm lifted a wry brow. "So tell me, then . . . just what in the bloody hell makes you think that *you,* of all people, will be the one to find Atlantis—and in the Caribbean, no less?"

"This, Mr. Northrup."

Heedless of the proprieties, she unfastened the top two buttons of her blouse. Plucking forth the chain from which dangled the Poseidon coin, she favored him with a small triumphant smile.

"My father discovered this artifact during his final expedition to the Biminis," she explained. "Unfortunately, I do not know the exact locale of the site he was exploring, since someone tore the page with the coordinates from the journal that he left behind. Perhaps I can find someone in the islands who served as his guide and who can take me back to the same spot."

Realizing that she had strayed from the original subject, she went on, "At any rate, Mr. Northrup, the coin dates from the correct time period and is inscribed with both the name and image of the Greek sea god. And Poseidon, as surely even you must know, was the patron god of Atlantis."

"Ah, yes, the earthshaker, I believe he was called. But I fear my acquaintance with the Greek gods is rather limited . . . save, of course, for an interest in the ways of Aphrodite."

His cool gaze deliberately dropped to the soft, pale flesh

of her exposed throat, and Halia blushed. Swiftly, she tucked away the makeshift pendant and refastened her lace collar.

"Jest if you wish, Mr. Northrup," came her stiff reply, "but I intend to recover whatever articles of historical interest there are to be found off the coast of Bimini. I have worked with my father on countless other such expeditions, and I am confident that the standard methods of archaeology can be applied here, despite the milieu."

Reaching for her book, she tucked it beneath her arm and stood. "If you have no further questions, I will be on my way. Christophe will be in to attend you in another hour or so. Until later, Mr. Northrup."

She did not linger for any parting words from the Englishman, but hurried to the cabin door and pulled it open. Not bothering with a backward glance, she shut the door behind her with a bang and started down the passageway toward her own cabin.

Malcolm waited until the louvered door had closed with an irritable click before he let his features settle into an expression of chill calculation.

Statues of gold.

A bloody hundred of them, just waiting somewhere beneath the waves to be discovered, or so the chit claimed to believe. This, not to mention a possible cache of gold coins like the one she had just shown him.

Slowly, he shook his head. He might have dismissed her as merely delusional, save for the evidence of the coin . . . that, and the fact that hers was the second recent opinion he'd heard that the fabled lost land was located somewhere in the Caribbean.

The first suggestion had come from the nameless gentleman who, but a week earlier, had sold him a certain document that hinted at the same possibility.

Malcolm let his thoughts drift to that night outside his Philadelphia hotel. His lecture earlier the same evening had met with even more than its usual success, so that it was almost midnight when his hack pulled up before the hotel's awning-covered entry. Wilkie had gone on ahead, leaving him behind to pay the driver. Barely had the carriage pulled away than a furtive figure behind him stepped from the shadows.

Growing up on London's back streets had developed keen instincts in him, so that Malcolm was poised for a fight well before he had gotten his first good look at the man. For once, his instinctive wariness had proved unnecessary. The man had turned out to be, not a desperate footpad, but a nervous gent of middling years possessed of a document he claimed would interest the ersatz Sir John.

His interest piqued by the possibility of yet another new scheme, Malcolm had stood the man a brandy and listened to his tale. What had unfolded was a wild accounting of Caribbean pirates and ancient treasures that culminated in a whispered offer . . . that for a sum, Malcolm could become the proud possessor of a paper detailing the coordinates of the long-lost continent of Atlantis.

The purchase price proved a modest thousand American dollars. Amused by the irony of it all—a con man unknowingly attempting to swindle his fellow practitioner of the game—he had countered with an offer of half that amount. To his surprise, his nameless companion had accepted with alacrity.

Malcolm frowned as he attempted to recall just what his five hundred dollars had bought him. The best he could remember was that it had been an unprepossessing page of penciled scrawlings, apparently torn from a journal. Among them had been what he presumed were a set of maritime coordinates—unintelligible figures, to him, but perhaps possessing some meaning for a seafaring sort of person.

Now, however, he wondered if the paper he had purchased with the vague idea of reselling it one day might instead serve a more useful purpose—that of turning the tables on one Miss Halia Davenport.

He settled against the thin mattress of his bunk, hardly noticing the discomfort of his bonds as he began turning ideas over in his mind. Atlantis or no, if there was gold to be had somewhere beneath the waves, he bloody well meant to get in on the deal. As he earlier had told Wilkie, the time had come to retire the fictional Sir John Abbot and set upon a new scheme.

Momentarily, he turned his thoughts to his absent partner. With any luck, the intrepid Wilkie had discovered just what devious sort of plans Miss Davenport had in mind for Malcolm, and was even now in pursuit. Once in Savannah, he need merely wait for the older man to arrive at a certain Mrs. Bluedecker's boardinghouse that had been their prearranged rendezvous spot for the past few months. Then, they would plan what steps to take next . . . though already, an idea was taking form in Malcolm's mind.

At the moment, a treasure hunt seemed just the thing to stave off the boredom that inevitably settled in once he had played out a con beyond its useful life. And his role as gentleman and scholar, was growing rather stale. He needed something challenging.

All that remained now was to convince a certain young woman that what she needed in her quest was a partner.

Damn the man, but he was infuriating . . . not to mention thoroughly treacherous.

Teeth gritted and fingers clenched into small fists, Halia hurried down the hallway toward her own cabin, the accompanying click of her heels against the wood deck pounding out an angry staccato. So caught up was she in her pique that she did not see the bearded and bespectacled middle-aged gentleman who innocently stepped outside his cabin door and into her path.

Had the man been less light on his feet, they would have collided. As it was, the edge of her book caught him in the ribs. "Oomph," he gasped out. That reflexive exhalation was followed by an equally breathless, "I do beg your pardon, miss."

"Indeed."

The scathing look she spared him as she gathered up her fallen tome was actually meant for a certain Englishman. Not knowing that, her luckless victim tipped his bowler and prudently scuttled back inside his cabin again.

A bit of her anger now spent, she continued down the passage at a more sedate pace. The time had come to put aside emotion in favor of logic, she told herself, trying to ignore Lally's prediction, for it still echoed in her mind.

Dat man, he be trouble.

Halia shook her head, though she could not dismiss the truth that lay in the woman's words. The fact that the Englishman appeared resigned to his fate did not reassure her. Twice already, she had been lulled into complacency by the rogue's apparent compliance with her wishes, only to be taken unaware a moment later. By now, she trusted Malcolm Northrup with the truth rather less than she would trust the ship's striped cat with a string of fresh fish.

"But it is just for a few hours more," she reassured herself as she reached her cabin door.

Once inside, she set down her well-thumbed copy of Plato's works on her bunk and gave the leather cover a fond pat. Reaching for her portmanteau, she pulled out her father's journal and laid it beside the other book, then flipped back its cover. The slim volume fell open of its own volition to the spot where a ragged strip was all that remained of the missing page that had recently been torn.

Determinedly, she began scanning the entries on either side in hopes of discovering some clue to the missing page's

A TOUCH OF PARADISE

contents, trying as she did so to forget the rest of Lally's prediction. She had no intention of giving her heart—or any
other part of her anatomy, for that matter!—to her unwilling captive.

She would be rid of Malcolm soon enough. Beyond that,
she would be possessed of sufficient funds to keep her expedition afloat—both literally and figuratively—for several
months. As for her enforced relationship with the Englishman, it would become an unpleasant memory that would
soon fade from her thoughts beneath the brilliant Caribbean sun.

Or would it?

With a sigh, she shut the journal and began gathering up
the few remaining possessions that she had yet to pack.
Thus far, her plans had unfolded with relative ease, so that
she was confident now that she had not erred in her
unorthodox course of action. Before the summer was ended,
she might well have made the discovery that would validate
her and her father's work . . . nay, their life's passion. Only
one minor stumbling block now remained on the road to her
success.

Someone else possessed Arvin Davenport's notes detailing the precise location of the long-lost Atlantis site.

Chapter 6

"Dat place, it be looking like some kind o' fancy dessert."

Lally's muttered observation broke the silence that had held during the short drive from the wharf. Discreetly dabbing a trickle of perspiration from her brow—for the hot Georgia sun had made their hired hack feel like a fully fired cookstove—Halia followed the older woman's gaze beyond the carriage window.

The vehicle was rolling to a halt before a sizable structure whose clean lines bespoke the subdued architecture of the previous century. What had caught her and Lally's notice, and no doubt the attention of even the least discerning passerby, was the fact that the building's well-tailored facade had been stuccoed an improbable shade of pink.

"It does rather look like a *petit four,*" Halia agreed. Silently, she determined that the distinctly tropical color was more than a little appropriate for the sultry heat that gripped the city. Indeed, the brilliant shade shamed the pale hue of her smartly tailored walking suit—dusty rose trimmed with black piping, a combination that always set off her golden complexion to advantage.

She gave the building another doubtful look. She might well have dismissed it as another of the Englishman's ruses, had she not spotted the unassuming placard above the columned entry. Its wording dispelled any doubt that this startling confection of a building was an official branch of the Second Bank of the United States.

"Quite an amusing color, is it not?" Malcolm observed from the seat across from them.

He had pulled out his pocket watch to check the time. Now, as he snapped the lid shut, Halia noted the engraved coat-of-arms that adorned it. Some sort of creature, she decided . . . a dog, perhaps, or maybe a wolf. No doubt in his role of baronet, the rogue claimed that hereditary device as his own.

If Malcolm noted her scrutiny, he gave no sign. In the same mild, cultured accents he'd affected in his role as Sir John Abbot, he added, "I understand the effect was entirely unintentional, merely the result of whitewashing over red Georgia brick."

She shot him a questioning glance, unwillingly noting as she did so that he cut a distinguished figure despite his borrowed attire. In keeping with his formal air, he had abandoned the white linen bandage he'd worn these past days. Her conscience was eased by the fact that the angry red welt where the bullet had creased his temple had faded. A lock of dark hair spilling over his brow concealed any evidence of his injury.

Once again, he was the dashing Englishman whom she'd met in her library a seeming lifetime ago . . . and as always, she was on her guard against him.

Now, he shrugged in response to her unspoken query and lightly explained, "I have found that it pays to learn as much as possible about one's surroundings, on the chance that information might one day prove useful—if only to impress the ladies."

"I fear it will take more than a smattering of local history to impress *me*, Mr. Northrup," she replied in a stiff tone that she hoped masked her sudden nervousness.

It was still not too late to change her mind, she reminded herself as she tore her gaze from him to focus on the bank's bright facade. All she needed to do was send the Englishman on his way—a bit worse for wear, perhaps, but otherwise unmolested—and her mad scheme would be at an end. She could return home to her New York City brownstone to spend her days amid her books, rather than indulge in what some might judge to be little better than a treasure hunt.

But if she did so, she would be letting her father's work vanish with him and that, she could not do.

She readjusted her black, high-crowned hat with its jaunty rose-colored ribbon. A stray wisp of blond hair had escaped her tight crown of braids to dangle damply against her brow. Resolutely, she tucked that lock back into place. She would see this matter through to the end, she vowed, no matter how many rogue Englishmen she had to face down in the process.

By now, the carriage sat sedately parked on the cobbled avenue. Christophe clambered from his perch alongside the driver and pulled open the door. Malcolm ignored his offer of assistance, however. With lordly grace, he climbed from the coach and then reached out a gloved hand to Halia.

She hesitated. What if the man had only pretended to co-operate with her, and even now was prepared to snatch her bodily from the carriage? How better a way for him to exact his revenge for the events of the past few days than by kidnapping *her*?

Then common sense reasserted itself. Surely even so bold a villain as he, would not attempt any such mischief with the stern-countenanced Christophe standing almost on his heels . . . especially since the Negro had her pistol tucked beneath his calico shirt. Chiding herself for her missish behavior, she raised her chin to regal angle. Then, clutching in one hand her oversized reticule—deliberately chosen for the fact it could readily hold a large amount of cash—she lightly clasped Malcolm's proffered hand with her other.

She promptly realized she had made a mistake.

Even with two thin layers shielding their flesh, the contact between them was nothing short of electric. *Like sparks crackling from a cat's stroked fur,* was her first unsteady thought as she half stumbled from the coach to meet his dark gaze with a wide-eyed look of her own.

Malcolm, she realized, must have experienced a similar jolt of sensation, for she glimpsed a swift play of emotion across his features. Surprise—a response he swiftly suppressed—and then a spark of some more heated sentiment burned in his whiskey-dark gaze.

They stood, fingers entwined, for the space of several heartbeats, and Halia fleetingly recalled that incident in the ship's cabin the morning before. Then, he had pinned her to the berth in a manner meant to be threatening but which instead had been fraught with an unfamiliar if exciting intimacy. Something of that same emotion now flowed between them again, a heightened awareness of each other that neither could escape . . . or deny.

Then Malcolm's expression rearranged itself into one of bland tolerance. Both relinquished their hold with more speed than good manners dictated, he with a muttered curse and she with a sighing release of the breath she had not realized she'd been holding. Fighting a blush, she drew aside and waited while Malcolm attempted the same courtesy with Lally.

Lally would have none of it, however. Disdaining his proffered hand, she fixed him with a glare that would have sent a lesser man stumbling back. With queenlike grace she alighted from the coach to join Christophe.

"We two, we be waitin' here for you," the latter assured Halia. His look was for Malcolm, however, as he gave the concealed pistol a meaningful pat and added, "And we not be expectin' any trouble."

"Might I suggest we proceed, then?" Malcolm replied. "The longer we stand here, the more notice we draw to ourselves . . . and I am certain that undue attention is the last thing Miss Davenport wishes."

With a mock gallant bow, he gestured her to proceed him. She swiftly complied, grateful that he had not compounded her earlier discomfiture by offering his arm. In that, at least, she had learned her lesson and would keep a good arm's length clear of the man from now on. As for what was to come, she must appear outwardly calm, no matter that her insides were churning like a storm-tossed sea.

A moment later, they stood inside. Halia blinked, waiting for her eyes to adjust from the blinding brightness of the street beyond to the churchlike dimness within. The heat seemed less oppressive here, no doubt because of the modern electric fans dangling from the ceiling above. Their faint whirring sound as the broad blades stirred the still air called to mind the chatter of cicadas that was an integral part of a Southern summer.

Soon, however, Halia could make out details around her. In counterpoint to its fanciful facade, the bank's interior reflected the stolid elegance of an establishment dedicated to the making and lending of money.

To one side stretched a gleaming brass railing, behind which lay an impressive length of mahogany counter. Manning each of its half-dozen windows was a young clerk accoutered in the requisite black sleeve garters and green eyeshade. Directly opposite them lay a series of glass doors etched with elegant gold script and leading to the offices of the bank's more senior employees.

Halia took in all this with a single—and, she hoped, casual—glance, before turning her attention to her fellow customers. Most were dark-suited, mustachioed gentlemen of middling years and humorless visages. All were conducting their business in the hushed tones normally associated with libraries and houses of worship.

A portion of her earlier tension eased away. These stern-faced men hardly appeared the sort who concerned themselves with others' affairs. As for the officious-looking guard posted before the massive steel door of the main vault, he appeared more bored than watchful. Not that she need fear him, she swiftly reminded herself. She was not here to rob the place, merely to relieve one of its customers of money that was not his.

Even as she made this determination, a balding, bespectacled man well past his sixth decade stepped forth from behind the glass door marked President. With a brisk nod, he drew himself to his full height—a mere half-head taller than Halia—and started in their direction.

"Why, Sir John," he greeted Malcolm in precise tones as he halted before them and offered his hand. "Indeed, it has been some time since we have last seen you."

"Six months, I would venture, Mr. Burnett. I fear my various ventures have kept me busy of late."

So he was Sir John to this man, as well, though she would not hazard to guess which surname he might be employing this time.

Frowning, Halia waited while Malcolm condescended to the democratic gesture that was the handshake. Then, deliberately, she stepped forward. Knowing the Englishman as she did, she would not put it past him to conclude their transaction with not so much as a reference to her presence.

But he did not ignore her, after all. Still, his tone reflected barely checked boredom as he waved a careless hand in her direction.

"I suppose I must introduce this charming young woman at my side. Burnett, might I present Miss, er, Bertha Jones-Smith, of New York City. And this, my dear Bertha, is Mr. Aloysius Burnett . . . late of that most charming city of New Orleans."

"Good day to you, sir," she said, swiftly transforming her grimace at Malcolm's words to a tight smile. Really, but the man was most trying! Before leaving the ship, she had instructed him not to use her true name in dealing with the bank officials. Though he *had* complied with the letter of her request, his choice of aliases left more than a little to be desired.

Burnett appeared to note nothing amiss in her manner, however, but merely made a dutiful bow over her hand. "A pleasure, Miss Jones-Smith. And might I take it that you are a friend of Sir John's?"

"Actually," Malcolm interjected before she could reply, "Miss Jones-Smith happens to be my . . . bethrothed."

He choked ever so slightly over that last word, and Halia suppressed another ripple of annoyance. Surely the idea of marriage to her was not so disgusting a fate as all that! As for the banker, his sour expression softened into what she guessed was meant to be a smile and turned back to Malcolm.

"Your betrothed? Indeed, I had no idea. My felicitations to you both."

"Quite," Malcolm drawled, effectively cutting short any further expressions of congratulations. "Indeed, I fear it is this current happy state of affairs that brings the two of us here today. There are a few . . . arrangements that we must make."

"But of course. Monies to be transferred, household accounts to be opened—"

"Actually, Mr. Burnett, what I wish to do is make an immediate withdrawal of all my money."

"Immediate withdrawal . . . all your money?" the banker choked out and visibly blanched, while a fine beading of perspiration promptly ringed his wide forehead.

Taking swift pity on the man, Halia sought to soften the blow. "Indeed, Mr. Burnett, we mean no ill reflection upon you or your establishment. It's just that the money is needed elsewhere at this time."

"A-All your money?" that gentleman faintly repeated, his gaze never leaving Malcolm as he whipped a snowy square of linen from his breast pocket. Using one hand to dab with the handkerchief at his brow, the banker gestured with the other in the direction of his office. "If we might perhaps take a seat and discuss the matter . . ."

With the air of a condemned man on his way to the executioner's block, Burnett escorted them past the glass door to a pair of tufted, red leather chairs set before a broad mahogany desk. He saw them settled, then shut the door again before all but collapsing into his own high-backed seat.

"All your money?" he ventured yet again, as if the repetition might finally bring him a different reply. When Malcolm merely inclined his head, the banker sank further into his chair.

"A sip of water, perhaps," he murmured to himself. He swiveled and reached an unsteady hand toward the pitcher and matching glass on the credenza behind him. Crystal clinked against crystal as he poured himself a shaky glassful and proceeded to down the contents in a single gulp.

While the man strove for calm, Halia shot Malcolm a surreptitious glance. *He* appeared quite unmoved by Burnett's plight, an expression of polite expectation blandly etched upon his face. For herself, however, she could feel the guilty color start to burn upon her cheeks. It had never occurred to her that, in carrying out her plan against the Englishman, she might be forced to cause others distress.

Finally, however, Burnett rallied enough to favor them both with a sickly smile.

"Ahem. Do I understand you correctly, Sir John, that you wish to close out your *entire* account with us?"

"Every bloody cent of it," Malcolm replied in a cheerful tone. "And I . . . we prefer cash, rather than a bank draft. And we should like to conclude the transaction immediately, if you do not mind."

"But that is quite impossible." The white handkerchief fluttered to the desktop in an unconscious gesture of surrender. "Why, we are speaking of almost one million dollars."

One million dollars.

Halia bit back an awed gasp. That was almost twice the

sum she had thought the Englishman to have had tucked away, money enough to fund a dozen such expeditions as she now planned. Why, with what would be left once she concluded her own venture, she could set up a scholarship for young women, dedicate a small wing in her father's memory to the New York City Public Library, fund an expedition to . . .

So caught up was Halia in sudden visions of philanthropy that it was a moment before she realized Malcolm was addressing the banker once more.

"—our charming Miss Jones-Smith is quite insistent on that point. There are all manner of furbelows she claims to require, not to mention her desire to refurnish my home from top to bottom prior to the wedding. And given the circumstances, I fear I am obliged to indulge her."

"But, Sir John," the banker persisted in a tone of growing desperation, "you of all people surely must realize what such a decision entails."

"Indeed, I do, Mr. Burnett . . . but I believe I shall charge *you* with the task of explaining the situation to my, er, betrothed."

"Explaining what?" Halia interrupted as confusion and no little trepidation began to take hold. "If the money belongs to Mr. Nor—that is, Sir John, why can he not just have it back?"

The banker cleared his throat. "It is quite simple, my dear. The money is not here to give him."

Chapter 7

"Not here!" Halia's eyes widened, and her anxious gaze flew from Burnett to Malcolm and then back again. "But where did it all go?"

"Why, it is invested, of course. Surely you did not think that we kept all that money simply lying about."

But that is what she *had* thought, why she had embarked upon this mad scheme, at all.

Rightly interpreting her silence as assent, the banker sighed and leaned forward with a self-important air. "Let me explain. This bank, like any other, makes its money by investing the assets of its clients in various trusts, real estate ventures, commodities trading, and so on. As the bank realizes a profit, it returns its clients a portion of those gains . . . payment, so to speak, for the use of their money. That, Miss Jones-Smith, is the nature of banking . . . and that is why I do not have the money to give you just now. In a few days, perhaps . . ."

He trailed off, and a cold hand of despair clamped over Halia's heart. Here, she had risked limb, if not life, to reach this point in her journey, only to learn it had all been for naught! If only she had thought to ask—

Then realization dawned, and she swung about to face Malcolm. He met her glare with a bland look, but Halia did not miss the gleam of satisfaction in his dark eyes.

"Why, you knew all along that this would happen, you fiend, you cad, you—"

She broke off when she caught Burnett's look of well-bred surprise. Reminded of the role she was playing, she choked back the righteous indignation that rose like bile in her throat and strove for composure, even as her thoughts swirled wildly.

No wonder the Englishman had not demurred at the idea of coming to the bank. He had known from the start that his ill-gotten funds would remain safe from her.

Malcolm, meanwhile, favored her with a conciliatory smile that neatly masked his triumph. He addressed her in fond tones. "Do calm yourself, my dearest Bertha, for all is not lost. Once we are married, you can fritter away my fortune to your heart's content."

"But that will be too late, *dearest*," she replied in a sugared tone that was quite the equal of his. "You know that I had certain . . . plans already in place."

"But one does not always get what one wants," he countered and settled with a satisfied air in his chair.

Halia slumped back in her own high-backed seat and swiftly considered her options. Should she expose him right now for the fraud that he was—losing any hope of recovering any of the ill-gotten money—or should she play out her role awhile longer?

In the end, Burnett's advice decided her.

"Please, do not distress yourself, Miss Jones-Smith," that man primly urged, his composure restored, now that he no longer risked the imminent loss of Malcolm's fortune. "I do believe Sir John has a small sum tucked away in one of his personal accounts that might serve for now."

"A small sum?" she repeated with a flicker of hope.

The banker nodded. "Approximately ten thousand dollars, I would venture."

Halia straightened in her chair, rapidly recalculating the basic expenses that her expedition would entail. The amount the banker had offered was sufficient to cover the cost of securing a boat, a crew, and supplies enough to last several weeks . . . or even months, if she were judicious in her expenditures. Though the sum was quite a bit less than she had planned upon, it likely was the most she could hope for by this point.

"I do believe you are right, Mr. Burnett," she finally said, allowing herself a small satisfied smile. "The amount will serve quite well."

"Ah, then our problem is settled. Shall I presume, Sir John," he added with a look back at Malcolm, "that you will authorize me to make this withdrawal in the young lady's name?"

Malcolm sat silent for the space of several heartbeats, his look of complacency momentarily stiffening into an expression that was less pleasant. Then, with a bored wave of one hand, he deigned to reply.

"Very well, give the bloody money to her, then," came his ungracious response.

The clipped words, so unlike the urbane tones he employed as Sir John Abbot, drew a small frown from the banker. Then, just as quickly, Malcolm regained his earlier air of bland congeniality.

"Do let us get on with it, then," he told Burnett. "I have no doubt that my, er, betrothed, is eager to begin spending my money."

"Quite so."

With alacrity, the banker rose and stuck his bald pate past the glass door, gesturing as he did so for one of the clerks to attend him. While Burnett engaged that young man in swift conversation, Malcolm turned back to her with the same convivial air.

"You see, my dear Bertha," he addressed her, "all has worked out as it should, after all. I would even venture that, once you have safely tucked away that bit of pocket change into your reticule, you will no longer feel the need to plunder any other of my accounts."

It was a neatly veiled warning, Halia knew, but she chose to overlook the threat. Much as she would have enjoyed relieving him of *all* his ill-gotten riches, she had what she needed now. Besides, once their business together was concluded, she had no intention of ever setting eyes on the Englishman again.

"You are quite right. I promise that this is the first and last time I shall trouble you this way."

So saying, she settled back in her seat, her gloved hands tightly clasped around her reticule strings while the three of them silently awaited the clerk's return. After a seemingly interminable delay, the young man reappeared with a brick-sized packet neatly wrapped in brown paper.

The banker rose to take the packet; then, with an almost courtly bow, he settled it into Halia's waiting hands. "Ten thousand dollars, Miss Jones-Smith."

"Thank you, Mr. Burnett," she breathlessly managed and stuffed the bundled cash into her reticule. Then, fearful lest Malcolm or the banker might think twice about this unorthodox transaction, she hurriedly stood.

"I do believe I must be about those errands that we spoke of," she explained and with a final nod for Burnett started toward the door.

"One moment, luv."

With that drawling command, Malcolm rose from his own chair. He moved with swift grace so that, quite before Halia realized what had happened, he stood between her and the glass door.

"Bertha, my dear," he chided her in a light tone as she reluctantly met his gaze. "Surely you did not intend to leave without one last word to me?"

The chill smile he gave her held nothing of "Sir John's" bland charm. Rather, it reflected a certain triumphant satisfaction, as if he and not she had been the victor here.

And why did she harbor a sudden, unsettling fear that such might well be the case?

With a mental shake, she dismissed her uncertainties. "Indeed, how thoughtless of me. Good-bye, then," she replied and unthinkingly offered her gloved hand.

Malcolm promptly grasped her fingers and pulled her toward him, so that she now stood inches from the starch-fronted expanse of his chest. Yet this time, it was not the touch of his hand that affected her, so much as the way his dark eyes glinted with some unnamed emotion that sent an answering shiver through her.

"My dearest Bertha," he countered in a caressing tone as he caught her by the shoulders, "is that any way to bid your intended farewell?"

She opened her mouth to reply, but before she could manage a word, Malcolm bent and claimed her lips with his.

The kiss was no formal token of affection but instead a heated demand that sent her reeling. His mouth against hers was hot, insistent . . . as if he might draw the very breath from her and leave her quite senseless, she thought in sudden alarm.

She made as if to pull free, but the abrupt tightening of his grasp recalled her to the role that she was playing. She must endure this indignity, she realized, or else risk unwelcome questions from Burnett. But even as she steeled herself to accept this barbarous treatment, a stirring of unfamiliar feminine awareness rippled through her.

And, suddenly, she was kissing him back.

An inner voice frantically reminded her that this was madness of the worst sort . . . that she had no love for this man . . . that she was making a public display of herself over a rogue, a thief. Yet here she was, pressed against him in a wanton manner, eagerly parting her lips so that he could better taste her. It was uncalled for, illogical.

Whatever could be wrong with her, that she was behaving in such a fashion?

But barely had such thoughts registered in her mind than
Malcolm abruptly drew back and released his hold. She
swallowed a small cry of protest and took a stumbling step
back, aware now that Malcolm's expression of triumph had
given way to something closer to uncertainty.

For her own part, her heart was pounding like a mare at
full gallop. The hot rush of blood she could feel rising in her
face was no doubt staining her cheeks a lamentable shade of
red. As for her breathing, it was none too steady now, as if
she had walked much too far and fast.

But even as she struggled for composure, Malcolm favored her with a bland smile. "And that, my dearest Bertha,
is what I would call a proper farewell," he commented and
then stepped aside, his tone as light as if he had done nothing more scandalous than tweak her nose.

Halia was saved from a reply—if, indeed, she had been
capable that moment of making one—by a muffled sound
from Burnett that might have been a cough. Gathering what
remained of her dignity, she turned her back on the Englishman a final time and smartly marched back past the glass
door.

Barely had she gained the main lobby than a smattering
of applause stopped her short. She glanced about her to see
that the attention of all six young clerks and a good dozen of
the bank's customers was fixed upon her. Some leered good-
naturedly, while the others wore expressions of righteous
disapproval. Sudden suspicion took hold, and she glanced
back the way that she had just come. Burnett and Malcolm
both were clearly visible behind the glass door that led to the
banker's office.

Which meant, she realized in horrified embarrassment,
that the men standing before her had been an audience to
Malcolm's audacious kissing of her just moments before.

The blood in her cheeks burned hotter still. It was all
Halia could do not to gather up her skirts and make an undignified run for the main door and the street beyond. As it

was, she made her departure at a pace slightly faster than might be considered decorous.

It was with an acute sense of relief that she pulled open the door and plunged out into the blaze of hot sunlight once more. Blinking against the glare, she saw that Lally and Christophe still waited with the hired coach.

"The money, you be gettin' it, den?" Lally demanded of her as Christophe held open the carriage door.

Halia did not pause for conversation but merely nodded and then clambered inside. "Let us return to the docks again, Christophe," she instructed him as Lally settled opposite her. "We must see about hiring a ship for the next leg of our journey."

With a nod, the Negro shut the door after them and took his place atop with the driver. The coach lurched forward, rejoining the numerous other carriages, carts, and riders on the busy thoroughfare.

Once the coach was well embedded within the swell of vehicles, Halia allowed herself a sigh. She had accomplished what she had set out to do, after all. She was more than halfway to her destination and possessed of an ample sum of cash, to boot! Moreover, everything—well, *almost* everything—had gone quite the way she had planned it. If only the remainder of her journey would unfold so smoothly . . .

"The spirits, they be right, again. Dat man, he be castin' a spell of his own on you."

"A spell?"

Puzzled, Halia glanced at the other woman to see her dark features set into lines of ill-concealed loathing. Why, it was as if Lally knew that some exchange besides a monetary one had happened inside the bank.

Memories of Malcolm's kiss taunted her, and she fought back a guilty blush. Even to herself, she would not admit that his ungallant gesture had ignited within her psyche a flicker of attraction quite at odds with logic. But she could not deny the purely feminine response he had somehow drawn from her body . . . a hot curl of restless energy that still lingered within her.

Perhaps the rogue *had* worked some sort of sorcery on her, after all!

Firmly, she shook off such fancies. "Spell or no, we finally are rid of Mr. Northrup," she replied, instead. "And as I do have his money—though perhaps not as much as I had hoped to lay hands on—it should be a simple enough matter to find a ship. So do not fret, Lally. All is well."

"Hmmph."

The single syllable held a Greek chorus's worth of doom, but Halia feigned deafness. No point in lingering over what was past, she decided. Once they had resumed their travel, she would soon forget all about the man.

For, surely the vague excitement she'd felt at the single bold kiss of a rogue Englishman would pale before the thrill of discovering the lost continent of Atlantis.

"I will be but a few minutes, Mr. Burnett."

With that assurance, Malcolm took a chair at the broad table that was the only other item of furniture in the windowless chamber. Plainly paneled and lacking any decoration, the tiny room bore more than a passing resemblance to a monk's cell . . . though the business undertaken within was decidedly worldly. Here, the better-heeled of the bank's customers conducted their own private transactions, safe from the common eye.

Malcolm waited until the banker had shut the door after him. Then, with the eagerness of a lad on Christmas Day, he applied a small iron key to the lock of the safety deposit box set before him.

The hinges gave but a whisper of protest as he raised the narrow lid to reveal its contents. Methodically, he began sorting out the objects . . . among them, a ribbon-tied bundle of stock certificates, authentic-looking if quite worthless;

half-a-dozen gold pocket watches; a pair of diamond cuff studs.

He picked up a gold dollar piece. With a careless bit of legerdemain, he maneuvered it along the knuckles of one hand, then tossed the coin back with a score more like it. Then, with a wry shake of his head, he drew forth a stack of bills the equal of the sum he had just relinquished.

The loss, while galling, had been a small enough price to pay for gaining the upper hand in the game. He might as easily have given up ten times that amount and not noticed the damage.

What had the more lasting impact on him, he reluctantly conceded, was his reaction to their kiss.

Malcolm gave himself a mental shake, but he could not quite dislodge the memory. He'd intended the kiss as a final, mocking reminder to Halia that he *had,* in the end, bested her at the game. What he had not expected was the unsettling physical reaction he experienced . . . a fierce, odd sort of hunger quite removed from anything so simple as pure lust. It wasn't just that he had felt in sudden need of a woman, having denied himself that particular pleasure for some time now in the face of more pressing matters. What unnerved him was the fact that, at that moment, he had wanted only one certain woman.

Deliberately, Malcolm shoved aside that moment of self-realization and its possible ramifications. He had more important issues facing him now, and but a short time in which to make his decisions.

With that in mind, he tucked away the cash into his jacket pocket, then reached back into the iron box to pull forth yet another prize. His fingers closed on a black velvet pouch securely bound with a sizable length of gold cord. Unraveling those knots, he spilled forth a blaze of cold green fire into one outstretched hand.

Poseidon's Tear.

Malcolm gazed with outright reverence at the rough-cut

emerald that nestled in his gloved palm. The size and shape of a plover's egg, the gem had earned its name almost a century earlier from its discoverer, an elderly Englishman with a penchant for Greek mythology. Within six months of his find, however, that gentleman had died quite suddenly . . . and quite mysteriously, it was claimed, though the details of his passing had been lost with time.

The emerald had changed hands two dozen or more times since then, Malcolm knew, accumulating with each new owner yet another bit of legend and superstition. Some tales claimed that Poseidon's Tear was but a cursed rock, bringing those who possessed it little better than misery—and, sometimes, death. Still other stories attributed great good luck to the gem and to those fortunate enough to lay hands on it. Needless to say, Malcolm subscribed to that latter body of superstition.

He allowed himself a small grin. That promise of good fortune, combined with the emerald's intrinsic worth, was what had led him to steal the stone from its most recent owner. The fact that this man had been one Seamus O'Neill, modern-day buccaneer and Malcolm's sometime partner, had only made the acquisition that much sweeter.

Malcolm admired the brilliant green jewel a moment longer. The coincidence of the sea god's name in connection with both the emerald and his enforced association with Halia was not lost on him. Gambler that he'd always been, he had learned not to ignore such omens. Fate had dealt him a new and quite interesting hand, and he'd be a fool not to play it.

Thoughtfully, he returned the gem to its velvet wrappings. Then, loosening his collar and cravat, he looped the gold cord over his head and tucked the pouch so that it settled beneath his shirt. Thus concealed, the emerald would be safe from theft yet close enough at hand to bring him its legendary good fortune. Chances were, that in the days to come he was going to need all the luck he could find.

With that thought in mind, Malcolm finally plucked from the strongbox the object for which he had come.

It was an unprepossessing document, merely a ragged-edged sheet of paper torn from a journal of sorts. Well-creased and liberally smudged with dirty fingermarks, it bore signs of having been carried about for some time. He'd only given it a single, cursory read the night he had bought it, having assumed the claim it made was but a hoax. Now, however, he read the few inked lines with care.

—*best of my knowledge. The coin, while admittedly a compelling exhibit, is hardly proof enough to support my claim. But my preliminary study of the formations in question convinces me that they are man-made, and not merely a function of Nature.*

As for Plato's account, it does not prohibit the Bimini Islands as being the possible locale of the lost continent. Rather, an enlightened reading of the original Greek supports this argument. All in all, it is my informed opinion that further exploration of the site is warranted and that such an endeavor will ultimately yield an archeological find unmatched in this or any other century.

Malcolm paused, a thoughtful frown creasing his brow. The reference to a coin brought to mind the gold disk that Halia wore about her neck. Perhaps her pendant was the same artifact the writer of this journal page had seen, or maybe there was a whole bloody cache of them lying about. But more telling than the mention of the coin was the series of numbers penciled beneath the text . . . a navigational coordinate, if his guess was correct.

He returned his attention to the page. Accompanying those numbers was a crude rendering of what he presumed to be the Biminis . . . an untidy cluster of two main islands, one of them little more than a sliver of coast, combined with several smaller islets to form a ragged C. Just off the northwest shoreline was sketched a series of squares laid out like a section of cobbled lane. In neat block letters beside those squares was written a single word.

Atlantis.

His frown eased into a chill smile. No doubt Miss Davenport would give much to possess a map that detailed the location of the supposed Atlantis site. Without these coordinates, she would be forced to plumb every inch of Biminian coastline, a task that might take weeks. With the proper heading, however, she could begin immediate recovery of the treasure trove buried beneath the Caribbean.

Momentarily, he considered simply taking the coordinates, hiring his own crew, and recovering whatever spoils there were to be had—without Halia's help. Just as quickly, however, he dismissed that plan. He had no love for the ocean, and the idea of his swimming beneath the waves in search of some elusive treasure held no appeal for him. Moreover, he hadn't the faintest idea of how to direct such an archeological expedition on his own.

Halia, however, did.

Partners, it is to be, then, he wryly told himself. Deliberately, he refolded the page and tucked it away with his cash, then returned the rest of his belongings to the strongbox. The time had come to take the offensive in the matter of Miss Halia Davenport. The chit owed him, she did . . . and he was bloody well ready to collect on that debt.

By the time he quit the bank and was strolling down the cobbled lane, he already had decided upon a rudimentary plan of action. With luck, the ever-resourceful Wilkie would have swiftly determined the reason for Malcolm's disappearance several days earlier. Chances were that he was already en route to Savannah and would be meeting Malcolm at the boardinghouse that was their prearranged rendezvous. Once that happened, the pair of them had only to learn on which ship Halia had booked passage for the next leg of her journey, so that they could make the same arrangements.

Sidestepping a pile of rubbish, Malcolm allowed himself a smug grin. Catching up with her again would be the easy part of his job. After all, how many beautiful blond young women bound for the Biminis could there be in this city? Moreover, how many of said young blond women were accompanied by a surly Negro giant of a butler/coachman and a Haitian lady's maid who likely was equally handy pinning up hair or casting voodoo curses?

Idly, Malcolm ran more details of his plan through his mind. Once at sea, he would confront the chit and make his offer . . . the Atlantis coordinates, in exchange for half of whatever treasure she might discover. She could hardly deny him, especially considering that it was *his* money she was using to fund her expedition. And if that argument did not convince her, he had another method of persuasion at his disposal, one that had served him quite well in the past.

If Halia refused to relinquish his share of the find, he simply would seduce his half right out from under her.

Chapter 8

" 'Tain't fair by 'alf," Wilkie grumbled with a longing look at the retreating shore. " 'Ere, I just 'opped off one boat, an' I'm right back on another."

"I quite concur," Malcolm acknowledged his companion's plaint with a wry twist of his lips. "The last place I care to be right now is aboard ship, particularly in light of my most recent sea voyage. Unfortunately, a carriage will not get us to the Biminis."

He plucked a handkerchief from his breast pocket and wiped the perspiration that ringed his brow as the morning sun ripened. In another hour or so, the temperature would be all but unbearable, even with the brisk sea breeze that tugged at his hat with briny impertinence. But the heat would not be the worst of it.

Gamely, he fought the queasy sensation that had settled in his gut ever since the ship raised anchor half an hour before. Damn, but he hated the bloody ocean and every mother's son of a bloody ship that sailed it! Why, even the name of the steamer on which they now traveled irked him to no end. The *Retribution,* it was called . . . a bloody unpleasant sort of moniker, under the circumstances.

Reminding himself that the emerald he carried would cancel out that trifling bit of ill omen, he gave Wilkie a resigned shrug. "Remember what I told you last night. In the end, you will find this voyage a small enough price to pay for the prize at stake."

" 'Ere's 'oping, then."

The doubt in Wilkie's tone indicated his belief that the chances of such an outcome were slim, at best. Still, Malcolm knew that his partner would follow his lead, if only from habit.

The older man had arrived in Savannah the night before, reaching their rendezvous spot several hours after Malcolm had quit the bank. Reassuring Wilkie as to the state of his health, Malcolm had gone on to relate the details of his capture and subsequent abduction. Wilkie's relief upon discovering that his partner was alive and in the city had given way to smugness as, for much of the remaining evening, he recounted the steps he had taken in the aftermath of Malcolm's unexpected disappearance.

An' a right fine piece o' work it was, too, he had opined with no little pride. With a wry smile, Malcolm recalled the rest of the man's tale.

When his partner had not returned to the hotel, as planned, Wilkie had assumed the worst. He first sent word to the benevolent society Malcolm was scheduled to address that night that Sir John had fallen ill, with his chances of recovery slim. Then, with the shrewd instincts of a man who had successfully outwitted any number of local constabularies, he began piecing together the details of Malcolm's abduction.

With no other clue at hand, Wilkie had made his way to the Davenport brownstone only to find the house locked and deserted. Making unorthodox use of an upper story window, he had gained entry and begun a swift search. The only evidence he had found as to Malcolm's fate had been more than a little alarming . . . several blood-soaked cloths left lying in a basin.

Fearing for his partner's health—if not his very life— Wilkie set out on their trail. He had managed to track down the hack driver whose carriage Christophe had borrowed to carry the trio to the dock. From there, it had been a matter of a few coins pressed into the right palms to discover which ship they had boarded. Within hours, he had been on a ship bound for the same destination as Malcolm, and he possessed a fair description of the three kidnappers.

Now, Wilkie heaved a gusty sigh and deliberately turned his back on the distant shore. "So, 'ow long do ye plan on waitin' afore ye let 'er catch a glimpse o' ye . . . that is, if she'll even recognize ye?"

"If the 'she' you are referring to is Miss Davenport, I would venture the two of us will cross paths quite shortly. After all, there is hardly room here to hide," he explained with an encompassing gesture at the tidy little steamer on which they were traveling.

In answer to Wilkie's other observation, he absently scrubbed a hand across his smooth upper lip, his mustache and bushy sidewhiskers having gone the way of the departed Sir John. Given the fact that he had affected that style for the better part of a year now, he had been hard-pressed to recognize himself in the mirror last night once he'd shaved away the last of his facial hair. Without it, he looked little older than a school lad, was his own private assessment. Still, the fewer ties he had to his most recent alter ego, the better . . . especially in this part of the world. With that in mind, he had also reverted to the use of his true name for this particular venture.

He returned his thoughts to that matter. This voyage, he had learned, would be brief—little more than two days to travel to Florida's southeastern coast, and then a short journey through the Straits of Florida to the Biminis. He knew nothing more of Halia's plans beyond that; still, it followed that she must hire a smaller vessel capable of plumbing the shoreline once they reached the islands. Those details, however, he would leave to her.

He fondly patted the breast pocket of his coat, where the

Atlantis coordinates were safely tucked away. He had learned the page by rote, lest some unforeseen disaster occur and he be forced to recreate its contents from memory. Either way, however, he held the trump card in this game of theirs . . . a card he was more than ready to play. It only remained now to be seen if she joined him willingly, or not.

Halia leaned against the railing of the steamer's upper deck and turned her face to the breeze. For the first time in these past nightmarish days, she felt almost at peace with herself. Her outlandish plan had proved a success, after all. Here she was, free at last of the Englishman, and well on her way to Bimini.

She tied the white ribbons of her straw hat more tightly beneath her chin and let her thoughts drift back to the past two days. With the money she had wrested from Malcolm, she had begun making preparations for the final leg of her journey. In addition to several weeks' worth of rations and supplies, she would be in need of a boat and crew. To that end, she'd send advance word to an acquaintance of her father's in the islands, one Captain Rolle.

Captain Rolle, the journal notes had indicated, was a native Bimini Islander and an experienced sailor, with a sloop of his own. True, he had not been with Arvin Davenport during that last, most important discovery of his—oddly, no ship or crew of any sort was mentioned in that account— but his knowledge of the surrounding waters would make the captain an ideal candidate for the job she had in mind.

She could only hope that her message reached him before she landed . . . and that he was not already otherwise engaged.

With the appropriate telegrams sent, she had set about purchasing the first of her supplies, having already booked passage on the *Retribution* for the following day. That accomplished, she performed her most difficult duty, saying good-bye to Christophe.

"Me, I can't be goin' with you," he had flatly stated the night before.

He had refused to elaborate, so that Halia had been at her wits' end. Vaguely, she recalled Lally hinting that her brother harbored some dark secret that had forced him to leave his native Haiti when he was but a young man. What it was, she could not guess . . . an illicit love affair, perhaps. Hardly reason enough to leave two women to travel on their own, Halia had thought in some pique. Still, she could hardly force the man to go where he did not care to go.

"Perhaps it is just as well," she had finally conceded as she counted out his return passage. "I would feel much better knowing our town house was attended, lest a certain Englishman of our acquaintance decide to pay a visit while we are gone. Besides which, once we make Bimini, Captain Rolle will see to our welfare."

Now, however, she realized that her concerns over her and Lally traveling alone were groundless. Indeed, there was a sort of freedom that a clear sky and calm, open waters brought with them that she'd never quite noticed while traveling with her father. She intended to revel in it.

With that in mind, she left her post at the ship's bow and strolled about the deck, greeting her fellow passengers who also were enjoying the ocean breeze. One of them—a portly, bespectacled gentleman of middle years whose most remarkable feature was his bushy gray beard—seemed familiar. Her first thought was that she might previously have met him at some lecture or another she had attended with her father. When the man gave no sign of recognizing her, however, she decided that she must have been mistaken.

But she was more certain of the identity of another of her fellow passengers whom she suddenly glimpsed across the deck from her.

"Oh, my," she breathed in horror and halted.

The deck beneath her feet seemed to tilt wildly, as if she were a landlubber unused to the ocean's movement. She clutched at the railing for support, a litany of denial now playing through her mind.

It couldn't be . . . no, surely this would be too cruel a trick for the Fates to be playing.

Some perverse sort of curiosity held her there, waiting for him to look her way. For she had not seen his face, as yet, given the fact that his back was to her and he was engaged in conversation with another, older man. She reminded herself that there still remained a chance that she was again wrong in her identification, that it might not be he.

Then she shook her head. She could never mistake the coolly arrogant set of Malcolm Northrup's shoulders or the understated elegance of his gestures.

As if feeling her gaze upon him, the man turned in her direction. Her instinctive gasp of dismay became a sigh of relief when she saw that, unlike her nemesis, this man was cleanshaven. *Just a silly mistake,* she scolded herself and made as if to continue her walk.

Then he favored her with a cool smile and a jaunty salute, so that her uncertainty came rushing back. What if it *was* he, and he had merely taken a razor to his face? Unwilling, all at once, to test that hypothesis, she spun about and headed for the sanctuary of her quarters below deck.

A moment later, white skirts aswirl and hat tilted at a precarious angle, Halia burst into the tiny cabin that she shared with Lally, not bothering to close the door behind her.

The Haitian woman was sorting the contents of a frayed carpetbag across one narrow bunk. Halia, despite her distress, noted an eclectic collection of items. A glance revealed a half dozen bundles of chicken feathers, carefully sorted by size and color; a dozen or so slim candles, some black, some white, some red; numerous paper packets of various herbs, fresh and dried, whose combined fragrances filled the cramped quarters with a heady perfume.

At the commotion, Lally replaced the squat bottle she held alongside a collection of similar such containers. Then, smoothing the skirt of her simple yellow shift, she favored Halia with a look of mild reproach.

"An' what be your big hurry, girl?"

"He's here," she gasped out, collapsing onto her own berth. "That is, I think it is he."

She shut her eyes and tried to catch her breath. She *had* to be mistaken, she told herself. She had left him safely behind in Savannah, had said nothing to him of her plans save her final destination. Perhaps the events of the past few days had taken their toll on her, and she had merely imagined she had seen Malcolm standing on the deck below her.

Lally, meanwhile, was staring at her in bemusement, the task before her momentarily forgotten. "Who be here?"

"He . . . him . . . Mr. Northrup."

"Dat man?"

Lally's ebony eyes widened; then, just as swiftly, they narrowed into dark, dangerous slits. Purposefully, she reached into her bag and pulled forth a clear glass vial, which she raised to catch the glimmer of daylight shining through the cabin's hand's-breadth of a porthole.

The bottle's liquid contents glowed a malevolent ruby hue. The Negress added, "This time, I be fixin' him good."

"Fixing him? No, Lally, wait!"

Halia leaped to her feet again and stared in horror at the slim bottle, her heart seeming to still in her breast. Just a few days earlier, she had nearly managed to kill the Englishman. She certainly had not nursed him back to comparative health only to let Lally dose him with some lethal brew.

"We've no need to take so drastic a step," she swiftly insisted. "Believe me, we'll find some other way to rid ourselves of Mr. Northrup. We can't just poison the man simply because he followed us from Savannah."

"Poison?"

Lally favored her with a sly smile as she uncorked the bottle. She gave its contents an experimental sniff. Then, with a shrug, she restoppered it and set it out with the rest of her potions. "Who be sayin' anyt'ing 'bout poison? Dat juice, it won't kill him. It just make him be *wishin'* he was dead."

"Oh. I see."

Relief set her heart to beating normally once more. She could ill afford the luxury of giving way to panic, she reminded herself. She had to determine just why the Englishman was following them . . . and what she must do about it.

"Perhaps he wants his money back," she hazarded aloud, the idea sending an uncomfortable shiver through her. "After all, ten thousand dollars is quite a sum to lose, even if one is wealthy. Or, maybe he thinks to follow us to the Atlantis site, and then abscond with whatever riches he can lay his hands on."

Then an even more appalling possibility struck her, one so outrageous that she did not even dare voice it except to herself. She recalled all too clearly their parting at the bank . . . that frightening, heady moment when he had pulled her into his arms and kissed her. Even as she had raged against such cavalier treatment, a small part of her had responded.

What if he had been equally affected? What if Malcolm had come, not in search of money or even treasure, but in pursuit of her?

"Here now, luv," came a familiar voice from the doorway, "Surely you don't think me as crass as all that?"

Halia's eyes flew open again, and her gaze locked with that of the Englishman as he stood leaning against the doorjamb, regarding her with a bland smile. For one painful moment, she feared she might have spoken that last thought aloud, and mortification swept her. Then she realized he simply was referring to her comment about riches, and she sagged with relief.

Never again would she even *think* about the other, was her silent, fervent vow. They were hardly lovers, but were instead enemies, in ideology if not in act. The only common ground between them was beneath their feet. It was a fact she would do well to keep in mind.

"Indeed, Mr. Northrup, this is quite a surprise," she managed, her tone not as unruffled as she might have wished.

She tried not to stare, though her feminine curiosity was piqued by his altered appearance. He looked younger without his mustache and sidewhiskers, even—dare she admit it?—more handsome. Now, she could see the firm line of his well-cut chin and the almost sensual cast to his mouth.

And he has dimples, as well, spoke up a flighty inner voice unlike her usual sensible self. Appalled by this lapse, she took a steadying breath and went on, "And what odd coincidence brings you here, Mr. Northrup? As I understood it, you have no great fondness for sea travel."

"Very true, Miss Davenport, but sometimes one must make sacrifices in the pursuit of one's goals."

"And just what might those goals be?"

"Money . . . treasure," came his lazy reply that quite accurately echoed her own earlier guesses.

He did not wait for Halia's reply but nodded toward his companion standing behind him—a lean man of middling years with a pockmarked face, whose wiry blond hair stuck out at right angles from beneath his bowler.

"Might I introduce you to my associate, Mr. Wilkie Foote. Wilkie, this is Miss Davenport, the charming young woman whom I told you about."

"Right pleased t' meet ye, miss," came that man's almost mournful reply as, sweeping off his hat, he made her a stiff little bow.

Halia's murmured acknowledgement was almost as dismayed. Malcolm, however, let his gaze travel about the tiny cabin.

"And, ah, yes, the redoubtable Lally," he finished his introductions and gave the Haitian woman a mocking tip of his own straw boater. Then, with a gesture at the paraphernalia she had spread across the bunk, he added, "Cooking up a bit of mischief, are you?"

"Dat's for you to be findin' out," Lally spat back with a glare that would have unnerved a lesser man. Catching up a bundle of red rooster feathers, she brandished them menacingly in his direction. Then, reaching for her carpetbag once more, she began shoveling her bottles and potions back within its threadbare confines.

Malcolm merely shrugged, then returned his gaze to Halia. "So tell me, Miss Davenport, are you enjoying spending my hard-earned money?"

"Hard-earned?" she retorted, righteous indignation reviving her powers of speech. "Indeed, that is hardly the term I would employ. And you know full well that my intent is not frivolity, but scientific study . . . which was, as you'll recall, the claim you made to those people from whom you swindled that money in the first place."

"Ah, then perhaps you will have some interest in the proposal I am about to make you. You see, I have given this notion of yours about searching for Atlantis some serious thought. I have concluded it would be to both of our advantages if you and I were to become partners in this particular venture."

"Parnters . . . with you?"

Her voice quivered on an emotion that lay somewhere between hilarity and horror. She glanced behind her to see that Lally had paused in her packing. The parcels of herbs in her hand seemingly forgotten, the older woman stood staring at Malcolm with the same expression of disbelief Halia knew must be written across her own features. As for Wilkie, his pockmarked face remained impassive, though his discreet cough might have been an expression of dismay . . . or else, amusement.

With a shake of her head, she turned back to Malcolm. A second searching look convinced her that he was quite serious in what he had proposed. But what could have made him think she would consider taking him up on so ludicrous an offer?

"It seems I have taken you by surprise," Malcolm broke the silence and favored her with an ironic smile. "Let me elaborate. I am proposing that we travel on to the Biminis together. Once we reach the islands, you will conduct your search for the Atlantis site, funded by the monies I have so generously advanced you. Anything you find, we divide into equal shares—half to me, and the other half to you."

"Equal . . . shares," she faintly echoed.

The words gave rise to her sense of the absurd, that emotion followed quickly by righteous indignation. Really, but the man had audacity! Not only did he think to follow while she conducted serious research, he expected *her* to do all the excavating while he no doubt basked upon the beach. Likely, he expected her to cook and clean for him and his partner, as well.

But more galling than Malcolm's high-handed suggestion was the fact that he regarded her scientific expedition as nothing more than a treasure hunt.

Masking her outrage with a cool smile of her own, she went on, "It does sound like an ideal partnership . . . for you, that is, Mr. Northrup. For my own part, I see no possible advantage to my entertaining your offer."

"Ah, but I disagree. You see, Miss Davenport, I just happen to have laid hands upon a certain document I believe you might find of interest."

"What could you possibly have that might prove of any interest to—"

She broke off as Malcolm straightened from his casual pose against the door frame and, with an infuriating smile, reached into his jacket. He withdrew a folded sheet of familiar-looking paper, which he dangled before her.

"—to you, Miss Davenport?" he softly finished her question. "Indeed, it just happens that I have in my possession the coordinates to your late father's so-called Atlantis site."

"Let me see that!"

Instinctively, Halia made as if to snatch the page from his hand. Malcolm was swifter than she, however, moving out of reach so that her fingers closed upon air.

"Not so fast, luv," he lightly chided and tucked the paper back in his pocket. "You'll see it *after* you've agreed to my terms . . . namely, that I provide the coordinates, you do all the work of recovering the treasure, and we split the profits fifty-fifty."

"But, that is a ludicrous notion," she choked out. "Why should I give half to you when you propose to do none of the work? Besides which, such a find will be of untold historical significance. Each item must be thoroughly documented and then turned over to a scientific institute or a museum, not bartered about on the open market."

"A noble sentiment, Miss Davenport, but hardly a practical one. We both know that you could spend weeks, or months, or even a lifetime searching the Caribbean and still come up empty-handed. With these coordinates"—he lightly tapped his breast pocket—"you can make your way straight to the site and begin recovering artifacts almost immediately. The arrangement *is* more than generous," he added, echoing the sentiment she had expressed to him a few days before.

Hearing her own words turned against her, Halia bit her lip in silent frustration. Why should she believe that Malcolm had the missing page from Arvin Davenport's journal, when he had made a career of duping the unwitting with similar schemes? She herself had told him that the pertinent page had been stolen. It would have been a simple feat for the Englishman to obtain a similar volume and tear a page from it, then make her believe it was the document she sought.

But someone *had* stolen the document, she reminded herself. Some unknown person had crept into her home and boldly torn a leaf from the book, and then vanished with it into the night. Who better to point to as suspect in such a crime than an admitted confidence man?

"But why make me such an offer?" she finally countered, seizing upon the most telling argument. "If those *are* the genuine coordinates, as you claim, why don't you simply fund your own expedition? Then, everything you find would be yours alone."

Malcolm lifted a wry brow. "But you already know the answer to that, luv. I don't propose to do any of the work, merely reap the benefits of your expertise. That is why I am willing to settle for half the treasure . . . as should you."

And half would be better than none, she reluctantly conceded . . . assuming, of course, that the page he'd showed her *was* the missing entry from her father's journal. And perhaps once Malcolm realized the immense importance of uncovering Atlantean artifacts, he might be persuaded to abandon his selfish notions and allow someone other than himself to benefit from his actions.

"Very well, Mr. Northrup," she finally ventured, "let us suppose I am willing to consider your offer. Surely it is only fair that I be allowed to examine the document and determine for myself whether or not it is authentic before I agree to your terms?"

"You can look at it all day, luv . . . that is, once we reach Bimini. I'm not about to hand over my trump card until I'm standing on *terra firma* again. Give it to you now, and I'd likely find myself tossed overboard by your loyal servants," he said with a wry glance over at Lally.

The older woman, who had been following their exchange in watchful silence gave a wordless sound of disdain. Halia bit back a snide retort of her own, for the notion of Lally ruthlessly shoving Malcolm over the ship's railing was satisfying, to be sure.

Instead, she replied, "Then let us strike a preliminary agreement. You shall keep your distance until we disembark at Alice Town, where you will then show me the page you are carrying with you. If I declare the document to be a forgery, we will part company and you will leave the islands on the next boat."

He nodded. "And if you agree that the page did indeed come from your father's journal, in exchange for its return, you will take me on as your partner in the Atlantis expedition. It sounds like an equitable deal to me, Miss Davenport. So now, do I have your hand . . . and your word on it?"

She hesitated, staring at the gloved hand he offered. Surely there could be no harm in this bargain. It would be too much the coincidence for him, of all people, to possess the one document she needed. This had to be another ploy on his part, a cruel game such as those he had played upon countless other victims in the past. By agreeing to his terms, she would at least buy herself a few days of peace on this journey.

"Very well, sir," she replied and took his hand.

This time, she was prepared for his touch, so that the pressure of his fingers against hers sent only the slightest of shivers through her.

The smile Malcolm gave her as their hands separated hinted at the cool satisfaction of a man who believed he had gotten the better part. His tone, however, was bland when he said, "Then I shall bid you a pleasant journey, Miss Davenport, until we dock in Bimini."

Chapter 9

It was as if they were gliding across a vast expanse of green and blue mottled glass, Malcolm thought, in something akin to awe.

Dressed in a dark gray morning suit and stiff-collared shirt and wearing his straw boater, he was seated in the stern of the skiff ferrying him and Halia from the *Retribution*. That ship lay anchored within the shallow, eastward-facing harbor formed by the C-shaped sprawl of Bimini's main islands. That vessel would remain there for the next few hours until the exchange of goods and supplies with the locals concluded.

Half an hour before, Lally and Wilkie—neither trusting the other to handle matters properly—already had set off with the luggage in another, larger boat. The rest of the passengers were bound for other destinations, and he and Halia were the last to put ashore.

It had been just after sunrise when the *Retribution* had begun crossing the fifty-mile wide strip of gray-blue water off Florida's southwestern coast that was part of the Gulf Stream. A misty dawn had clung to an austere sea quite devoid of welcome. Even when the sun finally burnt off the fog to reveal a sky of so blue a hue that it might have been taken from an artist's canvas, Malcolm was not impressed. He had remained that way for the next few hours until finally a sliver of land, riding low in the water, appeared upon the horizon.

From a distance, the island's green and white vista had appeared pleasant enough, if not the lush Eden he might have imagined it would be. As they drew closer and the water grew clearer and bluer, he realized that it was the surrounding sea that gave the place its beauty.

Now, he clung to the side of their single-sailed, flat-hulled boat as their guide, a taciturn Bimini Islander with skin the color of obsidian, expertly maneuvered them across the shallow reef. Their ultimate destination, he understood to be a point just to the north of the port city of Alice Town, where Halia had obtained a house for the duration of their stay.

By degrees, Malcolm allowed himself to relax. This was the part of any sea voyage that he usually dreaded. To his mind, only a bloody idiot could claim to enjoy bouncing about the waves in a teacup of a boat that was liable to sink at any moment. For once, however, he found himself almost at ease upon the ocean—not relishing the trip, mind you, but not in fear of his life.

For never had he seen so clear and peaceful a body of water.

Perversely, the sight also called to mind his London childhood. He had spent many of those years near the Thames—a muddy, garbage-strewn twist of river whose stench could fair knock a strong man to his knees. That alone would have been sufficient to give him a dislike of the water. A terrifying crossing over a storm-raked channel when he was but half-grown had instilled a permanent distaste for sea travel.

But this . . . this molten jewel of a sea, so clear that he could see straight down to the sparkling white sand far below, could pick out bright flashes of color that were tiny, impossibly-hued fish . . . this held an allure from which even he was not immune.

Then a flicker of movement beneath the glasslike green waves caught his attention. He leaned closer to the water's edge, then abruptly drew back and swallowed hard. A dozen or so feet below the water's surface, a shadowy figure half again as long as a man was tall had just swum directly beneath their boat.

A bloody shark!

Or was it? He'd never seen a live shark before. The nearest he had come to such an encounter was passing the sign outside a particular London waterfront tavern known as the Shark's Tooth. That lurid placard depicted a smiling hammerhead making a feast of a luckless sailor, hardly a pleasant image.

"Quite a sight, is it not?" Halia's voice drifted to him with the warm sea breeze, the first words she had spoken since they'd left the *Retribution.*

Malcolm started. Then, realizing it was to the scenery at large, rather than to that unknown sea creature that she referred, he weakly nodded. The tone of disdain that she normally employed when addressing him had vanished, he noted in some surprise. Rather, it was replaced by a note of almost joyous satisfaction. Thoughts of the shark shoved from his mind, Malcolm turned his attention from the sea to the young woman who would soon be making him his latest fortune.

She sat beside him, her broad-brimmed hat forgotten in her lap and a worn carpetbag propped on her knees, her face turned to catch the ocean spray. Dressed in a crisp yellow skirt and matching jacket, with wisps of blond hair playing about her face like seafoam, she appeared perfectly at home atop the gentle swell of waves. An expression akin to anticipation played across her delicately chiseled features.

As if she were awaiting a long-lost lover, Malcolm decided in a lapse into unaccustomed fancy.

The notion triggered a sudden, urgent ache within his loins that took him by surprise.

Keep your mind on bloody business, my lad, he silently warned himself. If there was one thing he'd learned in his long and successful career as a con man, it was never to let a bit of muslin distract him from the goal at hand. Mastering his unwanted reaction, he sought refuge in the mundane.

"It's a pleasant enough view, I suppose," he conceded with a gesture toward the approaching shore. "Perhaps you should tell me a bit about the place, since we will be making it our home for some time."

Halia's green eyes—their color so like the dancing waves—locked on his, her expression of anticipation replaced by angry resignation.

"Whether or not *you* stay remains to be seen. But perhaps it would do you well to know something about the islands, at that."

She settled back against the boat's edge, her gaze once more turned to the shore. A hint of irritation still evident in her tone, she began, "The Bimini Islands are, as you know, part of the Bahamas. They consist of two main islands and several small cays"—she pronounced that last word as "keys"—"but cover barely ten square miles, in all. The islands were officially discovered by the Europeans approximately four hundred years ago, as part of their colonization of the New World."

"Ah, yes, that Columbus fellow," Malcolm murmured.

Halia ignored the interruption. "The Spaniards came first, followed later by the English, who actually began settling here under charter. It was during that first colonization that the islands also became home to brutal privateers and smugglers . . . people of your own sort, Mr. Northrup," came her cool aside.

She was closer to being correct than she might have expected. When Malcolm only shrugged, however, she resumed her lecturing tone.

"These pirates found the islands an ideal spot from which to plunder merchant ships traveling between Europe and the Americas. They soon became a scourge with which to reckon, those pirates of the Caribbean. The English finally put a stop to it early in the previous century, but another equal evil continued to flourish."

"Slavery," Malcolm finished for her, with a sidling look at their dark-skinned oarsman. That man, however, appeared to be paying no heed to this history lesson but silently guided the craft past a floating clump of yellow gulf weed.

Halia soberly nodded. "Slavery was common in the West Indies for almost three centuries. Ships would arrive from West Africa on a regular basis, their holds overflowing with men, women, and children brutally torn from their homelands to work the canefields. That shameful practice continued until fifty or so years ago, when the English passed the Emancipation Act."

"Several decades ahead of you colonials," he pointed out when she paused for breath.

She gave a grudging nod at the truth of that last and went on, "Once freed, the greatest number of those former slaves elected to remain in the West Indies . . . some on the land that their former masters deeded to them. Others roamed throughout the Bahamas and settled on various other islands. They later were joined by escaped American slaves who were seeking sanctuary outside the United States while our own war for freedom raged on. Now, almost six hundred people—black and white—live here in the Biminis."

"Quite interesting," Malcolm drawled in a tone to imply the opposite, "but what about your Atlantis theory? Where do your wandering Greeks fit in here?"

"I am getting to that." She plopped her hat back on and tied its white ribbons beneath her chin. "The islands' earliest settlers were South American Indians—the Lucayans, to be exact—who may have inhabited the islands as much as five hundred years earlier than the Spaniards' first arrival . . . approximately 1000 A.D., if you have some difficulty with the arithmetic, Mr. Northrup. But if my father's theory is correct, a flourishing civilization had established itself here at the far reaches of the Atlantic thirty-five hundred years earlier than even that."

"But why travel thousands of miles from their homeland to settle here, of all places?" Malcolm asked, mildly curious, despite himself, to see where her arguments would lead.

Halia gave a dismissive wave of her hand. "As to why the original Atlanteans left their home, I can only conjecture. Perhaps their ideas on government and technology caused them to be persecuted . . . or perhaps, like many peoples, they traveled far afield simply for the adventure of it all. But as to why they came here"—she paused for an encompassing gesture at the sea and rapidly approaching shore—"I would think that self-evident."

"Defense," he promptly guessed. "The Biminis are far enough from the mainland to be easily defended from invaders, yet close enough so that travel back and forth would be a simple affair."

"Perhaps there is some merit in your reasoning," she conceded, "but that is not quite what I had in mind. As surely even you must agree, the islands are beautiful and peaceful. Too, they are well-situated on the Gulf Stream so that the weather is almost always pleasant. It could be an idyllic setting, given the suitable companions."

The faint curl to her full lips with that last remark implied that Malcolm did not number among that chosen. He had no time to reply to that unspoken insult, however, for land was upon them. The skiff sliced with knifelike ease toward a crude pier that jutted from the rocky shore.

"This be the place," their guide spoke up for the first time as he furled the sail and made fast the lines.

He pointed to a low bluff several dozen yards beyond, atop which sat a two-storied, white clapboard house with bright yellow shutters and a flanking of ragged green palms. An inviting-looking veranda, the sort where a man might lean back in a chair and prop his boots on the railing, stretched along both levels and overlooked the island's eastern coast.

Malcolm noted the trail of newly churned sand that led in a straight line to the house from where they stood. There, he made out several dark-skinned, brightly dressed figures all shouldering trunks and cases of various sizes and milling around an open doorway.

Not a bad spot to spend the next few weeks, Malcolm decided. Then he saw the dark-skinned man seated on a slab of rock at the foot of the bluff.

"That must be Captain Rolle," Halia declared as the man uncoiled himself from his casual pose and moved with pantherlike grace toward them.

His was the blue-black skin of unmixed African heritage, and Malcolm wondered if his parents might have been those former slaves of whom Halia had spoken. He wore a jaunty blue seaman's cap atop his close-cropped black hair, and a gold earring adorned his right lobe. He was dressed all in white, from the requisite baggy pants to the rolled-sleeved cotton shirt that stretched alarmingly over his massive biceps and chest.

Another bloody pirate, Malcolm thought with an inner groan.

Already, Halia had climbed from the skiff. Once their taciturn boatman handed her carpetbag over to her, she picked her way through the wet sand to a point beyond where the sparkling water was playfully lapping at the shore. She let her gear plop to the ground, then held out her hand to the dark-skinned man standing before her.

"You be Miss Davenport?" he asked in the now-familiar musical cadence of the islands as he took her hand.

She nodded. "I've been looking forward to meeting you, Captain Rolle. My father was impressed with your knowledge of these waters . . . and I do believe he quite liked you, as well."

"Me, I enjoyed workin' wit' Mr. Arvin," came the man's solemn reply. "I be sad to be hearin' dat he died."

Malcolm heard the catch in Halia's voice as she thanked the man, and he gave a speculative frown. *So she was still grieving for her father,* he realized, filing that thought away for future reference. Himself, he would not have cared a bloody fig either way if his own father lived or died.

Her moment of weakness seemingly passed, Halia turned her attention back to Malcolm. "Lally and your Mr. Foote must already have seen to the luggage," she briskly noted. "It would seem, then, that only one thing remains yet to be settled . . . a test of sorts, if you will." So saying, she bent and reached inside her carpetbag.

The sight of her rounded backside directed his way caused Malcolm, who had swung one leg over the vessel's edge, to halt. Forgetting his warning of a few moments before to himself, he did the only reasonable thing he could do, under the circumstances. He remained straddled over the boat's bow and enjoyed the view.

Enhanced by just the hint of a bustle, that portion of her anatomy held an unexpected charm that he had never noticed until then. It occurred to him, too, that she did not dress to flaunt her womanly attributes, nor did she slavishly follow the latest modes in dress. Rather, she favored simple styles that, to his jaded eye, were a refreshing change from those of the self-consciously fashionable females to whom he had most recently been paying court.

As Malcolm reached this conclusion, Halia straightened and turned toward him once more, a slim, cloth-bound volume clutched in one hand. Recalled to the present matter, he hurriedly scrambled out onto the sand . . . only to fall to his knees as a sugarlike spill of white beach lurched up to meet him.

"Haven't lost your sea legs, Mr. Northrup?"

Though her inquiry was polite, her tone held a note that was suspiciously like a suppressed snicker. For his part,

Captain Rolle did not bother to hide his amusement but flashed a brilliant white grin Malcolm's way.

Fighting the tide of hot color he could feel rising up his neck at this ungainly display he'd made of himself, Malcolm staggered to his feet. He would remain where he stood, at least until he regained his equilibrium. Damned if he'd give the pair another chance to laugh at him.

"The sand is a bit loose, I fear," he answered in a stiff tone. "Now, what is this about a test?"

"It is quite simple. You claim to hold the missing page from my father's journal. I just happen to have that journal with me."

She held out the volume in one palm, like a sacrificial offering, and flipped open its cover. The inner pages fell open to a place somewhere beyond the middle, where a ragged edge of paper sprang like a cock's comb down its center.

"All we need do is fit your page here, to the exact spot from which the missing page was torn," she went on. "If it does not match, then you will go right back to the ship. But if both edges align exactly, then I will concede that your find is genuine . . . and I will take you on as my partner."

"*Equal* partner," Malcolm clarified. With a flourish, he whipped the paper in question from his coat pocket and smoothed its creases.

Halia frowned. "Do hurry, Mr. Northrup. You would not want the *Retribution* to weigh anchor without you."

"She can set sail at any time. I'll not be on her," was his blunt reply as he took a few measured steps toward her and handed her the page.

So you think, Mr. Northrup, she silently answered him. With nervous fingers, she took hold of the page, glancing as she did so at the several lines of text there. It *did* resemble her father's work, she conceded, but that did not necessarily mean—

"Ah-ah, Miss Davenport. No fair reading until you match up the two pieces."

Malcolm plucked the page back from her; then, with all the drama that she had grown to expect from him, he fitted the paper to the torn edge of her book.

The two aligned exactly.

"Oh, my," Halia whispered and bit her lip, not daring to meet Malcolm's gaze. Until the very last instant, she truly had not believed he held the missing journal page. She had agreed to their ludicrous bargain merely to silence him, never dreaming she would be obliged to make good on her part of the deal.

Fighting a growing panic, she gave the page a more careful reading, recognizing in the phrasing as well as the handwriting her father's style. As for the entry itself, it continued in logical sequence from where the previous page's text left off. Even the black half-oval, where the writer had blotted an ink splatter, mated with another such mark on the torn edge.

"Well, *partner,* I guess we should make our way to the guest house and begin making plans," Malcolm interrupted Halia's frantic thoughts, triumph evident in his tone.

He made her a fleeting bow, then turned toward Rolle. "Captain, I shall see you on the morrow."

With those words, he began trudging toward the bluff. Halia stared after him, the journal and its long-lost page both safely in her grasp. She remained watching as he negotiated the rocky footpath that led up that rise to her rented cottage above. Once he reached the top, he turned and gave her a jaunty wave of his boater.

She bit back a few choice words of frustration and swiftly considered what was to be done. But what help was there for it? By her own words, she was stuck with this overbearing rogue as her new partner . . . or was she?

For did she not have what she needed right here in her very hands? The Atlantis coordinates were hers now, as was the knowledge of how best to utilize them. All she need do was rid herself of a certain Englishman, and everything would be back under her control.

She allowed herself a few moments to savor that scenario before slowly shaking her head. Doubtless, a few words to Captain Rolle and an appropriate sum of cash would readily solve her problem. Malcolm would find himself aboard the *Retribution* and out to sea again by midafternoon, with no recourse left him. Once he was gone, she would be free to recover the artifacts on her own and be certain that every item she unearthed found a safe haven in a museum.

But that would mean going back on her word to the Englishman . . . which, while no doubt justifiable, was something she could not do with an easy conscience.

"I believe we will all be staying in Bimini, after all," she addressed Captain Rolle. "If you are agreeable, I will meet you and your crew at dawn tomorrow morning on the main pier. We can make a preliminary search of the site and then decide where best to begin our exploration, just as I outlined in my letter to you. As I'm sure you realized, it is the same site that my father explored."

That last came out as something of a question, for she had no idea if Rolle had ever been privy to her father's work. In answer, the captain shook his head.

"Me, I never be takin' Mr. Arvin to dat spot, but dat don't mean he didn't be goin' there with someone else."

Halia bit back a disappointed sigh at his words. She had feared as much from the fact that her father had made no direct mention in his journal of the events leading up to his find. He must have captained his own boat and crew, or else, gone out on the sea alone . . . just as he'd done the day of his death.

Pushing aside those painful memories, she summoned a smile for the captain. "At any rate, I have maps and charts of the area we'll be searching, and I will supply you with the exact coordinates tomorrow. You have found experienced divers?" she asked, knowing that he should have many to choose from, since one of the island's primary exports was sea sponges.

He nodded, another fleeting grin showing bright white against his dark skin. "You already be meetin' Jeffers," he said with a gesture toward the hitherto unnamed sailor. "The rest, they be all set."

He paused for a glance over his shoulder at the guest house, then added in a jovial tone, "Me, I be curious to see how you an' dat one be gettin' along together."

Halia felt a blush steal over her cheeks. "If you are referring to Mr. Northrup, we will hardly be 'together,'" she hurried to clarify. "The guest house has several suites of rooms, I am told, so I expect Mr. Northrup will keep to his own quarters. Besides which, he will not be joining us in the morning, as he has already made clear his intent to let *me* do all the work."

"If dat's what you say. This skiff, it be belongin' wit' the house, so you can be usin' it if you want. Do you be needin' any help with dat bag of yours?"

Halia shook her head. "Thank you, but I can manage on my own," she replied and hefted it in demonstration.

With a shrug and a tip of his cap, Rolle started off down the beach, followed by Jeffers. Halia set down her carpetbag long enough to tuck the precious journal with its loose page back inside it. Then, sighing, she turned back toward the bluff.

Perhaps she could convince Malcolm to take up alternate quarters in the neighboring settlement of Bayley Town. Cheered by that possibility, she began the trek toward the house.

Chapter 10

Halia's walk was hardly pleasant. With the earlier breeze stilled and the sun directly overhead now, Caribbean heat lay in a steamy blanket across the beach.

She dabbed with the cuff of her shirtsleeve at the sweat that trickled down her temples, then lifted her skirts almost to midcalf in an attempt not to stumble on the uneven beach. Nothing, however, could keep the warm sand from seeping through her boot lacings and sifting between her stockinged toes. She gritted her teeth against the discomfort. This was to be expected, after all. Once she shed her traveling outfit for clothing better suited to the sand and heat, she would have no further difficulty . . . at least, not with the terrain.

But by the time she finally stumbled up what was little better than a rocky goat path to gain the bluff's summit, the combination of physical and mental distress had begun to take its toll. She paused for a moment to catch her breath, giving a closer look to the exterior of what would be her home for the next few months. From this angle, she could see that it was in the shape of a modest, two-storied L. The yellow wooden shutters at every door and window not only added a cheerful splash of color to its white facade, they were practical, as well. In the event of a hurricane, those louvered doors could be pulled tightly closed against the brutal winds and pounding rain such a storm would bring.

Once her breathing was almost back to normal, she wended her way down a path of crushed seashells that spanned the dozen or more yards from the bluff's edge to where the guest house lay. Dragging her carpetbag behind her, she mounted the wooden steps and called for Lally.

"You be takin' your time," that woman pronounced as she stepped past the open doorway to give Halia's disheveled appearance a wry look.

Not waiting for a reply, Lally gestured her inside. Halia found herself at the far end of an open foyer—a cool, dark room devoid of furnishings and whose walnut-stained wooden floors protested her every step. Just to her left, an open staircase curved in a modified J up to the floor above. To her other side, at the juncture where the house's two wings met at right angles, was a pair of carved mahogany doors. They opened, she saw, into a cozy-looking parlor that no doubt served as the gathering point for family and guests. Across from her, a row of French windows revealed a rectangular flagstone courtyard within the crook of the L that was the main house. Two low stone walls ran either length of the courtyard's outer reaches, so that the entire paved area was completely enclosed. Intrigued, Halia spared that small patio a closer look.

The courtyard was an oasis of shade in the midst of an abundance of sun. Its centerpiece was a twisted fig tree a full two stories high that spread welcome shadow across the hot stone. Wrapped around its substantial circumference like a starched white collar was a backless stone bench that could easily seat a dozen people.

The two exterior walls set at right angles to each other were made of the same white stone as the bench. In one of the opposite corners, just beneath the roof line, she glimpsed a cistern—a huge, stone jug tall as a man that served to catch and hold rainwater.

It and the rock walls were almost hidden by a tangle of green vines that wove up their heights and then cascaded over their tops with a shower of bright orange hibiscus petals. Other, more delicate blooms also peeked between the stones as a counterpoint to those showy flowers. In a final touch of whimsy, both walls were topped by a line of specimens of that ubiquitous, spiral-shaped creature of the Caribbean, the conch.

Halia smiled at the sight. As a child, she'd always thought their shells resembled huge mouths, the way their spiked white outer shells rolled back to reveal cheerful interiors of sleek, pearly pink. She still had a fondness for them, as well as for the tasty stew the islanders made from conch meat.

But even as she smiled in pleasure at this house that she had leased, sight unseen, Lally shot a dark look in the direction of the stairway. "You best be seein' what dat man"— she spat those last two words as an epithet—"be doin' up there. I be hearin' him wanderin' about, him an' dat other one."

"Doubtless, the pair of them are up to no good."

Her brief moment of satisfaction flickered out. She dropped her carpetbag and stalked toward the stairs, trailing a fine sprinkling of beach sand behind her. The last thing she needed was for the Englishman to think he had the run of the place. Now would be the perfect time to approach him about moving himself and his manservant to Bayley Town.

Barely did she reach the upper landing than she heard Malcolm's off-key whistling. *Some English drinking song, no doubt,* she decided with a sniff as she began tracking that raucous sound to its source.

She made her way down a narrow hall that ran the inner perimeter of the house and took an unexpected jump up half a dozen steps at the juncture between the two wings. At the top of those steps was an open doorway, through which the sound of Malcolm's whistling came still more loudly. She did not bother to knock but merely stepped inside.

Her first impression was one of spaciousness. This had to be the master bedchamber, she decided, for it took up almost the entire wing. Two open pairs of French windows leading to the oceanfront veranda were shuttered against the noon sun. Daylight lay in neat stripes across the gleaming wood floor stained the same mahogany hue as the main hall downstairs.

Hands on hips, and lips pursed in dismay, she strode into the center of this room that, by all rights, should have been hers. Against the far wall, a broad mahogany four-poster swathed in yards of mosquito netting stretched pencil-thin limbs almost to the ceiling. An oversized armoire and a low chest of drawers, both mahogany, and an old-fashioned, mahogany-framed divan upholstered in white brocade completed the furnishings.

But where was Malcolm?

Barely had the question flitted through her mind than that gentleman stepped through the door of what had to be an adjoining dressing room.

Dim as the light was, she had no trouble seeing that he had availed himself of that other room's facilities. He had exchanged his gray morning suit for a coarse white towel, jauntily wrapped about his narrow hips. Its fringed edge adding rakish emphasis to that portion of his lower anatomy where both ends of the cloth happened to overlap.

And, save for that towel, he was completely naked.

He caught sight of her at almost the same instant, and his whistling abruptly broke off. Irrelevantly, she noted that he wore some manner of leather thong around his throat with a velvet pouch dangling from it. Then she glimpsed the lazy grin that was spreading over his face, and she realized in horror that she had been staring.

"Oh, my," she whispered into the resulting silence and spun about.

She had seen him in a similar state of undress once before, that day on the ship, but circumstances then had been far different. Then, he had been no threat to her—recovering as he was from a head injury, tied to a berth and modestly covered with a bedsheet. But this . . . this was *different*.

In the moment it took her to regather her scattered wits, she heard the soft padding of his bare feet against the wood floor as the Englishman started toward her.

Her horror blossomed into full-blown panic, and she caught up her skirts to flee. Before she could take a step, however, an elegantly manicured hand clamped around her upper arm.

"I had wondered where you'd gotten yourself off to, Miss Davenport," he observed in smoothly cultured tones, as if he were not standing almost naked in the same room as she. "If you are looking for your room, it happens to adjoin mine. I do believe your luggage has already been stowed there—so, if you wish, you can avail yourself of the connecting door between our two chambers."

"A connecting . . . door?"

She swung about in his grasp, only to find her nose mere inches from his bare chest. And quite a respectable chest it was, her sly inner voice judged, comparing him to any number of bare-chested sailors or stevedores she had seen in her travels. Pale, perhaps, compared to the tanned skin of those men who spent their days in the sun, but still respectably muscled with just enough silky black hair to—

She broke off that train of thought and bit her lip . . . hard. What was she doing, judging him as if he were the prize bull at the county fair? Why, she was supposed to be chastising him for trying to usurp her role as leader of their expedition. What matter that she could breathe in the very smell of his flesh . . . a masculine scent of soap and fine linen combined with lingering traces of sea spray and honest sweat.

Resisting the almost overwhelming temptation to let her

curious eyes glance any lower, she dragged up her gaze past his shoulder. There *was* a narrow door that all but melted into the panel work along the far wall, she saw in no little dismay. Then, refusing to be distracted by such details, she returned to the matter at hand.

"That is what I have come to talk to you about—rooms, I mean," she went on, determined not to be intimidated by his manner or his mode of undress. "I think it would be preferable for you and Mr. Foote to find yourself another place to stay . . . in Bayley Town, perhaps. It is but a short walk up the King's Highway, and—"

"But surely you cannot expect me to abandon my partner our first day here? No, Miss Davenport—or perhaps I may more properly call you Halia, now—I intend to stay right here in this room."

"But it is *my* room," she persisted through gritted teeth. *"I* leased the house—"

"With *my* money, might I remind you."

"—and *I* am in charge here. Besides, even a scoundrel such as yourself must agree that it is not proper for you and I to share adjoining chambers."

Malcolm lifted a wry brow. "Then perhaps you might convince Wilkie to switch with you. He has taken one of the two other, smaller rooms down the hall from us. Or, I believe that Lally is in the second one. She might be inclined to exchange sleeping quarters with you . . . though I presume her sleeping there would cause an equal scandal?"

Thoroughly aggrieved now, Halia jerked free of his grasp. "You are quite the most appalling man I have ever met," she choked out, feeling the blood rise in her cheeks. "If you do not have the decency to consider my feelings, then I suppose there is no remedy for it. I will simply have to forego my reputation and sleep in the adjoining room for the duration of our stay."

When a flicker of triumph lighted his bland expression,

she hotly added, "But be forewarned, Mr. Northrup. The door between us shall remain quite firmly locked."

So saying, she turned to leave. Then, succumbing to bold impulse and a flash of feminine vengeance, she twisted back around. In a gesture that would stun her a moment later, she caught hold of the towel's fringed edge and gave it a vicious tug.

That length of cotton promptly fluttered to the floor, leaving Malcolm wearing nothing but a bemused expression and the leather thong about his throat. Then, with a dignified lift of her chin, Halia turned again and calmly quit the room.

It wasn't until she stood in the hall again, the door between her and Malcolm firmly shut, that the enormity of what she had just done hit her.

"Oh, my," she faintly managed and clamped her palms to her burning cheeks. Never before had she behaved in so scandalous a manner! To be sure, she had not realized what she was about until she had actually done it . . . besides which, she *had* been subjected to extreme provocation. Still, to actually have stripped the man of his towel like that!

Even as those thoughts crossed her mind, she heard a metallic click behind her. She shot a desperate glance over her shoulder to see the knob of Malcolm's door twisting from within.

Dear Lord, he was coming after her . . . and here she stood but a few feet outside his chamber bemoaning her folly.

Barely had his door swung inward than she was running toward the sanctuary of her own room. She fumbled with the latch, then half-stumbled over the threshold and slammed the door shut behind her.

With trembling fingers, she fastened the inner bolt; then, recalling the adjoining door, she flew across the room to barricade that entry, as well. To her relief, it was equipped with a similar lock.

She slid the bolt home with a firm click, giving silent

thanks as she did so to whichever former lady of the house had had the foresight to install it. The only other way in, she determined, would be through the French doors that led to the veranda. Luckily, their hurricane shutters had yet to be unlatched. Any forced entry would, of necessity, entail a not-inconsiderable racket, the sound of which surely would bring assistance swiftly running.

With a gasp of relief, she sagged against the bed, which was a smaller version of Malcolm's. To be sure, she would have felt even more secure had her carpetbag with its hidden pistol been among the luggage stacked in the room's center.

Uncertainly, she strained her ears for any sound from Malcolm's chamber. Likely, she was safe enough for now. She need only remain barricaded here until the Englishman left the house, or else Lally came to fetch her. In the meantime, she might as well pass the time by changing into more suitable clothing.

Her heart rate had returned to normal by the time she pulled open the smallest of her trunks and began sorting through her practical wardrobe. She chose a white cotton shirtwaist and a divided skirt of the same fabric, the latter so short that its hem grazed her ankles. The daring style required no corset and was cool enough for the tropical heat. In such attire, she could easily manage the island's beaches and rocky roadways, as well as clamber unhindered about Captain Rolle's boat.

Pleased with her choice, she made her way to her tiny dressing room and quickly stripped down to her chemise and drawers. The house staff had already brought up a towel and pitcher of cool water, both of which had been placed atop the mirrored washstand.

She poured a scant basin's worth—mindful that fresh water was at a premium on the islands—and then began to scrub the sand and salt spray from her body. But even as the cooling dampness refreshed her skin, the knowledge that only a thin wall separated her from Malcolm sparked an uncomfortable heat within her.

For, try as she might, she could not dismiss the image of his long, muscled body from her thoughts.

She bit her lip and scrubbed harder, as if the very action might wash away the unwelcome memory. *After all, you've seen naked men before,* her inner voice reasoned. *What difference does one more make?*

What difference, indeed! What she had seen before were marble and plaster depictions, some elegant, some frankly erotic . . . but all, in the end, merely images formed from some long-dead artist's imagination. Malcolm, however, was warm flesh and blood.

And, God help her, she had wanted to touch him.

The realization took her quite by surprise, so that her towel slipped unheeded from her hand. Then she shot a guilty glance at the narrow door connecting their two rooms. What if he knew? What if Malcolm had seen this shocking need fairly etched upon her face?

She gave a soft, despairing groan and searched her reflection in the washstand's mottled mirror. Her cheeks were pink with sun and guilt, while her lips were pale and faintly parted as anxiety now quickened her breathing. Uncertainty had darkened her green eyes, and they suddenly seemed to overwhelm her other features.

She frowned. Surely this was not the face of a woman in the throes of lust. Or was it?

Halia groaned again and turned from that unsettling image of herself. This was but a temporary aberration, a momentary lapse brought on by the stress of the past few days. She was, after all, a woman of good sense and logic, and not the type to let any man distract her from her work. She must simply take herself in hand and pretend that none of this had happened.

That resolved, she marched back into her bedroom and reached for her clothes. Much work remained to be done before tomorrow morning. She had maps to study, coordinates to chart. Let the Englishman tease and provoke as he might, she had more important matters to attend to.

Wrapped in righteousness and considerably cooler attire, she now felt herself equal to any challenge. Indeed, she had half a mind to march back into Malcolm's chamber and berate him for his earlier ghastly behavior. Prudence forestalled such action; still, her confidence had returned.

She gave a firm nod. The Englishman had intimidated her for the last time, she told herself. And if he dared ever flaunt himself before her again, she would not even blink, let alone be distracted by thoughts of those mysteries of the flesh . . . mysteries best left to the domain of women less firm of purpose than was she.

Malcolm straightened from where he'd stood pressing his ear to the connecting door between his room and Halia's. A wry smile was twisting his lips. The journey, thus far, was proving far more interesting than he could have hoped . . . and Halia, herself, a far more intriguing female than he would have guessed.

His smile broadened into a grin as he strolled back to the center of his room and snatched up the towel that lately had been wrapped about his midsection. Her parting gesture of defiance had truly taken him by surprise, so much so that he had let the chit walk away quite unscathed.

It occurred to him now that he had set a poor example for her future actions; still, he rather suspected she was equally appalled by what she'd done. By the time he had regained his wits and reached his doorway, she already was running down the hallway as if the Devil himself were in pursuit. He had not missed the sound of her shooting home both door locks a moment later, nor the restless patter of her footsteps that followed.

Now, Malcolm tossed the towel in the direction of his

dressing room and headed for his steamer trunk, which sat unopened in one corner. With both their identities in the open, he could hardly press Wilkie into service as his valet, which meant he'd be forced to shift for himself. Not that he wasn't perfectly capable of dealing with such matters, he reminded himself. It was just that he had grown rather used to his role of Sir John and its accompanying perquisites.

He pulled out the least wrinkled of his linen shirts, then searched the trunk again for a fresh cravat. The trousers he'd earlier worn would do for now, he decided as he tugged them on again.

All in all, the morning's events had worked out to his advantage, he judged. If nothing else, the fact that Halia had gotten an eyeful should set the chit to wondering what would happen if she accidentally left their connecting door unlocked one night.

For he would wager his share of the Atlantis treasure that Halia was still an innocent . . . and he would bet the same sum that she'd had a thought or two about changing that state of affairs since their first meeting.

Malcolm wryly shook his head. It was no misplaced vanity on his part that brought him to that conclusion. In his long career, he had pursued—and been pursued by—enough women to recognize the more common signs. It was all there, the blushing, the peevishness, the denials . . . even the chance stumbling into a gentleman's chamber while said gent was in a state of undress. With that groundwork already laid, so to speak, it would take little effort on his part to press matters on to their logical conclusions.

He resumed his whistling and continued dressing again. He paused, though, as he started to button his shirt collar. The emerald still clung about his neck like a frightened maiden, secure in its velvet pouch. Though it had brought him the expected added measure of luck, he was beginning to feel as if he had a miniature albatross looped about his throat. He might do better to stow away the gemstone, he decided, and untied the pouch.

Gem in hand now, Malcolm glanced about the room in search of a hiding place. He dismissed with a professional's eye the most obvious places—beneath the mattress, under the floorboards, stashed behind the armoire. Finally, he climbed onto one corner of the bed and reached up to where the mosquito netting was swathed around the bed post.

Grasping a handful of the sheer fabric, he knotted it around the pouch, then redraped the netting and stood back to admire his handiwork. There, the jewel would be safe from would-be thieves but readily accessible should the need arise for its retrieval.

Pleased with his cleverness, he started for the door. The next order of business would be a casual tour of the island, followed by a pleasant supper and a good night's sleep. And then tomorrow—

"And then tomorrow, my dear Miss Davenport," he murmured in the direction of her room, "I believe I shall allow you another try at seducing me . . . and perhaps I shall even let you succeed."

Chapter 11

Dawn had tinged the cloud-raked horizon a conch-shell pink and transformed the black waters of night back to a soft, pale blue. The heat had not yet settled its unyielding blanket over the island and the barest breath of a breeze carried a cool whisper off the retreating tide. It was the brilliant start to a new day . . . or, would have been, save that a certain English fly had buzzed its way into this smooth Caribbean ointment.

"You cannot come with us, Mr. Northrup, and that is final!"

With that chill pronouncement, Halia folded her arms over her chest and glared down at the man from her place in the bow of Captain Rolle's fishing boat. In contrast to her stern words, however, her emotions were a jumble of uncertainty. She had vowed yesterday not to let the man's presence unnerve her, but that was when a wall separated them. Now that she was face to face with him again, she did not quite know how to act.

Indeed, never had she faced the question of how an unmarried man and woman with little liking for one another behaved in company together, when the latter had seen the former without a stitch of clothing on!

If Malcolm was troubled by that matter, however, he gave no sign of it. No doubt he'd had his share of women over the years, so he was used to that sort of thing, she thought with a sniff. He had made no reply to her demand but remained boldly where he was, milling about with the fishermen and sailors gathered along the short dock.

They were in the midst of Alice Town, the most populated of North Bimini's several sparse settlements. It was a sandy, sunny, narrow little sprawl of a town that wended its way along two main streets running north and south: the Queen's Highway, which road hugged the eastern harbor; and the King's Highway, stretching atop the low, chalky cliffs that overlooked the Atlantic Ocean to the west.

Halia had spent the hour before sunset the previous day making the leisurely walk through town, transportation on the islands being either by foot or by dinghy. Alice Town, like the rest of the islands' settlements, was a relatively poor community, with fishing the main industry. Still, it possessed a buoyant soul that made up for its poverty.

On her walk, she had counted two churches and as many cemeteries, along with a handful of small shops and several clusters of houses. All but a few of the latter were single-story dwellings, some clapboard and some stucco. Cool white was the color of choice in this tropical climate, though a few owners had painted their homes yellow, pink, or blue.

Most of the houses, she categorized as cheerfully humble in appearance. Others verged on the whimsical in their owners' use of conch shells to decorate their doorsteps, entry gates, and walkways. Rampant clusters of flowered vines— hibiscus and morning glory were among the ones she recognized—added splashes of sunset colors to the green and yellow that predominated among the native flora.

The islanders, themselves, reflected that same air of humble cheer. While a few were of European descent, most were born of—or were, themselves—former West African slaves. The dark faces outnumbered the pale, yet all had toward their visitors an unfeigned friendliness unmatched by many more "civilized" people.

If only all of the visitors in question were worthy of such regard, Halia now sourly reflected.

She had not immediately recognized the Englishman among Rolle's ragtag crew, dressed as he was this morning in the same sort of baggy trousers, loose-cut shirt, and rope sandals as worn by the islanders. She had yet to get used to seeing him without his mustache and sidewhiskers. Only when he had clamped on his familiar straw boater—which looked ludicrously out of place topping such an ensemble— had she realized it was he.

Now, striving for calm, she appealed to the man beside her. "Captain Rolle, can you not have your men make that person"—she pointed indignantly in Malcolm's direction— "leave here?"

The Negro shook his head. "I can't be doin' dat . . . not when he be one of my own crew."

He paused for a few quick, shouted words of island patois that set those half-dozen men, Malcolm included, scrambling toward the splintered board that was the boat's make-shift gangplank. Then he turned his attention back to Halia, whose earlier glare had been transformed into an incredulous stare.

"One of your crew?" she echoed. "Why, there must be some mistake. You can't mean to say that you actually hired him."

"Not hired. Dat man, he be workin' for nothin'," Rolle explained with a quick flash of white teeth. "He say he be wantin' to do his share, but dat you be insistin' he be stayin' behind, instead. He says he's your partner . . . unless he be lyin' about that?" he demanded with a frown.

When Halia shook her head, Rolle gave an eloquent shrug and added, "If he be wantin' to work, den I say we be lettin' him. Better for you to be keepin' an eye on him, dat way."

Work . . . Malcolm Northrup? Why, it would be the same as if *she* had announced her intent to take up a life of crime!

Reluctantly, however, she conceded the sense of Rolle's last remark. Who knew what sort of plots and schemes the Englishman might become embroiled in if left to his own devices? So long as he kept his distance . . .

"Very well," was her less than gracious reply, "but I do hope that you explained to him the consequences of disobeying a captain's orders."

Rolle merely grinned again. Then, turning to his crew now assembled atop deck, he began clipping out orders. Halia returned to the bow, where she had stowed her carpetbag, and watched while the men prepared the boat to shove off.

The *Johnesta* was a neat little gull of a sloop—sleekly white with snowy sails that lifted with winglike grace from her single mast. She rode high in the water, a shallow-draft boat suited to the surrounding reefs. She was small enough so that two or three men could handle her, yet large enough to carry all the equipment that Halia had sent over to the dock the day before.

Her attention was reserved, not for the boat now, but for a certain member of her crew.

In imitation of the remainder of the crew, he had stripped off his shirt so that he was working naked from the waist up. That alone would have been enough to draw her attention had she not already seen quite a bit more of him the previous day. Rather, what caught her eye was the fact that his fellow sailors were all native Bahamians whose skin colors ranged from a light coffee shade to black. Malcolm was the only one among them who was of European descent.

Halia allowed herself a small smile. Already, the morning sun had lent a faint pink tinge to his skin. By noon . . .

By noon, he'll be burnt as Sunday's toast, was her satisfied prediction that almost made up for her embarrassment of the previous day. Though he was not as fair-skinned as many Englishmen, he would surely suffer under the sun more than she, given that she was used to the tropical rays.

All the same, she prudently had slathered her golden skin with one of Lally's ointments to protect against burning.

Her private amusement turned to grudging admiration, however, as she watched Malcolm assist with making the lines ready. He was handling himself with unexpected competence for a man who claimed no maritime experience. Equally surprising was the fact that his fellow crewmen, all of whom appeared to be seasoned sailors, seemingly bore no resentment at working with a neophyte . . . and a foreigner, to boot!

But then, was that not his profession, convincing the unwitting that he was their friend?

Moments later, the *Johnesta* was under way. Under Captain Rolle's firm guidance, she moved with slow if stately grace through the shallow harbor. Halia curbed her impatience, for she knew the reason for the boat's sluggish progress.

During the islands' heyday as a pirates' haven, the harbor had once been a veritable dumping ground for ballast stones, anchor chains, and like. Most of that debris had long since been cleared away by the first influx of legitimate settlers. Still, the occasional protruding anchor or other halfburied piece of wreckage still posed a danger to unwitting vessels.

She spent a few minutes gazing at the clear waters for something a bit more romantic than ballast, however . . . a cannon, perhaps, or else a pirate's chest spilling forth pieces of eight. When all she spotted was a prosaic section of hull and a pile of galley bricks, she turned her attention to her carpetbag. It held, among its collection of supplies, a sheaf of loose pages that was the sum of her previous night's work.

After a simple supper made all the more pleasant for the fact that Malcolm and his friend, Mr. Foote, were not present, she had spent the evening poring over her father's notes. From those entries and the crude maps she had of the

island and its surrounding waters, she had sketched out
their general course and the likely areas for a preliminary
search. The coordinates, she had already given to Captain
Rolle, but she had been vague thus far as to the purpose of
their search, lest she draw unwanted attention to the site.

She studied the topmost page, a tracing of the map she
had obtained from Malcolm. The original, she had left
safely behind, hidden with the rest of the journal in a recess
of her armoire. Partners or no, she did not trust the Englishman not to abscond with the entire volume, if it suited him.

"Full-and-by," she heard Rolle order his crew a few moments later.

She glanced up from her papers again to see that they had
cleared the narrow strait separating Bimini's north island
from its south. They were in Atlantic waters again, where
reefs stretched from the coast only to drop off with dramatic
suddenness into the cobalt-blue stretch of ocean that was
the Gulf Stream. There, Bimini played host to all manner of
ocean life, from tiny, bright-hued anemones to moray eels
and sharks.

Maps and charts in hand, she squinted across the smooth
turquoise sea which fairly sparkled beneath a brilliant
robin's egg blue sky. A brisk breeze had caught the sails, so
that the *Johnesta* now skimmed the water's surface at an ex-
hilarating clip. The sharp snap of the sails in the wind was a
counterpoint to the gossiping cries of the gulls that circled
above, while the rhythmic splash of waves against the bow
added a constant note to this ocean symphony.

Their destination was a point just off the island's northwest coast. By the time they reached the site, she doubtless
would be glad of her wide-brimmed skimmer, for the Caribbean sun would surely be well ablaze by then. For now,
however, she was content to enjoy the gentle rays that
warmed her face.

"Here now, luv, you're not avoiding me, are you?"

Halia stiffened, her pleasure in the morning churning

away like seafoam. Malcolm had caught her unawares, having abandoned whatever task he'd been put to by Rolle to sneak up behind her. With a haughty lift of her chin, she turned to face him . . . and then found herself blushing in confusion.

Try as she might, she could not banish the image of him standing naked before her the day before, like a classical statue come to life. Unfortunately, her thoughts must have shown in her face, for he favored her with a wicked grin that showed his dimples to advantage.

"What's the matter, luv? Don't you recognize me without my clothes on?"

"I recognize you quite well, Mr. Northrup," she managed with frosty dignity despite her heated cheeks. "I dare say it is the *particular* clothes you have on that took me by surprise. Did you perhaps steal them off some unsuspecting woman's washline last night?"

He promptly assumed an expression of mock-injury at the accusation. "My dear Miss Davenport, I haven't pinched a pair of trousers on washday since I was a lad in the East End of London. I'll have you know, I paid the woman in question a fair price for my new attire."

He paused to give her own clothing a considering look, then added with a sly grin, "But if I were you, luv, I wouldn't have the nerve to criticize anyone else's dress. Surely that is not what the fashionable set is wearing this season, is it?"

That was her own adaptation of the style that Amelia Bloomer had introduced years earlier with but middling success. It consisted of a pair of full-cut, dark blue serge trousers gathered at the ankle, a matching sleeveless shirtwaist, and a white, calf-length overskirt. A lightweight pair of canvas shoes allowed her safe purchase on slick boat decks and rocky beaches. It was a practical outfit and the most comfortable she owned . . . no matter that it was not the mode.

She smoothed her skirt and shot him a quelling look. "It is hardly my intent to be stylish. If you will recall, the Atlantis site is underwater. I do expect that some amount of swimming will be necessary to properly explore it," she primly explained. "But I must confess, I am at a loss to know why you are here aboard ship, and with the intent to work, no less."

"It is simple. It occurred to me that you might forget to share all the details about your various discoveries if I am not there with you."

"You mean, you think that *I* intend to cheat *you?*"

The outrage that swept her was genuine, so that she momentarily forgot her embarrassment. Before she could launch into any more voluble protest, however, he gestured in the direction of his fellow crewmen.

"The lads will be needing my help," he said, though the "lads" in question had paused in their own tasks to watch her conversation with Malcolm. He added, "I expect we shall confer again once we reach the site and you've noted your preliminary findings."

As he strolled back toward the bow, Halia gritted her teeth and resisted the temptation to fling some unladylike remark after him. *Confer, indeed. She* would decide what he did or did not need to know. Just because he had forced his way into a partnership with her did not mean he would have any say in how the expedition was conducted.

It was with a renewed sense of pique that she took up her own post again. The sea had darkened from turquoise to sapphire; still, it remained clear enough that she could spy the ocean floor far below the surface. The green and white Biminian shore remained in view, though it lay at some distance now.

They must almost be atop the site, she realized with a sudden surge of anticipation. They must almost be—

"Here," came Captain Rolle's clipped word behind her. At a quick command from him, the crew furled the sails, so that the boat slowed to an almost stationary pitch atop the gentle waves.

"We be needin' the water glass," he explained as Halia hurried to join him at the port side of the vessel.

He caught up what appeared to be nothing more than a large wooden bucket whose bottom was constructed of glass. Simple though it appeared, Halia knew it was an effective device, and one commonly used by Bahamian fishermen. One merely submerged its glass bottom a few inches below the surface and looked down inside it. Like an immense monocle, it eliminated the water's distortion and served as a porthole of sorts to what lay beneath the waves.

"Please, Captain, let me," she forestalled him when he unrolled a crude rope-and-driftwood ladder over the side and then made as if to descend.

With a gallant bow, Rolle stepped aside. Halia tugged off her shoes and untied her overskirt, leaving them in an untidy heap in her haste. Nimbly, she swung a leg over the side and felt for a foothold as the ladder lightly swung against the planking. Once she was balanced there, Rolle handed her the water glass. She descended several rungs until the waves lapped at her stockinged feet. Still clinging to the ladder with one hand, she crouched so that she could float the water glass atop the ocean's crystalline surface.

A knot of anticipation tightened in her chest as she took in the view below. The ocean floor lay a good three fathoms beneath her in water clear as a sultana's bath. Schools of tiny fish in a rainbow of hues—silver, blue, yellow, and red—flashed about in a silent, synchronized ocean ballet. Their backdrop was a rippled bottom of white sand littered with scores of conch shells, their pink mouths open in silent cries of welcome. Purple sea fans sprang from rocky outcrops and moved languidly with the current, their lacy display woven with ropes of thick green seaweed.

It was a scene of tranquil beauty . . . and it looked little different from any other Caribbean ocean floor she'd ever seen.

She glanced up at Rolle and shook her head. "Nothing here," she reported and clambered back up.

When she reached the top, however, it was Malcolm's hand that grasped hers and pulled her over the side again.

"What do you mean, nothing?" he demanded once she regained her balance. "I thought that with the coordinates, you could find the spot right off."

"There is still room for error," she coolly informed him, "besides which, it is possible that the ocean bottom has shifted since he recorded them. A storm or simply some unusual current patterns could disturb the sand enough to cover up the find."

She looked over to Rolle for confirmation. He nodded, asking, "And do you be knowin' what you be lookin' for, then?"

"No, not exactly. The journal was not clear on that point, but my guess from some of my father's notes is that it is likely a formation of some sort . . . perhaps the remains of a foundation."

"Likely . . . perhaps," Malcolm echoed and raised a wry brow. "Tell me, Miss Davenport, how exactly do you intend to identify this formation, then?"

"I'll know it when I see it," came her confident retort. Then, turning back to Rolle, she continued, "Shall we try another spot, Captain?"

A command from him brought the boat about. For the next hour, they moved in a concentric pattern, stopping at set intervals when Halia could descend the makeshift ladder and use the water glass to scan the bottom. Soon, her swimming costume was soaked to the waist and clung uncomfortably to her lower limbs, while the rope had begun to rub the flesh of her palms raw.

"Perhaps you'd care to take a turn, Mr. Northrup," she

offered now as the rope ladder was lowered for the half-a-dozenth time.

Malcolm shook his head as he clung rather desperately to the railing. He was looking pale now despite the growing heat, and the effort of that simple gesture appeared to tax him. Doubtless, he finally was feeling the effects of the gently tossing sea, she determined with uncharitable satisfaction . . . though, to his credit, he had managed thus far to hold down his breakfast.

"Not me, luv," came his blunt reply, though his tone was a bit more subdued than usual. "I don't know how to swim, and I'm bloody well not about to start learning now."

"I suggest that you be learnin'," Rolle interjected as he rejoined them. "Only a fool would be spendin' his time around the ocean wit'out knowin' how to be managin' himself in it. Perhaps Miss Halia, she could be teachin' you, then," he added with a look over at her.

Halia frowned. She was a strong swimmer, herself, and enjoyed a vigorous outing in the waves; still, the thought of allowing the Englishman to share her pleasure was more than she could bear.

"Really, Captain Rolle, I don't think I'll have the time to—"

"That sounds like an excellent plan," Malcolm cut short her protest and gave her a shadow of a grin that she countered with a quelling look of her own.

"I don't think I will have the time," she repeated, "though perhaps Lally will take on the task. She is, after all, native to the Bahamas and has been swimming in these waters since she was a toddler."

"But I could not impose upon her, as the two of us are hardly acquainted . . . while you, my dear Miss Davenport are surely the more appropriate person to approach for such a favor."

Halia spared herself the need of replying to that last outrageous statement simply by catching up the water glass and climbing over the side again. Unfortunately, she did not miss hearing the captain's muttered aside to Malcolm.

"Be givin' her a bit more time, then, and she'll be comin' around."

Decidedly out of sorts with both men now, she glanced into her water glass yet again.

"Same fish, same sand, same conch shells," she muttered, trying not to give in to disappointment as she scanned this portion of the sea floor. It was not as if she'd expected to find an entire sunken city the first time she peeked beneath the waves; still, she *had* assumed that they would have stumbled across some sign or another of the site, by now. Perhaps she had miscopied the coordinates, or her father had mistakenly recorded the wrong figures, or—

"Oh, my."

The words escaped her in a muffled cry of surprise. Blinking, she glanced up from the water glass to see Rolle and Malcolm leaning over the side, identical expressions of hopeful query etched on their faces. She bit her lip and gazed back down through the waves to the ocean bottom below, feeling her heart begin to pound faster in her breast.

It might just be a trick of the light, her rational inner voice warned. She took another look. Her instincts told her that her rational voice was wrong. Slowly, she gazed up again at the two men looming above her, feeling a triumphant smile spreading across her face.

Her tone was calm, however, as she called up, "You may drop anchor here, Captain . . . for I do believe we have found the remains of Atlantis."

Chapter 12

"Found it?" Malcolm echoed as Rolle gave the command to drop anchor. His seasickness forgotten, he clutched at the railing and stared down at Halia. Her only reply was the fleetest of nods . . . but it was enough.

Bloody hell, we've done it!

He gripped the rail more tightly still, visions of ivory columns and gold statues flashing through his mind. Shading his eyes against the splash of sunlight on the water, he gazed past the translucent waves in hopes of spotting the lost city. All he could see from this vantage point, however, was the rocky sand of the sea bottom.

By now, Halia was clambering back up the ladder. More impatient now than chivalrous, he offered her his hand and all but dragged her back onto the deck. Rolle, meanwhile, took the water glass from her and handed her a rough towel in exchange.

His restiveness growing, Malcolm waited while she toweled off the sea spray from her face and brushed back the damp tendrils of blond hair that clung to her forehead. She was, he determined, quite a bit worse for wear. Her ridiculous bathing costume had wicked up the occasional wave, so that the dark fabric wrapped about her lower torso and legs. The effect, some might find erotic . . . that was, if their taste ran to brine-soaked waifs.

His did not.

A proper American mermaid. He wryly dismissed her, trying not to concede that he found the picture that she presented rather endearing, after all. But surely it was only the thought of the riches lying almost at his feet that had softened his attitude toward her.

"Well?" he prompted when she had blotted away the worst of the sea water.

She turned a small smile on him, looking rather like a child who'd learned a marvelous secret that she was dying now to tell.

"Of course, it is far too early for us to judge the significance of my find," she primly began, "so I would suggest that we refrain from making any claims, at this point. The first thing we must do is let the divers begin clearing away the sand so we can get a better idea of the size of the site."

She paused to give her head a wistful shake. "If only we had some way to view it from above. A hot air balloon would be ideal, but perhaps with a bit of climbing we can make do with a perspective from the mainmast—"

"Bloody hell, I'll take a look for myself."

With those curt words, he tossed his boater at one of the crew, then snatched the water glass from Rolle's hands and swung a leg over the side. He groped a moment for a foothold; then, balancing with care, he made his way down the crude ladder.

A wave washed over his sandaled feet and soaked his cotton trousers to the knees. He ignored the sartorial damage, instead crouching at the lowest rung and submerging the lower edge of the water glass as he'd seen Halia do. Then, eagerly, he peered inside.

The translucent blue waters now appeared completely transparent. Indeed, every detail of this unknown world seemed to hang suspended from invisible cords, so that he had to fight the unsettling sensation that he was poised over some great abyss.

Frowning, he scanned in all directions, ignoring the lapping of the waves about his knees as he searched out some sign of a sunken city. All he saw, however, were bright colored fish by the score—some smaller than a man's thumb, others the size of a cooking platter—flitting atop a flat, rocky bottom dotted with trailing green and yellow grasses.

He shot a challenging look up at Halia. Along with Rolle and half the crew, she was staring down at him with interest from her post at the railing. No doubt she had done this on purpose, he sourly thought, pretending to find her lost island just to see how he would react.

"All right, Miss Davenport, you've had your fun," he clipped out as he started up the rope ladder. "I suggest that you and Captain Rolle have your little laugh, and then let's get on about business again."

"Whatever are you talking about?"

The indignation in her tone stopped him as he reached the upper edge of the planking. She stood but inches from him now, separated only by the railing. Her gaze was on a level with his, her green eyes narrowed in unfeigned pique.

He met her, sneer for sneer. "What I'm talking about is the fact that there's nothing down there but a year's catch of fish and a forest of bloody seaweed."

"Are you blind, Mr. Northrup? I would think that the evidence would be apparent even to an untrained eye such as yours. The scoring of the rocks is obviously manmade, as is their symmetrical arrangement . . ."

She paused, a look of cool amusement lightening her expression. "Surely you weren't expecting to see columns and statues down there? Oh my, you were, weren't you?"

"Not precisely," he hedged, praying that she would attribute the heat in his face to an overabundance of sun. When she merely waited in expectant silence, he gave his head a disgusted shake.

"All right, so that was what I thought we'd find." Still clinging to the rope ladder, he thrust the water glass into her arms, then proceeded up the last rung. "Hell, the whole of Greece and Italy is bloody littered with old temples. I even know a chap who had one brought over for his garden in Savannah, just so he could . . . bloody hell!"

So caught up had he been in his own defense, he had not noticed that the boat's pitching had increased. As he reached for the railing and went to swing his leg over it, he missed his grip and snatched a handful of air. For the merest heartbeat, he balanced on one leg like a Russian dancer, arms frantically flapping.

Then another wave caught the boat, and he dropped like an anvil into the clear blue waters below.

It was a relatively short fall, only half a dozen feet. Still, he had been taken unawares, so that his breath whooshed from his lungs as he hit the waves. The sounds from above—Halia's cry of warning, Rolle's careless shout of *overboard,* the resulting splash of his impact—all were muffled by the warm water that engulfed him as he plummeted, feet first, toward the bottom.

Eyes burning from the brine, he squinted up at the now-distant surface where a watery outline of the boat was still visible. An agonizing pressure began to build in his ears, while an iron band seemed to be tightening about his chest with his effort not to breathe . . . a battle he could feel himself rapidly losing.

Bloody, bloody hell!

He damn sure wasn't ready to die, not this way, but it looked like he wasn't being given much choice. The water around him had turned from the palest blue to green now—though whether that was because he was on the verge of losing consciousness, or simply because the sun's rays did not penetrate this deeply, he wasn't sure.

Vaguely, he was aware that a school of tiny, black-and-yellow striped fish was nibbling at his toes. One corner of his mind—the corner that wasn't giving way to outright panic—conceded the humor of it all. It seemed as if the long-ago prediction of the pirate Seamus O'Neill was about to come true.

He, Malcolm, was going to end his days as food for an ocean's worth of fish, just as his former partner once had threatened him.

But even as salty water began seeping past his tightly clenched lips, he realized that his downward progress had slowed. Moreover, he was actually beginning to rise toward the surface again. Renewed hope swept him, and frantically he began sweeping his arms up and down, as if to climb his way back to the top.

To his surprise, the motion *did* seem to speed his progress. He clawed at the water in a faster rhythm, watching as the water's color changed from green back to blue again, while the outline of the boat grew clearer. In a final burst of strength, he began kicking his legs as he'd seen swimmers do before. Just as the impulse to breathe in lungfuls of brine grew almost overpowering, he felt hands clutching at him, dragging him to the surface.

He burst through the waves with an ungainly splash, alternately choking out sea water and gulping down mouthfuls of blessed air. Someone had guided him to the rope ladder, and he clung to its lower rung like the lifeline that it was. A moment later, he was aware that someone was beside him, easily bobbing about the surface. He scrubbed the water from his burning eyes and looked over to see just who his rescuer was.

"You be all right now?" Captain Rolle asked, flashing him a bright white grin that Malcolm decided was the most beautiful in the world.

He weakly nodded in reply, then gasped out, "H-How long w-was I u-underwater?"

"Half a minute, maybe less," he said with a shrug, then grinned again. "You think you might be climbin' out all right this time?"

"I'm b-bloody sure not going to t-try that stunt again,"

he wheezed out in a stouter tone and reached for the rung above him. Haltingly, he climbed his way back to the top again; then, with the encouraging cries of his fellow crew members, he swung himself over the railing.

A slim pair of arms grabbed him just as he was about to collapse onto the deck.

"Thank God . . . I was afraid that you'd drowned," Halia cried as he sagged against her, her hold around his bare torso tightening into something suspiciously like an embrace. Reflexively, Malcolm pulled her to him.

Then he realized what he had just done and broke the embrace, hastily stepping to one side. Bloody hell, the sea water must have addled his brains! What was he doing, softening toward her like this? He was supposed to be letting her make all the overtures.

He caught up the discarded towel and scrubbed it over his face, all too aware of the interested stares of the crew who, like as not, had found the entire incident exceedingly entertaining. He must look the proper fool . . . and not just because he'd almost drowned himself.

Yet, more disturbing was the fact that his uncensored moment of need had awakened in him some far more complicated emotion that he could neither name nor deny.

Rolle, meanwhile, had made his own way up the ladder. He stood now alongside them, dripping sea water and good cheer. "So, the sharks not be eatin' today, after all," he commented to Malcolm, then turned to Halia. "Shall we be gettin' on wit' it, den?"

"Yes . . . certainly."

She shook her head as if to clear it of some unpleasant thought. Careful to avoid Malcolm's gaze, she caught up her overskirt and tied it over her now-dry clothes again, then started toward the bow.

Oh, my, whatever had just happened here?

Halia knelt beside her carpetbag and began searching through it, grateful for the distraction that she hoped would give her flushed cheeks time to cool. She had made quite the spectacle of herself, she miserably realized. Here, she literally had flung herself at a man who cared nothing for her, only to have him rebuff her . . . and before witnesses, to boot.

But then, her reaction had been one of pure relief, for she had thought for a few heartstopping moments that he must surely drown.

She briefly shut her eyes at the memory. She had been frightened nearly out of her wits when she'd seen Malcolm hit the waves and then drift steadily downward. To be sure, he *had* warned her that he could not swim, but it never had occurred to her that he could not even keep himself afloat for a time.

Her own first impulse had been to leap after him and drag him back to the surface—the sort of rescue she'd had occasion to perform once or twice before while traveling the islands with her father. Captain Rolle had forestalled her, however, and even administered a mild rebuke.

Let him be doin' what he can to save himself, before you be goin' in after him like his mama. Then, when she had opened her mouth to protest, he cut her short with the amiable reminder, *An' dat be an order, Miss Halia.*

Not prepared to mutiny against her hired captain, she had clamped her lips shut and frantically watched Malcolm's bottomward progress. Doubtless, he would concur with Rolle's assessment and resent her interference, for she had long since learned that most men believed pride took precedence over prudence.

But when seconds passed and he did not resurface, her uneasiness flared into outright panic. She had just decided to risk Rolle's ire and leap in to rescue Malcolm anyway, when she saw that he was making his own way back to the top. And Rolle—apparently satisfied that the Englishman was a fighter, if not a swimmer—then relaxed his own orders and had himself helped Malcolm back on board.

Sternly, Halia shook off the memory. She had done nothing amiss, after all. Indeed, she would have shown the same concern had it been any other of the crew that had been put into danger.

But would you have flung your arms around one of them in so heedless a manner? her sly inner voice wanted to know.

Not willing to dignify the silent question with a reply, she caught up her sheaf of maps and a handful of pencils, then returned to where Rolle and the crew were waiting. Malcolm, she noted from the corner of her eye, had dried off and once more donned his shirt and boater. He stood slightly apart from the rest, looking uncustomarily subdued and more than a little out of sorts.

Careful to avoid his glance, she spread the largest of her maps atop the closed hatch. "Here is our position," she began, penciling an X in the approximate spot.

She unrolled a second map that afforded a more detailed view of that section of coastline, then began sketching in a row of rough rectangles. "What I saw," she went on, "was a series of stone blocks. There were perhaps two dozen of them, arranged three and four across—like giant cobblestones, if you will. Of course, it is difficult to tell much from this vantage point, but they appear to me to be entirely too symmetrical to be a natural formation. Their edges are straight-cut and butt up against each other with almost no space between. They could well be the top of a broad wall—"

"Or maybe a road," Rolle interjected. He rubbed his chin and gave her a thoughtful look. "Seems how my granddaddy once be tellin' me 'bout a road beneath the water."

"You mean, there is an oral tradition concerning these rocks?"

He nodded. "Not many folks be seein' it, he says, because it be comin' an' goin'. He be seein' once, hisself, when he was a boy . . . but then a big gale be comin' through, an' the sea be swallowin' it up again."

"And did your grandfather say who built this road?"

"Nobody be knowin'. Seems that, before white folks be discoverin' this place, some Indian tribe be settlin' here. An' before them . . ."

He trailed off with a shrug, but Halia was too excited by this bit of intelligence to worry. Nowhere in her father's notes had he indicated that this section of rock had been documented by others. Still, if stories about it dated back to well before any official settlement of the islands, she would have a better chance of substantiating her own theory.

She gave Rolle a hopeful look. "I don't suppose that your grandfather . . . that is, has he already passed away?"

"Two summers ago, when we be out bonefishin'. But maybe I can be checkin' around to see if anyone else be rememberin' those stories."

"Very good. For now, I think we should have the divers begin marking boundary areas so we can begin measurements. And perhaps one of them might climb the mast and see what the site looks like from above."

Rolle proceeded to give the orders and, for the next few hours, Halia and the divers—the latter divided into pairs—settled into a routine. Using ribbons of sturdy red cotton cloth tied to rocks, they began laying out on the sea floor a checkerboard grid that stretched in four directions from the boat. That project, she had determined, should occupy them for the next several days. Once those preliminaries were completed, they would work within each segment of that grid, measuring the slabs and noting other unusual formations.

Settled comfortably in the bow, she watched wistfully as each team of divers took their turn on the bottom. In the next few days, she fully intended to make several dives. Still, she knew that she lacked the lifetime of experience that these men had in working below the ocean's surface for minutes at a time. Her skills would be turned to task aboard ship. In addition to directing the exploration, she would collect the data and update her charts and maps, as well as catalog any finds the divers might make.

And as for Malcolm, she thought with a sniff, he could either assist Captain Rolle or else stay out of the way . . . whichever he wanted, so long as he kept clear of her.

It was midafternoon when she called a halt, not wishing to tax the divers to their limits on the first day. Satisfied with their progress, she smiled as the boat skimmed over the glasslike waves heading back to the dock. They *had* found something of significance, she was certain.

Fondly, she clutched the coin pendant that she wore around her throat. Whether or not the rocks would prove to be the remains of the long-lost continent of Atlantis still remained to be seen. Before they had weighed anchor and left the site, however, she had sworn Rolle and the crew to silence. No need to risk anyone else knowing what they were about. She had emphasized that with the promise of a substantial bonus and the assurance of a mention for each man in her official account of the find.

All had taken a solemn oath to that effect—all, that was, save Malcolm.

I'm bloody well not going to tell anyone, and you know it, had been his sharp reply when she timidly had attempted to elicit a similar vow from him. She had not pressed the issue, affected despite herself by his wretched state.

Once they finally reached the harbor again and the *Johnesta* was safely docked, she allowed herself another look his way. His exposed skin was the same bright red as the cooked stone crabs she had seen the natives prepare, and his expression, equally pained. He *had* kept up with his shipboard duties, however, though she wondered if he would make it through a second such day tomorrow.

"You will be joining us for supper?" she ventured.

He gave a curt assent and started from the boat. In another moment, he was making his way down the pier, his gait steady if a trifle stiff.

"Oh, my," she murmured as she and Rolle started off in the same direction. "I do hope Mal—that is, Mr. Northrup can make it back to the guest house unassisted. Perhaps I should—"

"Now, don't you be runnin' after him, offerin' sympathy," Rolle mildly cut her short. "He be a tough enough man, for all he can't swim no better than a babe, an' ain't no man be wantin' to admit any kind of weakness."

"I suppose not." She gave a little sigh, then glanced over at Rolle as he allowed himself a chuckle. "What is it, Captain?"

"It's just that I be seein' now why you be likin' this Englishman. It's because he be remindin' you of your father."

"My father?"

She halted in midstep to stare at him, aghast. "Why, that is the most outrageous thing I have ever heard. My father was a scholar, a gentleman . . . and Mr. Northrup is rogue, a scoundrel. The two are nothing at all alike."

"If you be sayin' so, Miss Halia," he solemnly agreed. "I will be seein' you in the morning, then."

They parted ways at the end of the pier, Rolle heading into town and Halia towards the low bluffs on its outskirts. His last comment about Malcolm, however, had shaken her somewhat, so that she found her steps slowed.

He be reminding you of your father.

It was an outlandish charge . . . or was it? Frowning, she tried to see her father as a stranger might have. If she were to be completely honest, she could admit that he had always been a bit glib for a scholar. And perhaps a bit too much devil-may-care for a man who'd been left with raising a daughter alone. But those charges were all that she would concede.

"They are nothing alike," she stubbornly murmured. But then, what else was it that Rolle had said—that she *liked* the Englishman?

That assertion, she was less able to deny, though she in-

tended to stifle this fancy once and for all. For there was no
future for her or any other woman with his sort of man . . .
this, she knew with certainty. But for now, what was she to
do?

A smile flickered briefly on her lips as a possible solution
came to her. Perhaps it was time to give Lally and her voodoo spells a chance, she told herself. Had she not seen
countless other young women come to the voodooienne for
help with *their* love lives?

For, if Lally could conjure up a love charm guaranteed to
win a man's heart, why could she not cast a spell to ward off
the same?

Chapter 13

"Ye look bloody awful," was Wilkie's dour assessment as he stuck his head out of his room to watch Malcolm make his careful progress down the corridor.

Painfully, Malcolm halted and turned his head in that direction. He was in no mood for his partner's jibes, given the events of the day.

"I'd like to see how bloody *hearty* you'd look," he clipped out, "if you'd been burnt by a hellish sun, fallen off a boat and almost drowned, and then had to walk uphill all the bloody way home after it was over."

The older man shrugged, unmoved. " 'Tweren't my idea, comin' 'ere. I told ye from the start 'twas a lot o' foolishness. So, 'ow many pots o' gold did you find?"

Malcolm cleared his throat. "We did locate a rather promising site that we will explore further tomorrow—"

"Nothin', eh?" Wilkie cut him short with a look of sour satisfaction. "I won't say 'ow as I told ye so . . . but I told ye so. 'Tis a bleedin' goose chase we're on, for all yer Miss Da'enport claims otherwise."

Malcolm would have countered his partner's words, save that he had begun to fear the same thing. The brief glimpse he'd had of Halia's so-called Atlantis site appeared, to him, to be little different from the rocks that made up the island's

beaches and low cliffs. Only her certainty that she had discovered something special kept his hopes alive.

*But she'd bloody well better find something more interest-
ing than a pile of rocks before the week's end,* he grimly told
himself. He'd give it that long, at least, before deciding
whether or not to simply cut his losses.

To Wilkie, however, he merely said, "They'll be serving
supper in another hour or so. Make my excuses, would
you . . . and see if you can't get someone to send me up a
tray. In the meantime, I think I'll just stay in my room and
die of a bloody heat stroke."

"An' that's another thing," the other man indignantly
pointed out. "All this bleedin' sun, 'tain't natural—nor
'ealthy neither, by the looks o' ye. Give me a right civilized
pea-souper of a fog, any day."

With a promise to see about dinner, Wilkie shut his door
again. Malcolm slowly continued down the corridor, not especially cheered by the conversation they'd just had. This
was the first time Wilkie had not joined wholeheartedly in
one of his schemes, a sign that Malcolm found less than
promising. Still, perhaps he'd not made himself clear on the
whole point of this expedition . . . namely, for Malcolm to
seduce his way into Halia's good graces and then casually
help himself to any treasure she might stumble across.

It was a straightforward plan, he assured himself, requir-
ing no elaborate cover stories to tell or fictitious back-
grounds to embroider. All that was needed was for him to
be his usual charming self, and everything else would fall
into place.

Wryly, he glanced at the connecting door to Halia's
room. The only problem was that, at least for tonight, he
couldn't possibly summon the strength to seduce a dockside
trollop, let alone a reluctant virgin.

He reached his room and made his way inside. In his absence, someone had opened the louvered shutters that overlooked the gallery. He could see the sun extinguishing itself

in a showy splash of pink and orange as it slipped along the horizon and into the dark blue waves. A welcome hint of an evening breeze had risen, circulating the room and ruffling the yards of white netting draped across the four-poster. The white counterpane spread across its mattress beckoned him with the promise of peaceful repose.

Heeding that call, Malcolm eased off his rope sandals and shirt and headed toward the bed. He pulled back the coverlet; then, forgetting for the moment his sunburned flesh, he collapsed atop the cool white sheets.

All the fires of hell promptly flared across his back. He yelped and sat up again; then, recalling the connecting door between his room and Halia's, he shot a sheepish glance in that direction. He'd already looked the fool to her once this day, nearly getting himself drowned. He would be damned if he'd let her hear him whine over so minor a thing as too much sun.

Carefully, he eased himself back onto the bed, settling this time on his stomach. All he needed was a few minutes of rest to regain his strength.

Just a few minutes . . .

He awoke from vivid dreams of being flayed alive by a grinning, whip-wielding shark to find himself in a pitch black room. But even when the nightmare faded, the sensation of a hod's worth of hot coals being heaped upon his back remained.

"Bloody hell," he groaned out, not caring who might have heard him this time. He eased his way out of the bed—every twitch and turn fanning the invisible flames that were consuming his flesh—and lit a taper, then reached for his timepiece sitting atop the chest of drawers.

Midnight.

He caught up the candle and turned, then impulsively glanced over his shoulder at the mottled round mirror that was mounted atop the mahogany chest. Even in this flickering light, he could tell that his back was an unhealthy shade of deep red. Indeed, his skin seemed fairly to glow—a state of affairs that likely boded no good for his comfort the next few days.

"Bloody, bloody hell," he groaned again as, candle in hand, he shuffled to the hall door. The promised supper tray was in the corridor . . . had been sitting there several hours, in fact, given the appearance of whatever sort of fish stew it was that had congealed in its white china bowl.

His stomach roiling, Malcolm left that offering where it was and settled for the accompanying side dishes—a generous slab of brown bread wrapped in a napkin and a carafe of what appeared to be tepid ale.

He made a tolerable meal of the plain fare, though even the simple task of chewing seemed to exacerbate his pain. Swiping a few bread crumbs from his chin, he finished off the last of the ale, then shook out the napkin to its full length.

A water-filled carafe sat on his dresser. He liberally soaked the thin material with its contents, then lightly plastered the wet napkin across his back. It brought him a measure of relief . . . but not enough to allow him a peaceful night's repose, he was certain.

Clutching the napkin around him rather like an opera cape, he debated what to do. It crossed his mind that either Halia or Lally could suggest a remedy for his blistered skin. But, agonizing as his condition was, he'd be damned if he would entrust his abused hide to either woman's not-so-tender mercies.

So use your bloody wits, then.

Longingly, he thought of snowdrifts and shaved ice. Since snow was in short supply in the Biminis, however, he cast about for another solution. Butter, he'd always heard, was good for easing a blister and might do equally well applied to a larger area. But what were the chances that he'd find an ample store of fresh butter here in the guest house, or anywhere else on this benighted rock?

It's worth a try, Malcolm, my boy, he told himself as he tossed aside the damp napkin and opened his bedroom door again. He squinted down the darkened corridor, relieved to see no telltale sliver of light beneath any of the doors. The rest of the household was asleep. He could roam the place with impunity.

Like a man who had wandered any number of dark hallways in his time, he made his silent way down the L-shaped corridor to the staircase. He descended with nary a creak of a riser, then crossed the main hall to the parlor, nestled at the juncture where one wing of the house veered off at right angles from the other.

It was a quaint little room, he saw by the flickering light of his candle. It was furnished in a style popular at the turn of the previous century, right down to a japanned, three-paneled screen in one corner and an oil rendition of the late King George, hanging on one wall. The room reminded him of those musty English country houses—their furniture and tapestries unchanged since the Regent's time—where, in the guise of a guest, he once had plied his trade. In keeping with the illusion, heavy velvet drapes hung over both pairs of French doors on the far wall so that, drawn, they would obscure the view of the tropical courtyard beyond.

With another scornful glance, Malcolm dismissed the parlor as an affront to civilized folk and good taste. The original owners had an excuse, at least, in that they had been homesick for king and country at a time when this portion of the world was barely tamed. The subsequent inhabitants had no such similar justification, at least in his opinion, and should have taken it upon themselves to rid the place of such folly.

He shook his head and continued his search. Beyond the parlor was a small withdrawing room that had been set up as dining salon. A hint of the same fish chowder that had been left upon the tray for him still lingered in the air. Past the withdrawing room was a sort of butler's pantry that, upon closer inspection, also doubled as a larder.

Triumphant, he commenced a swift search. The lowest of the shelves held a tiny stone crock covered with a length of damp cheesecloth. A lump of white butter—slightly rancid by the smell of it—lay within.

He wrinkled his nose, faintly aghast at the idea of anointing himself with such a substance. Still, beggars could not be choosers, especially when his only other choice was soliciting a cure from Halia or else her she-devil of a servant. Weighing that latter option as the more appalling, he snatched up the crock and carried it back through the dining salon into the parlor.

He paused as he reached the French doors. One hung slightly ajar, letting in a hint of breeze and the faint, soothing rumble of the distant surf. It would be cooler outside than in, he judged and silently padded his way into the courtyard.

He settled on the stone bench that ringed the fig tree. Uncomfortably hard as it turned out to be, its chiseled surface still was surprisingly cool beneath his lightly clad buttocks. Too bad he couldn't transfer a bit of that relief a bit higher up.

He set down the butter crock and then pinched out his candle, for he did not need its faint glow here, in the open. A three-quarter moon peered down at him from between the sprawl of branches above, dappling him with enough silvery light that he might have read the latest novel, had he wished. All he wanted to do, though, was find some measure of relief from the burning pain of his blistered back.

Gingerly, he raised the butter crock to his nose again, then tasted a fingertip's worth of the white spread. *Bloody rancid,* he confirmed with a grimace. Still, it couldn't be any worse than that foul-smelling ointment Lally had slathered on him as he lay unconscious that first day. He started to scoop up a palmful when he heard a faint rustle behind him.

He swung about, half-suspecting who it was even before
Halia stepped from the house's shadow. "Afraid I sneaked
out and went searching for treasure on my own?" he wryly
inquired. "Perhaps you would feel more comfortable tying
me to my bed at night, so that you wouldn't have to follow
me about at all hours."

"I was *not* following you," she protested in a low if heated
tone. "That is, I woke up and heard someone moving about
the hallway, and since yours was the only door open . . ."

She broke off momentarily, looking a bit dismayed as her
gaze took in his bare torso. Then she shook her head, so that
her mass of blond hair, hanging loose about her shoulders,
glinted in the moonlight.

"Really, Mr. Northrup, you are quite a trying man. I suspected that you were awake and in some pain because of
your sunburn, so I thought to bring you some relief."

"Relief, eh? And just what did you have in mind?" he
asked, cocking an ironic brow as he let his gaze travel over
her in renewed interest.

She wore a modest wrapper of what he judged to be blue
flannel, cinched so that her slim waist appeared even smaller
and her hips more enticingly round. Its lapels had likely
been tugged snugly across her breasts when she had left her
room. Now, however, those edges gaped enough to expose a
tantalizing bit of flesh, while the moonlight created all manner of interesting shadows in that seductive valley. But what
truly caught his eye was the flash of pale ankle and calf as
the breeze caught at the hem of her dressing gown.

Did the proper Miss Davenport sleep attired in nothing
but her chemise and drawers, he wondered . . . or maybe, did
she instead sleep in nothing at all?

That idle speculation stirred in his loins an unexpected response that belied what he'd told himself earlier in the evening. Given a proper bit of encouragement, he might just be
able to seduce the chit, after all. Besides, he'd always had a
fondness for coupling in unconventional places. Granted,

the bench was bloody uncomfortable, but he still might manage—

"—hardly what I meant," her hasty protest interrupted this most interesting line of thought. He grinned as she swiftly clutched with one hand at the sprawling neckline of her wrapper and, with the other, thrust a squat jar at him.

"I asked Lally to make this up for you," she went on in an offended tone. "Spread it over the burn several times a day, and it should ease the pain, as well as hasten the healing process. You do realize, don't you, that you never should have exposed yourself to the tropical sun in that fashion?" she finished in the stern tone of parent to child.

Malcolm suppressed an evil grin, enjoying baiting the chit. "I assure you, Miss Davenport, that I shall be quite careful as to how I expose myself in the future," he replied in a soft yet deliberate tone.

He suspected that she blushed as she took his meaning, though in the moonlight it was difficult to tell. He watched in no little amusement as she opened her mouth to reply, then snapped her lips shut again. "Do take this," she finally managed and again proffered the jar.

"Ah, but I already have a cure," he smoothly answered and indicated the crock beside him.

Halia eyed it with suspicion. "But surely this is butter"— she marched over and snatched up the container, then gave its contents a sniff—"and rancid butter, at that. Would you rather not try Lally's ointment?"

"Perhaps . . . if you would spread it on for me."

He lightly flung the challenge and waited to see how she would react. She stood but a handsbreadth from him now, and he could see the look of alarm that washed over her face. Then, as if coming to some sort of decision, she gave a hesitant nod.

"I suppose it *would* be a bit difficult for you to reach all the burned spots. I'm not sure that this is proper, mind you, but given the circumstances, there could surely be no real harm in it."

"Then have at it, Miss Davenport, but do use a gentle hand," he replied and scooted around on the bench so that his back was toward her.

He listened to her soft rustling behind him as she set aside the crock and then fumbled for several moments with the jar lid. Finally, when she must have decided that she could delay no more, she said, "If you might turn just a bit more, Mr. Northrup, so you are in the moonlight—"

She broke off with a sharp gasp. "Oh, my, that *is* a serious burn," she breathed in a tone of what he judged to be genuine concern. "Even with the salve, it will likely be several days before the worst of it fades, and several more beyond that before you dare expose yourself to the sun again for even a short time. Perhaps I should—"

"Perhaps you should shut up, luv, and see about spreading that ointment on me, instead."

He allowed himself a grin at her muffled sound of pique. Then, without warning, icy fingers seared his shoulder.

He gave an undignified yelp. "Bloody hell, that's cold!" he choked out and shot a glance back at her.

It was Halia's turn to look amused. "That *is* the general idea, is it not? Shall I proceed?"

"Go on," he replied and braced himself for the onslaught.

This time, however, the sensation of cold was less startling. Indeed, it was rather like a blacksmith thrusting a newly forged bit of glowing iron into a bucket of water to cool it, the way the ointment subdued the painful heat of his burned flesh. By stages, he began to relax and enjoy the sensuous feel of her hand lightly moving over his back.

"So, what's in this ointment, anyway?" he lazily asked as her fingers moved down his shoulder blades and along his ribs. "Some of Lally's voodoo powders, no doubt."

"No, not at all," came her swift assurance, the words warm against the back of his neck. "It's a concoction of aloe and other plants, all of which are found here in the islands. It is a traditional cure, so you need have no fear."

Fear, however, was the last thing he was feeling.

Even as the heat seemed to fade almost magically from his back, a more interesting warmth began to settle in his loins. He shifted against the bench in response to the growing fullness of his manhood as it pressed against the confining fabric of his trousers. By the time her fingers reached his lower back, he was painfully erect and in need of some drastic relief.

"There, that should take care of you," he heard her say in soft satisfaction as, all too soon, she ceased her ministrations and set the jar down with a light clatter. "I will leave the rest of the ointment for you, so that you can—"

She broke off as he awkwardly rose and moved to face her again. Before she could take a step back, he caught both her hands in his. "I'm afraid, my dear Halia," he softly countered, "that I will need something more than a bit of ointment to—how did you so charmingly put it?—take care of me this night."

"Really, Mr. Northrup, I hardly think—"

"Malcolm," he softly urged and drew her steadily closer. "Call me Malcolm, luv. It's so much more . . . friendly. And we are friends, are we not?"

He watched as moonlight and uncertainty played across her features. Suddenly, her answer—the right answer—was important to him.

"I-I do suppose we *are* friends," she finally agreed in a breathless tone, her lips now inches from his.

His smile held more than a hint of satisfaction. "I'm glad of that, luv, for I'd hate to think I was about to kiss an enemy," he murmured and bent to claim her.

Chapter 14

The kiss was nothing like the punishing caress Halia recalled from the bank. Rather, it was the merest brush of his lips against hers, so brief a gesture that she might have imagined it, yet it sent a wanton shiver through her that left her weak. But none of this was supposed to be happening . . . not if Lally had done what she had said she would do.

Uncertain all at once, she tugged her hands from his grasp. "I-I don't think this is at all proper."

Even to her own ears, the breathless objection sounded more like a question than a statement of fact. He gave a soft laugh in reply and reached up to brush back a wisp of blond hair from her cheek.

"Who said anything about proper, luv? I'm fair to bursting with need for you, and I rather suspect that you feel quite the same. So why not allow ourselves this bit of pleasure?"

"Oh, my," she weakly murmured as he pulled her close again. This time, his kiss was more demanding, literally drawing the very breath from her so that she had to clutch at him for support.

Then he deepened his kiss, his tongue expertly probing the delicate inner flesh of her mouth in a manner both unfamiliar and thrilling. Hesitantly, she returned that caress, parrying each thrust of his tongue with her own tentative gesture that drew a low moan of satisfaction from him.

His hands slid to her breasts now. She bit back her own soft cry as, with his thumbs, he lightly caressed her through the thin barrier of fabric until her nipples had tightened into small buds of pleasure. Bolder now, she followed his lead, sliding her own hands over his chest. It was a heady sensation, feeling the silken scatter of hair beneath her fingers and the sleek expanse of muscle that played beneath his taut flesh.

Something *had* gone wrong, she vaguely realized even as she gave herself up to pure sensation. The healing ointment that Lally had concocted supposedly contained an additional ingredient—an herb said to dull male desire. Surely she had applied enough of the salve to him for it to have taken effect, yet the mixture seemed to have inflamed his need . . . and hers, as well.

Abruptly, she struggled free from his embrace to meet his expression of masculine satisfaction. She shut her eyes, fervently wishing she had never searched him out this night. The ointment had been an excuse. What she truly had wanted was a few moments alone with the man. She had needed to prove to herself that she could be coolly logical about this unseemly attraction she felt for him.

Instead, she had succumbed to the traitorous desires of her body . . . desires that now swept her flesh in waves of cold and heat.

He must have sensed her determination beginning to waver, for she felt him lightly tug at the sash of her dressing gown. "It's warm out," he murmured as the knot slowly pulled free, leaving her wrapper hanging loose about her. "Let's rid you of this thing, shall we?"

Not waiting for her reply—if, indeed, she had been capable of making one—he slid the dressing gown from her shoulders. His fingers were warm against her suddenly chill flesh as he eased the garment down her arms. Finally, with the barest whisper of fabric, it settled in a blue flannel pool about her feet. That obstacle gone, he lightly gripped her buttocks and pulled her to him, then once more claimed her lips with his.

Even as she opened her mouth to him, she was aware of the hot, throbbing bulge of his manhood as it pressed insistently against the juncture of her thighs. An answering warmth began to build in her—a tight, curling heat centered low in her belly. But even as she acknowledged the sensation, he broke free of their kiss.

She gave an instinctive cry of protest and opened her eyes, only to hear his soft chuckle in return.

"Don't worry, luv," he murmured, lowering his head to nuzzle the soft flesh of her throat. "I'm not through with you, yet."

Before she realized what he was about, he had slid one hand between her thighs. Heedless of the thin barrier of her pantalets, he began quite boldly fondling her woman's mound, lightly stroking at the swollen nub of flesh where every sensation seemed suddenly centered.

She gave a soft, strangled cry and would have pulled away, save that his other hand clutched her buttocks and held her still. "Don't fight it, luv," he urged. "Let me pleasure you for a moment."

Pleasure?

Indeed, it seemed the sweetest sort of torture, this kaleidoscope of sensation that was spreading through her in a way she'd never felt before. Vaguely, she was aware that her pantalets were soaked now with her own hot juices, while the lips of her woman's flesh had swollen like a bud ready to flower. How this was happening, she was not quite certain, but she prayed it would never stop.

But it must stop. It must.

Abruptly, Halia pulled away from him and caught a painful breath. Dear Lord, had she been that ready to surrender him her innocence? And she would have, in another moment, save for her sudden return now to her senses.

With a muffled sound suspiciously like a sob, she shook her head and took an unsteady step back. "No, Malcolm, this is a mistake. I don't . . . that is, I cannot—"

She broke off abruptly at the expression of bewildered masculine outrage that flashed across his face. It occurred to her that, once, such a reaction surely would have drawn her satisfaction. Why, then, was she racked with an odd sense of guilt, as if she had betrayed some sort of trust? An explanation on her part surely was in order . . . yet she could never hope to spell out her reasons to his satisfaction, when she could not understand them, herself.

Hastily, she bent to retrieve her discarded dressing gown. Then, with a silent look imploring him not to despise her for this sudden change of heart, she whipped that garment about her and fled the dark courtyard on coward's feet.

Malcolm stood within the fig tree's maze of shadows, his stunned gaze fixed on the French doors through which Halia had just disappeared.

What in the bloody hell had just happened here? All he knew was that he'd reached the point of wanting her almost beyond bearing, only to have her figuratively dash him in the face with a bucket of cold sea water.

With a groan, he adjusted his trousers across the bulge of his erection, which still strained against the confining cloth in hopes of relief. He waited a few moments more, until his almost painful need had eased into a less urgent throbbing. Then, reflexively, he shifted his bare feet against the rough flagstone, cursing under his breath when a sharp rock caught his heel. Until a moment ago, he could have been standing in a pile of broken glass and not noticed, so aroused was he.

As she had been, he bitterly reminded himself. He had not

forced himself upon her—that much, he knew. Hell, she'd
been more than bloody willing, clinging to him like some
dockside trollop who'd been paid an extra shilling to pretend that she liked it.

So what had gone wrong?

A mistake. That was what she had said, though moments
before she had been as eager for his touch as he still was for
hers. Perhaps it had been the thought of losing her maiden-
head that troubled her, yet why should that matter? After
all, he intended to wed her just as soon as—

"Bloody hell," he choked out and abruptly sat down on
the hard stone bench as he realized what had just passed
through his mind.

What in blazes had possessed him to consider—even
briefly!—so ludicrous an idea? He had no intention of mar-
rying the chit, now or in the future. Just because he happened to want her like he'd never before wanted any other
woman didn't mean a bloody thing!

He gave his head a sharp shake to clear it. It had to have
been too much sun earlier that made him susceptible to such
fancies. The idea of marriage—to her or any other woman,
for that matter—had been an aberration, and one he intended to put from his mind forever.

That firmly settled, he stood again. At least, fiery pain of
his back had subsided to a tolerable ache. He caught up the
jar of ointment and started for the door, grudgingly deciding that he owed Lally a word of thanks on the morrow. As
for what to do about Halia . . . hell, maybe he should take to
wearing the emerald around his neck again. It did seem that
he had lost control of the entire situation with her at about
the very time he had shed the lucky gem.

As he reached his bedroom, he knew that sleep would
likely prove elusive for the remainder of the night. For all he
might deny it, he was finding himself obsessed by her.
Chances were he would lie awake tonight and in the nights
to follow, wondering what it would have been like to bury

himself deep inside the tight warmth of her . . . and knowing that Atlantis would surely rise from the sea again before that would ever happen.

Bleary-eyed, Halia stood apart from the rest of the *Johnesta's* crew, hardly noticing the glory of early morning and the cool sea breeze that was a respite from the island's usual heat. Her unseeing gaze was fixed on the passing shore as the boat skimmed the shimmering blue waters leading to the Atlantis site. But right now, the last thing on her mind was her search for that long-vanished city.

What haunted her was memories of last night.

It was not until she had reached her room and latched the door behind her that the hot tears she had not realized she'd been holding back spilled over her lashes.

Lally and her spirits were right, she had told herself in despair. Malcolm *was* trouble. Worst of all, he *had* cast a spell on her . . . a sensual spell that left her traitorous body yearning for him, for all she knew that it was wrong.

Dashing the moisture from her cheeks, she impulsively had stripped off her dressing gown and undergarments, so that she stood naked in the heated darkness. Not caring that she splashed the floor with precious fresh water, she had filled her washbasin. With a coarse towel she brutally began scrubbing every inch of her body as if to eradicate the very memory of his touch. But instead of easing her yearning, the rough feel of the cloth against her smooth flesh had only intensified her need.

With a moan, she had flung aside the towel and pulled on her nightrail, then clambered beneath her sheets. Sleep proved elusive, however, because, moments later, she heard Malcolm moving about the adjoining chamber. What if he sought her out, since all that stood between them was a single door?

Half-dreading and half-hoping that he would, she had

tossed and turned almost until dawn, awakening unre-freshed and well past her usual time. As a consequence, she had arrived almost half an hour late to the dock.

It be a good thing you be payin' the wages, Captain Rolle had jovially pointed out, *or me an' my crew, we be gone a long time ago.*

She had acknowledged his good-natured gibes with a strained smile and a mumbled excuse about too much sun the day before. And then she'd caught sight of Malcolm.

For he had been there, after all, though she had half-suspected he might not be. He apparently had learned his own lesson from the tropical sun. Not only was he wearing a shirt today, that garment was buttoned to the throat. His familiar straw boater was pulled low over his brow, its brim shadowing his face so that she could not guess his thoughts. She could only hope that they were as unsettling as her own.

Still, an odd sort of relief had swept her at the sight of him. She told herself it was the fact that his absence on top of her own late arrival might have given rise to talk among the crew. With the success of the expedition at stake, she could ill afford undue attention focused on either of them. She would maintain her usual cool distance from him, she had vowed as the boat had set sail.

So caught up was Halia in her thoughts now that, when she finally returned herself to the present, the *Johnesta* had already reached her destination. Once more, they were at a spot off the island's northwest coast, not far from where yesterday's discovery had been made.

The anchor sliced through the water's calm blue surface with a muffled splash, that sound followed by the creak of timber masts and the soft splat of waves against the boat's hull. The peaceful rhythm was punctuated by the squawking laughter of gulls who dipped and swirled like carefree children at play.

Determinedly, she prepared for the job at hand. As the crew gathered around, she unrolled her charts and began marking off sections. She finally settled on one square on the main map that corresponded to a spot just off the bow.

"We'll begin here. Garnet"—she addressed the young sponge diver whose lighter, almost ruddy complexion had earned him that sobriquet—"you and Jeffers take the first group of measurements. I believe we should move in the direction of shore," she went on, turning her attention back to the map. "It seems logical that these blocks we've found might be the remains of a road, or even a harbor. Once we've moved a bit more sand—"

A muttered sound of disagreement made her break off abruptly. Not needing to look up to identify her dissenter, she asked in a chill tone, "Are you questioning my conclusion, Mr. Northrup?"

"Not your conclusion, just the whole bloody way you're going about this."

"Indeed?" Her lips thinning in irritation, Halia glanced up to meet his gaze.

He stood apart from Rolle and the rest of the men, arms crossed over his chest as he leaned against the rail. His comment was the first sign he had given of acknowledging her existence this morning. Doubtless, he had not forgiven or forgotten what had happened between them in the courtyard.

As if reading her thoughts, Malcolm favored her with a humorless smile. "As I said, you're going about this whole thing all wrong. All we have found thus far are several large, flat rocks embedded in the ocean floor—hardly evidence of a lost civilization, to my mind. Hell, I've seen rocks just like them in every stream bed I've ever stumbled across."

"I have already told you that we're not looking for columns and temples," she countered. "Whatever is here is buried beneath the sand."

He ignored the interruption. "I suggest that before you have these men dig up the entire sea bottom, inch by inch, you broaden your scale a bit."

"I hardly think you are qualified to make that judgment, Mr. Northrup. I am trained in these procedures, so I suggest that you let me run this expedition as I see fit."

"As *you* see fit?" He pushed away from the rail and stalked over to join them. "Might I remind you, Miss High-and-Mighty Davenport, that it is my money funding your little adventure, not to mention the fact I'm the one who supplied you with the correct coordinates, in the first place."

"Indeed?" Outwardly calm although seething now within, Halia set down her pencil and stood so that their gazes were closer on a level. "I have no idea how you stumbled upon the coordinates, but they are mine by right, since they came from my father's journal. As for the money, it wasn't yours to begin with. You stole it."

"That's beside the bloody point. We're equal partners in this venture."

"Only because you shoved your way in, *not* because I wanted you."

"That's not the impression I got last night, luv."

His words held a sneering implication that was not lost on her . . . nor, from the interested expressions on the faces of the crew, on anyone else. The mortifying thought occurred to her that anyone watching would think this was a lovers' quarrel.

Halia felt wash over her cheeks a sudden heat that had nothing to do with the tropical sun. She and Malcolm were standing almost nose to nose, now, so that she could see glinting in his eyes an anger that matched her own. Her own emotions ran almost as high. But she would not sink to his level, no matter how he goaded her.

She took a calming breath and squarely met his gaze. "Perhaps I was remiss in not explaining to you more fully just how a dig such as this is accomplished. To properly excavate the site—even considering that it is underwater—we must mark off quadrants and then thoroughly investigate each one in sequence. That way, we can intelligently link any evidence to its surroundings. It is a tedious process, I will admit, but it is the correct way. So unless you think you can do a better job—"

"Bloody right, I can."

Fairly snatching Halia's pencil from her hand, he leaned over and stabbed at the spot on the map that she previously had indicated.

"I'll make you a new deal, Miss Davenport. We'll divide the site like this"—he paused to slash an arrowed line north and south from the circle—"and we'll each conduct our own treasure hunt. The *Johnesta* will serve as our joint base of operations, with all supplies and equipment to be evenly shared."

He paused to scrawl her name to the right of that penciled line, then his to the left. "You will take half the divers and search the side closer to shore using whatever strategy you see fit. I'll take the other three men and search the waters west of our imaginary line in my own way. If I find the first actual evidence that we've discovered something more here than a pile of rocks, we will remain equal partners, but with the excavating continuing under my direction . . . though I will, of course, solicit your advice from time to time."

"And if *I* make the first find?" she countered, ignoring that last patronizing concession.

He shrugged. "Everything is turned over to you—lock, stock, and barrel, including the rest of my money and the sole use of the *Johnesta* and her crew. I'll relinquish any claim to my fifty-percent share and leave the island without a murmur."

Leave the island?

What should have been a welcome possibility suddenly left her feeling strangely bereft, but she would throw herself overboard before she let Malcolm know that. Instead, she coolly asked, "And who will determine whether or not any object either of us uncovers is a genuine Atlantean artifact?"

"We'll let Captain Rolle make that judgment; that is, if he is agreeable."

As one, she and Malcolm turned to the seaman, who shrugged and nodded. "If you be wantin' to do it dat way, it be fine by me, but I warn you I'll not be playin' any favorites."

"Then it's settled," he pronounced with a challenging look back at her, "unless you are afraid to take me up on my proposal."

By way of answer, she stubbornly lifted her chin and stuck out her hand. "I accept, Mr. Northrup, starting this very moment. But I believe we also should agree that neither of us will search without the other. We will avail ourselves of Captain Rolle and his boat only."

"Done," he replied and grasped her fingers in his.

As always, his touch sent a warm shiver through her senses, but she met his triumphant gaze with a look of stony resolve. This time out, she vowed, she would conquer her womanly weakness and keep her thoughts firmly on her goal. For she had the advantage of knowledge and experience that should surely give her the edge over Malcolm's haphazard approach.

Why, perhaps by day's end, she would have made her first discovery. It might be as soon as the morrow that a certain rogue Englishman would finally be out of her life . . . and this time, for good.

Chapter 15

Five days had passed since she and Malcolm had agreed to divide the Atlantis site. To Halia's dismay, nothing had yet come of her tedious hours spent directing her small team of sponge divers. In pairs, with Halia taking an occasional turn, they continued her approach of measuring each quadrant before carefully sifting through and then removing its cover of white sand. Though a pattern had begun to emerge—a road, perhaps, or maybe the top of a wide, long-buried wall?—she had as yet found no telling artifact such as the Poseidon coin that her father had found.

Her only consolation was that Malcolm seemingly was faring no better.

Having commandeered the *Johnesta's* dinghy, he and his crew of three had spent much of their time observing the site from above the waves. She had been surprised the first time she'd seen him clamber into the tiny boat with his men and take to the waves, given his propensity for seasickness and his previous unpleasant experience overboard.

But he continued to row out with them, even taking his own turn at the oars. Though still proclaiming his neutrality, Captain Rolle had taken pity on the fact Malcolm was a poor sailor and given him an ample supply of a local herb—the root of which, when chewed, helped combat unpleasant symptoms. She'd noticed, too, that he was no longer burning beneath the tropical sun but was beginning to turn as brown as she.

Sourly, she guessed that his next step would probably be to take swimming lessons from Garnet or one of the others, further narrowing her advantages over him.

With the line between them literally and figuratively drawn, they both had taken pains to feign disinterest in the other's actions these past days. They arrived at the dock independently and went their separate ways immediately as the boat returned. In between times, they each kept to their own side of the ship—hers, starboard and his, port—both addressing any point of concern to the captain, who found himself in the unlucky role of go-between.

It *was* all quite childish, she conceded to herself, but such was the stuff of competition . . . and this game was one she could not afford to lose.

Still, a dose of feminine curiosity prompted her to covertly observe Malcolm and his men. From what she could tell by way of casual glances, it appeared that he was using the water glass to get an overview of his portion of the site. He would send his men on seemingly random dives throughout the day, sometimes more than once in the same area.

He also was plotting out a map of his own, or so she presumed. What actually was written between the covers of the notebook he'd somehow procured was anyone's guess. Like a spoiled child, he took elaborate pains to keep her from seeing what he was writing down, though he took equal steps to make sure she saw him scribbling. Only her fear that he might stumble over some Atlantean artifact while conducting his haphazard operation kept her from taking any amusement in the situation.

But today, neither of them would make any progress in their search, for it was Sunday.

"Me an' my crew, we not be workin' on the Lord's day,"

Rolle had gently rebuked her the night before even as she had been making plans for the next morning's search.

She had been swift with an apology, recalling that most of the Biminians were devout Christians. Indeed, she knew that they were unique among the Caribbean peoples in the fact that, with few exceptions, their religious life had no underpinnings of African-based spirit worship.

Rolle graciously accepted her quick words of regret and countered by inviting her to join him and his family for Sunday dinner following services. Knowing that this sort of hospitality was rare among the islanders—the usual custom was to entertain outside and often in a public place—she agreed to his offer with alacrity.

Rolle's reminder that this was a day of rest had pricked her conscience. At home, she was an indifferent member of the Church of England, attending services only on holy days. Something about the island's unhurried pace, however, seemed conducive to matters of the spirit. Feeling as if a bit of such nourishment might do her no harm, she impulsively decided to attend services before joining Rolle and his family.

She learned that her host's house lay not far from Saint Stephan's Anglican Church, though Rolle explained that he himself attended the Methodist chapel farther down the road. She had asked Lally to accompany her but, as usual, the Haitian woman declined, assuring Halia that she would worship in her own fashion . . . which meant exploring the island in search of new herbs.

Wilkie had been within earshot of their brief exchange. According to Lally, the dour Englishman had spent most of the past few days lounging on the veranda playing patience, so that Halia wondered what had induced him to follow Malcolm here in the first place. He had caught her by surprise this morning as he expressed a desire to accompany her to church.

"That is, if ye don't mind, miss," the man had haltingly

offered. "Malcolm, 'e ain't much o' a church-goer, but I can do wit' a bit o' spiritual comfort e'ery so often."

Swallowing back her opinion that Malcolm was probably more in need of spiritual guidance than either of them, she had summoned a smile.

"I'd be pleased for your company, Mr. Foote," she had replied, realizing as she did so that she spoke the truth. Wilkie's blunt if dour personality could only prove a pleasant change from the self-serving attitude of a certain other Englishman.

Now, she caught up her broad-brimmed boater and tied it firmly over her tightly braided hair, then reached for her reticule. She already had donned a prim, white starched shirtwaist and sensible gray skirt, along with a pair of sturdy boots. Though less comfortable in the tropical heat than her usual garb, the outfit was more appropriate for the Sabbath.

She and Wilkie made the walk in short time. Saint Stephan's proved to be a rather impressive hilltop structure with its own school and cemetery. Built almost entirely of planking from wrecked ships—or so Halia learned from chatting outside its doors with various members of the church—the house of worship could seat almost two hundred. Its spiritual shepherd for the past twenty years had been one Father Philpot, whose ringing oratory Halia later decided was the reason for his burgeoning congregation.

Unfortunately, his sermon that morning was on the subject of tolerance and forgiveness . . . virtues she'd not much cultivated of late. When services finally ended at noon, she left the church rather more ruffled in her mind than she had been when she entered.

Wilkie noted her mood, offering his blunt assessment of the situation once they stood on the avenue again.

"Right stubborn, the both o' ye," he declared with a dour air as they strolled beneath the hot noon sun. "Ye bark an' snap at each other like a pair o' pups over an old shoe, an'" for what? 'Tain't nothin' out there but fish, if ye're wantin' my opinion."

"If, by pups and old shoes, you are referring to my relationship with Mr. Northrup, then I believe you are exaggerating," Halia countered in a stiff tone. "As for what is out there, I am convinced we are on the verge of a major discovery."

When Wilkie only made a sound of disgust, she heatedly went on, "You surprise me, Mr. Foote. I thought you and Malcolm were partners, that he could talk you into any manner of wild schemes. This, at least, is a scientific venture. Don't you want your share of whatever treasure he finds?"

"All I want is a bit o' peace an' quiet," he retorted, then looked mildly surprised at his own answer.

He knitted his blond brows, his pockmarked face taking on an even more doleful expression as he continued, "'Tain't that I don't enjoy the life, takin' from them wot's got too much to begin wit'. 'Tis just that Malcolm, 'e ain't never satisfied. We make ourselves a potful o' blunt one day, an' e's off lookin' for more the next."

"Indeed? I wonder why that is so?"

With an effort, Halia kept her tone free of anything other than polite interest, though in truth Wilkie had piqued her curiosity. She knew nothing of Malcolm but what she'd read of him in the unsigned letters, along with what she had observed first-hand these past days. All that she really knew for certain was that he was a charming scoundrel . . . a coolly dangerous dandy.

Suddenly, she had a keen desire to learn just what lay behind the man's contradictory facade.

Wilkie appeared to be giving his answer more than casual thought. Finally, he replied, "'E wouldn't admit it, were ye to ask 'im. But e'ery time 'e takes a few bob off a rich bloke, 'e's takin' a stab back at 'is father."

The thought of Malcolm's having any family was surprising enough, but before she could pursue Wilkie's last words, the man continued, " 'E comes from right good stock, 'e does. 'Is father is Charles Northrup, Earl o' Sherebrooke."

"Earl of Sherebrooke?" She stopped to stare at Wilkie, recalling the coat-of-arms she'd seen engraved on Malcolm's pocket watch. "Then he wasn't lying, after all. He really is—"

"—a bastard, right enough," Wilkie unexpectedly finished her statement. " 'Is Lordship 'ad an eye for the ladies. An' Malcolm's mum, she were a right pretty girl, for all she were just an upstairs maid."

"So the earl seduced her?"

Wilkie nodded. "When she turned up in a family way, 'er Ladyship were all fer turnin' 'er out, but 'is Lordship said no. Malcolm grew up fer a time wit' 'is 'alf-sister, which is 'ow 'e learned to talk like 'is betters. But then 'is mum died, an' the earl left for Dublin to take care o' some business. 'Er Ladyship saw 'er chance an' bundled the poor lad off to London town. She left 'im there in the streets, threatenin' to 'ave 'im 'orsewhipped if 'e ever came back. 'E were but twelve years old. That's when 'e an' I hooked up."

"But how horrible," Halia cried, filled with sympathy for the boy that Malcolm had been. "Did his father never come after him?"

" 'Er Ladyship told the earl that Malcolm 'ad run off o' 'is own free will, an' I'd say 'Is Lordship were probably right relieved. Malcolm, 'e were a wild lad an' too clever by 'alf. 'Tweren't until ten years later that 'e an' 'is father met again. That were the day that Malcolm pinched 'is Lordship's gold pocket watch," Wilkie finished with a grin.

Halia, however, saw little to smile at in this tale. "So that's why he so despises the upper class. But can he truly believe that his ill-gotten gains somehow make up for Lord and Lady Sherebrooke's sins against him?"

Wilkie shrugged and resumed his leisurely pace. "I only know wot 'e tells me," he said as she fell in step beside him again. Then, with a sharp look at her, he added, " 'Ere, now, ye're not to let on to 'im wot I said."

"I'll not breathe a word," she agreed and, indeed, she could imagine no time when she might bring up this remarkable bit of conversation to Malcolm. Still, it had given her a whole new outlook on the man.

By now, they had reached the side street that led a brief, twisting length up to the King's Highway. Bidding Wilkie farewell—he would spend the afternoon, he informed her, fishing in the harbor—Halia started up the narrow, sandy avenue.

Like the Queens Highway that ran parallel to it, Kings Highway proved quite a bit less grand a street than its royal name implied. It overlooked North Bimini's west coast so that, had she wished, she might have managed a glimpse of the area where she had been searching the waves these past days.

Almost before she knew it, she was standing before the address that Captain Rolle had given her. Like the neighboring houses, his was a neat, single-storied cottage. It was whitewashed and set back behind a low stone wall, the top of which was lined with dozens of conch shells. A lone silver-thatched palm provided welcome shade, while yards of trailing hibiscus blanketed the hard-packed dirt yard in a flurry of green vines and yellow flowers.

All the shutters were thrown open to catch the late morning breeze that made the day's heat almost bearable. From one window wafted the delicious spicy aroma of conch stew, and Halia's stomach gurgled in anticipation.

She made her way past a short wood gate, upon which someone with more enthusiasm than skill had rendered the word *Johnesta* in bright paints. Rolle already stood waiting for her in the open doorway, minus his usual blue cap and dressed in his Sunday best. Only the glinting gold loop in his ear hinted at his seafaring profession.

"Do be comin' in, Miss Halia," he urged with a flashing

grin. "The wife an' the childrens, they be waitin' to meet you."

He urged her inside to a neat parlor of whitewashed walls and bare wooden floor. It was sparsely furnished—as was common in tropical homes, to preserve a sense of airy coolness—and served double duty as a dining salon. Eight places had been laid atop the round table in the corner, and Halia frowned as she did the swift arithmetic. Surely that was one place setting too many.

She put aside the question, however, for Rolle's wife and four small children stood, like a regiment on drill, in a dignified line against the far wall. The woman stepped forward and offered her hand. "I be Esta Rolle, Miss Davenport," she announced in quiet satisfaction.

Standing half a head taller than Halia, though still far shorter than her burly husband, Esta was a striking woman of middle years. Flashing green eyes against *café au lait* skin proclaimed her mixed heritage, as did her straight black hair caught in a neat bun at the nape of her neck. In her simple red calico dress, she appeared to Halia's eyes far more regal than any New York society woman wrapped in silks and satins could ever hope to be.

Smiling, she grasped the older woman's hand. "It is a pleasure to meet you . . . and do call me Halia," she added before turning to the children.

The quartet, two boys and two girls, stood stair-stepped in height from the oldest—a solemn boy of perhaps ten years—to the youngest—a grinning toddler in pink calico who clutched the next older girl's hand. All shared their father's dark skin, and all had the earnest, well-scrubbed look that bespoke stern but loving parents.

Esta took her hat and reticule for her, then indicated the foursome. "Let me be introducin' you, Miss Halia," she said, giving her brood a proud smile.

Briefly resting the palm of her hand on each curly head,

she moved down the row from oldest to youngest, announcing, in turn, "Willis, Maxwell, Winifred, Viola."

With a shy chorus of "Pleased to be meetin' you, miss," all save plump little Viola made their respective bows and curtsies. Halia gave each child a nod and a smile in return.

"What a lovely family," she told Esta. "You must be proud."

"That we be," the woman replied, then addressed Rolle. "And where be our other dinner guest, then?"

So she had not miscounted, after all, Halia realized and shot the captain a questioning glance. He returned her silent query with a look of bland innocence, and foreboding swept her. Dear Lord, surely he hadn't invited—

"Sorry I'm late," came Malcolm's familiar voice from the direction of the open doorway, confirming her suspicions. "I had a bloody time even finding—"

He broke off abruptly as he stepped across the threshold and caught sight of her. She met his gaze, allowing herself a niggle of triumph as surprise, anger, and resignation all struggled across his features in hasty sequence. True, his reaction mirrored her own feelings, but she would not give him the satisfaction of knowing that.

Even as the two of them remained unmoving, Esta and Rolle hurried to greet their other guest. Esta gave no sign that she noticed anything amiss, though the captain's face reflected amused satisfaction, so that Halia knew the man had carefully planned his guest list, after all. As for the four children, they giggled and stared at the newcomer.

Malcolm evenly accepted his hosts' greetings, a look of bland disinterest having finally settled over his features. "I hadn't realized we were making a party of this," he said, raising a wry brow. "If we're rather too crowded today, I would be happy to stop by another time."

"We be wantin' you now, Mr. Northrup," the captain jovially countered and motioned him closer. "Here, you must be meetin' my family."

He began the introductions a second time for Malcolm's benefit. Standing to one side, Halia watched in silent disapproval as the latter made the swift change from reluctant caller to accommodating guest.

In honor of the occasion, he had returned to his usual formal garb and had exchanged his now-battered boater for a more appropriate felt bowler. His first move was to sweep off his headgear and bend over Esta's work-worn hand with a nobleman's lazy grace.

He proceeded to shower her with a profusion of compliments that, coming from his practiced lips, sounded surprisingly sincere. Halia was dismayed but not surprised to see the older woman fall victim to his easy charm, protesting his bantering words with smiling demurrers that only underscored her pleasure at his nonsense.

The four children, Malcolm won over quite as easily. He produced from his waistcoat pocket a handful of sweets—procured from where, Halia could not guess—and presented several to each youngster, in turn, with great fanfare. In a matter of moments, he was allowing little Viola to examine his pocket watch even as, with a surprising bit of sleight of hand, he plucked a silver dollar from young Willis's ear.

Charlatan . . . scoundrel, Halia thought, rolling her eyes and forgetting the earlier sympathy she had felt for him. If she had not been there as witness, he doubtless would have contented himself with a nod and a handshake for the lot of them, rather than summoning up this blatant display of good-fellowship.

It was while she was indulging in such uncharitable thoughts that Malcolm chose to glance her way. "Ah, yes, Miss Davenport," he murmured in conspicuous afterthought and gave her the barest of nods. "I presume that you have already met everyone here?"

"I have, Mr. Northrup," she replied with an air of equal unconcern. *"I* was on time, you see, and—"

"I think we should be sittin' down now," Esta hurried to interject, apparently aware of the tension between her two guests. "We don't want the stew to be gettin' cool. Children"—she turned to her now fidgeting brood—"you be helpin' our visitors to their chairs."

Halia promptly found either hand clutched by small and—courtesy of Malcolm's candy—sticky fingers as young Winifred and her baby sister crowded around her. The boys made an equally swift beeline for Malcolm, urging him toward the table. Esta and Rolle followed at a more sedate pace.

Like an India rubber ball, Halia bounced from place to place as the children battled for the honor of sitting beside their guests. Once the scraping of chairs subsided and the urgent pleas—"do be sittin' by me, miss . . . you have to be takin' this chair, mister"—were silenced, Halia somehow found herself wedged in against the wall and seated directly beside Malcolm.

Though she carefully kept her gaze averted, the fact that she sat practically shoulder-to-knee with the man made it difficult for her to ignore him. Despite the welcome cross-breeze the room was warm, and the heat of his body warmer still. She was close enough to him to detect the faint masculine scent of him—a scent that was oddly comforting even while it evoked a score of disturbing memories.

But she had no wish to be on such familiar terms with him. It was almost frightening, the idea of being able to recognize him almost by instinct. Why could not her traitorous body simply follow the dictates of her mind and know the man for what he was?

She had no time to indulge her dismay, however, for Esta spoke up. "Mr. Malcolm, might you be wishin' to say grace for us?"

Halia sensed with satisfaction that the request had taken him aback. But even as she expected him to decline the request, he smoothly replied, "But, of course."

Rather than say a traditional prayer, however, he launched into an invocation worthy of the Reverend Philpot himself. From their recent successful voyage to the sweet potatoes on the table, he counted every imaginable blessing. Uncertain whether to laugh or be appalled, she settled on offering her own silent prayer for strength.

"—may we be truly thankful," he finally finished, earning a hearty round of *amens* from the assembled Rolles.

"Show-off," Halia muttered under her breath amid that chorus and then raised her bowed head.

Now, serving bowls were being passed her way. She was no longer quite so hungry, given her unsettled state of mind. Still, not wishing to offend Esta, she made certain to spoon a portion of every dish onto her plate.

And food, there was plenty of. Along with conch stew—a thick, savory blend of chewy mollusk combined with herbs, tomatoes, and peppers—she helped herself to peas and rice, sweet potatoes, and fried bananas. Their drink was refreshing peppermint tea, a common beverage in the islands for it boasted both agreeable flavor and medicinal benefits.

By the time the bowls and platter of food all made their rounds, Halia had regained most of her composure and some of her earlier appetite. With the entire Rolle family at hand, she told herself, surely she could avoid any interaction with the man beside her.

She swiftly found, however, that she had no need of initiating discussion. Her hosts and their offspring kept up a stream of chatter that made her feel quite at home. Between mouthfuls, she answered questions put to her about her home in New York. Malcolm, she noted, received equal treatment, so the conversation never lulled.

Indeed, she wryly thought, anyone watching the sprightly chatter would have been hard-pressed to notice that neither of the guests of honor was actually speaking to the other.

Reassured that the burden of dinner conversation did not rest solely with her, she set herself to doing justice to the delicious fare before her. Halfway through her stew, however, she exclaimed, "John."

When the rest of the table turned questioning looks her way, she blushed and directed a hasty explanation to Rolle. "Indeed, Captain, I just realized that I did not know your first name. Then it came to me that if your wife is called Esta and your boat is the *Johnesta,* it only followed that *your* name could not be anything else but John."

Rolle grinned. "You be right 'bout dat. Me, I just be wantin' to call my boat *Esta,* but she"—he gave an affectionate nod in his wife's direction—"she be sayin' no, dat it be too big an honor. So I be tellin' her, we be sharin' everyt'ing else, so I be namin' the boat after the both of us . . . an' dat be it."

"An admirable compromise," Malcolm lightly commented. "You are fortunate, Captain, to have found a woman of both modesty and good sense. Few men are that lucky."

"Luck has little to do with it," Halia coolly countered what was, she knew, a barely veiled barb directed at her. Addressing Esta but speaking to Malcolm, she went on, "Most men are so blinded by their own shortcomings that they are hard-pressed to see their partners' virtues."

Then, not allowing Malcolm the chance to contradict, she turned the conversation back to the subject uppermost, as always, in her mind—the Atlantis site.

"Tell me, Captain Rolle, have you discovered anyone else on the islands who has knowledge of the submerged rock formation that we found?"

"I found a few people—some who be seein' them, an' some who be hearin' they're somewhere about. But no one be knowin' what they is. They just be here."

"And that be it," Malcolm murmured beside her.

Halia ignored the interruption. "But that is what I cannot understand," she told the captain. "In almost every case where similar such discoveries were made, there was always some sort of oral tradition surrounding it. Much of the time, the people had simply dismissed the stories as nothing other than fables and legends . . . but still, those tales existed."

"Like the Healin' Hole," Esta spoke up. "It be a place in the mangrove swamps on the far side of the island. Some folks, they be thinkin' it be the Fountain of Youth dat Ponce de León, he be lookin' for."

"Exactly," Halia agreed with a nod in her direction, only to catch Rolle's thoughtful frown. Suddenly suspecting that he was keeping something from her, she persisted, "But *you* know something, Captain, do you not . . . If not about the stones, then perhaps about my father?"

"It's not what I be knowin', Miss Halia, it's what I be guessin'. But you be hirin' me for a job, an' I be doin' it, wit' anyt'ing else not bein' my business."

"But I want to know what you think. Please, Captain."

He paused, as if searching out the right words, his usually jovial face taking on a serious expression. Finally, he went on, "I be thinkin' about dat coin you be showin' me, an' how you say your father be findin' it. An' then, I be wonderin' how it be dat no one else ever be findin' anyt'ing except him—not even you an' Mr. Malcolm. An' a coin, it be so little a t'ing, dat a man, he would be more than lucky to find it in this big ocean."

He hesitated again, and Halia felt a sudden foreboding well up inside her. Never had she questioned her father's conclusions, save to wonder why he had been so secretive in his final entries. But now, she heard a note of doubt in Rolle's tone that rested uneasily upon her ears.

"Are you saying, Captain," she carefully asked, "that you believe my father was mistaken in his idea that those rocks are the remains of Atlantis, that perhaps the coin is not genuine, after all?"

Rolle shrugged. "Me, I'm not the one to be sayin' if dat coin, it be real or not . . . nor the rocks, either. But sometimes, a man, he be chasin' after somet'ing so long an' so hard, he be losing track of the truth along the way."

At his words, Halia's feeling of foreboding flared into outright alarm. She quelled her rampant emotions a moment longer, persisting, "You talk about losing track of the truth. What exactly do you mean?"

Like a bitter conscience that refused to be silent, Malcolm spoke up beside her. "I believe what our good captain is trying to say is that your father was obsessed with locating the remains of lost Atlantis. And when all his searching came to naught, in his disappointment he set about convincing you—and perhaps even himself—that he actually had found something, after all."

"But that is ridiculous," Halia shot back, turning a heated look on the man beside her. "My father was a scholar of note. He contributed much to the scientific community, presenting papers and lecturing, developing new theories. Why, he—"

"Hear me out," Malcolm cut her short, his tone holding an odd note that she'd never before heard from him—of pity, perhaps, or even compassion? Grudgingly, she kept silent and nodded for him to continue, though she suspected whatever explanation he delivered was sure to be self-serving.

"I've given the matter quite a bit of thought these past days," he told her, then gave her a wry little smile that unexpectedly twisted at her heart. "You see, luv, this is what I do best . . . play upon other people's dreams. And since Atlantis was your dream as well as his, I began to wonder if perhaps your father wasn't doing the same thing."

Then his smile faded. "I can assure you that it would have been easy enough for him to do. Once he'd procured his coin, he could search about for an appropriate spot for his so-called find. It would have to be a place with an identifiable underwater formation and possessing some of the attributes of Plato's account. Then, he would just have to forge a journal of his supposed discoveries, an easy enough task for a man of literary bent."

"I . . . see," she replied, gripped by the oddest feeling that she was falling quite slowly from some unseen precipice toward some rocky outcrop below. "So what this means—"

"What it means, my dear Halia, is that it is quite possible that your entire Atlantis expedition is based upon nothing more than a hoax."

Chapter 16

"A hoax," Halia dully echoed . . . and then she hit the figurative stones at the bottom of her mental cliff.

Her breath tore from her in a gasp that verged upon a sob, and she shut her eyes. *It couldn't be true, it just couldn't. How dare Malcolm presume to judge her father, when the two had never even met. Surely she, as Arvin's daughter for almost a quarter century, knew him better.*

Determined not to give way to the torrent of emotion that threatened, she clenched her hands into tight fists, so that her nails dug into the tender flesh of her palms. The pain gave her something to focus on. Deliberately, she opened her eyes again.

"But you have no proof of these claims," she countered in as calm a tone as she could muster. "You are judging my father by your own way of doing things. Unfortunately, as he can hardly defend himself against such slander, you are free to spread about any manner of story that you wish."

"Just a bloody moment." He met her gaze, his dark eyes narrowed in anger. "I have no wish to destroy your father's good name or sully your fond memories of him. I am merely pointing out another possibility here . . . one that makes perfect sense, I might add."

"Indeed? For all I know, Mr. Northrup, you might simply be trying to rattle me so with your wild tales that I give up my search and leave the treasure to you. Until I find reason to believe otherwise, I will give my father the benefit of the doubt."

She flashed a quick look at Esta and Rolle, silently asking their support. They met her gaze with expressions of sympathetic concern, but she noted that neither had yet disputed Malcolm's wild theory. As for the children, they realized something was wrong, for they had halted their squabbling and sat staring at her, eyes and mouths rounded in silent question.

With a final chill glance for Malcolm, she neatly folded her napkin and set it beside her half-full plate, then addressed her hostess.

"It was a lovely luncheon," she managed in an even tone, "but I fear I feel a bit unwell at the moment. I hope you will forgive me if I take my leave early."

"You be goin' on, then," Esta softly agreed, motherly concern written upon her face. "But you be comin' back any time, chile, if you be needin' to talk."

But talking was suddenly beyond her ability, at least, for now. With a quick nod, Halia shoved back from the table. She caught up her hat and reticule and then, with as much dignity as she could summon, started for the door.

She heard behind her what sounded like a whispered question from Rolle, and his wife's murmured reply, but to her relief no one followed after her. She stepped quickly through the shaded yard past the painted gate and back onto the dusty street. The noon sun gave her a blinding welcome.

The heat evaporated the tears that threatened to spill down her cheeks, so that she managed the walk back to the guest house dry-eyed. Stubbornly, she repeated her earlier arguments to herself. Her father was no pot hunter or adventurer, but a scholar. Surely he would never have thought to sully his reputation or that of the academic world at large by such a deception.

But what about those last few weeks just before his disappearance at sea, when he had acted so oddly? Perhaps his behavior had been an indication all was not right. Why else would he have procured a pistol and then refused to let her accompany him on what proved to be his last voyage?

Firmly, she thrust aside the tiny serpent of suspicion that had uncoiled in her heart. She would not believe what Malcolm had said, that her father had deliberately deceived her, and that was that.

For, if it *were* true, she would be forced to wonder what other lies he might also have told her over the years.

By the time Halia reached the guest house, her head seemed quite ready to burst with too much sun and too many unanswered questions. She hurried inside to the sanctuary of her room, grateful that Lally already had left in search of her herbs. She could never have faced the woman and pretended that all was well.

She poured a scant basin of tepid water and soaked a corner of a towel, then wiped her flushed cheeks. But even as she began to regain her composure, a chilling thought struck her.

What if father's death at sea had been tied somehow to his Atlantis search? What if it had not been an accident, but suicide . . . or even, murder?

She dropped the towel, which landed in a damp tangle at her feet, and wrapped her arms around her, suddenly cold despite the heat. She stood that way for several moments, staring unseeingly at the ocean view beyond the French doors as several scenarios played themselves out in her mind.

Her father, finding proof of Atlantis's existence only to be murdered by someone out to usurp his glory.

Her father, fleeing some unknowns who had forced him into this deception, falling victim to their murderous wrath.

Her father, remorseful at the deceit he had perpetrated,

rowing out into the Caribbean and then flinging himself into the waves.

"No, stop this!" she cried aloud and gave herself a firm mental shake. There was only one way to satisfy her doubts, and that was to prove her father's theory true.

An idea hit her, sending swift, angry relief rushing through her. No matter that Captain Rolle and his crew did not sail on Sundays. She simply would take the skiff and spend the rest of the afternoon at the site, searching on her own for the evidence that would prove her father had not betrayed her.

She matched thought to deed, exchanging her boots, stiff shirtwaist and tailored skirt for her bathing costume, then tying on her overskirt. She spared another look out the French doors to the blue sky and emerald water beyond.

She had fully half a day left to her, she assured herself, plenty of time to sail out, make several dives, and be back by dusk. While a few high clouds now scuttled across the sun, the wind was light and sea was calm. She could easily manage the skiff on her own. As for diving alone in those shallow waters, it would not be much different from bathing by herself off the beach.

Swiftly, she shoved aside memories of her father's warnings against taking out a craft alone. This was too important, she told herself, trying not to remember what had happened when he had ignored his own advice.

As she started from the room, she caught sight of the tiny photograph of her and her father that she had placed on her bedside table. Impulsively, she caught up that sepia image, taking comfort from this last link to her father. She stared at the beloved features a moment; then, with a fleeting smile, she laid the picture on the bed and then turned toward the door.

"I still believe in you, father," she murmured as she started down the hallway. "And I promise, no matter how long it takes, I *will* find something out there beneath the waves to prove you right."

"An' don'tcha be givin' dat girl any grief," Esta warned with a final stern look at Malcolm as he started out her door half an hour later. "Miss Halia, she be needin' a friend right now."

"I promise to comfort Miss Davenport as best I can," he agreed, though he knew full well that he would simply leave the chit to her own devices.

For it wasn't his place to soften the blow of her father's deception, he reminded himself, ruthlessly shoving aside all memory of her stricken face. In fact, he already had done his part simply by awakening her to that unpleasant if necessary bit of knowledge. Of course, if she found herself in need of some other, more tangible comfort—say, the sort that might be had in the privacy of her bedchamber—then he might be prevailed upon to assist her in that.

Esta must have read something of his thoughts, for her frown deepened. "You be listenin' to me, Mr. Malcolm. Miss Halia, she don't be needin' someone dat only want to be breakin' her heart. Besides, I be suspectin' dat you be carin' for her more than you be admittin'."

His first impulse was to disagree, but he knew that to do so would make him appear the cad in her eyes. And, suddenly, he was not prepared to fall from her good graces. He contented himself with a smile and a compliment, instead.

"That was one of the best meals I've had in sometime, Mrs. Rolle," he truthfully informed her. "As for the company, it was even finer."

He gave little Viola, who was clinging like a barnacle to his leg, a final pat on the head. Then, gently, he detached the tot's sticky fingers from his trousers and handed her to her father.

"Captain," he said with a nod, "I shall be seeing you in the morning, then."

"Me an' my crew, we be there," Rolle agreed, "but there be somet'ing I best be tellin' you, first. I didn't want to be sayin' not'ing in front of Miss Halia."

He indicated the blue sky above, where a scattering of high white clouds had gathered like playful lambs, then gestured to the barometer hanging by the doorway.

"The weather, it be fine for another day, maybe two, but then it be changin'. A storm be movin' in . . . maybe even a gale."

"A gale?" Malcolm frowned. "You mean, a hurricane?"

The seaman shrugged. "Like I say, maybe yes . . . maybe no. This is the time of year they be comin', though they be missin' the island most times, so all we be gettin' is rain. When the rains pass an' the water settles, then we can be goin' back out again."

"But what if there is a hurricane, and it doesn't miss the island?"

"Then we be havin' trouble."

While Malcolm listened in carefully concealed alarm, Rolle regaled him with tales of times when the islands had suffered a hurricane's full fury. Sometimes, they had been lucky and suffered no loss of life. Other times, a handful or more islanders fell victim to the gale, drowned in the flood waters or killed by falling debris. And always, there was the damage—homes flattened as if by a giant fist, tree after tree torn from its roots, boats sunk.

"So you see, we be takin' this serious," the captain finished as he hoisted Viola onto his shoulder, then flashed Malcolm a grin. "Now, don't you be frettin'. Chances be good, this just be a tiny little storm a-comin'."

Not much relieved by that last assurance, Malcolm took his leave of the Rolle family and began the dusty trek back through town.

Bloody hell. What was he, a good Englishman, doing in

this land of blistering sun and killing gales, anyway? He should have listened to Wilkie and cut his losses back in Savannah. Had he done so, right now he would be ensconced in some elegant hotel with all the modern amenities, including chilled champagne and a welcome artificial breeze from an electric fan dangling from the gilt-trimmed ceiling.

But then, his inner voice mockingly reminded him, he never would have seen Halia again.

He tried to squelch that thought as swiftly as it came, but to no avail. Instead, the images began crowding in his mind, building on that idea.

Halia sitting in the bow of the boat, looking the prim sea sprite with her blond hair billowing about her.

Halia, in that ridiculous bathing costume of her that, when wet, clung to her slim frame in the most interesting manner.

Halia, half-dressed and pliant in his arms that night in the courtyard, evoking in him an unfamiliar swell of emotion that had seemed to spring from something more than physical need.

And she was what this entire adventure of his was all about, he suddenly realized. Not a lost city . . . not some long-hidden treasure . . . just her. And it had been that way from the first moment they'd met, though he had tried his damnedest to deny it.

The revelation stopped him in his tracks.

"Bloody hell," he groaned out, desperately waiting for his inner voice to speak up again and argue the point. For surely he hadn't escaped the clutches of any number of marriage-minded young women over the years, just to succumb to the doubtful charms of the only woman who had turned him down flat when he tried to seduce her.

He stood there a few minutes beneath the hot sun, vaguely aware that his collar was wilting in the heat and his sweatsoaked shirt beneath his waistcoat was rapidly plastering itself to his back. Finally, when no mental arguments were forthcoming, in a swift gesture of frustration he whipped off his bowler and dashed it to the sandy ground.

Bloody, bloody hell! He *had* succumbed, no doubt about it, though for the life of him he couldn't imagine why. He had made it his business over the years to remain free of emotional entanglements, most especially those involving attractive young women. And he'd always succeeded in that goal—that was, apparently, until now.

The sound of childish giggling from behind a low wall recalled him to his senses. He glanced over at the cottage beside him to see half a dozen shiny little black faces peeping over the rocky ledge at him. Sheepishly, he bent to retrieve his battered hat, when something in the dirt-packed yard caught his eye . . . a strutting red rooster with tail feathers like a New Orleans showgirl's plumes.

Slowly, he brushed off his bowler and put it back on, his gaze never leaving the gaudy fowl. *Rooster feathers.* He'd seen bundles of them and other more esoteric items in Lally's possession the day they'd left Savannah. And then, a few days later, the Haitian woman had prepared an ointment just for him—ostensibly to relieve his sunburn.

But what if she'd had an ulterior motive in offering her services? What if that healing ointment had contained something else . . . such as a voodoo love potion?

It was an insane notion, Malcolm firmly told himself and continued down the sandy lane. If anything, any spell of Lally's would likely be designed to push him and Halia apart, not bring them together as lovers.

Still, the superstitious corner of his mind that subscribed to lucky emeralds and watch fobs-as-talismans was not placated. After all, he could argue it the other way—that Lally might *want* him to fall in love with Halia so that he would not be tempted to steal her blind, as was his intent. And how else to explain his uncharacteristic behavior, save that some external force was in control of his emotions?

Mentally, he assembled the evidence at hand. First, he

hadn't been looking to fall in love and, indeed, the possibility of such a happenstance had never even crossed his mind. Moreover, he'd always made it a rule never to become emotionally involved with any female connected with his work, a rule that he had never once broken. But the greatest inconsistency lay in the fact that he hadn't even bedded the chit yet . . . surely an important precursor to falling in love.

That settled it. He *had* been hexed.

Not certain whether to be relieved or outraged at this revelation, he settled on a plan of action. As soon as he reached the guest house, he would track down Lally and demand that she effect some sort of cure for this malady of the heart. And it would go badly with her, he vowed, if she refused.

But by the time he reached the guest house, he realized that the sharp sword of his earlier resolve had been blunted. Perhaps the cause was the hot blanket of humid air that the tropical sun had laid across the town. Or maybe Lally's spell had an even tighter grip upon him than he feared, and he was succumbing to an unwilling sense of compassion. For, try as he might, he could not forget Halia's look of carefully checked anguish when she had learned the likely truth about her father.

"All right, I'll have a bloody talk with Halia, first," he muttered, as much to the absent Esta as to himself. With any luck, the chit would rebuff his overtures and, as was her habit, make him angry enough to dispel any more tender emotion. Then, he'd visit Lally.

He made his way into the dimness of the main hall. The French doors along the far wall were open, allowing a cross-breeze that was a welcome respite from the early afternoon sun.

A glance out onto the courtyard and an equally quick search of the lower floor yielded no sign of Halia. Likely, she had sought the sanctuary of her room, he told himself and started up the stairs. Once outside her chamber, he paused a moment to debate the wisdom of what he was about to do. Then, reluctantly, he knocked.

Her unlocked door skittered open a few inches beneath his touch, but no Halia appeared. Curious, he pushed the door open a few inches wider and peered inside. The room was empty.

Had she not come home . . . or had she returned and then already gone back out again?

Unwilling concern supplanted curiosity, and he strode inside the chamber that was a smaller version of his own. He promptly noticed atop her bed a jumble of clothes he recognized as the skirt and shirtwaist she earlier had worn. As to what, if anything else, was missing or left behind, he could not guess.

"Miss Halia, she be gone."

Nearly jumping out of his skin, Malcolm turned to meet Lally's censuring gaze. Then, swiftly assuming the casual air of one who'd been caught, uninvited, any number of times in someone else's room, he shrugged.

"Gone?" he politely echoed. "Do you mean that she's stepped out for a breath of fresh air, or are you trying to tell me that she has fled the island entirely?"

He promptly regretted his attempt at levity, for the Haitian woman's obsidian eyes narrowed into catlike slits, and she muttered an unintelligible imprecation. *Bloody hell, she's trying another one of her hexes,* was his first panicked thought.

Then, mentally reproaching himself for letting himself be intimidated by a woman—never mind that she might possess uncanny powers—he assumed his best Sir John air and flashed her a stern look.

"I asked you a civil question, madam," he clipped out, "and I trust you will do me the courtesy of a civil answer—preferably in a tongue that I can understand."

A look of sly humor flashed across her dark features. "What I be sayin', Englishman, is dat she be gettin' the bet-

ter of you again. Here you be, wanderin' about like a lost
dog, an' she be out lookin' for her treasure. An' my spirits,
they be tellin' me dat today, she be findin' out there what she
be wantin' the most."

"You mean, she's out at the site? But Rolle and his crew
aren't working today, so how—"

He broke in midquestion and slapped a hand to his forehead. "Bloody hell, she took the skiff, didn't she!"

At Lally's cool nod, he spun back around and stalked
over to the open French doors, making his way out onto the
gallery. Squinting past the bluff in the direction of the Atlantis site, he made out against the sparkling blue and green
water a tiny blur of white that had to be the sail of her boat.

He tightened his jaw against the stream of invectives that
threatened. He'd be damned if he would let Lally think her
mistress had bested him. Still, the woman's last comment indicated she thought Halia was onto something. Had the chit
perhaps found some new clue in her father's journal and not
bothered to share the knowledge?

With an effort, he kept his tone light as he stepped back
inside and addressed Lally again. "I believe you said something about your spirits claiming that Halia was going to
find some sort of treasure today. I don't suppose they bothered to tell you exactly what it will be?"

"Ignorant Englishman," she spat back. "The spirits, they
not be tellin' everyt'ing . . . not like some people dat can't
never be keepin' their mouth shut."

He raised a wry brow and ignored that last insult. "What
a shame. I would have hoped your spirits would have been a
bit more forthcoming. But then, vagueness is the hallmark
of any good fortune-teller, is it not?"

With that pleasant barb, he started for the door, only to
halt in midstep as he caught sight of something he'd not noticed before. A tiny framed photograph lay on the bed
alongside the bundle of her clothing. Curious, he paused to
pick it up.

He immediately recognized Halia's aristocratic features rendered in sepia. As for the older man beside her—

Frowning, he studied that other image a moment longer then slowly shook his head. He could be mistaken, he told himself. After all, it had been dark that night.

No, not wrong, insisted the instincts that had served him so well these many years.

His fingers tightened on the picture frame; then, with deliberate casualness, he held it out toward Lally. "This photograph of Halia . . . who is the man with her?"

"Dat be Mr. Arvin, her father," she replied, regarding him with suspicion though it was apparent she could not see any harm in passing on that bit of wisdom.

"Her father," he softly repeated and allowed himself a small smile of triumph. *Bloody hell, this shed a whole new light on things.* His tone still one of unconcern, he asked "So how long ago was it that he was lost at sea . . . two months, three months?"

"Maybe," was Lally's cryptic reply.

It was enough, though. He tossed the picture back onto the bed. Giving wide berth to Lally, who continued to eye him like the local fishmonger examining a week-old catch he headed out the door and down the corridor. No matter that he'd not taken time to question the woman about her voodoo activities, in general—and about love spells, in particular. He had other concerns now.

Indeed, what held his thoughts was the photograph of Halia and her father. Whether all of his suspicions would prove correct, he could not guess—not until after he talked with Halia.

And talk with her, he intended to do this very day . . . even if it meant waiting all afternoon on the dock for her to return.

Chapter 17

Malcolm had been waiting all afternoon on the dock for Halia to return.

More accurately, he had spent the past several hours watching in turn from the dock, which jutted into the shallow harbor on the island's east side, and from the bluff with its view of the reefs off the western coast. It had been from that latter vantage point that he had thought he'd glimpsed Halia's sail several hours earlier. But whether it had been her or merely a distant flock of gulls atop the waves, he could not say with certainty.

All he did know was that dusk was fast approaching, and she had not yet returned.

"Bloody hell," he muttered for the dozenth time now as he gazed over the bluff from his uncomfortable perch atop a flat rock. He had wasted a good half a day; still, given what he now knew, he wasn't about to let either of them continue their search until he'd had a chance to speak his piece to her.

And what he had to say to Halia, she was not going to like . . . of that, he was certain.

He shook his head. At least, his enforced wait had given him plenty of opportunity to think over his theory and reassure himself he was correct. He'd had his suspicions from the very start, to be sure. It was the photograph in Halia's bedchamber, however, that had clinched it. He knew without a doubt now that this entire Atlantis expedition truly *was* a hoax.

For what else *could* it be, when it had been Halia's own father that night in Philadelphia who had sold Malcolm the missing coordinates?

Sourly, he plucked out his already-soaked handkerchief and swiped at his forehead. At least, he'd had the sense to snatch up his boater on the way out, so that he'd had some protection from the blazing sun. Another saving grace was the fact that a few more clouds had scuttled in. That, combined with the setting sun, had dropped the temperature by a few degrees from intolerable to just barely endurable.

Restless, he rose and stretched his cramped frame, squinting against the orange sun as it made its way toward the waiting blue waves. Maybe it would be cooler down by the water, he told himself. Besides which, maybe he'd find himself on the good side of Lally's spirits, and a marble figure of Poseidon would wash up on the beach and into his waiting hands.

A few moments later, he had made his way down the bluff to the water's edge. The waves were eagerly lapping at the narrow strip of beach, spilling one after the other across the white sand as the tide began its inexorable climb toward the rocks. A welcome breeze had risen, as well, combining with the almost hypnotic sight and sound of the surf to make him relax . . . just a little.

Frowning, he once more scanned the water in the direction from which she'd likely come. By now, the sun had dropped to the horizon and was slowly extinguishing itself in the deep blue waves. A few free-wheeling gulls still lingered atop the sea foam, while an occasional splash made by some enthusiastic fish broke the monotony.

But of Halia, there was no sign.

His frown deepened as he debated whether to give way to frustration or concern. For all he knew, the chit might have made her way to another landing point without his seeing

her. Worse, maybe she'd taken an entirely different route to
begin with, perhaps had gone to South Bimini, instead. He
was debating whether or not to give it all up and head back
for the house, when a shadowed movement in the shallow
waters but a few yards from him caught his attention.

Shark! was his first instinctive thought. Then, upon a second look, he realized that the silhouette was wrong. What
had appeared to be a shadow was actually a diamond-
shaped black creature that was as flat and wide across as a
carriage wheel. Two hornlike protuberances adorned what
he presumed to be its head, while a long tail trailed from its
opposite end. It skimmed the reef with a flapping motion of
either winglike edge, as if it were flying beneath the waves.

"A devil fish," he determined aloud, mentally matching
its description to that of several unusual varieties of fish he
knew were more properly known as manta rays.

Early into the expedition, one of his divers had made
mention of those fish. Relatively harmless creatures, the
man had assured him—save for certain smaller of the spe-
cies. When threatened, they could deliver with their whip-
like tails a painful sting capable of causing temporary
paralysis, or even death. Still, their human victims were few
and usually were unwitting swimmers who, wading in the
shallows, accidentally stepped atop one of the ugly beasts.

Intrigued by this fish that looked like something out of a
nightmare, Malcolm forgot about Halia as he simply
watched the manta making lazy circles along the shoreline.

It moved with an economy of effort, barely rippling the
water as it propelled itself in silence through the darkening
waters. Back and forth it swam, hugging the white sand for
a time. Then, changing course, it would rise to skim the sea's
surface, gliding close enough so that he could make out the
faint pattern of circles against its brownish-black hide.

And then it was joined by a second manta.

The pair glided in the shadowy shallows in a tropical ballet, first circling about as mirror images of each other, then

each breaking free to swim in an independent pattern. They
were grotesque and yet beautiful, repellent but utterly fascinating. He could have watched them forever, he realized,
save that daylight was almost a memory now—and something from the corner of his vision now had caught his attention.

He tore his gaze from the mantas and squinted at the dark
shape bobbing atop the cobalt waves. It was moving closer,
drawn toward shore by the inexorable tide. Finally, he made
out a mast with a furled sail and realized what he saw was
no ocean flotsam, but a boat.

Halia's boat!

For surely it was the very same craft that had brought
him to the island that first day. He frowned and moved to
the water's edge for a better look. Why would the boat be
adrift, he wondered, rather than be moving under sail? And
was he imagining things, or did the tiny craft appear to be
empty?

A chill feeling of dread settled in his gut. No, not necessarily empty, he told himself. It could be that she had been
taken ill and was lying in the bottom of the boat. Maybe
she'd been injured, perhaps badly enough so that she had
been unable to raise the sail again and been forced to drift
her way back to shore. Or maybe—

The mantas forgotten, he pulled off his boots and waded
knee-deep into the water until he was several yards from
shore. "Halia!" he called, his voice sounding abnormally
loud over the gentle rush of the surf. "Damn it, Halia,
what's wrong? Halia?"

He cupped his hand behind his ear, straining to hear
something—anything!—from the silent craft. Closer it came
to shore, so that in another minute he finally could see
within. And then the cold sensation in his belly spread like
winter's ice to his heart.

Empty.

"Empty," he murmured in disbelief. "Bloody hell, it's empty."

With a strangled, guttural sound, he grasped the edge of its hull and began to drag the drifting craft behind him toward shore. A moment later, gasping, he had dragged it as far onto the beach as he could, so that the tide would not reclaim it. Then, dreading what he might find, Malcolm clambered into the grounded boat to look for clues.

The first thing he noted in the dying light was that the craft appeared normal. Halia's familiar black carpetbag was tightly lashed to the side, the sail neatly furled. Her neat little black boots sat primly on one bench, as if she had taken them off to swim. No crimson splashes of blood stained the skiff's pale boards, no gashes in the hull hinted at some mysterious violence. Everything was in order . . .

Or was it?

By now, his initial, uncharacteristic reaction of shock had given way to his usual chill logic. If the craft had simply been set adrift, then the anchor and its line should be coiled up at the ready. Yet there was no sign of the anchor, only a line dangling over the hull.

He swiftly caught that rope and hauled it from the water, only to be brought up literally short. A portion of the anchor line remained—that was all, with the anchor presumably at the bottom of the Caribbean.

Frowning, he twirled that short end in one hand, studying it in the half-light of dusk. The remaining bit of line was not frayed, the way it would have been if age and exertion finally had combined to snap the line. Rather, it appeared to be a neat severing, as if someone—or something—had simply cut it in two.

But, whether accidental or intentional—it did not concern him for the moment. What mattered was the fact that Halia must still be out on the water somewhere.

The realization jerked him from his refuge of cool calculation and sent a surge of barely controlled panic through him. He snatched up his boots and, half-running, half-hopping, had tugged them back on by the time he reached the foot of the bluff. That low barrier, he scaled with a mountain goat's speed.

In another minute, he had covered the short distance to the courtyard leading to the guest house. Not pausing to open its low wood gate, he instead caught the top edge and swung over it. Then, boots clattering across the uneven flagstone, he headed for the open French doors and made his way to the makeshift dining salon.

The rest of the household—Wilkie, Lally, and the middle-aged Biminian husband and wife who served as the staff—were already seated at the table. Two additional place-settings that were his and Halia's remained untouched.

As one, the foursome turned to stare as Malcolm burst through the doorway.

"Halia . . . she's missing . . . got to send for Captain Rolle," he gasped out, then paused and leaned against the doorjamb to get his frantic breathing back under control.

Wilkie was the first to react to Malcolm's abbreviated account of matters, pausing in midbite to demand, " 'Ere, now, wot are ye sayin'?"

Lally slowly rose from her place at the head of the table. The only sign of distress she gave was the slight widening of her dark eyes—that, and the way she unheedingly let conch stew drip from the wooden spoon she was holding.

"She be gone?" the woman softly echoed. "You mean, her boat, it not be comin' back?"

"That's the whole bloody problem!" Malcolm exclaimed in frustration. Bloody hell, why was it taking them so long to understand? "The boat *did* come back—but she wasn't with it."

Lally's spoon hit the table with a clatter, faintly echoing the scrape of wood against wood as Wilkie abruptly shoved back his chair from the table and stood.

"Ye mean, she fell o'erboard?" he exclaimed, his pock-marked face turning ashen.

Malcolm helplessly shook his head. "I don't know what the hell happened," he admitted, praying he did not sound quite as desperate as he suddenly felt. "All I can tell you is that she took the skiff out this afternoon, and while I was there waiting on the beach for her, the bloody boat came drifting back all on its own."

He ran a quick hand through his disheveled hair—his boater had fallen off during his frantic flight—and turned to the manservant.

"Levar," he hurriedly addressed the Negro, who had already set aside his plate and risen to await orders, "take Sadie and locate Captain Rolle—he should be at home with his family—and tell him what has happened. Tell him that we'll need his crew and his boat to search for Miss Davenport."

"We be gone now, Mr. Malcolm," Levar swiftly agreed and started out the door at a trot. A murmured agreement rose from his wife, her dark face wearing a look of equal concern, as she promptly untied her apron and departed the room on his heels.

Malcolm turned back to Lally and Wilkie. "We'll be needing supplies—blankets, lanterns, and the like."

The next half hour saw several minutes of frantic action as the three of them searched out the items in question. The remaining time was spent in impatient if unavoidable waiting, each caught in their own thoughts. It was fully dark, then, by the time they finally heard Rolle's heavy footfalls upon the veranda.

"Tell me what be happenin'," he demanded without preamble once he was inside.

Malcolm related in a rush what little he knew, then swiftly went on, "Even if she fell overboard, or if the anchor line broke while she was making a dive, she might still be afloat. She's a strong swimmer, you know. She might even have found something to hang onto . . . a piece of driftwood, maybe. If your crew can be ready to sail—"

"Me an' my crew, we not be sailin' my boat nowhere . . . not tonight."

The blunt statement caught Malcolm off guard, and he searched the man's face to see if perhaps he were joking. Rolle's usually jovial features, however, were drawn into grim lines that forestalled any such misunderstanding.

"Not sail?" Malcolm choked out in disbelief. "Bloody hell, man, she's out there somewhere waiting for us to find her. Who gives a damn if it's Sunday."

"You not be understandin' me, my friend. We can't be sailin' dat harbor, at all, not in the dark. It be hard enough in the day, wit' the reef bein' so shallow. But at night . . ."

He trailed off, and Malcolm's disbelief fast turned to outrage. He'd never counted Rolle a coward or a quitter, but maybe he had been wrong. Fixing the captain with a look of chill disdain, he replied, "Then I'll bloody well go myself."

Though how in the hell he would actually manage that feat, he did not care to mull over . . . not just yet. If he had to, he'd pound on every door in Alice Town until he found a man with a boat willing, for the right sum, to risk the night. And if he couldn't find a boat and crew, then he'd locate a dinghy and paddle out there himself.

But one thing, he did know—he damn sure wasn't going to sit by and do nothing until dawn.

Even as Malcolm swung about to leave, Rolle put a beefy hand of restraint on his arm.

"You be waitin', my impatient friend. All I be sayin' is dat we not be takin' *my* boat out. I did not be saying dat we not be lookin' for her. All we be needin' is an anchor, an' we can be takin' the skiff."

" 'Ere, now," Wilkie interjected in a hopeful tone. "There's a shed out beside the 'ouse. Maybe there's something inside wot we could use."

"Check it, then," Malcolm clipped out. Once Wilkie had

hurried off in search of his makeshift anchor, he turned back to Rolle.

"Thank you," he simply said.

He dared not say more, lest he break down and fling his arms about the man in gratitude. The captain merely nodded in return, lamplight glinting off the gold loop in his ear.

"Don't you be worryin' none," he replied, folding his immense arms across his chest and looking more the pirate captain than ever. "If anyone can be findin' her, it be you an me."

Almost two hours later, however, Malcolm had begun to wonder at the captain's optimism.

For the dozenth time, they had furled the sail and dropped anchor—Wilkie's foray into the outbuilding having met with success—to call Halia's name and scan the waves for any sign of her.

Oversized lanterns lashed fore and aft spread a yellow glow that was their only source of light, for clouds had wrapped the moon and stars in a blanket of pitch. As for the inky waters, tonight they were choppier than Malcolm could ever recall seeing them. Still, sound seemed to carry farther than usual across the water in such darkness, so that he felt certain that they would hear any cry for help.

Twice, now, they had spotted a dark shape atop the water resembling a body. Both times, however, the shadowy figure had proved to be a drifting clump of seaweed. By now, Malcolm's nerves had been stretched almost to the breaking point as fear and frustration battled it out within him.

Damn the chit! It was *her* fault he had missed his dinner to spend the night out here on the darkened sea. If she'd only kept to the rules—or at least, asked him to come along with her—this never would have happened.

So what the bloody hell worries you the most, his inner

voice demanded, *the fact she cheated . . . or the fact that she might be dead?*

The question sent a chill through him. Yet, though his mind conceded the possibility, his heart refused to accept it. Halia could not be lost to him forever . . . not now, not before they had settled matters between them. The fact that his feelings for her might be nothing more than the result of Lally's conjuring—and, thus, quite as fraudulent their Atlantis search—no longer mattered.

He loved her . . . and he bloody well was going to find her and tell her so!

By his estimate, they had covered the entire Atlantis site, moving in regular, ever-shrinking circles. Every muscle of Malcolm's body ached with the effort of looking and listening. Now, he ran a frustrated hand through his hair and slumped back against the bow, dragging his gaze back to meet Rolle's. Conversation between them since they'd shoved off had been sparse, each man caught up in the urgency of their search.

But it had reached a point where Malcolm needed to know something of the man's thoughts . . . most specifically, did *he* hold out any hope of Halia's still being alive. Rolle knew the winds, the shoreline, the tides. Surely with his lifetime of experience in these islands, he must have some theory as to what could have happened.

"Do you think we'll find her?" he bluntly asked, the question echoing against the gentle lapping of waves against the boat.

Rolle's dark face had taken on a mystical glow beneath the flickering lamplight, so that he appeared to Malcolm like some pirate-god presiding over his watery kingdom. He did not speak for some moments. Then, just as Malcolm feared he would keep his thoughts to himself, he shrugged.

"Me, I can't be tellin' you dat, not unless we be knowin' what happened to her. I be thinkin' dat, if she be fallin' from the boat, there be three things dat can be happenin' to her.

Maybe she already be swimmin' back to shore, or maybe another boat, it be rescuin' her."

"Or maybe she drowned," Malcolm harshly finished the list. "But that doesn't explain how the boat broke free. Only a knife could cut the line that neatly. Maybe someone only wanted us to think she's dead."

A scenario flashed through his mind of some band of island cutthroats seeing her out there alone and seizing her for their brutal pleasures.

"—maybe a shark," he heard Rolle say.

That last word abruptly jerked him from thoughts of imaginary brigands. Bloody hell, how could he have forgotten the ominous creature he'd seen swimming in the harbor the day of their arrival? A fish that bloody big could have attacked her and severed the line in a single bite.

But even as another picture flashed through his mind—this one of Halia's slim form being mangled in the jaws of swimming death—he realized Rolle was still speaking.

"—don't be thinkin' dat's what happened. A shark, it mostly be feedin' at night, an' in the shallows. Besides, no one here be gettin' killed by a shark for years, now," he finished with a shrug.

If that last was meant as assurance, Malcolm was not comforted. Still, which was the more frightening thought, that she'd been savaged by a killer fish or been abducted?

He gave his head a sharp shake to clear it. This sort of wild speculation was doing no one—least of all Halia—any good.

"So what do you suggest we do, Captain?"

"I be thinkin' dat we should be headin' back to shore. If she be here to find, we already be findin' her. An' maybe someone else already be bringin' her home. An' if not, then we be doin' better to search again in the daylight."

It made sense, Malcolm conceded. If she were out there, they would have found her by now . . . or else, she surely would have spotted their lanterns or heard their shouts and called out to them. And with luck, maybe she *was* already back at the guest house.

Still, it was with guilty reluctance that he bowed to the other man's judgment and gave his nod of agreement. A minute later, Rolle had pulled up the anchor and raised the sail once more. Breeze caught canvas with more than usual vigor, so Malcolm recalled the captain's prediction of a storm moving in.

Shivering slightly now against the wind and spray, he kept his hopeful gaze on the water's surface as they started back to shore. By the time they reached the beach, he had quite convinced himself that Halia had already been rescued and would be awaiting their return. The first thing he would do when he saw her, he vowed, would be to roundly chastise her for the mental anguish she'd put him through.

And then, he would drag her off to his bedchamber and make love to her until they both were sated.

He reached the top of the bluff to see light blazing from every window in the guest house. A renewed surge of hope lent him speed as he covered that distance for the second time that night and made his way through the courtyard. He reached the French doors and flung himself through them into the main hallway, all but colliding with Wilkie.

"Where is she?" he breathlessly demanded as he clutched his friend's arms, reading a look of relief in the older man's pockmarked face.

That expression abruptly faded, however, as Wilkie freed himself from Malcolm's grip and shook his head.

" 'Ere, now, wot do ye mean? The way ye was runnin', I thought ye'd found 'er."

"Then no one brought her back?"

The realization knifed through him with an almost physical pain, so that he almost missed the other man's questioning, "Will ye be goin' back out to look for 'er?"

"Not until morning," was Malcolm's bleak reply. "We covered every bloody inch of water between here and the site, but there was no sign of her. We were hoping maybe someone else had found her.''

He broke off with a muttered curse. Damn it all, they should have stayed out longer. Now, he had the whole of the night stretching before him to worry and wonder . . . and all the while, maybe Halia was still waiting for him to find her.

By then, Rolle had made his own way back to the guest house. Malcolm only half-listened as the man recounted for Wilkie what they'd done. Instead, his attention was drawn to the clusters of lit candles—some graceful tapers, others mere stubs—that sat in every window. The faint aroma of beeswax combined with another, sweeter smell that curled about the room.

He shot a questioning look at Wilkie, who glanced from him to Rolle and then shrugged. "It be 'er—Lally—wot done it. 'Tis some sort o' voodoo, I'm thinkin'.''

Bloody wonderful, was Malcolm's first thought. The way things were going, she'd probably set the house on fire before the night was through. Rolle, he noted, was shaking his head and frowning.

"Here in Bimini, we not be holdin' wit' such things," was his disapproving comment. "We all be good Christians, prayin' to Jesus for help, not the spirits.''

"I'll have a word with her.''

Leaving Wilkie and Rolle behind, he started up the stairs. The door to the small bedchamber that was Lally's stood ajar. The scent of burning incense and herbs that emanated from it was almost overpowering.

Lally stood in the room's center, surrounded by a small circle of lit candles. Her back was to him, and her usual neat bundle of tiny braids had been freed to twist Medusa-like over her shoulders. She had exchanged her flamboyant garb for some white, loose-fitting wrapper that looked rather like a monk's robe. Its trailing hem floated dangerously close to the burning tapers.

"Are you searching for answers from the great beyond,''

he coolly addressed her, eyeing that potential disaster with more than a little wariness, "or are you seeing how close you can come to turning yourself into a human torch?"

"Ignorant Englishman," she responded, not bothering to look his way. "I be tryin' to learn from the spirits what be happenin' to Halia."

"Indeed."

With that wry observation, he took a few steps closer. Now, he could see the makeshift altar she had set up along one wall. Still more candles sputtered upon it, while a shallow sort of metal basin served as a centerpiece. In the center of that bowl, she had placed the now-familiar photograph of Halia and her father.

"So, what do they say?"

Knowing as he did the woman's dislike for him, he still was shocked at the barely veiled venom that spilled from her lips as she replied, "It's not what they be sayin' dat you need to be knowin'. I be tellin' her dat you be nothin' but trouble, but she not be listenin'. If she be dead, then it be your fault."

"*My* fault?" he choked out. "What in the bloody hell is that supposed to mean? This whole expedition was her idea, so if you think you can blame me—"

He broke off abruptly as Lally finally deigned to look his way. Her dark eyes were narrowed to obsidian slits, but he sensed the pain beneath her anger, recalling him to the fact that Lally had been a part of Halia's family for years. If he was distraught over her disappearance, then what must Lally be feeling?

"All right," he conceded, tempering his anger with an unfamiliar emotion that he supposed must be compassion. "Talk to your spirits, then . . . just try not to burn the bloody house down around us in the process. The rest of us will be heading out again on Captain Rolle's boat to search at first light. So be sure to let me know before then if your spirits say anything that might be of help."

He had turned to leave, when Lally's voice stopped him. "Wait, Englishman. They did be tellin' me somet'ing."

He glanced back over his shoulder at her, suppressing a superstitious chill at the picture she presented—white robe against dark skin, surrounded by a plethora of lit candles that easily betokened either Christian or pagan worship. The line she walked lay somewhere between evil and benevolence, he was certain. Still, her next words gave him his first bit of comfort this night.

"The spirits, they be sayin' she still be alive . . . but dat you'd better be findin' her fast."

Chapter 18

Piracy, it seemed, was a profitable occupation even in these modern times.

Such was Halia's first thought as the door to the captain of the *Golden Wolf's* private cabin locked behind her. From the curtained berth in the corner to the neat rolltop desk, every inch of the quarters was teak, trimmed out in gleaming brass. The accouterments were as richly apportioned.

Along one wall ran a broad shelf filled with leather-bound volumes, their spines stamped in gold. A second shelf held crystal decanters and matching glassware, each item set into its own snug recess to withstand the ship's rolling. Along a narrow side table were assembled the tools of the seafaring trade—sextant, compass, and a handful of other instruments whose purpose she could not guess—all appearing to be of the finest craftsmanship.

Indeed, these quarters were a far cry from the dank, dark berth below deck where she had spent last night. But then, Seamus O'Neill was something quite other than childhood tales of pirates had led her to expect.

A gentleman privateer, was how he had described himself to her yesterday afternoon, after his crew had literally plucked her from the sea to haul her aboard his ship. Having never before met a member of that breed, she'd had to take his word for it.

She guessed his age to be the same as Malcolm's. In height, they were equal; indeed, their features were vaguely similar, too. In contrast to Malcolm's sleeker form, however, O'Neill possessed a more muscular build that bespoke a man used to physical exertion.

His coloring was that of so many Irish men she'd seen in the streets of New York City—black hair, dark skin, and blue eyes. Combined with a hint of musical Irish brogue, it was a devastating mixture . . . at least, to the female sensibilities.

But she had refused to be swayed.

Halia gritted her teeth at the memory. She had made one attempt at rebellion last night, soon after she'd been brought aboard. She had refused to join her abductor here in his private cabin for the evening meal, reluctant to give even the appearance of cooperation. What the pirate wanted from her, she was not yet certain, but she did not intend to make his task easy.

She had been allowed but that one refusal.

With a chill smile, O'Neill had ordered her hauled below deck, where she had spent the remainder of the night tensely listening for approaching rats, both human and rodent. The wee hours of the morning came, yet sleep eluded her, so that she drifted somewhere just beyond the point of wakefulness.

It had been then—frightened, chilled, and uncertain what the morning would bring—that she finally had allowed herself to come to a conclusion about her relationship with Malcolm. Quite simply, she had fallen in love with him.

The realization had given her something warm and solid to cling to as she pondered her fate. To be sure, loving him was hardly the logical thing for her to do—dear Lord, the man was a scoundrel, a betrayer of hopes!—but suddenly she did not care. The only concern she had was that, when it came down to it, she had no idea what his feelings were for her.

She had awakened at dawn—unrested, hungry, her bathing costume stiff with sea salt, though buoyed by last night's revelation. By then, she also was convinced that the Irishman was not to be trifled with.

With that in mind, she had not refused his invitation a second time. Neither had she rejected his offer of a dress and undergarments to replace her own sodden clothes. The only thing lacking had been some manner of footwear, for her own smart boots had been left behind in the skiff, which in turn had been cut adrift.

The frilly lavender gown the cabin boy had brought proved far too formal for morning, with its exaggerated decolletage and rows of flounces. Still, it was better than parading before the captain in her bathing costume, especially since she'd somehow lost her overskirt during her struggle with the pirate crew. Though certain O'Neill's plans for her did not include ravishment, she did not care to test her theory.

Even as that last thought crossed her mind, the cabin door swung open.

"Sure, and 'tis a pleasure to see that ye've come to yer senses this fine morning," O'Neill observed with cool satisfaction. He gestured to the square table to one side of the cabin, where two places of the finest English china were set. "Do have yerself a seat, me darling, and join me for breakfast."

Warily, Halia complied, managing not to flinch as his strong hands brushed her bared shoulders while he assisted her into her chair. Now, she noticed a bearded sailor standing nearby at silent attention and laden with a tray stacked with covered platters. At a signal from O'Neill, he trotted to the table and dealt out the serving dishes like a hand of rummy, then began removing silver covers from the assembled collection.

Halia watched in something akin to amazement as a veritable feast began piling up before her. The largest serving platter overflowed with kidneys, sausages, and sliced ham.

A second dish held eggs cooked in two different styles, while a third tray boasted tropical fruits—this not to mention the basket of breads and tarts.

Halia shook her head. Pirate or not, O'Neill certainly knew how to eat.

The seaman-cum-butler stepped back, and O'Neill nodded in satisfaction as he spooned up a portion of eggs.

"Faith, but I have never understood why anyone would starve himself just to prove a point . . . have ye, Weedle?" he addressed his man.

Weedle shook his bushy head, the gold loop in his ear bobbing. "No, Cap'n, I ain't."

"Then neither of you has ever been a prisoner before," Halia retorted as she snapped open her linen napkin and laid it in her lap, then reached for a sticky bun. Surely the man must realize that at least one such an act of rebellion was all but mandatory when one was held against one's will.

O'Neill met her defiant gaze and gave her a crooked smile that—just for the briefest instant—reminded her of Malcolm.

"Ah, but I have been a prisoner, me darling," he softly countered while helping himself to a rasher of ham. " 'Tis not a memory I relish, but I do recall that I choked down every bite of the moldy bread they saw fit to give me . . . just so I would have strength enough when the time came to make me escape."

"Oh," was the only reply she could muster. That was the rationale she finally had seized upon to justify dining with the brigand. She prayed he could not hear her stomach gurgling in anticipation of the bounty placed before them.

"Will ye be having tea, Miss Davenport?" he inquired, as if this were a social call, and carelessly indicated the elegant silver service that Weedle now produced.

No doubt stolen from someone, was Halia's reflexive thought as she gave a grudging nod. Though if he expected her to take on the role of hostess and pour, she silently assured herself, the brigand would be sorely disappointed.

The captain must have read something of her thoughts in her face, for he gave another chill smile and gestured for Weedle to do the honors.

They ate in silence, ostensibly companionable on his part and deliberately sullen on hers. She barely tasted the food, however, for she was concentrating instead on covertly studying her new adversary.

Unlike his pirate crew, O'Neill dressed as if preparing for formal company. His navy trousers were fashionably tailored and his white linen shirt beneath an embroidered blue waistcoat was the product of an expert tailor. Only the gold loop in his right ear and the oversized knife in his belt gave any indication his profession was not quite orthodox. Once again, she was reminded that most other women would have found this man devastatingly handsome . . . as she would have, under other circumstances.

The clink of china against china recalled her to the situation at hand, and she realized with a blush that she had been staring. Luckily, O'Neill appeared otherwise occupied, lacing his second cup of tea with a liberal dose of milk and sugar. Once he'd tasted it and apparently found it to his satisfaction, he set aside his plate and turned his attention to her.

"I suppose ye have been wondering why I've made ye my guest," he began with a cool smile. "Let me assure ye that I am not in the habit of kidnapping young women and sailing off with them. Sure and to be honest, ye are the first female I have been obliged to take by force."

She quite believed that last statement. Indeed, she suspected that women flocked to his ship in large enough numbers that, when in dock, he probably had to post guards to keep them out.

Aloud, she said, "I must presume, then, that in seizing

me, you were desirous of something other than companion-
ship."

"That I was, me darling."

His reply fell somewhere between an insult and a warning, so that she felt herself blush and grow cold all at once.
To hide her confusion, she choked down a quick swallow of
her tea, then swiftly asked, "So then what *are* your plans for
me, Captain O'Neill?"

"Much as I regret it, ye are but a lovely means to my
end," came his soft answer. "Ye see, I have some unfinished
business to attend to with our mutual friend, Mr. Northrup.
And since I've been unable to convince him to meet with me
of his own free will . . ."

O'Neill trailed off, then gave a shrug. "Quite simply, me
darling, I intend to use ye as bait."

In the gray dawn light, Malcolm stared down a moment
at the folded sheet of foolscap with his name scrawled across
it in a familiar hand. He broke the seal to read the few lines
it contained. Relief and outrage came washing over him in
equal waves. Then, swiftly refolding the missive, he raised
his gaze to the young Biminian boy of perhaps twelve years
standing on the dock before him.

"Who told you to give this to me?" he demanded, trying
unsuccessfully to keep the urgency from his voice.

The dark-skinned lad frowned and then shrugged. "I not
be knowin' him, an' he not be tellin' his name."

"Then perhaps you might try describing him," Malcolm
suggested with barely checked patience. "White or
black . . . young or old?"

"He be white," the boy decided after a moment's thought.
"An' he be old . . . older than you, even. His hair, it be white,
too."

*A white man with white hair somewhere above the age of
thirty.* Not much of a description, he told himself. Still, with

so many black faces on this island, a pale one would tend to stand out.

"And did you perhaps chance to see where this particular man happened to go?" he persisted, though without much hope.

To his surprise, the boy nodded. "He be givin' me this"— he held up a silver dollar—"an' the letter, an' then he be walkin' away there."

He pointed down the pier. Squinting, Malcolm glimpsed a light-haired man in a dinghy setting off across the harbor.

"Bloody hell," Malcolm breathed, his fingers tightening on the page he held. It was too late to stop the man now, but at least he knew where the stranger was headed.

Absently, he reached into his waistcoat pocket and plucked out a coin, which he added to the silver one already in the boy's hand. Then he turned to Rolle and Wilkie, who along with Rolle's crew had been silently watching this drama unfold.

"Halia's alive . . . and that bloody pirate has her," he baldly announced.

Rolle frowned. "Pirate? My friend, there are not bein' any pirates in these waters for fifty years."

"If yer talkin' about Seamus O'Neill, 'e's a bleedin' pirate, all right!" Wilkie exclaimed and spat on the dock in disgust. "But 'ow did 'e track us 'ere, I wonder?"

Malcolm shook his head. "All I know is that he did, and this is why."

So saying, he held out the offending note. Rolle took it and, squinting, slowly read the contents aloud.

"I've managed to lay hands on something valuable of yours. You already have absconded with something valuable of mine. It would be in everyone's best interest to make a trade. The Golden Wolf *is anchored just outside the harbor. Come alone . . . and come soon. O'Neill."*

The Negro shook his head and handed the letter back. "I

be understandin' this first part, dat he be holdin' Miss Halia. But what do you be havin' of his?"

"A mere trifle," Malcolm returned with an evasive flick of his fingers, "just a little something I pinched from Seamus when his back was turned."

Wilkie snorted. "A trifle? 'Ere, now, that's not wot I would call it." He turned to Rolle and explained, " 'Tis an emerald the size o' yer thumb an' wot's worth a bleedin' fortune. 'Tis e'en got its own name."

"Poseidon's Tear," Malcolm clarified when Rolle's frown deepened. "Seamus was a bit distressed to find it gone, and he's been trying to track down it—and me—ever since."

"It sounds as if this man, he be meanin' business," the captain opined. "Me an' my crew, we can be gatherin' some guns. Now bullets, they might be harder to find, but dat pirate, he not be knowin'."

A rumble of assent from Garnet, Jeffers, and the other crewmen backed up Rolle's offer.

Malcolm surveyed the men with gratitude even as he grimly shook his head. "I appreciate the offer, but this matter is between Seamus and me. Besides, his crew is armed to the teeth. A handful of untrained men would never stand a chance against them."

"Then wot do ye plan t'do," Wilkie interjected, "go out there all by yer bleedin' self?"

"What other choice do I have?"

For he knew Seamus well enough to be certain that his veiled reference to Halia's safety was no idle threat. If he did not turn over the emerald, the pirate would kill her . . . and even making the trade would not necessarily guarantee Halia's life.

Rolle, meanwhile, was gesturing to the harbor and the horizon beyond. "Then you must be goin', my friend, but you had best be hurryin'. The storm I be warnin' you about, it be movin' this way."

Sensing urgency in the man's tone, Malcolm spared a

closer look at the sky and waters. The waves, he saw, were even choppier than last night and had taken on a dull pewter shade unlike their usual turquoise hue. The sky, too, was leeched of its familiar brilliant blue, while the rising sun was wrapped in a huddle of dirty clouds in contrast to the white wisps that more commonly drifted above. To be sure, the temperature had not abated; still, this morning it was a different sort of heat . . . cloying, oppressive, so that a man was hard-pressed to take a breath.

Thoughtfully, Malcolm tapped the edge of the folded note against his palm, his gaze fixed on the harbor entrance. The weather be damned, he decided. Surely the storm was far enough out not to be a factor—at least for today.

"I'm more concerned with settling this matter than worrying over a bit of rain," he flatly stated. "Now, as I see it, I've got two advantages over my old friend. The first is that he can't know what sort of relationship Halia and I have." He shook his head and gave a humorless smile. "Hell, I'm not bloody certain on that point, myself. But that means he's only gambling that I care about what happens to her."

"An' the other advantage?" Rolle prompted.

Malcolm allowed himself a chill smile. "The other is that I happen to be the only person who knows where the emerald is hidden."

O'Neill lowered his spyglass and gave a satisfied smile. "Ye can be putting your mind at ease now, Miss Davenport. Sure, and yer gallant rescuer is on his way."

"You mean, Malcolm?"

Gathering up her skirts, Halia rushed to the railing and stared out toward the harbor. Sure enough, slicing through the rising waves in their direction was a skiff resembling her vessel that the pirate crew had set adrift after abducting her.

So he had not abandoned her, after all!

For that had been her fear, that Malcolm would leave her

to her fate. She gave a small sigh of relief. Not wanting to appear overly anxious, she hid that emotion with a shrug.

"I told you before, Captain, that Mr. Northrup and I are merely business partners . . . and not very amicable ones, at that. And recall that you sent your message to him just after dawn, while it is now almost noon. Surely that is proof that I mean little to him, that he does not view his role in this matter as rescuer."

The pirate quirked a wry brow. "So ye have been telling me since this morning. So why am I not believing ye?"

"Believe what you will, Captain," she boldly countered. "I only wish to spare us all disappointment when he proves unwilling to negotiate with you."

"Ah, but 'tis ye who will be disappointed. It will not go well for ye if he does not cooperate."

O'Neill's words were soft, but something in his bland expression sent a sudden chill sweeping through her despite the heat. Determined not to let him see that he had shaken her, she lifted her chin in a fearless gesture. But before she could make a reply, a third voice spoke up behind them.

"Here now, we had a deal," the newcomer protested. "You assured me that if I brought Northrup to you, my daughter would come to no harm. Well, sir, I intend to see that you honor your word."

Chapter 19

Halia clutched at the railing, shutting her eyes as a sudden dizziness swept her. She must have been imagining things, she frantically told herself. She had to have been mistaken. It was impossible. The voice *couldn't* have been that of—

"Sure and that was a careless thing to do, Arvin," she heard O'Neill's mild rebuke, "though as for harming your girl, ye can see for yerself that she's healthy. But, 'twould have been better for ye both if she still thought ye dead."

"Fabricating my untimely end was *your* idea," came the bluffly insistent voice of her father. *Her father!* "Damn you, O'Neill, did I not do everything you asked of me? Why did you have to involve her, as well?"

With a muffled cry, Halia clamped her hands over her ears, unwilling to hear more. This was too much to bear, her inner voice cried. She had thought her father dead, had mourned him, and then acted the felon to carry out his life's work. Yet, if she were not imagining things, it had all been but a game, a farce.

Vaguely, she was aware that the two men were arguing, though the words spun by her, unintelligible. All she could focus on was the fact that the parent she loved and trusted had betrayed her . . . and for what?

But—reason or excuse—it did not matter, her inner voice

raged. Nothing could justify what her father had done to her.

Or could it?

Guiltily, she recalled her own actions of these past weeks—kidnapping, near-murder, theft. Had she not told herself that the end had excused the means?

"Wait," she choked out and lowered her hands to her side. Then, slowly, she turned to face her father.

His blue gaze met hers, but she saw a glimmer of tears in his eyes as he tried to smile and failed. "Halia, child," he began in a husky voice. "You must believe me, I had my reasons . . ."

She stared at him in silence a moment, numbly noting that his blond hair had gone white in these past weeks, while his face was creased by lines she hadn't seen before. He looked older, thinner . . . and blessedly alive.

All at once, the hot rush of her anger began to seep away beneath a sudden onslaught of joy. Stubbornly, she tried to reclaim her outrage. What he had done was cruel, unforgivable. He no longer deserved her love, only her contempt. But even as her inner voice raged on, she knew—all that mattered was that her father had returned to her.

"Oh, Papa," she softly cried, and flung herself into his familiar arms.

She caught but a glimpse of his grateful smile before he pulled her to him. "I'm sorry, child, I'm sorry," he murmured, his voice breaking on a sob, as well. "I never meant to hurt you, and the entire time I kept an eye on you as best I could."

"You did?"

Abruptly, she pulled back to stare at him as realization struck. "Why, that was you on the ship to Savannah . . . and later, on the *Retribution*," she exclaimed with a choked little laugh. "You were the man with the bushy beard and with your hat pulled halfway over your face."

"I was rather proud of that disguise," Arvin admitted.

"The only one who recognized me was Christophe, on the way to Savannah, and only because I took my hat off once."

"Christophe?" she echoed with a frown. "Then that must have had something to do with why he refused to accompany us the rest of the way."

Arvin nodded, then lowered his voice as he explained, "I felt obliged to confess to him and enlist his help. If your Mr. Northrup did not take the bait and follow you on to Bimini, then Christophe had instructions to use whatever means necessary to put him on that boat. You see, I could not risk failure . . . not at that point."

Before Halia could make any reply to that equally unexpected revelation, however, O'Neill broke in on their conversation.

"Sure and 'tis the touching scene, this father and daughter reunion," he said with a chill smile, "but 'tis time now to greet our new guest."

Malcolm. Dear Lord, she had almost forgotten him.

Halia glanced off the side to see the skiff was almost upon them. Malcolm was alone, and one corner of her mind marveled at how well he managed the small vessel for a man who professed ignorance of anything related to the sea. By now, he had maneuvered the boat up alongside them.

An ungainly thud told the tale, that he had overshot his mark and rammed the *Golden Wolf's* hull. With a cry, Halia rushed to the side to see if he had capsized.

"Bloody hell," she heard him curse in disgust.

The skiff was intact and, apparently, so was he. She smothered a relieved smile and watched as one of the crew tossed him a line. He had managed to furl the sail and was lashing the tiny craft to the larger vessel.

By now, a good portion of the *Golden Wolf's* crew had sauntered toward the side to watch this doubtful display of seamanship. O'Neill, too, joined her and Arvin at the rail. She noted in some surprise that, rather than taking umbrage at the injury to his vessel, the captain appeared amused.

"Malcolm, me boy, did you not learn any better all the time we spent together?" he called down as he tossed over a rope ladder. "Sure, and 'tis fair embarrassed I am, to call ye my brother."

"Brother!" Halia gasped out.

She stared at O'Neill, wondering if this were some jest on his part. To be sure, she had noted a resemblance between him and Malcolm, but she had chalked it up to coincidence. Never had she suspected that they were—

"Half-brothers, actually," Malcolm coldly corrected in his best Sir John accents as he swung a leg over the railing to stand before them. "Our mutual father, the Earl of Northrup, had a way with the ladies, for all that he proved a singularly ineffective parent. Speaking of which—"

He broke off to glance at Arvin, who had the good grace to look somewhat abashed. "Ah, yes, Mr. Davenport," he went on. "You and I have already met . . . outside a tavern in Philadelphia, was it not? I believe there is the small matter to be resolved of that five hundred dollars I paid for a spurious set of coordinates."

"Sure, and that's something the two of ye can work out later. Right now, we have more pressing issues to discuss," O'Neill interjected, his tone lazy though his blue eyes held a chill glint.

Malcolm matched him with an air of equal unconcern. "Ah, yes. If I understood your note correctly, you seem to think I have something that belongs to you."

"I bloody well *know* ye have it. I'll be wanting me emerald back, and no more of yer tricks."

By now, he and Malcolm had moved away from the rail, positioning themselves slightly apart from the crew as they faced each other like a pair of pugilists. The logical corner of Halia's mind reflexively fell to comparing them.

O'Neill, she decided, was the embodiment of the beast from which his ship, the *Golden Wolf,* had taken its name. She could sense in him a barely checked ferocity that, once loosed, surely could not be readily calmed. With the pack that was his crew at his command, he would prove a formidable enemy.

As for Malcolm, he had the sleek lean grace of the panther that walked alone, by choice. Cunning, rather than ferocity, would be his watchword . . . though whether he could prove a match for O'Neill, she could not guess.

Now, Malcolm shot his half-brother a wry look. "Even if I did have your bauble—and I'm not saying that I do—suppose that I'm not inclined to give it up?"

"Then yer pretty young friend will be paying the price."

Before Halia could react, O'Neill spun about and caught hold of her, the crook of one arm tightening around her throat as he drew her in front of him like a shield. With his other hand, he whipped out his knife and pressed the tip of its blade to her cheek.

She stiffened in his grasp, all other sensation lost in the feel of cold steel against her tender flesh. Vaguely, she was aware of her father's cry of protest, quickly cut short. What Malcolm's reaction was, she could not tell. If she shifted enough to meet his gaze, the blade would surely draw blood.

O'Neill's breath was warm against her ear as he softly said, "I'll not be wishing to harm her, but I will if ye won't be doing as I ask."

"Not to tell you how to conduct your business," Malcolm lightly countered, "but it seems you've taken quite a lot for granted, here. What makes you think I care a bloody fig for what happens to the chit?"

By way of reply, O'Neill increased the pressure on his blade, so that the tip nicked her flesh. Halia bit back a reflexive cry of pain and tried not to flinch when she felt a warm drop of what could only be blood slide down her cheek.

"Ye may not care for her, me boy," came the pirate's equally cool reply, "but I know ye've a weak stomach. Sure, and I don't think ye'll care to stand by and watch me slice her pretty face to ribbons. Now, tell me, what have you done with Poseidon's Tear?"

"Ah, well, let me think."

His tone held deliberate challenge, so that she nearly swooned in panic. Why was he taunting the brigand, when her very life might be at stake? Had she been wrong, and Malcolm had no feeling for her, after all?

She sensed rather than saw the two men's gazes lock, felt rather than witnessed the almost palpable tension. Brothers or not, no love was lost between them . . . of that, she was certain.

Her fear now was that, caught as she was in the middle of this long-fought battle between them, *she* might prove to be the ultimate victim.

Finally, Malcolm broke the stalemate.

"Indeed, it has just occurred to me that I do have the emerald, after all," he carelessly conceded. "I suppose I might be persuaded to give it up for a fair price . . . say, twenty thousand American dollars. And perhaps you might throw in Miss Davenport, for good measure."

" 'Tis no time for jests, me boy," the pirate softly countered, even as Halia, mindful of the blade to her face, choked back a sound of outrage. *Throw her in, indeed!* "Ye'll give me the emerald for the girl, and no dickering about it."

Malcolm lifted a wry brow. "If that's your best offer, then I suppose I must accept it. Why don't I just take the skiff and—"

"Sure, and ye don't think I'll be letting you sail off, just like that? Ye'll wait here aboard the *Golden Wolf* while yer man Wilkie goes back to Savannah for the emerald."

"Actually, it won't be necessary to send anyone anywhere. It just so happens that I brought Poseidon's Tear to Bimini with me . . . for luck, you might say."

Surprise—or else certainty that he had gained Malcolm's cooperation—caused O'Neill to drop his knife from Halia's

face. Though he kept his grip firmly about her throat, she
was able now to watch the proceedings.

"Ye mean, yer carrying about a bloody king's ransom in
yer waistcoat pocket?" O'Neill demanded.

Malcolm gave the ghost of a self-deprecating smile and
shook his head. "Not exactly. The stone is back at the guest
house—and hidden quite well, I might add."

O'Neill stood silent a moment before allowing himself a
bark of a laugh. "Only ye, me boy, would be so bold . . . or
else, so foolish. But ye've saved us a good deal of time, for
all that. Ye'll send word for someone to bring it, while ye
wait with us here."

"I suppose I could. Still—"

He broke off to glance heavenward. Halia followed his
gaze, the small sigh of relief she'd allowed herself at regaining a bit of her freedom dying on her lips.

The sky was completely overcast now, she realized with a
frown. Moreover, so preoccupied had she been these past
minutes, she had not noticed the breeze strengthening into a
wind that now was tugging at her skirt and ruffling the loose
wisps of hair about her face.

She decided with a flicker of unease that a storm was definitely moving in.

"—would suggest you let me go back for the emerald,
myself," Malcolm was saying. "Otherwise, I would first
have to get a message to Wilkie. He, in turn, would have to
track down the gem and then find some way to bring it out
to the ship. We might well be in the midst of a nasty gale by
that time."

"Sure, and ye think I would trust ye not to make a run for
it?"

"But where would I go? This *is* an island, and you've seen
for yourself that I am no sailor. And one more thing," he
persisted in a reasonable tone when the pirate remained silent, "given the poor luck you've had of late, even if Wilkie
could manage his way out here, he might end up being

washed overboard—and the emerald, with him—if the storm hits early."

" 'Tis a valid point, and one that bears thinking on," O'Neill replied with a careless shrug of his own. "Ye'll not be trying to take the skiff back to the mainland in these conditions—not if ye value yer hide the way I know ye do."

"Then do we have a deal?"

"Ye have two hours. I'll meet ye ashore, at the west entrance point to the harbor. Come alone with the emerald, and we'll make our trade there—the gem for Miss Davenport. But keep in mind that, if ye don't show up, the girl will suffer for it."

Malcolm briefly consulted his gold timepiece, then carelessly tucked it away. "Fair enough," he conceded, "that is, if you agree that it will be just the three of us ashore. I don't care for these odds"—he gave a dismissive gesture toward the gathered crewmen—"and I'm bloody well not going to give you the chance to make off with the emerald and Miss Davenport, both."

"Malcolm, me boy, do you think I'd do me own brother that way?" O'Neill softly replied in a tone of mock injury. Then, with a shrug, he finished, "Just the three of us, then . . . and Poseidon's Tear."

Halia found herself suddenly freed as, with that decisive reply, the pirate released his grip and carelessly thrust her in the direction of her father. Arvin, who stood near the railing, reached to steady her.

"Don't worry child," he murmured, his fatherly embrace reassuring. "O'Neill is harsh but, to this point, he's been a man of his word. You'll be safe enough, I warrant—that is, if Northrup makes good on his part of the bargain."

But what if he doesn't? a quavering inner voice asked as she clutched at her father for reassurance. *What then?*

For she had no idea of Malcolm's true feelings for her. Though her own emotions had undergone a change since their first meeting, she had no guarantee that his had, as well. For all she knew, those few moments of shared passion that night in the courtyard had been but an aberration on his part. It could well be that he would have no qualms about keeping his emerald and leaving her to her fate.

Then, for the first time since O'Neill had seized her, Malcolm glanced her way. She saw with a sinking heart that his dark gaze was expressionless . . . the bland, unsettling look of no man with no stake, one way or the other, in the outcome.

Even as she vowed not to let either of them see her fear, Malcolm had crossed the few steps back to the railing, where the rope ladder still was tied. He paused before her, then drew his handkerchief from his pocket.

"Nice gown, luv," he murmured as he lightly dabbed the trickle of blood from her cheek, "but a bit formal for this time of day, don't you think?"

Then, tucking the silken square back into his jacket, he swung a leg over the side and began climbing down the rope ladder.

"Mind ye, two hours and not a moment more," O'Neill called down to him as Malcolm shoved off in the direction of the harbor again. Then, turning back to Halia and her father, he shrugged. " 'Tis fair aggravating, having a brother that'll steal ye blind, given the chance."

Halia made no reply to his facetious observation, for her gaze was focused on the departing skiff as it inexpertly mastered the choppy waters. Though Malcolm's tending to her nicked cheek had seemed a gesture of concern—or even tenderness—the mocking words that followed had cut just as surely as had O'Neill's knife.

"Come, child," Arvin gently insisted, interrupting her uneasy thoughts as he took her by the arm. "We'll wait in my quarters until it is time."

She nodded, sparing another look for the skiff and then glancing O'Neill's way once more. The pair of them seem-

ingly forgotten, he had turned back to his crew and was issuing curt orders to counter the changing winds.

Surely he would not harm her over a gem, valuable as it
might be, she reassured herself as she and her father started
toward below deck. His chilling words had been just a
threat, but a means to bend Malcolm to his bidding.

Then the pirate's cool blue gaze settled on her once more,
and she knew she was wrong. Should Malcolm not show,
O'Neill would dispatch her with the careless ease of a man
ridding himself of a pair of boots that pinched. As for her
father, chances were he would suffer the same fate.

A chill sense of hopelessness washed over her. She could
not begin to predict which role Malcolm would take in the
next two hours—that of savior or scoundrel. All she knew
with any certainty was that her fate lay in his hands . . . and
that she simply would have to trust him to do what was
right.

She was counting on him to do what was right, Malcolm
wryly realized as he guided the skiff back toward the slip
where Wilkie and Rolle were waiting for him. What a
bloody joke *that* was, considering how he'd spent the
greater portion of his years doing the opposite. And in this
case, the right thing meant trading his hard-won emerald for
Halia's release from his brother.

Thoughtfully, he plucked his handkerchief from his
pocket and studied it. The snowy white cotton was marred
by a crimson smear of blood. Halia's blood.

His reaction to that bit of drama on Seamus's part had
taken him by surprise. He'd needed every ounce of self-con-
trol he could muster to remain calm as he watched the pirate
nick her golden skin with his blade. It had been the sight of
that single drop of blood, tracing a tearlike path down her
cheek, that had almost been his undoing. In that moment,

he could have easily murdered Seamus with his bare hands, half-brother or not.

"Fool," he muttered, though whom the word was meant for, he was not certain.

Christ, he didn't even know what his true feelings for Halia were. For all he knew, Lally's voodoo spell still had him in its grip, so that this odd emotion that held him might be nothing but an illusion. Should he give up the emerald, he might well find he had sacrificed a fortune of a gem for a woman that, when the potions wore off, he might learn he despised.

On the other hand, he might realize after the fact that he'd had it in his power to rescue the woman he truly loved but had done nothing to save her, after all.

As the skiff reached the pier and Rolle caught the line he tossed, Malcolm grimly made his decision. One day, he might regret taking such a course; still, he could not concern himself with the hazy future.

What he had to do, he would do . . . and as for the consequences, he would just have to live with them.

Chapter 20

"Sure, and I knew I was fool to trust him," O'Neill said in disgust as he flipped shut the cover of his pocket watch. He rose from the flat rock where he'd made himself comfortable, then spared a glance at Halia. " 'Tis a quarter hour past the time we agreed upon. It seems my brother has made his choice . . . and yers for ye."

"But maybe he's just been delayed," she protested as a shiver that had nothing to do with the cool rising wind that swept her. "Give him another few minutes, and I'm sure he will come."

But would he?

Clenching her hands together to still their trembling, she rose from her perch on a driftwood log. Barefooted still, she padded a few steps from the shoreline off which the *Golden Wolf* lay anchored, then surveyed the area before her.

O'Neill had landed his ship's dinghy on the island's southernmost point, a broad sandbar dotted with limestone outcroppings and littered with broken conch shells. She guessed that under normal conditions it would be a peaceful spot. Today, however, pewter-colored waves slapped at the shoreline with uncommon impatience, sending white foam splattering onto the beach.

Clumps of scrubby, dark green vegetation interspersed with patches of anemic-looking grasses bravely resisted the onslaught. A few yards inland and past the high-tide line, the white sand gave way to an almost forestlike vista of mangroves and vines. Malcolm would have to negotiate his way through that maze, surely no easy task for someone on foot.

"Yer faith is quite touching, me darling, but sadly misplaced," she heard O'Neill softly say above the sound of the rising wind. "And with the storm moving in, I fear I cannot wait any longer."

She swung back again to face him, dread forming a fist-sized lump in her throat as her gaze traveled from the pirate's chill blue gaze to the thick hilt of the knife that hung from his belt. Reflexively, her fingers sought the tiny crescent cut on her cheek, and she shivered.

Dear Lord, he means to kill me, after all.

Her first panicked instinct was to flee. With an effort, she suppressed that reaction. Dressed as she was in a ridiculously tight gown, she would take no more than a step before he would be upon her. Her sole recourse was to stall him, either until he reconsidered his plan of action or else Malcolm appeared.

But Malcolm was not coming . . . that, she now knew. The knowledge sliced through her heart with a far deeper pain than even O'Neill's knife was capable of inflicting. Until a moment ago, she had felt certain that he would not betray her. But now, But now, it seemed she had been proved wrong—and she and her father would suffer for it.

"If it's just riches you want," she frantically tried, "then perhaps you and I can make a bargain."

She paused to fumble with the neckline of her gown, plucking forth her gold coin pendant to show him. "Surely you must know that I—and my father, before me—have been searching these waters for the lost city of Atlantis," she went on in a rush. "My father found this coin not long ago, and I suspect there are far many more treasures still to be discovered. I could offer you half . . . no, two-thirds of whatever I bring up—"

"Ye could be offering me the whole lot, me darling, and I'd not be interested," he coolly cut her short. "I know there's no treasure to be found, not here. Ye see, yer father got that coin from me."

"From you?"

Her knees wavered like seafoam, and it was with an effort that she held her ground. Once more, she recalled Malcolm's words of the day before. *Nothing more than a hoax,* he had said, though she had refused then to believe him. But now, O'Neill claimed to be part of that very deception, and surely he had no reason to lie.

So all of this has been for naught, she wearily realized. *All of this.*

With unsteady hands, she raked aside the locks of blond hair that the wind had wrapped around her face, then spared a glance towards the water. The waves had risen to a pitch as frantic as her thoughts, assaulting the shoreline with even greater urgency than a few minutes before. If O'Neill intended to row back to his ship before the storm hit, he would have to leave now, before the burgeoning swell made that an impossibility.

Which meant that her own time had run out, as well.

"Sorry I'm late," called a familiar voice from the tangle of mangroves behind her. "It's a bloody long walk to here from the guest house."

Just as realization pierced her fear, O'Neill seized her by the arm and swung her about to face Malcolm. This time, the Irishman's blade was at her throat, but she hardly noticed as a single cry echoing in her mind.

He came, after all!

If Malcolm noticed her relief, he gave no sign. Indeed, he spared her but a look before turning his attention to O'Neill. "I trust you hadn't given up on me . . . not after I swore I would be here."

" 'Tis more than giving up. Another minute, and yer Miss Davenport would have been past saving," the pirate clipped out, an edge of barely checked anger adding heat to his usually cool tones.

Malcolm merely shrugged. "But I am here now. And as it appears that Captain Rolle's gale is also headed in on schedule, why don't we get on with business before we're drenched to the skin. If you'll just allow Miss Davenport to go free—"

"First, ye'll take off yer coat and turn around," the other man cut him short. "Even knowing yer too fine a gent to think of using a pistol, I'd not put it past you to be carrying one, anyway."

"Your lack of trust wounds me," Malcolm replied, though he did as asked and slid off his jacket. Tossing that garment aside, he turned to show that no weapon was concealed in the rear waistband of his trousers.

"Yer either smarter than I gave ye credit for, or yer a bleedin' fool—I'm not sure which," the Irishman coolly told him. "Now, let's see the bleedin' emerald, and be quick about it."

"As you wish."

So saying, Malcolm reached into his trouser pocket and withdrew a black velvet pouch. It was the same cloth bag that Halia recalled seeing hanging from a gold cord around his neck the day she had confronted him in his bedchamber. Deliberately, he tugged at the knot holding it; then, with a flourish, he spilled the gem into his outstretched palm.

It glowed with the same deep green as a sunny Bimini sea and was the size and shape of a sandpiper's egg. Despite herself, Halia could not hold back a gasp. Never had she seen an emerald that large or that brilliant a color. No wonder that each man coveted it with a single-minded passion.

O'Neill nodded in satisfaction and lowered his knife. " 'Tis Poseidon's Tear," he conceded. "Now, toss it over to me, and I'll let yer girl go."

Malcolm did not immediately answer. Instead, he paused to whip his handkerchief from his pocket and swipe at his brow. Then, tucking away the white cloth square, he returned the gem to its pouch.

"I rather think I'd prefer you to release her first, and then I'll give you the emerald. After all, how am I to know that *I* can trust *you?*"

His question was punctuated by a sudden gust of wind and a sprinkling of raindrops, as if Poseidon himself were indeed weeping over them.

If O'Neill noticed that the rain had begun, he gave no sign but merely replied, " 'Tis a bloody risk ye'll have to take . . . or have ye no faith in yer own brother?"

"I trust you as much as you trust me, Seamus," was the bland reply. "Unfortunately, time appears to be at a premium here, so I must act contrary to my instincts."

So saying, Malcolm tied the gold cord more tightly about its pouch and sent the tiny bundle flying. It spun in a graceful arch and landed directly at Halia's feet.

"Pick it up," the pirate softly ordered as he loosed her. His tone admonished her not to attempt any tricks.

Awkwardly, given her tight gown, she bent and scooped the velvet-wrapped package from the sand. Though her first impulse was to fling the cursed rock far into the waves, she heeded his unspoken warning and dropped the emerald into O'Neill's waiting palm.

His fingers closed over it, and he gave a satisfied smile. "Sure, and 'tis a pleasure doing business with you, brother. Now, take yer Miss Davenport and be off with ye."

"But what about my father?" Halia addressed him in a rush. "Will you let him go, as well?"

Both men turned to stare, as if she'd taken a role in this drama that was not rightfully hers. Then O'Neill shook his head.

"Arvin and I, we have a few matters left to settle," he said with grim finality. Tucking the tiny packet into his waistcoat pocket, he turned into the wind and started toward his dinghy.

A frantic plea rose in her throat as she watched him shove the tiny craft back out into the waves. What had transpired between her father and the other man, she could not guess; still, she could not just walk away, knowing that her father remained the Irishman's captive.

But even as she took the first impulsive step in the same direction, a hand clamped over her bare arm.

"Now's not the time to worry about him, luv," Malcolm said, the sound of his voice almost drowned out now by the wind and waves. "The storm is almost on us. We have to get to shelter, and soon."

"But, no one has answered me. What about my father?"

"Later."

He tugged her back around to face him, and she saw grim purpose in his expression. Already, the light mist had dampened his dark hair and begun to plaster his white shirt to his torso. In another few minutes, the rain would begin in earnest.

She spared a final glance over her shoulder at O'Neill's dinghy as it was tossed like a child's toy atop the foaming waves. The tide was rising, and the usually tranquil green sea was now a churning frenzy of gray water. The pirate would be lucky to make his way back to his ship without capsizing, though she could spare little sympathy for the pirate. And as for her father, there was nothing that she could do to help him for now.

"You are right," she conceded with a small sigh of despair, the words bitter upon her tongue. "Maybe when the storm has passed—"

"If we don't get moving now," Malcolm bluntly cut her short, "in another minute, we'll have seawater up to our arses and be in need of help, ourselves."

He paused, his gaze momentarily fixed on her nicked cheek as an odd stillness settled over his features. Then, his tone diffident, he asked, "Are you . . . that is, did that bloody brigand hurt you, at all?"

Halia returned him a puzzled look. Why, Malcolm had been right there when, to prove his point, O'Neill had drawn blood. Then comprehension washed over her, so that she felt herself blush scarlet.

"If you want to know if he forced himself upon me," she stiffly replied, "then the answer is no. While I can hardly say that he lavished every courtesy on me, he did behave with the utmost propriety."

His shielded expression relaxed. "I'm glad to hear it. It would be a bloody nuisance to have to kill my own brother."

She stared back at him, uncertain just how to take that last statement. But even as she told herself that it meant he must care about her, if only a little, he slanted her a wry look. "So tell me, luv, are you wearing anything under that charming purple gown of yours?"

"Am I wearing anything?" she sputtered. "Of course, I . . . that is, what business is it of—"

She broke off with an outraged shriek as he reached both arms around her and unceremoniously rent the back seam of her dress, sending buttons flying.

"Are you mad?" she gasped out and grabbed at her bodice, which had slipped halfway off her shoulders to expose her camisole. "If this is your idea of a joke—"

"I'm serious as a bloody constable," he shouted back over the rising wind. "With all those frills and furbelows dragging behind you, you'd be drowned long before you could make your way to higher ground . . . *if* you did manage the climb. And since there's no bloody way I'm going to carry you all the way back to Alice Town, I suggest you take off the dress."

Swiftly, she conceded the logic of his argument. Better to be alive if mortified than quite proper but drowned, she decided and promptly began shedding the ruined gown. A moment later, she stood there in nothing but her borrowed silk camisole and lace-trimmed pantalets.

To her relief, he neither leered nor laughed but merely snatched up his discarded jacket and tossed it in her direction. "Let's try for the guest house," he urged as she gratefully pulled on the large coat and hugged it to her. "With any luck, the worst of the rain will hold off a bit longer."

Barely had the words left his mouth than, just to prove him wrong, the pewter sky above erupted in a chilly downpour.

"Bloody hell!" he choked out and, grabbing her hand, headed for the rise and the trees beyond.

Blindly, Halia stumbled after him. With her free hand, she raked at the curtain of blond hair that the onslaught had plastered to her face, concentrating as she did so on keeping her footing. Shards of broken conch shells and splinters of driftwood sliced at her bare soles, but fear dulled the pain. A cut foot was of little account compared to the havoc a gale could wreak.

She'd heard countless tales of seawaters that could rise with astounding speed to all but submerge an island. Just as frightening was the wind that, like a runaway locomotive, would roar over the land to flatten every tree and shack in its path.

What chance would the two of them have out in the open, pitted against nature's fury?

For the moment, however, the wind was almost a blessing, literally pressing them onward into the tangle of mangroves beyond. Once there, they found some small shelter from the blinding rain, though by now the ground beneath their feet was little more than an immense puddle.

"Come on," Malcolm urged, his grip tightening on her as he pulled her steadily onward. "We have to keep moving."

Now she was grateful for his insistence that she rid herself of her borrowed gown, for the footing here was even more treacherous than the sand and rock. More than once, she went sprawling over an exposed tree root. Each time, Malcolm dragged her upright again. How he knew where to lead her, she could not guess. She only prayed they were moving inland, and were not circling back toward the shore.

Even as that unwelcome possibility flitted through her mind, she lost her footing yet again and slipped down a rocky grade, dragging Malcolm after her.

By some miracle, she remained on her feet until she reached the bottom of that slope. There, an upright slab of limestone put a painful and unceremonious halt to her descent. She wound up in a sitting position, her back against that rectangular outcropping. An instant later, Malcolm, with an equal lack of grace, landed lengthwise atop her like a sprawling supplicant, his face buried in her lap.

Halia gave a strangled cry and stared down in horror at the back of his head. Dear Lord, what if someone saw them lying together, no matter how unintentionally, in such an intimate pose?

She promptly realized the irony of entertaining such a concern in the midst of more immediate dangers. But even as she chided herself for her folly, she realized that he had not moved since their tumble.

Hesitantly, she prodded his ribs with one finger in attempt to rouse him. When that proved ineffective, she shook him by the shoulders, but to no avail.

Frantic now, she caught his face with her palms and lifted his head, searching his features for some sign of life. His eyes were closed, his skin an unhealthy gray hue . . . but surely that was a groan now issuing from his slack lips.

"Bloody . . . hell," she heard him wheeze out a moment later. To her relief, he half-raised himself from her lap to dash leaves and rainwater from his face with the back of one hand. "Knocked the . . . bloody breath . . . from me."

Not thinking what she was doing, she raised a hand to tenderly brush back the dark hair plastered to his brow. Then his gaze met hers, and she felt a blush heat her face.

What was she thinking, to use such a loving gesture on him, when they were anything but intimates.

A wry grin spread across his face as he regained control of his breathing. "Mind, I'm not complaining about the outcome," he went on as he pulled himself into a sitting position beside her, rain spilling over his brow. "The only thing is—"

He broke off with a choked curse, his eyes widening in dismay. Even as Halia feared that the fall had truly addled his wits, he gasped out, "The only thing is, we're sitting in a bloody graveyard!"

She spared a look at the limestone slab against which she was so heedlessly leaning. It was, indeed, a headstone, which meant they must have stumbled into the public burial ground that she knew lay near the island's southern tip. All around them, crude markers—some of carved and painted wood, others of rock—indicated the final resting places of numerous deceased Biminians.

She glanced back at Malcolm, who now wore a look of distinct apprehension at finding himself in such a place. For her own part, a sudden uneasiness gripped her, but not because of any misplaced fear of the dead. Rather, she was recalling how she'd overheard one of the *Golden Wolf's* crew speaking of another gale, years earlier, that had vented its fury on the tiny island. That time, the rising waters literally had washed several corpses from their graves in this very cemetery.

"We have to move higher," she declared and scrambled to her feet. "We're still too close to the shoreline."

"I'm with you, luv."

So saying, he rose and caught her hand again. They wended their way through the maze of trees and irregularly spaced grave markers until they reached its end. The trees gave way to a clearing where, by dint of squinting, she could make out several tiny houses—the nominal outskirts of Alice Town.

Away from the shelter of the trees, the rain once again pelted them with a blinding fury. The wind, which for a few minutes seemed to have died, now resumed blowing with even greater intensity. It brought with it a veritable garden of leaves, broken vines, and small branches. Leafy debris plastered itself to Halia's jacket and clung to the soggy curtain of blond hair that painfully whipped about her face.

Doggedly, she clutched at his hand as they stumbled their way up an unpaved little avenue that resembled a creek bed. Water flowed unchecked down it, washing about their ankles and carving ruts in the sandy soil. Squinting through the downpour, Halia noted that the few cottages lining the trail all had their hurricane shutters pulled tight against the onslaught. As for their inhabitants, they were either snug inside or else had already moved to higher ground.

"How much farther?" she gasped out, stumbling against Malcolm when she lost her footing inside a water-filled rut.

He paused to steady her, shielding his eyes with one forearm as he glanced about them. "Let's try for Captain Rolle's place," he called back to her, the words just audible over the roar of the wind. "It can't be more than another— bloody hell!"

With that shouted curse, he grabbed her to his chest and swung about. An instant later, a broken tree limb as big around as a man's arm and twice the length pelted past the spot where they'd just been standing. A second, much larger branch followed, the butt end of it grazing his shoulder.

"That does it!" he exclaimed and grabbed her by the hand again. "We're going to find shelter now, before a bloody tree does us both in!"

So saying, he dragged her in the direction of a white, thatched house half the size of the captain's modest cottage. Reaching its shuttered entry, he did not bother to knock. Rather, he flung open the wooden doors and half-tossed Halia inside before pulling the twin shutters closed again after them.

Chapter 21

Halia shoved her dripping hair from her eyes and swiftly glanced about the single-room cottage. No lantern shone within, while the shutters and storm-darkened sky without only added to the dimness. Still, she could see past the shadows well enough to tell that no one was home—not that it mattered. Island hospitality dictated that Malcolm and she were welcome to the refuge they had found.

"They must have gone elsewhere, perhaps to one of the churches," Malcolm opined, echoing her thoughts. He spoke in a more normal tone now, for the wind's steady howl was subdued by the thick stucco walls around them.

She nodded in reply, watching as he doubtfully took in the puddles rapidly forming on the wooden floor where rain filtered through the shuttered windows. A series of steady drips where the thatched roof above had worn thin added a rhythmic undertone to the muffled howling of the wind outside.

Not that there was much inside the neat little room that a few leaks could damage. A pair of brightly patterned blankets hung from the ceiling, dividing the cottage in half. One side apparently served as a joint parlor, larder, and dining room. Its furnishings were sparse—a long table, four chairs, and a tall open cupboard. The opposite side, she saw, was used for sleeping—and boasted a bed, crude washstand, and a large wooden chest. Conch shells and fishing gear served as decorations of sorts, in addition to the collection of skillfully woven baskets in all sizes scattered about the place.

"Home, sweet home," Malcolm muttered, then gave a wry grin as his gaze returned to her. "Here now, luv, you look like something the bloody cat dragged in."

"You don't look much better, yourself," she retorted, allowing herself a smile as she took in his appearance.

Wet leaves adorned his equally wet dark hair like a laurel wreath torn asunder, while his white linen shirt and his trousers were plastered—most uncomfortably, she guessed—to his torso. A growing pool of rainwater not unlike the puddles at the windows was forming at his feet, and a glance at his expensive boots showed them all but ruined.

He followed her gaze and ruefully tugged off the offending footwear, spilling still more water around him. He tossed the boots into the far corner, then cocked an ear in the direction of the gale without, his expression growing sober.

"I suppose we'd best start searching for supplies . . . matches, candles, blankets—"

"Water," Halia interjected.

He raised a brow and indicated the growing pool around him. "I'd say we already have enough of that, already," came his ironic reply.

She shook her head. "That's the worst danger of these storms here on the island," she explained. "Fresh water is already in short supply, and if the flooding is too bad, the few wells and springs can all become contaminated. That brings the danger of contracting typhoid or cholera . . . or of simply dying from thirst."

"Good point," he conceded with a shrug. "And we'll be wanting food, as well."

A few moments later, they had searched the humble dwelling and gathered what they needed. Malcolm proceeded to light the tiny lamp that hung from the center of the ceiling, turning up its wick as far as was practical. It gave out a feeble circle of yellow light, yet Halia took more than a little comfort in that glow.

Malcolm, meanwhile, plucked a blanket from the stack he'd accumulated, and he tossed it in Halia's direction. "You'd best dry off, while I make things snug."

Gratefully, she stripped off the sodden jacket and tossed it alongside Malcolm's boots, then began briskly toweling her wet hair. The weave of her borrowed coat had been such that her undergarments had escaped much of the damp, though the legs of her pantalets were soaked to her knees. She wrung out what water she could from the latter, then wrapped the blanket around her like a shawl and turned a curious look on Malcolm.

He had stripped off his wet shirt and had draped a blanket about his shoulders. Now, he dragged the table from its spot beneath one shuttered window and turned it on its side, then shoved it over to the opposite wall. He positioned it so that all four wooden legs butted up against that whitewashed surface and the scarred tabletop faced outward. That accomplished, he crossed to the far side of the room to snatch the blankets and thin mattress from the narrow cot there. He bundled the bedding and carried it back to the upended table, then spread the blankets and ticking in a neat pallet against the wall.

"There we are," he said with pride as he stood back to survey his handiwork. "Just in case these shutters don't hold, we'll have an extra bit of shelter against the wind and rain."

Halia bit her lip as she eyed the makeshift billet. Indeed, they would practically have to pile atop one another just to fit behind the table! But rather than dismay her, the idea of climbing back there with him sent a pleasant shiver through her. But would he think her too bold if she agreed to this plan?

An abrupt crash, followed by a harsh metallic squeal that

was the sound of a window shutter being torn from its moorings decided her. She spared a look at the narrow opening, where the missing shutter's mate unsuccessfully tried to hold back the storm. Then, sudden fear gripping her, she made for the shelter . . . Malcolm at her heels.

A moment later, the pair of them sat cross-legged atop a tangle of blankets behind the table. Somehow, she had ended up with his arms snugly about her and her head pressed to his partially bared chest. But rather than pull away, she clung more tightly to him.

"Comfortable, luv?" he murmured against her hair.

She nodded. True, the wind was howling all around them like a pack of angry hounds, and she could feel a misting of rain from the open window even behind the barrier of the table. Still, an odd sort of contentment had settled over her despite her growing anxiety.

"I still cannot believe that Captain O'Neill is your brother," she spoke up a moment later, then slanted him a guilty glance. "I said I would not mention this, but Wilkie told me a bit about your past. Did you also first meet Seamus in the streets of London?"

"We met quite by accident about five years ago, in a charming little tavern on the London docks known as the Shark's Tooth," he replied, seemingly unconcerned about her confession. "Seamus didn't have a ship of his own, then, but was a mate on another vessel that had just put into port. We'd both been drinking, and we got into a bit of a brawl over a comely little serving wench that we both fancied."

Halia suppressed an irrational flicker of jealousy at the thought of his battling for some other woman. "And which of you ended up with the barmaid?"

"Neither," he replied with a wry grin. "By the time we had beaten each other half-senseless, the chit had made off with another gent. We sat back down and had another ale to drown our sorrows, and he noticed the Sherebrooke coat-of-arms on my timepiece. We discovered then that we were half-brothers . . . each with a different mother but the bastard son of the same father. As you might guess, it came as something of a shock to us both."

"But I would think that would bring the two of you together, when it seems you don't harbor much brotherly affection for each other."

Malcolm shrugged. "We're too much alike to get along for more than a short time. I have sailed a time or two with him on the *Golden Wolf,* which is where I learned what little I know about seamanship."

He shifted closer to her then, and something hard-edged pressed into the side of her leg.

"Ouch," she inelegantly declared, forgetting for the moment Malcolm's checkered lineage as she pulled free of his embrace. "Whatever do you have in your pocket?"

In the dim light, his face took on a look of smug triumph as he rose to his knees and reached a hand into the offending pocket. He pulled forth the bundle that was his handkerchief and began unwrapping whatever it was that he'd secured within it.

She scrambled to her own knees to look, then gave a gasp of disbelief when she realized what he held. For nestled in his palm was a familiar lump of icy green fire that gleamed with an almost unearthly light under the lantern's yellow glow.

"Poseidon's Tear," she exclaimed and stared up at him. "But I saw you give it to your brother, so how—"

"A simple bit of legerdemain, luv."

Grinning, he wrapped the handkerchief over the emerald again, then whipped away the cloth to reveal his palm now empty. Even as Halia watched wide-eyed, he opened his other hand to show the gem neatly palmed. It was the same sort of sleight-of-hand he'd performed with young Willis Rolle and the coin, she realized.

"A handy little trick I picked up when I was a lad," he went on by way of explanation. "With Seamus, I merely showed him the real emerald and then substituted a chunk of limestone that I'd picked up beforehand and stashed in my handkerchief. As I suspect he won't have time to inspect his prize until after the gale blows over, he'll never know the trick I pulled on him until he is well out to sea."

"No, I suppose he shan't," she agreed, her gaze fixed on the emerald in outward calm.

Inside, however, a cold little fist of anger tightened beneath her ribs, so that for the moment she ignored the storm around them. He'd not cared enough for her to give up his precious stone . . . not even knowing that it could have meant her life.

Her reaction to that bitter realization was instinctive. She reached up and slapped his face, hard.

The impact of her blow, combined with the fact that she had taken him completely unawares, sent him reeling. He pitched over backwards and landed on his rump. His expression reflected astonishment as he gingerly rubbed his bruised jaw with one hand, while the other clutched his emerald.

Then his dark brows twisted into a frown, and he demanded, "What in the bloody hell was *that* for?"

"What if he *had* looked?" she challenged him with equal heat. "What if your brother had opened the pouch before he left and discovered that you had tricked him again? Why, he might have killed me right then and there."

Malcolm scowled and gave his head a disgusted shake. "He wouldn't have killed you. Hell, if he'd killed anyone, it would have been me. The worst he might have done to you was take you back with him to the ship so he could sell you to the highest bidder in some Mediterranean port."

"And that's not a fate as bad as death?"

The planking on the flimsy cottage rattled in swift echo of her anger. She paid the sound no heed but scrambled to her feet, planting her fists on her hips as she stared down at him.

He promptly stood so that he again had the advantage of

height over her. "Don't worry, I wouldn't have let him carry you off." His tone implied, however, that he might be reconsidering the matter for future reference. "But the point is, Seamus didn't look, you're safely away from him, and I still have the stone. I don't see what's so bloody awful about that."

"What's so bloody awful about it," she hotly echoed, emphasizing each word with a poke of her forefinger at his bare chest, "is the fact that you care more about your silly emerald than you do me."

"Do I, now? Well, we'll just bloody see about that!"

So saying, he let the blanket slide off his shoulders as he climbed over the table and stalked toward the same window where the shutter had earlier torn loose. He spun about to face her, ignoring the rain that gusted over him as he thrust out his palm to display the gem in question.

Then he clenched his fingers around it and wordlessly turned. Barely did she realize what he was about than she glimpsed a final flash of green fire as he flung the emerald through the open window to join the wind and rain.

Open-mouthed, she watched as he stalked back over to where she waited. He climbed over the table edge and halted before her, displaying both hands in the exaggerated manner of a stage magician.

"It's gone for bloody good now," he clipped out. "And since I'm not wearing a shirt, you can be certain it's not up one of my sleeves. So, does that settle the question of which I want more, you or the emerald?"

She simply stared, not quite trusting herself to speak.

With an impatient sound, he caught her by the shoulders and roughly pulled her to him. "All right, so tossing away a bloody fortune didn't convince you. Maybe this will."

Then his mouth was on hers—entreating, demanding. She eagerly responded, splaying her hands across his bare chest as she pressed herself to him and opened her lips to him.

Remembering her previous lessons at his hands, she flicked her tongue across his, tasting him. He answered with a low growl of satisfaction, his fingers tangled in her wet locks as he pulled her closer still.

Then, abruptly, he pushed her away. His voice ragged with emotion, he told her, "If you want me to stop, luv, tell me now. Otherwise . . ."

He trailed off, but his meaning was all too clear. She hesitated only a moment, then softly answered, "I don't want you to stop, not this time. But you must tell me what to do."

"Just follow my lead," he told her and then claimed her lips once more.

This time, however, he did more than kiss her. Pulling aside the blanket still thrown over her shoulders, he began to pluck at the tiny ribbons of her chemise, untying each one in swift succession. She made no protest as he eased the fine spun cotton off her shoulders and let it drift to the ground. Then, that barrier gone, he moved his hands down her hips, lightly gripped her buttocks, and pulled her to him.

Once more, she felt the hot, throbbing bulge of his manhood as it strained against the thin cotton of his trousers. The now-familiar heat began to build low in her belly, the sensation only heightened by the feel of her breasts pressed to his chest. The silken hairs caressed her nipples that had tightened into tiny buds of pleasure. Instinctively, she rubbed herself against him like a spoiled feline wanting attention.

He gave a muffled groan and broke free of their kiss. Before she could protest this loss, his fingers caught at the waistband of her drawers. With practiced efficiency, he untied the ribbon that held them and swiftly slid that last garment down her hips. Now, she wore nothing at all save for the gold coin necklace about her throat.

He nuzzled that silken flesh, and the warmth within her settled between her thighs in a hard, hot ache. Seeking relief but unsure how to gain it, she moaned in sheer need.

"You're ready for me, aren't you, luv?" he murmured and slid one hand between her thighs.

She shut her eyes and almost sobbed in relief as he gently caressed that slick flesh, stroking her until her whole body quivered in response. Then, before she realized what was happening, he lightly inserted one finger inside her.

The sensation made her cry out in wanton delight. She clutched at his arms, her breath coming from her now in tiny gasps of pleasure as he began moving his finger in and out of her tight core. Each stroke seemed to bring her closer to some sensual crescendo. Then, just as she feared she might swoon from the sensation, he pulled away his hand from between her legs.

She moaned and opened her eyes.

"I-Is it over, then?" she whispered, unable to keep the disappointment from her tone.

In the yellow glow of the lamp, she saw a look of strained amusement pass over his face. "Not 'ardly, luv. There's much more, I promise you."

His hoarse voice recalled to her those other times when she had heard him lapse into a milder version of Wilkie's rough accent. Then, he'd been injured or under some other sort of stress. Perhaps what was happening now was unfamiliar to him, as well, she faintly thought.

He fumbled a moment with the fastenings of his trousers, cursing under his breath when his fingers proved clumsy. A moment later, he had tugged off his trousers and freed his swollen manhood to her stunned gaze.

"What's the matter, luv?" he asked with a crooked grin, stroking his erect, turgid length with obvious pride. "You've seen me without me pants on before."

She blinked, knowing it was not proper to stare but unable to look away. "That is quite true," she managed in a strangled whisper, "but somehow you looked quite . . . different then."

His grin broadened. " 'Tis your own fault. You've done

this to me, with your kisses and sweet moans. And now, you'll 'ave to repair the damage."

Gently, he caught her hands in his and guided her fingers around his stiff rod. "Run your fingers down me, luv," he urged, moving her hand along his length. "Pleasure me like I did you."

She hesitated, wondering if she dared do this. She could hear the wind beyond whipping across the tiny cottage with an urgency that seemed to mirror both their needs. Now, the roaring in her ears was not so much the storm without but the tempest within that buffeted her with sudden desire. And if this was what they both wanted, surely there could be nothing wrong with touching him this way.

With light strokes, she did as he asked, reveling in the feel of velvety soft flesh wrapped around a veritable saber of hardness. But more compelling was his reaction to her tentative touch.

He'd caught her by the shoulders now and leaned back, his legs apart so that she could reach the whole of him. With every stroke she could feel his manhood quiver beneath her fingers. Emboldened, she lightly flicked her thumb across the swollen head of his shaft, and her fingers grew sticky with a few drops of warm fluid not unlike her own hot juices.

"You're fair to killin' me," he hoarsely muttered, "but don't stop . . . not just yet."

She was doing to him what he'd done to her, bringing him to the brink of some sensual peak. A surge of feminine triumph washed over her, and she felt a renewed heat flare between her thighs. Reveling in her power, she continued her exploration of this unfamiliar if delightful masculine landscape, her fingers roaming lower to the base of his staff. Lightly, she cupped the heavy, twin pouches of flesh that hung there.

He gave a muffled groan, and she felt his balls tighten in her grasp even as he pressed himself more urgently into her palms. With gentle strokes, she continued what she'd begun until, all at once, Malcolm eased himself from her grasp.

"Sorry, luv, but I can't wait any longer," he choked out as he grasped her around the waist and lifted her.

"Now, wrap your legs around me," he urged, his fingers cupping more securely beneath her bottom.

Clutching at his arms for support, she did as he asked. For a moment, she felt the hot pressure of his manhood as it throbbed against the warm, moist entrance to her body. Then, with a single thrust, he penetrated her.

There was a moment of sharp pain, so that she cried out and reflexively scored his arms with her fingernails. She shut her eyes and pressed her forehead to his shoulder, waiting for the burning sensation to fade. It did so swiftly, to be replaced by an unfamiliar fullness that seemed to stretch her woman's sheath to its limits.

Uncertain what to do next, she opened her eyes. Her face was on a level with his now, and she could see the beading of perspiration that dampened his taut features.

"I'm sorry I had to hurt you," he murmured and brushed a kiss against her lips. "If you think you can stand it, we'll go on now."

That last was more of a question than a statement, so that she could not help but smile. Even had she been in mortal agony, she could not have refused the very masculine desperation in his tone.

By way of reply, she wrapped her legs more tightly around him so that she drew him even more deeply inside her. He groaned. "Hold on, then, and I'll make us both more comfortable."

With his manhood still sheathed deep within her, he lowered her down to the tangle of clothing and blankets beneath their feet. Now, he was poised atop her, resting his weight on his forearms as he settled himself between her spread thighs.

"Now, move with me, luv," he urged as he began a slow

rhythm, easing his shaft from the tight core of her, only to plunge more deeply within her again.

She needed no further encouragement. Her arms wrapped around his waist, she followed his lead as he pumped into her, each stroke a delicious agony. She closed her eyes and gave herself up to sensation.

Then, abruptly, he went still.

She gave a small cry of protest and her eyes flew open. Her questioning gaze met his as he stared down at her, his features taut with desire. He managed, however, to sound quite nonchalant as he murmured, "I believe there is still one small matter to be settled before we finish. I was trying to convince you that you matter more to me than the emerald. Have I managed, yet?"

"Must we speak of that now?" she gasped out. Indeed, she felt hardly capable of rational thought, let alone conversation.

He nodded, then clarified, "That is, if you wish things to continue."

Dear Lord, the man was quite insane. But then, perhaps she was, as well, since right now she would gladly admit to anything short of murder if only he would keep doing these wonderful things to her body.

"You have managed. I believe you," she said in a rush. "And now, can't we go on?"

"As you wish, luv," he replied and promptly obliged her.

Within moments, all sensation flared into a single burning need that continued to build with every thrust. And then, unexpectedly, she exploded in a fiery climax of sensation.

Even as she gave a breathless cry of pleasure, she heard Malcolm's harsh groan of completion as he thrust into her a final, shuddering time and found his own climax.

Afterwards, they lay tangled together in the shadows for several minutes, the only sounds besides the twin beating of their hearts that of the relentless wind and the driving rain. Finally, Malcolm eased off and settled alongside her.

"I believe I took unfair advantage of you a few moments ago," he conceded with a wry grin as he idly toyed with a stray lock of her damp, tangled hair. "I made you answer a question while in the throes of uncontrollable passion."

"Uncontrollable?" she squeaked out, feeling herself blush scarlet. Shy now, she tugged one of the blankets over her nakedness.

"What question?" she asked, though she knew full well to what he referred. The trouble was, she had not quite decided if she believed her own earlier answer or not.

He quirked a wry brow, his expression telling her that he knew she deliberately was dithering. "Perhaps I should be asking another question," came his casual reply. "Maybe I should find out instead what *your* feelings are for *me.*"

Oddly enough, this was the easier query to answer. Taking a deep breath, she said, "But that is quite simple. I love you."

There. She had said it. But what if he laughed . . . or worse?

He did neither. Instead, he shook his head a little, as if her words were not quite the ones he had expected. Then he gathered her closer and arranged the blanket so that it covered them both.

"Maybe we should stop talking and save our strength for other things," he suggested as his manhood stirred against her.

"Do you mean that you would like to make love again?" she asked, striving for a diffident tone, though the prospect sent a wanton shiver through her.

She must have sounded far too eager, she realized, for he grinned. "Again . . . and yet, again. That is, if you are agreeable."

By way of answer, she kissed him. And together, they once more countered the gale beyond with a tempest of their own making.

Chapter 22

It was the silence that awakened Halia.

Groggily, she opened her eyes to find herself lying on an unfamiliar floor behind an upturned table and wrapped in a tangle of blankets. It was morning. That much, she judged from the gray light spilling in from the open windows and unshuttered entry. But whose house was this, and what was she doing here alone and quite as naked as a sea sprite?

Then memory came rushing back, and she sat up, clutching a worn cotton blanket to her breasts as she gazed about the empty cottage.

She and Malcolm had taken refuge here from yesterday's storm. Indeed, puddles of rainwater remained on the uneven wooden floor beneath each window. Frightening though it had been, however, the storm turned out to be something less than the predicted gale.

Never had they encountered the storm's eye, that period of calm when the winds and rain abruptly died for a time before resuming with equal fury. Still, the heavy rains had continued through the afternoon and into the night, so that they both had agreed it made more sense to wait until daylight to make their way back to the guest house. To that end, they had passed what would have been tedious if fearful hours occupied in a most enjoyable activity, finally falling asleep to the frantic accompaniment of wind and rain.

But where was Malcolm now . . . and why had he left her like this?

She tamped down an inner flicker of alarm and swiftly searched the rumpled blankets for her discarded clothes. His, she noted, were missing, which probably meant he had left of his own accord. Chances were he had just stepped outside to survey the storm's damage, or else to take care of his physical needs.

She attended to that last need, herself, her steps ginger as she abandoned her makeshift pallet and availed herself of the tin bowl she saw tucked away beneath the cot for that purpose.

Perhaps Malcolm was merely being considerate of her feelings, she told herself a few moments later as she began pulling on her camisole. Indeed, now that she thought about it, she was rather relieved not to have awakened with him beside her. It was one thing to have passed a stormy night with him in such wanton abandon, and quite another to find herself lying naked in the bright light of morning in the arms of that same man.

A blush warmed her cheeks as she glanced down at herself to see the lingering juices of their lovemaking that had dried upon her thighs. She would have to wait until later to bathe, she told herself as she reached for her pantalets. Until she knew how much damage the storm had wreaked, she did not dare waste precious fresh water.

But putting on that last garment proved a bit harder than she had expected, given her battered feet. She bit back a pained cry as she balanced her weight on first one injured sole, and then the other, leaving faint smears of blood on the wooden floor where she'd stood.

During their frantic flight yesterday, she had paid little heed to the abuse that her bare feet had taken. Now, she was rather too squeamish to check for damage, despite the fact that it seemed the more she stepped about, the greater her pain.

Ruefully, she also acknowledged that her feet were not all that was sore this morning. The lingering ache between her thighs and the stiffness of her limbs were the price of her most enjoyable introduction to the physical side of love. To be sure, she did not regret it. But for the first time now, it occurred to her that something other than sore muscles might come of last night.

Indeed, it was not beyond the realm of possibility that she might have conceived as a result of their coupling.

The idea sent a shiver of mingled trepidation and wonder rushing through her. She had always hoped to have children of her own, one day, though she had always assumed that a husband would have been part of the bargain. Now, the first part of that wistful dream might be within reach. As for the second, however, she could not picture Malcolm in the role of either father or spouse.

Not that he had asked her to marry him, she hurried to remind herself.

With a sigh, she returned her thoughts to other, more immediate concerns. After she located Malcolm, they would have to make their swift way back to the guest house to let everyone there know they were well. Once she was assured that all the household had safely weathered the storm, she would then wait for word of the *Golden Wolf's* fate. But before she began any sort of search, she would first have to find something to wear over her undergarments.

Gritting her teeth against the pain of her feet, Halia tiptoed to search her unknown hosts' belongings. The wooden chest near the cot produced two simple if clean calico shifts—one yellow, one blue. She caught up the latter.

The dress proved to be cut for someone far more round of figure than she. Its neckline gaped alarmingly to expose most of her camisole, while its waist was large enough so that she could grab a large fistful of cloth on either side and have dress to spare. Still, it was better than walking the streets of Alice Town in her unmentionables.

To her relief, she also discovered a wooden hair comb, which she promptly put to use in unsnarling her hair. By the time she managed to smooth the worst of the tangles, she heard through the open windows the bright sound of a man whistling. Recognizing the cheery notes as belonging to Malcolm, she hurried to greet him as he appeared in the open doorway.

He halted there abruptly, an expression rather like guilt flickered across his features. He reminded her of a schoolboy caught at some mischief, that image strengthened by the fact he was dressed in yesterday's clothes that looked far worse for wear than hers. Then he grinned and started toward her, and her heart gave a giddy little lurch.

"Nice gown, luv," he lightly declared as he halted before her and brushed a kiss over her lips, "but just a bit unfashionable. I think that when we finally return to New York, we should see about finding you a proper dressmaker."

Was he hinting that he saw a future for them together? She dared not press the issue now, but merely echoed his careless air as she replied, "I will be happy if I can just manage to keep my own clothes on my back."

He slanted her a wicked glance. "I'm disappointed, luv. I'd rather hoped to see you with them off on a regular basis," he said and pulled her into his embrace.

This time, his kiss was one of sensual demand, and she eagerly complied. When they finally broke apart a few long moments later, her entire body was aquiver with need. She saw the same desire etched upon his face, as well, and the regret in his tone echoed her own.

"Much as I'd prefer to spend the rest of the morning making love to you, we'd best be going," he said and lightly put her from him. "It looks like we only got the edge of the storm, but there is damage enough, all the same." He paused, then added, "There's something else I must tell you."

"If you wish—but first, I have something for you."

So saying, she caught the narrow chain around her neck and pulled off the makeshift necklace. Even as he stared at her, puzzled, she pressed the Poseidon head coin into his hand.

"A gift," she explained with a shy smile. "It's a small thing, I know, and hardly worth the price of your lost emerald, but I want you to have it."

He stared down at the rough gold disk, and she wondered if her impulsive gesture had perhaps been a mistake. Then, with an odd sort of smile, he tucked the coin into his pocket. "You're wrong, luv," he softly replied. "It's worth far more . . . at least, to me."

His answer gladdened her heart, and her smile grew wider. "I feared you might think me unduly sentimental. But now, tell me, what did you wish to say?"

He gave a careless shrug. "It will keep. Right now, let's put this place in a bit of order before we're off."

"I'll fold the blankets."

She turned to match deed to word, then broke off with a muffled cry of pain as another step finally proved beyond her ability. Concern flashed over Malcolm's features, and he promptly caught her arm.

"What's wrong, luv?"

"I fear that I managed to cut my feet rather badly last night," she conceded with a wavering smile.

Swiftly, he scooped her up in his arms and deposited her in one of the chairs. The next moment, he had knelt to cradle one of her bare feet in his hands. He examined both soles, then sat back with a scowl.

"Is it bad, then?" she managed in a faint voice.

He shook his head. "You'll not die," came his ironic reply, "but why in the bloody hell didn't you say something last night?"

Though his expression was accusatory, the mingled concern and admiration she heard in his tone served as a balm to her sore feet and uncertain heart. "I supposed I was too frightened to think of anything but the storm. Perhaps if you might find some rags to wrap around them, I might be able to walk a little easier."

"You're not taking a bloody step. I'll carry you back . . . that is, as soon as I set things right here."

She watched as he righted the table and dragged it back to its spot along the wall, then began folding the bedding. She would have argued against his plan, save that logic dictated she probably would not make it half-a-dozen steps before she would be begging his assistance, anyway.

Moreover, the prospect of having him literally sweep her off her feet and carry her through the streets brought with it a small shiver of feminine appreciation.

Still, it was with prim restraint that she looped her arm around his neck as he lightly hefted her. Then he glanced down at her, and the possessive glint in his dark gaze sent a sudden shyness through her, so that she felt her cheeks grow warm.

To cover her confusion, she summoned a careless smile. "Don't worry, I'll not expect this of you again," she assured him. "I am certain Lally has some sort of salve that should dull the pain and heal me quite quickly."

Barely had the words left her mouth than an expression she could not identify momentarily darkened his features. Then, blandly, he replied, "Yes, she does seem to have quite a way with settling matters, does she not?"

They were the last words he spoke to her. She sensed a sudden withdrawal in him, a coolness that had not been there a moment before, but she was at a loss to understand it. Had they not just kissed, not just spent the night before making love?

Then he carried her outside into the morning light, and she promptly forgot her concerns.

It was as if some giant hand had wielded a scythe and lopped away at every treetop, leaving the island blanketed in tree limbs and torn leaves. As Halia stared, aghast, Malcolm picked his way through the tangle of battered greenery toward the road leading to the Queens Highway. Their progress was slow, however, and not only because of the fallen limbs. Though much of yesterday's rain had drained to the sea, water still stood in low spots and the sandy soil remained boggy, so that traveling by foot was treacherous.

By the time they reached the road, she could see that the damage to the landscape was even greater. Uprooted trees had splintered wooden fences and tumbled stone walls. In some places, the debris was such that Malcolm had to set her down beside the road to clear a path, then scoop her up again and continue.

Neither had the surrounding houses gone unscathed. As they drew closer to town, Halia saw that many humble little shacks and cottages had lost shutters or even whole sections of roof. An entire wall of one such home, she saw, had collapsed entirely. She clutched at Malcolm's arm in concern, fearful that its inhabitants must surely have been injured, until she saw a man and woman with their brood of laughing children calmly clearing away the worst of the damage.

For, with the rising of the sun, the islanders had left the safety of their homes to see what damage the winds and sea had wrought. To her surprise, the collective attitude was not despair but cheerful acceptance. Doubtless they were accustomed to such brushes with nature's fury and calmly shrugged off the inevitable backbreaking aftermath, at least, so long as there were no dead to bury.

And from the bits of conversations she overheard, it did seem that no islander had been washed into the sea or even suffered any worse injury than a few bruises. Halia offered a silent prayer of thanks for that, even as she frantically wondered if the storm's benevolence had extended to the ships off the coast. If only she had some way of knowing whether or not her father was safe!

By the time they were in sight of the guest house, Malcolm's face was flushed a dull red and his brow beaded with perspiration from the effort of negotiating the climb with her in his arms. He had ignored her repeated suggestions that she try to walk a part of the distance, or else wait beside the road while he brought additional help. The sun had risen enough so that the island seemed wrapped in a suffocating blanket of moisture, and yesterday's rains seemed almost preferable by comparison.

As for making the trip cradled in his arms, it had turned out to be rather less than the romantic journey she had envisioned, given his unexplained silence. By the time he deposited her on the steps of the guest house veranda and collapsed beside her, her sigh of relief was as heartfelt as his had been.

" 'Ere now, we were just goin' out to look for ye," exclaimed a familiar rough voice from the door beyond.

Halia turned with Malcolm to see Wilkie hurry out onto the porch, his pockmarked face split by a wide grin. " 'Ere, I thought we'd be buryin' ye both come mornin'. 'Twas unnervin' enough, lettin' ye go off alone to meet that bleedin' pirate, but then we get a bloody 'urricane on top o' that . . ."

He trailed off with a shake of his head, and Malcolm gave him a weary grin. "I was a bit concerned, myself, I must admit."

"So wot 'appened, then?"

As Halia listened, Malcolm briefly recounted for the other man the events of the previous afternoon and night, save for mentioning how he and she had passed their enforced confinement. Wilkie made no comment, but the shrewd look he briefly turned on her told her that he guessed at the truth, nonetheless.

"So, we're back safe and sound, for the most part," Malcolm finished with a shrug, "though Miss Davenport did manage to stomp about on broken glass or some such and cut her feet."

"It was conch shells," she stiffly countered, "and it was

completely unintentional, I assure you. So perhaps, Mr. Foote, you might be so kind as to summon Lally to assist me."

"An' what you be doin' to dat poor girl, leavin' her sittin' there like dat?" the Negress sternly demanded from behind them. "You be bringin' her inside now, so I can be takin' care of her."

A few minutes later, Halia was settled against a mound of pillows in her own bed, Malcolm having carried her upstairs, as well. He had declined Wilkie's offer of assistance with a muttered, "She's my bloody responsibility, not yours." His expression had reflected that such a burden did not rest at all well with him.

Though a dozen sharp retorts had risen to her lips, Halia had found that, all at once, she felt too battered in body and spirit to care *who* carted her about. She had accepted without protest the sweet-tasting tonic Lally insisted she sip. Then, while the older woman smeared a pungent if soothing salve on her abused feet, Halia gave her an account of her abduction and what followed afterwards.

"Your father, he still be aboard dat ship?" Lally wanted to know once Halia had finished.

She nodded. Lally had shown no surprise at the earlier mention of Arvin's name, so doubtless Malcolm already had told the entire household that he'd also located the senior Davenport, alive and well, aboard the *Golden Wolf* with her.

"The pirate, O'Neill, said that they still had some unfinished business to settle, and he refused to let Papa go with me. But no ships have yet been reported lost in the storm, so I am certain he is fine."

She paused to meet Lally's dark gaze, and something in the woman's expression spoke of a deeper knowledge. Halia frowned, then softly exclaimed, "The entire time, you knew what he'd done, and even that he was alive. But how could you have been sure?"

"Sometimes, what a woman be knowin' about a man, she be knowin' with her heart."

That simple statement, and the look of fierce pride on the other woman's face, spoke of years' worth of secrets kept. And she, Halia, had been too blind to understand the truth, until now.

"Why, you and my father, you love each other!"

Her astonishment was not over the fact that these two people of different races and ideals had found each other. Neither was she appalled that her own father might still be enjoying the physical side of love at his age. What took her by surprise was the fact that they had kept their secret so well and for so long.

"But why did you never say anything to me?" she wanted to know.

"Your father, he be wantin' to tell you, but I be sayin' no," Lally declared as she tied the last strip around Halia's foot and sat back, hands folded defiantly in her lap.

Halia shot her a look of hurt accusation. "But surely you did not think that I would object, just because your skin is not the same color as his. Why, I would have been happy for the both of you."

"I be knowin' dat, chile," she softly replied, and a small smile played upon her lips. "But sometimes, it just be hard enough to be lovin' someone, without you be worryin' about everyt'ing else, too."

"Yes, I know," Halia said with a small sigh and sank back against the pillows again.

Lally rolled her eyes heavenward. "So you be lovin' dat man, after all," she declared. "I should have been givin' you dat potion, not him. An' I suppose dat, last night, you an' he be doin' what a man an' woman supposed to be doin' together."

"We did, and more than once," she admitted with a blush . . . and to her horror, promptly burst into sobs.

Lally leaped up and settled herself alongside her, wrapping motherly arms around her shoulders. "It will be better the next time, I be promisin' you. Some men, they be so eager to take what they can, they don't be thinkin' about they woman."

"But it was wonderful," Halia protested with a sniff, dashing the tears from her cheeks even as she stifled a sudden yawn. Doubtless, Lally's potion was making her act in such an uncharacteristically emotional manner. "And he even threw away his emerald just to prove that he cared more about me than about it. That's why I don't understand why he seems so distant . . . even angry."

"Most men, they not be knowin' why they be thinkin' what they be thinkin', themselves. All you can be doin' is to be waiting for him to be comin' to his senses."

"But what if he doesn't?"

"Den dat be dat," Lally declared with a sage nod and stood. "Now, you be gettin' a bit of sleep, and when you be wakin' up, maybe things, they be better."

"But I just woke up, so how can I be tired?" Halia protested, even as her eyelids began to droop. Barely had the question left her lips than she slipped off to dreams of emeralds and ecstasy.

Chapter 23

" 'Ere now, ye can't be bloody serious," Wilkie exclaimed, his pale brows beetling into a frown. "Ye can't be sailin' off like that."

"I can, and I will," Malcolm coolly declared as he stowed away the last of his clothes in his trunk and shut the lid. "You can join me or not, but, come this afternoon, I'll be on my way—westward, I do believe. I think San Francisco might prove an interesting destination."

"Yer 'eartless, ye are. First, ye try to take 'alf 'er bleedin' treasure, then ye 'ave yer way wit' 'er . . . an' then, when ye find out there's no gold, ye run off an' leave 'er behind."

"And just what would you have me do—marry the chit, perhaps?"

" 'Tis a thought."

It was, indeed, a thought . . . and one that Malcolm had found himself entertaining ever since he and Halia had made love. For he realized he had found with her something more than simple physical pleasure. A hollowness of his soul that he had not known existed had been filled. And, just as a man who lived on bread crusts was satisfied with that simple fare until he tasted cake, so Malcolm had thought himself content with his lot until he'd glimpsed a different sort of future open to him.

Last night, he'd been tempted to continue feasting on

cake the rest of his life. Thankfully, he had come to his senses this morning.

"I appreciate your concern, Wilkie," he replied, careful to keep his expression bland as he paused in the midst of buckling the trunk's final strap and glanced at his friend. "Unfortunately, I have no wish to marry anyone, least of all Miss Davenport. And as we have been partners for many years, I do hope you'll take my side in this matter."

"I'll take yer bleedin' side, but that don't mean I'll like it."

So saying, Wilkie turned on his heel and stomped out. Malcolm waited until the door had slammed after him. Then, with a muttered, "Bloody hell," he crossed the room to the open French doors and strode out onto the gallery.

In the distance, he could see Bimini's wide harbor, where beneath a bright sun, numerous boats and ships that had fled to the open sea to avoid yesterday's storm were now limping back to port. Had the *Golden Wolf* and her crew made it safely through, as well? More to the point, had his half-brother survived the waves?

If so, then Seamus would be coming back in search of him.

Idly, Malcolm reached into his trouser pocket, his fingers closing on a familiar, sharp-edged object, the talisman that had gotten him through this whole bloody mess. He had not realized just how much it meant to him until he had wakened from an unbelievable night of passion to a single panic-stricken thought . . . that he'd tossed away Poseidon's Tear as casually as he might have discarded a worn pair of boots.

He had tried to dismiss that thought, reminding himself that he had done it for a reason, and that he did not regret the gesture, in the least. But finally, pragmatism and old habit had superseded sentimentality.

He'd stealthily eased himself from Halia's sleeping embrace and pulled on his clothes, then hurried out into the garden to search for the lost gem. He had walked in a straight line from the open window, frantically searching for a different sort of green among the verdant tangle. Whether by luck or by fate, he had stumbled upon the emerald within minutes, scooping it from where it lay half-buried in the sand.

Oddly enough, he had regretted this bit of deception the minute he returned inside to Halia's sweet kiss and her most enticing embrace. He had nearly confessed, then and there, would have done so if Halia had not cut him short with her gift.

Now, he reached into his other pocket, plucking forth the chain from which dangled the Poseidon coin. Gold glittered beneath the sunlight, reminding him of the treasure that could be his, if only he would take it.

And he might have, too, had not Halia inadvertently reminded him of one fact about their relationship that had slipped his mind . . . that his feelings for her likely were not genuine, but a product of Lally's voodoo hexes.

With another muttered epithet, Malcolm shoved the coin back into his pocket. Turning his back on the bustling harbor scene, he headed into his room. Now was the time to make good his departure—*his cowardly escape,* an inner voice taunted—while Halia slept and Seamus remained at sea. He'd send the manservant, Levar, to find someone with a boat willing to take himself and Wilkie back to some sort of bloody civilization today.

For he'd be damned if he'd let himself be held hostage by a love potion, no matter how much joy it brought him.

With a sigh of pure bliss, Halia settled into the hip-deep little tub of hot water that Sadie had left her. She had slept all the morning and part of the afternoon, Lally's potion having had its intended effect. She had awakened quite rested, the ache of her injured feet having subsided to merely a twinge.

The only thing the woman's elixir had not done was to ease the uncertainty of Halia's heart.

She bit her lip and reached for the sliver of scented soap beside her, determined not to give way again to weak tears. Neither would she cravenly pursue the man and insist he declare some tender feelings to match her sentiments for him. For she could not force him to love her, that much, she realized . . . just as she knew she could not make herself stop loving him, despite it all.

She sank back into the warm water and shut her eyes, recalling their night of lovemaking. Never had she known that a mere touch could bring her to such rapture—nor, that having once experienced it, she would find herself wantonly craving more. But though she suspected he might oblige by bedding her again, she could not bring herself to settle for just the physical pleasure he might give her.

She wanted his heart, as well.

It was with a sense of regret that she scrubbed away the scent of him from her flesh and rose from her hasty bath. Still, by the time she had dried off and dressed in her own clothes again—the borrowed shift having been sent back to its owner via Sadie—she had come to a decision.

First, she would make her way down to the docks to wait for word of her father's fate. Indeed, perhaps the *Golden Wolf* had already returned to port, and her father even now was on his way to see her. Once that was settled, the second thing she would do was seek out Malcolm—for perhaps, as Lally earlier had suggested, he might have come to his senses in the intervening hours and would be waiting for her, as well.

Of the two possibilities, the former seemed the more likely, she decided with a sigh. No matter, she would still give the infuriating man another chance. If he proved unwilling to discuss their personal relationship, she would approach Malcolm with a purely business proposition, that they continue their previous partnership.

It would be quite straightforward. She'd continue her exploration of the underwater site which, though perhaps not the ruins of lost Atlantis, might still prove to yield important finds. All the work would fall to her, while half of whatever she discovered she would turn over to Malcolm, to do with as he chose.

Of course, chances were that the surrounding waters had been churned into a sandy pool by the storm, which would mean that the work could not begin until the sea had settled. And if the ocean bottom had shifted, that also would mean that she would have to begin her digging all over again.

She gave a small, satisfied smile. The project might last several months, she judged. Surely that would allow sufficient time for him to come to the obvious conclusion—that he could not do without her in his life.

"That's it. That's the *Golden Wolf!*"

Halia stood on the bustling dock two hours later, clutching Lally's arm as she spied the familiar ship sailing into harbor. Even from a distance, she could see that the pirate's vessel had sustained damage, so that they must have been caught in the worst of the storm. What remained now was to learn if all hands had also survived yesterday's cruel onslaught.

Trying to divert her impatience, she scanned the harbor waters. The setting sun spread a pink glow across the waves that appeared far different today than usual. For, as she had suspected, the storm had churned the sea bottom until a haze of fine sand was suspended in the island's blue-green waters, turning them a milky white. It could take days or even weeks for the ocean to settle again back to its familiar translucence.

But would her battered heart rebound as swiftly?

She had learned the bitter truth but an hour before. Impatient to confront Malcolm, she had finally given in to the inner voice that urged her not to put this off any longer. She had hurried to the door that connected their two chambers and unbolted her side of it, then slipped into his room.

The first thing she had noticed was that the doors to his wardrobe were swung wide open to reveal an empty interior.

A sudden trepidation seizing her, she had taken a closer look about her. His clothes *were* gone, she saw, as was his traveling trunk. A glance at the dressing room showed the mirrored washstand clear of any razor or shaving brush. Indeed, any sign of his earlier presence was gone save for one thing . . . her gold Poseidon coin neatly placed upon his pillow.

With an anguished cry, she had snatched up the coin and fled his room for Wilkie's chamber. The older man's belongings were gone, as well.

With another sound of disbelief, she swung about and almost fell into Lally's arms.

"Dat man, he be gone," the older woman had simply said. "Levar, he be takin' the two of them to the dock this morning."

This morning. Why, that had been hours ago! "But why did you not wake me?"

"Because it wouldn't be makin' no difference," was her blunt reply. "A potion, it can be helpin' a man along when he's already of a mind to be doin' somet'ing, but it can't be makin' him go against his heart."

Though her own heart cried out that this was not true, that she could convince him to love her, the logical corner of her mind conceded the wisdom of Lally's words. He had made his choice . . . and she was not it. All she could do was gather up the scattered pieces of her pride and go on with her life.

Now, a cry from the approaching vessel returned Halia to the moment. At the ship's railing, a white-haired man stood waving.

"Papa," she breathed in relief, turning to the woman at her side. Though her expression was calm, Lally's black eyes gleamed with what looked suspiciously like tears.

The woman caught her look and proudly lifted her chin, shrugging as she did so. "I told you, he be on dat ship."

They waited as the ship dropped anchor a short distance out. Then, after a seemingly interminable delay, the *Golden Wolf's* dinghy was lowered. By dint of squinting, Halia made out two figures in addition to the seaman who was rowing.

Her father's white-blond mane was bright against the dying sun, so that he was easy for her to distinguish. The other man was dark-haired, and something about the way he held himself was hauntingly familiar.

The frisson of hope that had risen in her breast died, to be replaced by a sense of unease as the dinghy drew closer. The second man was not Malcolm, as she had prayed, but was instead his half-brother. The boat pulled even with the pier, and the pirate gracefully clambered onto the dock, closely followed by Arvin.

Rushing as fast as her cut feet would let her, Halia hurried to embrace her father.

"Halia, child, I was afraid I would never see you again," he softly exclaimed as he threw his arms around her. "All O'Neill could tell me was that he had left you on the beach. I could only pray you had made it to higher ground before the storm hit."

"We were fine, Papa," she replied, drawing back from his hug to meet his familiar indulgent gaze. "I was more worried about you, because *he*"—she shot a condemning look at O'Neill—"said he would not let you go. He claimed you two had some matters to settle between you, still."

The pirate's blue eyes reflected an expression of chill unconcern as he shrugged. "So we did, but no more. Sure, and yer father is a brave man—or else, a bleedin' fool."

Halia frowned. "Whatever are you talking about?"

" 'Tis quite simple. Yer father, he saved me life."

"It was by mistake, I tell you," Arvin interjected, his face turning a dull red as he glanced from the pirate to Halia. "The waves were high and his dinghy capsized just as it reached the ship. I saw him hit his head on the hull and knew that was my chance. I jumped into the water, hoping to get to the dinghy before it sank. The only reason I ended up saving him was because his men threatened to shoot me there in the water if I didn't."

"Intentional or not, he saved me life and evened the scores between us," O'Neill finished the tale. "I told yer father he was free to go."

"Thank you," Halia stiffly replied. She took her father's arm, urging him on ahead of her. "Now, if you will excuse us, we must get back to the guest house."

"Not so fast, me darling."

His soft words lashed out like a whip, so that despite herself she let her father continue on while she turned again to face the pirate. He reached into his trouser pocket and drew out an egg-shaped stone, which he tossed onto the dock at her feet.

" 'Tis a small matter of an emerald that I'm still owed. Now, why don't ye be good enough to tell me where me brother has run off to."

"Run off is the correct term, Captain O'Neill," she retorted. "He and Mr. Foote packed their belongings and left from this dock sometime earlier today. I have no idea where they have gone, nor do I care."

Those last words trembled a little on her lips, proving them for the lie that they were. O'Neill quirked a wry brow, momentary amusement warming his chill blue gaze.

"So, he pulled one over on ye, too," he softly replied. " 'Tis typical of him, I might have warned ye. And I suppose he had the emerald with him?"

Halia returned him a cool smile. "As for your jewel, Captain O'Neill, I fear I have a bit of bad news for you, as well.

You see, Mr. Northrup tossed it away during the storm last night.''

"Tossed it away?" The pirate's blue eyes narrowed, any trace of earlier amusement now quenched. "Sure and I don't believe ye. Why would he do such a thing, throwing away a bloody ransom like that?"

Proudly, she lifted her chin. "He did it to prove—that is, it makes little difference, now. But I assure you that Poseidon's Tear is gone."

She braced herself for some sign of anger, praying as she did so that the pirate would not vent his rage over Malcolm's outlandish behavior against her or her father. She was stunned, then, when O'Neill burst out in the first genuine laugh she had heard from him.

"Sure, and knowing me brother, I'll wager that he went back later to find it."

With those words, the pirate climbed back down the ladder to where his dinghy was tied. As his seaman shoved off, however, O'Neill leaned forward.

"I'll make ye a promise, me darling," he called back to her. "The next time I see me scoundrel of a brother, I'll be sure to tell him what a fool he was . . . that he chose the wrong jewel to keep."

Oddly enough, O'Neill's wry compliment brought her a bit of comfort. Her heart somewhat lighter than it had been a moment before, she started back up the pier to where her father and Lally stood, hands clasped. Catching sight of her, Arvin promptly loosed his grip on the woman.

"I, er, was just telling Lally that I appreciated her looking out for you these past weeks," he gruffly explained, avoiding both her and Lally's gaze as another dull flush darkened his features.

Halia halted before him and planted her hands on her hips, giving her head an impatient shake. "Really, Papa, why don't you stop acting foolish and just give her a proper greeting, for once?"

Arvin's mouth dropped open. Then, comprehension lit his face with an even brighter blush, and he began a word-less stammer as he groped for an explanation. Before he could manage an intelligible phrase, however, Lally grasped his arm.

"She be right," the woman declared as, heedless of the milling islanders, she raised her lips to his.

Chapter 24

A week had passed since the *Golden Wolf* had limped back
to port, returning Arvin to his family. As for Malcolm,
Halia had heard nothing more of his fate save for what the
manservant, Levar, had told her.

Sitting at the supper table idly toying with a bowl of
conch stew, Halia let her thoughts drift to the past few days.

I be findin' dem a boat, and dey be climbin' aboard, the old
man had related with stark simplicity. He had seen the skiff
shove off into the harbor, he admitted, and he had seen that
same vessel return late that day. As to its final destination,
he had not asked.

Though tempted to track down the boat and demand
some more concise answers from its owner, Halia refused to
play the scorned woman bent on tracking down her seducer.
He knew where to find her, if he so chose . . . not that she
would necessarily take him back now.

Reconciled to the fact that he was not coming back, she
had decided to wipe all thought of him from her mind. It
would be a simple enough task, she assured herself, since
nothing of his was left behind as a reminder of their time
together. Her father, she was certain, did not suspect what
had passed between her and Malcolm, so she did not have to
face the prospect of his playing the outraged parent. Indeed,
the only person she had taken into her confidence was Lally.

And then Lally pointed out the one possible outcome of her failed romance with Malcolm that she conveniently had forgotten about.

"What if there be a babe?" the woman had demanded. "What do you be doin' then?"

With the same blunt manner, Lally had also explained that there were herbs that could be distilled into a potion that would end a pregnancy in its early stages. It was for Halia, though, to choose whether or not she wanted to solve any such possible problem that way. When Halia promptly rejected her suggestion, Lally had spoken of the subject no more.

But one source of heartache Halia had not anticipated came of watching her father and Lally together. Now that their secret was common knowledge, they had gone from the formality Halia remembered in New York to acting much like a long-married couple. The heated looks they exchanged when they thought Halia's attention was elsewhere, however, better befitted a pair of newlyweds.

Though her delight for her father and Lally was sincere, Halia could not suppress a twinge of envy as she watched them together. For a few brief hours, she had known a similar sort of joy, which made witnessing the pair's obvious affection all the more difficult for her than if she'd never known what it was like to love.

As to whether or not she had *been* loved, she was still not sure.

He chose the wrong jewel to keep.

O'Neill's words of the previous week continued to echo in her mind until she feared she would go mad. Had he truly made a choice? Why had he not just taken both her and the emerald? Or maybe he *had* wanted her but simply had feared that she would not have him.

"—was a foolish thing to do, I'll admit, but I can explain," came Arvin's sheepish voice now, the words breaking in on her doleful thoughts.

Halia straightened in her chair at the supper table and gave her father her full attention. This was the first time they'd had time to talk. For the past several days, Arvin had been up at dawn to assist with setting the island back in shape again, only to return well after dark each night. As for Halia, her feet had healed sufficiently so that she was able to lend her own help to the cause, sharing food and water from the guest house with those in need.

"I'll be leavin' you two to talk," Lally declared and rose from her own spot. She glanced over at Arvin, then warned, "An' we be havin' a talk of our own, later."

The next moment, the tiny dining room was empty save for father and daughter. Arvin, she saw, looked distinctly uncomfortable.

"You've already told me some of it," she prompted when he continued silent. "I know that O'Neill gave you the coin, and that he helped you out of some sort of trouble. But why did you claim that you had found Atlantis, in the first place?"

Arvin shook his head, his expression that of a man who had seen his fondest dreams crumble. "You know better than anyone else, child, that finding the lost city has always been my secret hope. And after our last trip together, I had conceived of a new theory that placed the lost continent here, in the Caribbean."

"That was the monograph you wrote, the one that rebutted Ignatius Donnelly's claims."

He nodded. "The trouble was, I had no money left with which to begin a new search. I feared that someone else would come along and take off where I had left off, make the great find that I should make . . . so that all my years of research would have been for naught."

"And so you went in search of someone who would act as a sponsor of sorts," Halia exclaimed as the circumstances began to come clear.

Arvin shook his head, his lips turned down in wry memory. "Oddly enough, they came in search of me. Soon after our return home, a group of South American gentlemen appeared on our doorstep. One of them—Señor Gutiérrez, as he called himself—had seen the monograph and was intrigued. He and his friends were willing to put up a considerable sum to finance an expedition to locate the remains of Atlantis. All they asked in return was a certain percentage of whatever I found. But first, they wanted some assurances that the site I had chosen was a likely one."

"And so you showed them my Poseidon coin," she guessed, indicating the uneven gold disk that she was once more wearing about her throat.

"I had two coins, actually," Arvin corrected, "both of which I had procured from our good Irish captain. The one, I gave to Señor Gutiérrez and his friends, and the other I saved for you."

"But why lie?" she wanted to know. "Why not wait until you had some genuine find to show them."

"But that was the trouble. Without their backing, I could not make any extensive explorations, and unless I produced some sort of artifacts from the site, they would not advance me the money."

"But I was certain of my theory," he went on, "so much so that I was willing to take any risk. And so I concocted my journal entries and turned over the coin to Gutiérrez, who proceeded to advance me my financing. Unfortunately, it was not until I accepted the money that I learned the sort of brutal men that he and his friends truly were."

Halia frowned, trying to sort this through. "But I don't understand. If you had the money, why did you not simply begin the search?"

"Because, child, our good friend O'Neill informed the South Americans that they had been duped."

She dropped her fork with a clatter. "O'Neill did this? But why?"

"He was after Poseidon's Tear, which your Mr. Northrup

had stolen from him, and he needed a way to lure his half-brother someplace where he could hold him captive awhile, if necessary. And since Northrup just happened to be involved in a swindling scheme involving Atlantis, O'Neill decided to throw the lot of us together. You—with my unseen help—would be the bait to lure in the Englishman. But first, O'Neill had to remove me from Gutiérrez's clutches, so he helped me to contrive my own death."

Halia shook her head, mentally trying to unravel the threads of this bizarre tale and then weave them back again into something that made sense.

"But I truly thought you were dead," she told him, remembered pain adding a catch to her voice. "You could have confided in me. I would have kept your secret and helped you."

"I know that, child," Arvin replied and reached out to pat her hand. "But it was to keep you safe that I did what I did. If the South Americans had suspected something was amiss, they might have harmed you to get back at me."

Halia conceded the truth of that last, recalling the struggle between Malcolm and O'Neill that had ended with her in the middle. How much more terrifying would it have been for her to have found herself in those other men's grasp, instead?

"I wrote those anonymous letters," Arvin went on, "the ones that revealed Northrup for the fraud that he was. I knew that you would not let the matter rest . . . though I did not expect you to kidnap the man."

"It was the best plan that I could settle on," she protested, feeling herself blush.

Arvin gave her a fond smile. "And you know the rest, how I followed you in disguise. It all went quite well," he conceded, "save that your Mr. Northrup saw fit to complicate matters at every step."

"Well, you can hardly blame Malcolm," Halia rushed to

defend him. "How was he to know that all of this was nothing more than a fraud?"

The question sent a spark of indignation through her, so that she shoved back her chair and stood. *She* was the one who had been poorly used here . . . first by her father, then by O'Neill and, finally, by Malcolm. Suddenly, it was all quite more than she could bear.

"I need a bit of fresh air. If anyone needs me, I shall be out in the courtyard," she told him and made her way out the French doors.

She settled on the familiar stone bench beneath the sprawling fig whose immense, ragged shadow dappled the silver moonlight streaming from above. The air tonight was cooler than usual in the wake of the storm, and she welcomed the mild breeze on her heated cheeks.

What she was doing out here, she was not certain, she decided after a few minutes of simply soaking in moonlight. To be sure, this courtyard held only unsettling memories of another night. She shut her eyes, recalling how Malcolm first had snared her in a sensual trap from which she had yet to escape. But honesty compelled her to admit that, given another chance, she would not have done anything different, even knowing how it must end.

She swallowed hard, determined not to give into angry self-pity. Besides, it could have been far worse, she reminded herself as her fingers crept reflexively to the coin dangling over her breast. The rogue might have married her before leaving her behind.

The faint, shuffling sound of shod foot against stone interrupted her thoughts. Cautiously, she opened her eyes again. No doubt her father or Lally had come in search of her. Why she should be alarmed, she was not certain, save there had been something almost furtive about that sound.

A glance about the courtyard, however, showed it empty save for herself. She realized at the same moment that the noise she heard had not come from the direction of the

house. Rather, it emanated from one of the outer walls—or
had it? Sternly, she told herself that she was imagining
things, that all she had heard was a branch scraping against
the guest house.

And then the sound repeated itself, and she realized that
someone was attempting to climb inside.

She swallowed back a cry, images flashing through her
mind of the unknown Señor Gutiérrez seeking vengeance
against her father . . . or else, Seamus O'Neill returning to
kidnap her again. Whoever was out there did not belong
here, that was certain, else why had they chosen to sneak in
over the back wall?

She remained where she sat, hardly daring to breathe as
she stared at the spot from where the sound had come.
Chances were that this intruder did not even know she was
there, hidden as she was in the fig tree's broad shadow. Once
in the courtyard, he might even pass by without seeing her—
but even if he did not, better to get a glimpse of whoever was
out there, first. If she gave way to fear now, and tried to flee
to the safety of the house, she risked being struck down
from behind and never seeing her assailant.

A sudden movement along the top of the wall sent her
heart lunging into her throat. Next moment, some unknown
person was crouched atop the wide wall, looming menacingly in the dim light.

Halia's fingers flew to her mouth to hold back a reflexive
cry. Dear Lord, surely he must hear her heart beating, the
way it was slamming against her ribs. Her nerves stretched
almost to the breaking point now, she waited for what must
come next.

And then, one of the numerous conch shells lining that
stone perimeter tumbled from its perch to shatter on the
flagstone below.

"Bloody hell," a familiar voice muttered in disgust as the
shadowy figure leaped down.

She realized it was Malcolm at the same instant that he

stepped out into the moonlight. It was the moment for which a single hopeful corner of her heart had prayed . . . and it was a moment that had come far too late to suit her.

Joy and anger simultaneously welled up in her as she leaped to her feet, those emotions building until they exploded from her lips in a single accusing word.

"You!"

Chapter 25

Malcolm halted in midstep, and she sensed that he was quite as shocked by her presence as she was to see him. His words when he answered, however, reflected a cool nonchalance that only fueled her outrage.

"Here now, luv, you ruined my little surprise," he remarked as he started for her. "I thought to slip inside and then out again without anyone seeing me."

"And what were your plans—to rob us quite blind?"

He shook his head as he halted before her. "Surely you don't think quite so ill of me as all that? It simply happens that I forgot something of mine and wished to have it back."

Even as she guessed his meaning, he reached out and lightly caught the dangling coin between his fingers. She gasped in outrage and reached up her own hand to pull the necklace free.

She promptly realized her mistake, for he clamped his other hand across hers. Now, the chain and her fingers were entangled between both his hands, effectively binding her to him.

"Here now, luv, you gave it to me," he murmured, his lips mere inches from hers.

She stubbornly lifted her chin, determined not to let herself be distracted by his nearness or the familiar warmth of his touch.

"But *you* left it behind. Besides which, it was meant to replace the emerald that you cast away . . . and since I suspect you already have recovered that gem, it seems a pointless gesture now."

"You know me a bit too well, luv," came his rueful reply as his fingers tightened over hers. "As a matter of fact, I did go out that morning after the storm to look for Poseidon's Tear. I'd just found it and was coming back inside when you appeared in the doorway. I very nearly came clean and confessed what I'd done . . . but then, you gave me this"—he glanced down at their clasped hands, where moonlight illuminated the gold coin showing between their fingers—"and I found I could not."

"Was that why you acted so strangely then?" she cried. "It was but a small token, I know, but I thought somehow that you might be pleased with it."

"It was quite the nicest thing anyone has ever given me," he softly answered, "save for the gift that you had given me the night before."

Knowing that he referred to their lovemaking, she felt herself blush. Oddly, though, her anger had drained away now, leaving confusion in its wake.

"But I still don't understand. Why did you leave like that, without even a word? I-I thought that you had begun to care for me just a bit."

"That's where you're wrong, luv."

At those bleak words, she bit back a cry and shut her eyes. Despite her earlier vow, she felt a single hot tear slide down her cheek as shame washed over her. She'd been worse than foolish. She had given herself to him, thinking that he harbored some tender emotion for her, and all the while she had been deceiving herself.

"Here now, luv," she heard him lightly chide her, "it's fairly difficult for a man to tell a woman that he loves her when she won't even look at him."

Her eyelids flew open. "What-what did you say?"

"I said that I bloody love you," was his wry reply.

A frisson of hope sparked in her breast, but she refused to fan it into flames. "If that is true, then I still don't understand. Why did you leave . . . and where have you been this past week?"

"In answer to your second question, as soon as Wilkie and I reached Miami that first day, I had the boat turn around and take us back here again. We've been staying with Captain Rolle ever since, helping out a few of the islanders whose homes were the most badly damaged. And as for your first question . . ."

He broke off on a strangled note, then shook his head and plunged on. "It was just that I finally figured out the truth, that it wasn't me but Lally's bloody potion that made me fall in love with you."

When she merely stared, he explained, "It had to have been in that salve you gave me that first night here in the courtyard. Afterwards, I realized that Lally had done it for a reason. She probably hoped that I would be so besotted with you that I would give up my share of the treasure. And it nearly worked, except that I told myself I'd be hanged if I would be manipulated that way. And, besides that, I didn't want to know what would happen when the blasted stuff wore off."

A giggle escaped her, and he scowled. "And what's so bloody funny? Here, I'm telling you I've been hexed, and all you can do is laugh?"

"It's just that I have something to confess to you," she replied, a sudden, joyful lightness washing over her. "You were right, there was something in that ointment. But I fear that adding it was my idea—not Lally's. You see, I asked her to mix up a special sort of potion to go with it . . . but it was not a love potion."

Malcolm coolly regarded her. "What was it, then?"

"It was something that would make you lose all interest in me," she admitted in a rush. "I-I was afraid that *I* was falling in love with *you,* and I thought it best for the sake of the expedition that we keep our distance.''

In the faint moonlight, she saw a series of reactions—realization, dismay, anger—flash across his features. She feared for a moment that she had made a grave error in confessing her culpability. Then his expression settled into one of bland unconcern as he carefully addressed her.

"So what you're telling me, then, is that any feelings I have for you are genuine?"

"Correct," was her wary reply.

He shook his head. "I'm afraid your word is not good enough, luv, not after what I've been through. I believe I will require some more substantial proof."

"Proof?" she echoed in confusion. "What sort of—"

She never finished the question, for suddenly his lips were on hers, hot and demanding. With a muffled cry of relief, she eagerly complied with that unspoken want.

When they finally broke free of their kiss, several delightful moments had passed. "Very well, luv," Malcolm conceded, his breathing ragged as he flashed her a wry grin and pulled her down to join him on the stone bench. "I believe that you have quite convinced me."

"Perhaps *you* are convinced," she countered with an impish smile and shifted about to face him, "but I fear *I* will require more persuasion."

"As you wish, luv."

He promptly drew her onto his lap so that she straddled him, her skirts bunched wantonly about her thighs as his fingers clutched her buttocks. Through the thin barrier of her pantalets she could feel the heat of his engorged shaft as it pressed urgently against her. Sighing, she rubbed herself against him, the sensation sending waves of pleasure through her.

He groaned. "I'd suggest we move upstairs to your chamber," he hoarsely told her, "but I don't think I can make it that far."

"Neither can I," she breathlessly agreed, "so let's not wait."

Barely had the words left her lips than he reached between them to unfasten his trousers. His erect shaft sprung free of the confines of the fabric, urgently throbbing against her. With the same quick moves, he caught at the fragile fabric of her pantalets and rent the inner seam to expose her woman's flesh, damp now with her own juices. Eagerly she spread her thighs, and he thrust himself deep inside her.

Her soft, welcoming cry was echoed by his own harsh sound of satisfaction as he moved within her. This time, their lovemaking was the swift, urgent joining of two people who realized what they had almost lost between them. In moments, they had both found their release.

They remained for several moments quite scandalously entangled upon that bench. Finally, with a sigh, Halia eased off him and rearranged her crumpled clothing. Malcolm did the same with his, then slanted her a wry look.

"If you're in need of further persuasion—"

With a groan of mock protest, she cut short what she was certain would be a most improper suggestion and sat back down beside him. "I fear I am quite completely convinced," she told him. "Besides, my father or Lally might come wandering out in search of me."

"Ah, yes, that reminds me."

With a lazy grin, Malcolm rose and reached into his trouser pocket, withdrawing a folded sheet of age-browned parchment. "I almost forgot to tell you that I paid my half-brother Seamus a visit today. It seems that the *Golden Wolf* is in need of some repairs, so she is still anchored in the harbor. At any rate, I had begun to feel a bit guilty about cheating him of his emerald twice now, so I offered him a trade."

Halia frowned. "What sort of trade?"

"Quite a one-sided deal, I fear. In exchange for Poseidon's Tear, he gave me a certain map he had in his possession . . . one purportedly showing the site of a certain lost tribe that some people claim was descended from the ancient Atlanteans. I rather thought that would make an appropriate wedding gift . . . that is, if you would like me to step inside and have a word with your father."

Halia barely heard those last words, for she leaped to her feet and snatched the document from his hands. Her fingers trembling in anticipation, she unfolded the page so that a stray ray of moonlight illuminated it.

It was a crudely linked rendition, little more than a ragged section of coastline and the suggestion of a mountain range.

"Brazil," she softly pronounced, glancing up for his confirming nod before she returned her attention to the document.

A dotted line wound from the shore to the foot of that range to an X, the coordinates of which were scripted in an ornate hand. It was dated, as well . . . the year being fourteen hundred and ninety-three.

"Are you quite certain this is genuine?" she asked, trying to contain the note of excitement in her voice.

He shrugged. "Wilkie took a look and judged it real enough, though all he could vouch for was the parchment. It might be a modern forgery . . . but then again it might not."

Slowly, Halia looked up again to meet Malcolm's gaze as the import of his earlier words sunk in. "A wedding gift, you said?"

"A wedding gift," he softly confirmed.

She bit her lip, considering. "If we are to marry, then I would have to insist that you give up your fraudulent ways and turn your hand to some honest profession."

"I rather suspected you would say that," he replied with a wry smile.

She frowned. "And I would be quite uncomfortable living off the proceeds of the money you've already obtained by means of deception. I would want that money go to some charitable cause . . . scientific research, perhaps."

"I feared that, as well," he answered, looking pained. "Any other conditions, luv?"

"Just one, Malcolm. I would prefer that you wait a few minutes more before going inside to talk with Papa."

As she flung herself into his arms, the map fluttered from her fingers. For a moment, it drifted like a fallen palm leaf on the soft Caribbean breeze. Then, gently, it wafted to the ground between them, marking the spot where a lifetime of love was just beginning.

Epilogue

"Sounds like a right good crowd, it does," Wilkie Foote allowed, propping open the door of the tiny anteroom off the sanctuary. He peered past the resulting gap to gaze at the assemblage, then gave a satisfied nod.

Indeed, St. Stephan's church fairly hummed now with anticipation. The majority of the Bimini Islanders were in attendance, dressed in their Sunday best. Brightly dyed cottons and deep-hued calicoes rivaled the flamboyant yellow and purple hibiscus blossoms that decorated the sanctuary. Near the front, Wilkie picked out Captain Rolle and his family, then noted the crewmen of the *Johnesta* scattered toward the rear of the church with their respective families. A welcome breeze wafted through the open windows, adding to the stir from the numerous handheld fans of woven palm leaves that fluttered in brisk counterpoint to the murmured conversation.

Wilkie stepped back from the open doorway and glanced over at his partner, who nervously smoothed a nonexistent wrinkle from his waistcoat, only to frown.

"Damn it all, Wilkie, I forgot my lucky watch fob," Malcolm muttered as he transferred his anxious glance from the waiting sanctuary to his flat midriff. "I can't go out there, not without it."

" 'Ere now, it's just a cheap bit o' stamped metal," Wilkie

reassured him in an indulgent tone. "Besides which, ye've done right well these past weeks wit'out it."

Malcolm nodded and relaxed into a wry grin. "I guess I have, at that."

He had only just returned from South America to the Biminis two days earlier, having spent the greater portion of a month tracking down a certain Señor Gutiérrez. Upon finally locating the man, Malcolm had presented him with a sum twice the amount of his original investment in Arvin Davenport's aborted expedition. That, and a few persuasive words, had now made possible the scholar's resurrection from his ersatz watery grave.

Now officially returned to the living, Arvin was putting the finishing touches on his latest monograph regarding the Bimini Atlantis site . . . which, following the gale, had been reclaimed once again by the sand. No proof of any tie to that lost continent had been discovered, he stated, even as he decreed that the site remained an area of scientific interest and should be studied again at a later date.

Arvin also had launched an overt campaign to convince Lally that the two of them should, after almost a dozen years together, finally be married. Lally had yet to give him a reply, to Malcolm's private relief. While he and the Haitian woman had declared a truce of sorts following his return the week after the gale, he was not prepared as yet to address her as *mother*.

His half-brother Seamus had long since sailed from the islands, though he had casually left behind wedding gifts for the newly engaged couple. His present to Malcolm proved to be a set of emerald cuff studs, while Halia's was an elegant emerald pendant in the shape of a tear.

" 'Ere now," Wilkie broke in on his thoughts, "it's time."

"I suppose you are right."

Malcolm took a steadying breath and, with his partner beside him, strode past the door and out into the sanctuary.

A beaming Reverend Philpot joined them, and the waiting congregation fell silent. Then, a stir rose from the rear of the church as Arvin and Halia—dressed in a simple white gown like a charming figure from an ancient Grecian fresco—started down the aisle.

Malcolm's uneasiness promptly faded, replaced by a sense of proud anticipation as his gaze met the radiant face of his bride. And her glow, he knew, was not just the result of today's ceremony. Only last night she had confided to him her suspicions that, in a few months, she might be forced to curtail her role as an explorer of lost islands . . . at least, until the new baby was old enough to accompany them.

A teary-eyed Arvin relinquished her into Malcolm's care, and he clasped her hand. The sensual spark that always accompanied their every touch was not lost with familiarity, he was glad to realize. Rather, it had been joined now by a warmth that reached his very soul.

They took their places before Reverend Philpot, who launched into an opening prayer the equal, Malcolm realized, of any of his own bombastic forays into that dominion. He suppressed a wry smile and bent his head toward Halia's golden mane, caught up into loose curls atop her head and adorned with a single white hibiscus.

"I have been thinking of names," he murmured as the good reverend droned on. "If the babe is a boy, I believe I should like to call him Charles . . . after my father."

Halia met his gaze with a look of pleased surprise. "I think that would be most appropriate," she whispered back. "I fear, though, that I have been more unorthodox in my choices."

She paused and slanted him a passionate look that, had Reverend Philpot glimpsed it, would surely have scandalized that upright clergyman. For Malcolm's part, it found him suddenly anxious for this ceremony to end so that they could begin the wedding night . . . no matter that it was still afternoon.

"If the baby is a girl," she continued in an undertone, charmingly unaware of the effect she was having upon him, "I had thought that, given the circumstances under which she was conceived, we might call her Tempest."

"Tempest," he softly echoed. "I believe that I rather like that."

To the enjoyment of the congregation, Malcolm called an unofficial halt to the proceedings as, well before the prescribed moment, he bent to kiss his bride.

Author's Note

Atlantis.

The very name has sparked the imaginations of countless men and women since Plato first recorded his tale of that lost continent more than two millennia ago. Convinced that Plato's account was no mere legend but instead a scholarly account of a vanished people, so-called Atlantologists have placed that island all across the globe . . . from the Mediterranean to the British Isles to the South Pacific.

These believers have built cases for the existence of Atlantis upon the Biblical Flood, comparing it to various legends among diverse cultures concerning a long-ago and devastating deluge. Why would so many such accounts have survived, they ask, were the stories not based on truth? Other would-be scholars—among them, the eccentric former U.S. Senator Ignatius Donnelly, who published a popular volume of his theories in 1882—seized upon similarities in language and customs world-wide to claim that the majority of nations all descended from a common ancestral root . . . that of the Atlanteans.

Indeed, theories concerning Atlantis abound. Two more recent discoveries, however, have put a new slant on the question. One concerns the Mediterranean island of Thera, off the north coast of Crete.

Since the early part of this century, scientists have been

piecing together the circumstances surrounding a cataclysmic volcanic eruption that occurred in that region sometime around 1450 B.C. That catastrophe is blamed for the destruction of the ancient Minoan civilization of Crete, a prosperous society known for its advanced technologies and its contributions to law, religion, and art. Excavation of that island and the surrounding waters has turned up the remains of a city, canals, and harbor, the layout of which coincides with Plato's description of Atlantis. Were the Minoans perhaps the model for the Atlanteans of legend, then? Some scientists believe so.

Another, equally intriguing theory had its start with the American psychic, Edgar Cayce. Between the 1920s and 1940s, Cayce did "life readings" of hundreds of people whom he said were modern descendants of the vanished Atlanteans. Moreover, he claimed that the remains of Atlantis would rise from the sea somewhere between Florida and the Bahamas in 1968 or 1969.

Some believe that Cayce's prediction did come true. In the late 1960s, divers discovered a series of huge rectangular stones along the sea bottom in the shallow waters off of Bimini . . . the very spot where Halia and Malcolm conducted their search. Dubbed the "Atlantis Road," it sparked the interest of scholars, as well as Atlantologists. Some dismissed the stones as nothing more than a natural rock formation; others pointed to the stones' regular arrangement and sharp-cut edges as evidence that they were hewn by an ancient people—perhaps, the long-vanished Atlanteans?

To date, no official determination as to the formation's origin has been made. Easily accessible by boat, the "Atlantis Road" remains a popular side-trip for visitors to Bimini. There, amid the sparkling turquoise waters that surround the island, it is easy enough to believe in legend . . . and in love.

If you want a taste of Alexa Smart's next book, turn the page for a look at Blood and Roses . . .

Chapter One

I fear, dear friend, that my life has grown Exceedingly Dull since you and your Dashing Young Poet left the city in search of adventure abroad. I have not yet found the Grand Commission as an artist for which I have hoped. Alas, mending lace and teaching small children to sketch are hardly the proper sort of careers for a Modern Woman. Lest I sink into Perpetual Boredom, I shall write often and share even the smallest fragments of news . . .

—letter from Miss Amaryllis Meeks to Miss Mary Godwin

London . . . May, 1816

"Now then, gentlemen, I believe you will find this next demonstration most edifying."

A murmur of anticipation rose from his fellow physicians as the speaker—a thin, intense man barely into his third decade—stepped aside from the wooden table. He stood in a circle of yellow light, illuminated by the dozen lamps strategically placed about the makeshift platform. Those lamps emitted heat enough so that, even though the drafty, high-ceilinged stone chamber lacked any sort of furnace, he could feel the sweat beading upon his forehead. He began removing his black frock coat.

As always, Talbot Meeks drew out this moment deliberately, aware that a sense of the theater was not amiss here. Indeed, standing before the score or so men of medicine who had paid a crown each to watch, he wryly realized that he bore an unfortunate resemblance to some Drury Lane actor.

The only difference was that his fellow player upon this particular stage was a naked corpse.

Having shed his jacket, he caught up a pair of porcelain-handled copper probes from which trailed lengths of thin wire. Those wires were, in turn, connected to a box-like device the approximate size of a linen chest. The assembly of wire, metal rods, glass discs, and liquid-filled jars appeared innocuous enough to the untrained eye; a few cranks of its handle, however, produced a charge that could knock a man off his feet.

Coolly, Talbot once more faced his audience. They were seated in the carved wooden pews that were a legacy of the building's previous function—namely, a chapel. Though cloaked in shadows so that he could not make out their faces, he could hear their impatient rustling and catch the occasional murmured word being exchanged. The air was thick with challenge and skepticism, as it was every time he offered his anatomy lessons.

He felt a muscle in his cheek twitch as he struggled to contain his irritation. His demonstrations were conducted in the strictest of scientific fashion, with his intent to dispel the superstition and ignorance that still pervaded his profession. For too many of his fellow physicians cared little about their patients and even less about plumbing the workings of the human body. Rather, they prescribed noxious concoctions and let copious amounts of blood to treat every condition from gout to childbed fever . . . and then afterwards extracted an exorbitant fee for their services. For most of the physicians here this night, then, attendance had been motivated more from idle curiosity than any true urge to learn.

Here now, gentlemen, I'll give you your crown's worth and more, he thought. He did not betray his emotions by so much as a lifted brow, but instead took a step forward.

"The apparatus you see behind me is an electrical generator based upon designs first developed by Messieurs Ramsden and Ingenhousz before the turn of the century. With these probes"—he paused to raise them like a priest offering up the Host—"I shall demonstrate how a current of electricity applied to the appropriate nerve centers of our subject can simulate living movement."

So saying, he inserted one rod into the grounding plate installed on the table, then momentarily pressed the tip of the other rod to the cold, white flesh of the dead man's lower torso.

The withered leg promptly kicked heavenward.

Talbot waited for the muffled exclamations to die before continuing. "We see similar results with other nerve centers," he explained and applied the probe to the corpse's upper chest. This time, the dead man's waxen right arm shot out, as if he were a pugilist blocking a swift jab.

To the accompaniment of growing murmurs, Talbot moved the probe across that dead flesh until his subject fairly twitched like a man with the ague. The demonstration lasted no more than half a minute, but by then the pungent scent of discharged electricity filled the converted sacristy. Eyes burning, Talbot set aside the probes and let the unprotesting corpse subside into his previous graven stillness.

"Quite fascinating, Dr. Meeks," spoke up a man with a reedy Edinburgh burr, "but hardly more than parlor tricks. I dinna ken what medical purpose that generator of yours serves."

Talbot glanced toward the darkened arena before him.

He recognized the speaker by his voice though the man's face was hidden in shadow.

"Dr. McArdle, your presence honors me," he answered. "As to your objection, might I remind you that many of our esteemed colleagues here and elsewhere have begun experimentation using electrical current. I presume you are familiar with the work of Doctors Malham, Fursey, and Kent, to name but a few? Though the results of their work are now inconclusive, future applications will surely prove to be many. For example, with the use of electric generators, we will one day restore function to lame limbs . . . provide relief from melancholia . . . perhaps even stimulate the regrowth of hair."

That last suggestion drew a ripple of laughter from the audience, for the balding McArdle's attempts to disguise his receding hairline had long been a source of amusement to his fellow physicians.

"Aye, jest all ye wish," the Scot countered, "but ye canna change me mind. Ye're dabbling wit' heathen powers, an' no good will come of it."

"I must disagree," spoke up another voice from the darkness. "Every major advance in human history came only when men of vision were willing to stride past their prescribed boundaries of knowledge into strange and wondrous new territories of learning."

"Aye, Dr. Cramer," McArdle sourly addressed that man, "an' if that be the case, then the Barkshire Demon does the Lord's work, ridding the city of fallen women."

That acerbic mention of the unknown killer who had been stalking London's backstreets these past months quelled further comment. Talbot took advantage of the silence to regain control of the conversation.

"And now, gentlemen, we will continue with a study of the internal organs," he said with a cool smile and reached for the leather case containing his surgical instruments.

*   *   *

From her perch in a curtained alcove directly above the makeshift stage, Amaryllis Meeks set down her charcoal stick and allowed herself a sigh of relief. She had feared that, goaded by the Scot, her brother might have given way to the cold anger that of late seemed ever to bubble just beneath the surface of his usual gentlemanly mildness. Instead, Talbot had handled the situation with an aplomb that made her proud.

While her brother arranged scalpels and surgical knives along the examining table, Amaryllis took a moment to flip back through her sketchbook. Her presence here, hidden within a dusty, velvet-curtained alcove once reserved for titled personages to observe Sunday services, had been Talbot's doing. For the converted chapel was his, housing this tiny amphitheater, an examining room, and private chambers in which he had lived since his wife first had taken ill.

She turned yet another page, squinting in the half-light. Even had the sun been brightly shining without, the hall would have been dark. For the stained glass windows—save for the circular one in the ceiling above them—had all been boarded over to keep prying eyes from seeing within. Talbot had allowed her but a single candle lest someone note her presence, and that faint glow had made her work difficult. Still, she gave a satisfied nod as she looked over the studies of legs and torsos that she'd thus far managed.

Her subject was the corpse upon Talbot's examining table. Unlike most young women, she was not discomposed by the sight of a dead man. That sight was commonplace to her, since her father was the sexton of St. Pancras Church and she had grown up practically within the churchyard. Indeed, she had already succumbed to whimsy and mentally dubbed the deceased fellow George, given his passing resemblance to the current monarch.

This cadaver was no Adonis-like model with a smoothly

muscled physique. Instead, the table held a wizened old man with a scrawny chest and limbs, his only feature of note a full head of silvery hair. He would have to do, however, as this would be the closest that she would ever come to a life school. As a woman, she could hardly be admitted to such a gathering, where a nude model posed for the benefit of the assembled artists. Thus, she deemed herself sadly deficient in several crucial areas of anatomy . . . so much so that she even once had stripped down to her chemise before a mirror and used herself as a model.

Talbot, however, respected her work as a painter and watercolorist. Unlike their father, he never laughed at her declarations that she would one day earn her keep with her artwork, perhaps because he considered himself something of an artist in his own field. Whatever the case, he understood her need to study the human form. It had been he, in fact, who suggested she attend his next anatomy lesson. The only restriction was that no one—most particularly, their father—must ever know she was there.

Now, the sound of Talbot's voice pulled her attention back to the makeshift stage. Impatiently, she brushed aside an auburn curl that had come loose from its pins to hang rakishly over one of her eyes. Then, she twitched aside the curtain again.

Lamplight glinted from the scalpel her brother held in one hand, and she bit her lip in consternation. Earlier, he had warned her that the greatest portion of his lesson involved the dissection of a human subject. At the time, she had been too excited by the opportunity he was affording her to consider just what that meant. Now, however, as she watched him make the first incision into George's sunken chest, she felt her stomach lurch.

By the time he had split open the dead man like a Christmas goose primed for stuffing, she felt distinctly faint. Swiftly, she pulled on her cloak and gathered up her drawing materials. Seeing a dead man was one thing. Watching his innards being removed and cataloged was quite another. But as she prepared to pinch out the candle and grope her way to the curtained exit, she recalled Talbot's final admonition as he had settled her in the alcove.

Wait here for me until after the lesson, and I will escort you home. After all, it's far too dangerous these nights for a young woman to wander the streets alone.

He was right, of course. Over the past six months, the Barkshire Demon already had claimed four victims. All had been young impoverished females of various occupations—from prostitute to shop girl. Her gender and humble station in life left her uncomfortably close to being the sort of woman that attracted the Demon's attentions. Indeed, anyone would say she was a fool to consider making her way home alone and on foot.

Or was she? Amaryllis bit her lip again, considering. The tabloids all had made note of the fact that the Demon struck only on foggy nights. This evening was clear, and her way home well lit by streetlights, so that she would be safe enough. Moreover, it made no sense for her brother to make the long walk to St. Pancras and back simply to ease her fears. For she was a modern woman, after all, adhering to Mary Wollstonecraft's dictums regarding women's rights. Surely she possessed the sternness of mind not to be frightened by phantoms.

For, while wandering the fog-shrouded streets was unnerving, the thought of returning inside and witnessing poor George being served up like Sunday dinner was equally distressing. Even if she shut her eyes, she would still be able to hear everything. And poor George, through no fault of his own, had already developed the ripe odor of a corpse left unburied too long. She would still be able to smell him, as well. And while she might be stern of mind, she most definitely was weak of stomach.

The distinctive sound of a saw ripping through brittle bone that now rose from the stage below goaded her to action. Swallowing her queasiness, she tore a page from her sketchbook and dashed off a note of explanation to Talbot. Then, posting the paper on a convenient splinter just outside the alcove, she tiptoed her way down a narrow flight of steep stone steps and slipped out the back way.

Once outside, however, she halted in dismay. In the intervening hour since the anatomy lesson had commenced, a serpentine fog had oozed its way off the Thames to wrap chill white coils about the city streets. Now it was the sort of night when a person could hardly see his hand before his face. Indeed, it was exactly the sort of night when the Barkshire Demon walked the city.

Sternness of mind, she reminded herself. For she was well away from that unsavory area near the river where the Demon prowled. And, should she become unnerved once she had walked too far to turn back, the solution was simple. She would simply flag down a passing hack and spend a few precious coins.

The matter decided, then, Amaryllis plunged into the fog.

Glimmers of the gas lamps' yellow light had escaped the fog's grasp and that fitful illumination was sufficient for her to negotiate the walkway. Even so, by the time she had covered a block she could scarcely make out any detail of her surroundings. Only the fact that she made this walk on a regular basis kept her from stumbling, hopelessly lost, through the anonymous streets. A few minutes later, however, the fog lifted long enough for her to glimpse a millinery shop where she occasionally shopped.

Halfway home, she thought as she let out a breath she had not realized she was holding. And then footsteps echoed in the distance behind her.

Reflexively, she halted. By chance or design, the other set of footfalls fell silent, so that she wondered for a moment if she simply had imagined them. For, indeed, they had sounded nothing like ordinary footsteps. Muffled by the night and the burgeoning fog, they had been reminiscent of tree limbs being slowly dragged across the damp cobbles. Steeling herself, she turned for a look at whoever was behind her.

No one was there.

After a moment, she resumed her pace, though her heart was thrumming at a quicker rate than before. Surely it had been but her imagination that had conjured phantom sounds. Indeed, had she and her friend Mary not often made a game of frightening each other with fearsome tales, so that she was predisposed to hearing ghostly noises?

But now, the only sound was the soft click of her own sensible boots against the walk. The dull rhythm was unnerving in its own way, announcing her presence more loudly than she would have wished, but it was a far preferable sound to the unearthly gait that she'd imagined had echoed her steps.

A few moments later, however, she almost wished for the company—unearthly or not. For the fog had thickened again, leaving her to strain her eyes against the swirl of white in hopes of spotting some landmark—a signpost, perhaps, or else another familiar shop front. This time, though, none rose out of the fog.

"Blast." Her unladylike mutter now held a small note of desperation. Even had she wished now to flag down a hack, none was to be found. She would have to keep on going.

Hesitantly, she extended one arm. The tight sleeve of her bottle green gown stretched the limits of its seams as she groped before her. When her gloved fingers closed over nothing more substantial than mist, she cautiously swung her arm to one side, only to connect with brick.

A wall. She edged closer to it, relieved she had not managed to wander into the middle of the lane. Now, should she remain where she stood and hope that the fog might lift a bit, or should she guide herself by following the building's edge? Yet even as she inwardly debated the question, she heard a faint, unnerving shuffling somewhere behind her.

Her flesh prickled at the furtive sound. *It was the same person . . . and he was still following her.*

Frantically, she shrank back against the wall and strove for calm. She had no proof, after all, that this unseen person was in pursuit of her. And if he were hidden from her by the night and the fog, then it stood to reason that he also could not see her. Unless, of course, he were the Demon.

For the tabloids had attributed almost supernatural powers to the fiend who seemingly wandered the foggy nighttime with the same aplomb a regular man strolled about on a sunny day. The fact that no one had ever witnessed his crimes, nor had he yet left any sort of clue behind as to his identity, only added to the mystery.

Even as a thrill of horror swept her, she determinedly embraced common sense. Again, she reminded herself that the Demon had never struck this far north of the river. Indeed, his fanciful sobriquet had come from the fact that each of the murdered women had been found in an alley off a narrow little twist of a dockside street called Barkshire.

But what if the Demon had decided, this night, to venture farther afield in his fearsome hunt?

Then she simply would outwit him, she told herself with a stoutness she did not entirely feel. Using the wall as a guide, she began moving away from the source of those shambling footsteps with as much speed and silence as her sensible boots and limited visibility allowed.

Rough stone bit through the worn kid of her gloves, and she stumbled half-a-dozen times on a protruding doorstep or a section of wrought-iron handrail. To her despair, none of the barred doorways or shuttered windows spilled forth any welcome light from beneath stoop or sill. No one was within . . . that, or the inhabitants were simply asleep within the dark, shuttered safety of shop and home.

And still the unseen walker followed after her, neither gaining on her nor falling behind. Yet even while she moved with frantic haste, her ears straining to track his menacing progress, her thoughts were fixed on the lurid newspaper accounts she had read of the bloody crimes.

Another Horrid Murder.

Demon's Rampage Continues Unchecked.

Police Officials at a Loss.

Though the tabloids vied with one another to uncover ever more outlandish details of the case, a few facts had remained constant. Each murdered woman had been found in an alley several days after her disappearance, naked and with her clothes neatly bundled beside her. The cause of death in all four cases had been deemed strangulation, for each victim's neck bore marks of brutish hands.

But that was not the worst of it.

Amaryllis shivered again, wishing she had heeded her brother's opinion that proper women did not read newspapers. Had she been less diligent in keeping up with such stories, she might have been spared the knowledge that now taunted her. For, if those accounts were to be believed, the killer had not contented himself with merely killing the women.

Afterwards, the fiend had cut them open with almost surgical precision and neatly plucked out their hearts.

The shuffling sound behind her rang closer now. She stifled a moan of pure terror . . . and then the wall she had been using as a guide abruptly fell away beneath her hand.

A street corner, she realized after an instant of fear. Thankfully, she rounded it. Perhaps she could lose her pursuer now. Even better, she might find an occupied building in which to take refuge. But a dozen paces down that side street, a second brick wall suddenly loomed out of the fog before her.

Too late, she realized her mistake. She had turned down what must be a blind alley. The rank smell of rotting garbage around her confirmed her suspicions. Frantic, she groped her way down the length of this second wall until, but a few feet farther, she reached the corner where it butted up against a section of wooden fencing.

Trapped.

She choked back a panicked cry, sagging against the damp planks as she debated whether to take refuge here or retrace her steps. This shallow passageway could prove the ideal hiding place, for her pursuer might well pass by its narrow entry and continue on into the night.

But what if he didn't? What if he stumbled across her, instead? She would have no place to flee to, no chance at escape. Hers would be the next name to appear in the tabloids as the Barkshire Demon's latest victim.

Better to keep running than risk being cornered, she decided and started back in the direction of the main road. For, did she not have an advantage over the Demon's previous victims? Doubtless, none of them had been modern women such as she, capable of rational thought and—unencumbered by impractical footwear—swift flight.

She paused once again at the alley's narrow mouth . . . and that was when a hellish face appeared from out of the fog.

That face! Skin a waxy, grayish shade . . . black eyes dull and yet ablaze with brimstone. And the smell that clung to him, the sweet sickening scent of decay that could never be mistaken for anything else. Dear God, it was the face of a corpse—the face of some creature that had been disgorged from the ranks of the dead!

What swept through her mind was less coherent thought than it was reflexive impression, and so fleeting that she barely had time to register its meaning. She took a step back and opened her mouth to scream.

And then the creature extended a corpse-like hand at her.

The scream died on her lips. *Run!,* a frantic inner voice shrieked, but her feet remained firmly planted on the uneven cobbles. She could merely watch while, like some fumbling swain, the being made an ungainly swipe at the hood of her cloak.

The woolen covering slipped from her head, while her tangle of waist-length auburn hair, loosened from its pins by her earlier exertions, spilled past her shoulders in a fiery blaze. At the sight, a flicker of emotion—triumph, perhaps?—passed over the slack gray face. Then, with a guttural sound of satisfaction, he reached out both pallid hands toward her.

Inwardly, she screamed, a piercing wave of unadulterated terror. Outwardly, however, she remained unmoving, as if the fog had wrapped her in innumerable misty threads that held her firmly as chains. No sound escaped her, not even when the cold, dead fingers wrapped themselves around her throat.

Was this how the Demon's other victims had faced their end? Had they, too, been paralyzed with fear and unable to make even a token attempt at resistance?

She should struggle, should claw at his hands . . . yet the thought of touching that corpse-like flesh was more than she could bear. Even as she gasped for breath, even as red sparks exploded before her eyes, all she could manage was a frantic wish that it would be over, and quickly.

She heard it then—the clatter of wheels against stone that was an approaching carriage. At the sound, the brutal grip on her throat abruptly loosened. She felt herself drifting toward the chill ground like a laundry bundle carelessly tossed aside.

Talbot, she thought. *He realized I was gone and came after me.* But hardly had the words formed in her mind than the cobbles rushed up and darkness enveloped her. She would have to wait for consciousness to return to find out how very wrong she was. . . .

Amaryllis Meek's adventures are only beginning! Be sure to watch for Blood and Roses, *coming in fall, 1997 from Pinnacle Books.*

**If you liked this book, be sure to look for others
in the *Denise Little Presents* line:**